EVEN ODDS

FBI JOINT TASK FORCE SERIES (BOOK THREE)

FIONA QUINN

EVEN ODDS

FBI Joint Taskforce

Fiona Quinn

THE WORLD OF INIQUUS

Ubicumque, Quoties. Quidquid

Iniquus - /i'ni/kwus/ our strength is unequalled, our tactics unfair – we stretch the law to its breaking point. We do whatever is necessary to bring the enemy down.

The Lynx Series

Weakest Lynx

Missing Lynx

Chain Lynx

Cuff Lynx

Gulf Lynx

Hyper Lynx

Marriage Lynx

Strike Force

In Too DEEP

JACK Be Quick

InstiGATOR

Uncommon Enemies

Wasp

Relic

Deadlock

Thorn

FBI Joint Task Force

Open Secret

Cold Red

Even Odds

Kate Hamilton Mysteries

Mine

Yours

Ours

Cerberus Tactical K9 Team Alpha

Survival Instinct

Protective Instinct

Defender's Instinct

Delta Force Echo

Danger Signs

Danger Zone

Danger Close

This list was created in 2021. For an up-to-date list, please visit FionaQuinnBooks.com

If you prefer to read the Iniquus World in chronological order you will find a full list at the end of this book.

*To my daughter Devin who models intelligence,
strength, and grace in all she does.*

DIA

- Raine Meyers aka Clara Edwards, Cammy Burke, Paisley Moorhead, Oscar, Storm
- Javeed Hasan

FBI

- Damian Prescott
- Amanda Frost
- Lisa Griffin
- Rowan Kennedy
- Steve Finley
- Bruce Michaels

Delta Force Operators and Their Wives

- Ty – Echo
- T-Rex – Echo
- Havoc – Echo
- Nitro and Laurel— Echo
- Jeopardy and Pam – Echo
- Dice and Lucy – Echo
- Pelt and Theresa – Lima
- Budge And Kendra – Lima

Iniquus: Strike Force

- Striker
- Deep
- Lynx
- Jack
- Gator
- Blaze

Crime Families

- Prokhorovs – Bulgaria
- Todor Bilov and Frédéric Marquette
- Sergei Prokhorov
- Zorics – Slovakia
- Anna (Zelda Fitzgerald)

1

Act innocent.
~Moscow Rules

FRIDAY

RAINE PRESSED the bell long enough to hear it ringing somewhere in the back of the house.

By force of habit, she shifted to knife her silhouette next to the doorframe.

Raine never knew what would come blowing through a door, a terrorist, or a spray of bullets.

That wasn't on her list of possibilities today, she reminded herself as the cold cement from the front porch radiated through the soles of her tennis shoes and up into her calves.

The sudden plunge in today's temperature wasn't given priority when Raine was picking out her yoga pants and ski jacket. The purpose of her clothing was to give her ample maneuvering flexibility while letting her develop her cover as an urban millennial who woke up this morning to a breakfast of avocado toast and a six-step coffee order.

Raine had, in fact, eaten avocado toast this morning with an egg and some salsa, but her coffee had been home-brewed—black and industrial strength.

Looking over her shoulder, Raine's eyes searched past the minivan she'd borrowed from the pool for this assignment. She'd parked it one door down and across the street in the quiet Northern Virginia neighborhood. Mid-century architecture. Conscientiously manicured lawns. No movement. Empty driveways. Not even a dog loping through his early evening circuit.

Spinning back to the door, Raine focused through the side window to the darkened interior where Lucy McDonald was housesitting for a friend. The windowpanes reflected Raine's image back to her.

Raine looked properly incognito. Her facial features were hidden in the shadow beneath the visor of her ballcap. She'd tucked her ponytail through the back opening, doubling it into the elastic to make a messy bun. The blonde ends flicked against her perspiration dampened neck.

Her body—lit up with the anticipation of possible violence on the other side of this door—was revving Raine's survival motors.

She wasn't quite to the point where she'd pull her gun from her ankle holster. But the house exhaled anxiety.

Why wasn't Lucy coming to the door?

Raine pressed the bell again, extending her index finger for a longer, more imperative *buzz*. Starbucks venti cups filled each hand, keeping her fingers warm. She'd grabbed the cups from the kitchen shelf back at her office, leftovers from some meeting. She'd used a Sharpie to add "Paisley," her undercover name, to one and "Lucy" to the other.

This kind of detail was part of the pocket litter that she developed, props that defined her undercover role for the observant. If she was playing a mom, she might crumble goldfish crackers to powder the bottom of her purse, along with random broken crayons, maybe a plastic car, and a child's action figure.

When playing a role, it was all in.

Everything had to fit the puzzle.

Mistakes couldn't be tolerated when lives were on the line.

Still no Lucy.

Raine edged over to the little wrought iron table, where she set the coffee cups down and pulled her phone from the flex pocket on her thigh, double-checking. This *was* the address Lucy had texted. And this *was* the right spot according to her GPS…

Lucy had called Raine's "Paisley Moorhead" phone number and followed up the conversation with the text that included this address.

For some reason, Lucy had decided to leave the relative safety of Fort Bragg to come hide at a friend's house here in D.C.

When Lucy called Raine's Paisley Morehead cell phone number to let them know she was running for her life, she was frantic.

Raine had staged her cover and gotten here as fast as physics would allow. She hoped she wasn't too late.

It occurred to Raine that, never having met the woman, Lucy might not feel safe opening the door.

She sent a quick text to Lucy. **I'm here. Can you let me in?**

Raine didn't wait for an answer. She sniffed a deep breath then skipped down the brick steps.

On the way to the carport, Raine lifted her chin, arching back so she could cast a quick glance at the second-floor windows.

No lights on a gray, dreary day.

Maybe Lucy had decided to lie down. Pregnancy could be exhausting.

So could unremitting anxiety.

Still, no sign of interior lights was concerning.

Raine edged past where the blue Santa Fe was parked, scanning toward the backyard. She considered looking through the windows, but if there was anyone surveilling the house, that would give her away.

It could also let the bad guys know Lucy had broken their rules and reached out for help.

Partially hidden by Lucy's car, Raine tried the kitchen door.

Locked.

Another sweep of the area. Office workers would start trickling back to their homes soon. Mid-January, and the sun was setting. The first of the street lamps were blinking awake.

Raine reached under her ponytail, where she had clipped her ubiquitous specialized barrettes with their integrated lockpicking tools.

The knob lock on the door handle was quick work. Tumbling the deadbolt was much more finicky. Raine had to spend more time and use more focus than she would have liked.

Before she pushed the door wide, Raine crouched to pull her gun.

She paused outside. Centering herself, she sucked in a lungful of air then popped the door open, swinging her XDS around the room in a two-fisted grip.

Her heart beat in her ears. Her senses expanded like tentacles feeling around the space, searching for anything that posed a threat.

Everything was still.

It looked like dinner prep had been interrupted. There was a cutting board with diced onions. A bowl of already chopped red pepper and mushrooms. A pile of scraps. An open box of eggs.

Raine slid into the room and touched the stove. Cold.

"Lucy?" Raine called. "It's Paisley. I brought you a decaf with all the bells and whistles." Raine shut and locked the kitchen door before moving around the bottom floor, checking the hall closet and a tiny guest bathroom.

Pausing with her back to the wall, Raine could keep an eye on the front and back doors as she tugged her phone out again. She quick dialed Lucy's cell and tipped her ear toward the stairs, trying to acoustically locate Lucy.

It went right to voice mail.

While the house gripped its silence, Raine felt someone's attention prickling her awareness. It was a ghostly whisper in the still air.

She stepped cautiously to the front door, opened it, leaned back into the shadows, and scanned. Placing her gun on the entry table, ready for a quick grab, Raine tossed a laugh over her shoulder as if she was mid-conversation while she pushed the screen wide to retrieve the coffee cups. It wouldn't do to leave them out front where a set of inquisitive eyes could be keeping track.

The neighbors didn't need a heads up that something odd was happening here.

This close to D.C., there would be government worker bees who lived within sight. Raine made a mental note to run down the names of the neighborhood homeowners and their occupations when she got back to the office. She didn't need chatter at the company coffee stations to put a bug in someone's ear. The wrong ear.

Raine set down the coffee cups, then turned to shut the door and throw the deadbolt.

She retrieved her gun from the table, pressing the grip between her palms, finger riding the trigger guard as she moved down into the basement where laundry had been sorted into two piles of dirty clothes—toddler shorts and men's boxer briefs. They must be from the family, letting Lucy housesit while they were down in Florida.

No Lucy crouching in a corner or behind the hot water heater.

Raine stopped to compose a second message on her phone, then tapped send: **Lucy, should I finish chopping the onions for dinner?** That should tell Lucy that "Paisley" was in the house.

Even using a dedicated cover phone, Raine didn't want to break character, lest the bad guys were sniffing the air for communications.

Lucy's phone wasn't secure.

Raine's next text went to Iniquus's Strike Force: **I stopped at my friend's house on the way to yoga class. You two might hit it off. She's new to town.** Raine needed to give her back-up team a heads-up that something was off; they had already been apprised that she was heading over here.

This wasn't the first time Raine had partnered with an outside security group. But it was rare.

Her agency tended to hold their cards tight to the vest.

The DIA, Defense Intelligence Agency—like the CIA, Central Intelligence Agency—didn't do law enforcement.

Much of the way the DIA and CIA operated was the same. She was, for example, employing "Moscow Rules," rules developed by the CIA during the cold war so operators could function in the non-permissive atmosphere of the USSR capital. Even though she was here in Washington D.C., her adversaries came from the KGB tradition.

Also, like the CIA, the DIA's job—under the umbrella of the Department of Defense—was to gather intel and pass it on to those who *could* slap cuffs on wrists, as well as those who shaped necessary policies, and those who developed military actions.

Boy, did the military need to take action.

Someone was targeting the wives of Delta Force Operators with threats of violence and death.

Very specific Deltas.

The targeted wives, like Lucy McDonald, had two things in common. First, their husband's contracts all needed a re-up signature in the next three months—which meant they would be extending their special forces contracts with Uncle Sam. Second, the husbands were downrange on missions, leaving their wives home, alone and vulnerable.

What the DIA had gleaned so far: The goal of the threats was to stop the Delta Force operators from signing on the dotted line, discontinuing their work in the military. The terrorists wanted the wives to pressure their husbands, by any means necessary, into civilian life.

The situation had come to the DIA's attention when two of the wives had broken the rules set out by the terrorists and confided in each other. They decided they needed help.

One of the women had a familial connection to General Elliot, an owner of the highly lauded Iniquus Security Group here in Washington.

Iniquus brought the issue to the DIA, which was the right thing to do.

Quietly, the DIA visited each Delta wife, who met these two criteria.

Silently, each woman had nodded her head. They were all being threatened. They would suffer dire consequences if their husbands re-upped. The consequences would be equally tragic but torturously slow, instead of quick and humane, if the women reached out for help.

To anyone.

Even their husbands.

Especially their husbands.

Military wives knew that presenting home front problems to their husbands risked distracting them from their missions, putting their husbands and their units in danger. These wives would never tell their spouses that they'd been threatened even if the communications hadn't specifically warned them against such action.

The DIA started their investigation. They thought this might well be tied into other instances of cyber threats to military wives, which were being investigated by DIA Officer Raine Meyers.

As this new case unfolded, Raine had made sure each threatened Delta Force wife had her contact number, as Paisley Moorhead, so they could apprise her of any new threats. Raine didn't want the details to be lost in some game of agency phone tree.

I can come over now and bring pizza. Is this a good time? Though it felt like ages ago Raine had texted Iniquus about her "friend in town," the reality was that Strike Force responded almost immediately.

Raine noted the elasticity in her perceptions, recognizing that her limbic survival system was playing with time in her brain. Though it seemed like she'd been here all day, the fact was, only a few minutes had passed since she'd broken into the house.

Raine looked down at the text. Did she need them? Could be the house was empty… though where Lucy could have gone—eight months pregnant and without her car—was a mystery.

So far, it didn't look like there had been a struggle.

Yeah, this whole scene… Raine felt eyes on the back of her neck. Someone was watching. Backup might be helpful.

But if Raine sent a **Yes, thanks! Pepperoni and extra cheese** to Strike Force to get them en route. She wasn't sure who would show. If it was the woman on their team, Lynx, that would be fine. But the men were all six feet plus. They all had the bearing of warriors who had seen action and survived. Right now, the priority was on keeping things normal looking to Lucy's neighbors.

No curiosity.

No hard questions.

No. This wasn't the time for Iniquus to show up. Too many people were coming home from work, too many eyes would be scanning up and down the street.

Raine decided not to answer their text.

The Strike Force team would be monitoring from their war room at Iniquus Headquarters, possibly even staging someone at the strip mall around the corner and down the way.

Yeah, that was enough for now.

Raine raised her gun to a low ready position and started up the stairs.

If things went down, she only had her XDS, with nine rounds, eight in her magazine and one in the chamber.

Raine just didn't understand what she'd stumbled upon. She'd come here for a calm chat, having gotten a call that Lucy had changed locations. This was supposed to be a status conversation, not an exfiltration event.

The stair creaked under the weight of her foot.

Suddenly, at the end of the hall, a stifled sob skated out from under the door.

2

Keep them relaxed.
~ Moscow Rules

FRIDAY

RAINE'S HEART PUMPING, her t-shirt dampened with sweat under her armpits. She filled her lungs in a well-practiced rhythm of combat breathing, patterned to keep her nervous system from overriding her training.

Brains could screw you up if you let them. Raine knew this from hard-won experience.

Her gun pressed between her palms, her finger riding along the trigger guard, Raine proceeded systematically down the hall, taking each door one at a time, popping it open, doing a sweep, moving to the next. What looked like a guest bedroom and then a full bathroom next door.

Now, a gasp.

It seemed to have come from behind the last door on the left, sporting a wooden toy train, hanging from a hook. It was brightly painted with the name Pete billowing up from its smokestack.

With her back to the wall, Raine tried the knob. This was the only door in the hallway that was locked. It was a cheap hardware store system meant to warn others that privacy was desired and not meant to stop someone if they wanted in.

She decided not to kick the door open. One-handedly, Raine tugged the lock pick barrette from the back of her hair.

Inserting the slender awl into the opening, she pressed in.

Pop.

The release sounded large against a silent backdrop like the crack of an evergreen branch breaking under the weight of snow.

Raine stuck the barrette into her pocket so she could two-fist her gun as she pushed the door open with her toe.

Legos peppered the bright green rug.

Toy cars were toppled in a line as someone had rushed toward the bed.

Raine checked the closets anyway. This was no time for surprises.

"Lucy," she called, trying to ease the angst that swelled and billowed, filling the tiny bedroom. "It's Paisley. It's okay. You're okay." Raine crouched and lifted the leg of her yoga pants, sliding her gun back into the ankle holster. She pulled out her phone, karate chopped the flashlight on and pressed her cheek against the carpet.

"Lucy," she called again as she lifted the bed skirt and shined her light underneath.

In the back corner, Lucy's rounded form was wrapped into a hyperventilating ball.

"Lucy, it's Paisley. I'm the only one in the house." Raine wished she had more control over her voice, that she could make herself sound friendly and warm. But she had lost that ability from her war zone injuries and had to modulate the flatness of her words with loud and soft instead. "The doors are all locked. All is well. Let's get you out from under there."

Raine had hoped Lucy would reach out a hand for help. But instead, she mewled and pulled herself tighter in a full-blown anxiety attack.

Raine knew what these felt like. Awful. Unsurvivable. Waiting for imminent death.

And certainly not good for the mother-to-be. Raine was afraid if this kept up, Lucy might throw herself into premature labor.

Raine tried one more time. This time she put more command in her voice. "Lucy, it's time to come out. Give me your hand."

Lucy's leg kicked out reflexively, and Raine was done pussy-footing around.

Vaulting to her feet, Raine caught up the top of the mattress and flung it upward, the tails of the choo-choo sheets flapping about. Lifting and hugging the cumbersome form, Raine jostled the mattress over to the wall, where the covers slid off like melted ice cream down a cone.

Quickly, Raine stacked the box spring alongside the puddle of comforter and blankets.

That left only the wooden slats between Raine and Lucy. "I'm almost to you, Lucy. I'm getting you out of there. I'm going to help you."

As the slats came off, Lucy scrunched her eyes tight and slung her arms over her head. She curled there in the framework of the otherwise empty space.

Raine climbed in and started a medical assessment. Swiping her hands over Lucy, she'd check her fingers and palms for blood, then sweep again, making sure she'd covered Lucy's form, front, and back, at least all of her that Raine could reach.

Raine rested her hands on Lucy's eight-month pregnant belly. It was as tight as a basketball. Raine thought that Lucy's fear was probably giving her Braxton-Hicks contractions. Though, Raine wasn't trained for anything other than assisting emergency births, so she didn't really know.

Raine had helped to deliver babies on four different occasions. Those had been desperate circumstances. Twice she'd crouched on dirt floors while an Afghan village was under attack, and once in a ditch on the side of the road where the teen mother was left because she couldn't walk anymore. The last time had been in prison because she was the only other female within a hundred miles.

But it wouldn't come to that here. Hospitals and trained medical care were nearby.

Lucy still had a ways to go until her due date.

Stress, though…

Kneeling, Raine petted her fingers through Lucy's hair. "Lucy, I'm Paisley. We've talked on the phone. You asked me to come over and see you. On the way here, I checked your neighborhood," she said softly. "I checked your house. It's just you and me. I'm Paisley. Come on." Raine pushed back to come to a crouch. "You need to get it together for your baby's sake. Let's think of your baby now. Let's think about your little one and getting her comfortable by getting your blood pressure down. Get you breathing deeper."

Step one, secure the location, find and assess Lucy: Check.

Step two, calm Lucy down.

Raine stepped behind Lucy. She planted her feet wide and solid before she squatted down, wrapping the woman's arm around her neck. Rayne clasped Lucy's wrist and pressed up from the squat, dragging Lucy to her feet.

Side by side, they held there for a long minute while Lucy trembled against Raine.

Fear slicked off Lucy in waves of sound and vibration.

Lucy was a civilian; Raine couldn't lose sight of that.

In the taped phone conversations that the DIA had shared with Raine, Lucy seemed to be a shy and delicate woman, perhaps more so for going through her pregnancy by herself. She was introverted and didn't like to hang out with the other Delta Force wives, preferring the seclusion of her home and the company of her books.

Living the life of a Delta operator's wife required being made of stronger stuff than Lucy seemed to have in her.

In the game of life, Lucy hadn't been pragmatic in choosing her husband. Perhaps she'd have been better off marrying someone who could come home every night, someone with smaller burdens and a less dangerous role to play.

But when it came to the heart, few people were pragmatic.

And when folks were rational and practical about love, perhaps those results didn't unfold any better.

Raine's love life being a prime example. For her, matters of the heart were mostly about keeping her heart beating in her chest. She didn't have the time or attention for much else.

Stepping now, with Lucy's arm held tightly around Raine's neck, Raine guided Lucy over the bed frame, out the door, down the stairs, and into the kitchen, where Raine deposited Lucy on a chair.

"I'm making you tea," Raine announced, putting a hand on Lucy's belly. It had softened now. She'd keep a watch for if and when Lucy touched her belly and stilled; she'd look for a rhythm that told her to get this woman to the hospital. "It looks like you started dinner." Raine turned to the cupboards, searching for and finding a mug and a box of tea. Mint lavender that sounded like the ticket. "I know you probably don't feel hungry. But I'm going to finish cooking this up." She put the mug filled with tap water into the microwave oven. "And then we'll see if you can't take a couple bites for the baby's sake."

Lucy nodded.

"Is there anything in particular that sent you into an anxiety attack?"

"I heard a car stop outside," Lucy murmured, her first words since Raine arrived on the scene. "My friend, Martha, the one who owns this house, said that no one's around here during the day."

"You knew I was coming."

"Yes." She didn't speak again until Raine placed the mug in front of her and dropped the tea bag into the hot water. "I panicked," she said, wrapping her hands around the warmth of the mug.

Raine cast a glance over to the chopped vegetables and stopped blinking as her thoughts settled. She didn't want to get caught up in Lucy's angst, but the tickle on her neck told her to keep her guard up. Without a specific threat, Raine wasn't going to take Lucy from the house.

Not tonight anyway.

Raine needed to consult with Iniquus and see if a safe house could be arranged. Staying this fearful would surely put both mother and baby at risk.

This was a juggling act.

While her mission was to protect the Delta Force wives and identify the threat source, Raine was acutely aware that being here as "Paisley" might get her image in someone's camera lens, putting her other identities at risk.

As she thought that, a sense of foreboding wafted through the kitchen. Raine watched as it sent a shiver through Lucy, painting fear into her eyes.

3

Everyone is potentially under opposition control.
~Moscow Rules

Friday

Special Agent in Charge Damian Prescott settled his six-foot-two frame into a seat to the right of Deputy Assistant Director Amanda Frost at the highly polished table in an FBI Headquarters conference room in Washington D.C.

Two years ago, he'd been pulled away from his role in the FBI Critical Incident Response Group—CIRG—where he and his teammates had worked as specialists, responding worldwide to high-stakes events, including terrorist activity, hostage rescue, and child abductions. With the new Cyber Wars taking the place of the Cold War with the Kremlin, Prescott's Russian language skills—that he'd developed during his tenure as a Delta Force Operator—helped him lead a team tasked with identifying unconventional threats to the United States from crime families associated with the old USSR regime.

Prescott's gaze slid around the table of meeting participants. Steve Finley, domestic terror; Lisa Griffin, cyber; Rowan Kennedy, an East European attaché. Each had been part of exposing the attempted attacks from crime families out of Slovakia and Bulgaria. They'd thwarted the crimes and tied the families back to Russia.

Asymmetrical warfare was being waged: Poisons that could kill someone without showing up in an autopsy, efforts to use computer gaming systems as vehicles for terror, and other efforts to pit Americans against each other, driving the us/them narrative, fomenting anger and distrust, sowing the seeds of civil unrest—each of these plots were thwarted without public knowledge.

Solved, punished, buried away from the press.

To function effectively, their task force needed to operate under the radar and out of the limelight, as Steve Finley had discovered when his face showed up on an endless news loop last year, effectively sidelining him from deep undercover work.

Prescott turned his attention to Bruce Michaels, who was at the podium fussing with his computer, getting it connected to the big screen.

Michaels worked in signals intelligence, monitoring targeted foreign national suspects in the United States who communicated with those in foreign countries. Today, he was presenting information they'd been gathering. One of the targets they'd been surveilling overseas had a tie to a Pentagon civilian employee. Michaels was here to catch the joint task force up to speed, so they could decide what actions to take.

Was this a full-blown mission or another name for their tickler file?

"Okay," Michaels said as he squared his shoulders. He touched his palm to his chest. "Bruce Michaels, Signals Intelligence. I've been tasked with presenting you with a file of data that we've accumulated, to brief you on the contents, and to answer any technical questions that you might have." He focused over on Frost and waited for her nod.

Clearing his throat and adjusting his tie, Michaels reached for the remote and pointed it at the computer. The names Todor Bilov and Camila (Cammy) Burke appeared in bold lettering.

"Todor Bilov is a Bulgarian national, living in Geneva and working for a nonprofit that spreads literacy to developing and emerging economy countries. Todor is also a member of the Prokhorov family."

Rowan Kennedy leaned forward. Kennedy had been involved in a mission last fall that put his face squarely in the sights of the deadly Prokhorov crime family connected through marriage to a Russian oligarch. Kennedy would have to step warily if this developed into a mission with a public face.

"Cammy Burke," Michaels continued, "works in human resources at the Pentagon."

"How did you land on Bilov?" Frost asked.

"We, along with our allies, have been monitoring international phone calls associated with the Prokhorov family." Again, Michaels waited for Frost to nod before he continued. "Through these calls, we've discovered that Todor is coming to Washington." Michaels pressed a button, then used the laser pointer to circle an icon. "We have Todor's flight information and the name of his hotel. It's in the file." He tapped a button, and an audio icon moved onto the screen. "The reason this individual and his trip got flagged was the following conversation that took place yesterday between Todor and Cammy. And I should stipulate here," Michaels continued nervously, "that it's really three flags that went up surrounding Todor's visit. One, his close familial ties to the Prokhorov family.

Two, Cammy's job at the Pentagon working with sensitive personal materials concerning special operators. Three, that Todor lies to Cammy about the trajectory of his stay." Michaels looked at his feet as the audio began playing:

"I called to let you know that I'm coming to D.C." Todor spoke in English with an East European accent, but he was easily understood. His voice held a smile and a bubble of excitement.

"Oh, I'm so happy," Cammy responded. Her voice, in return, was rather flat. "When? Do you have a schedule? I'd like to make plans to show you around."

"Friday evening, tomorrow, that is to say, I will make my arrival."

"So soon? Is this an unexpected trip?" Cammy's voice was mechanical, almost robotic, sounding. Prescott thought she might be talking through an audio program that would protect her voice from being analyzed for identification. That would be flag four and a significant one. Innocent people didn't take steps like that.

"Unplanned, yes. A colleague is unable to make trip, and I am to take her place. In this capacity, Saturday night, I have philanthropic dinner to attend, representing my organization. If it is not too tedious, or too spur of action, no. Too…last minute. Yes, this. If it is not too last minute of invitation, I would love to escort you there. We can slip out after dessert and go elsewhere. Perhaps somewhere quiet so we can talk and enjoy each other's company. You say this? Enjoy each other's company?"

"Yes. We say it. We rarely mean it."

"I mean this," Todor continued. "I wish this. Time with you."

"Well, thank you. Then, yes, I would like to join you Saturday. Is this a formal event? Shall I meet you? I can drive if you'd like."

Prescott focused on Rowan Kennedy. Stress tightened the muscles in his face; Kennedy knew at least one of the people on this call.

"This is black-tie affair. I will have car pick you up." There was a pause. "I must warn you that my family becomes nervous when family member travels in America."

"Why?" Cammy asked.

Todor sounded mildly embarrassed when he said, "You have much random gun violence, for example."

"Oh."

"When any of us is in the United States, my family provide security."

"Oh?"

"I have two men team guarding us. Close protection, I think, is phrase. One will serve as chauffeur as well as protector."

"What? Will they have guns?" she gasped out. "You didn't have *any* security in Switzerland."

"Your country is very different. I, for myself, would not travel with security. But my family feel very strong for this."

"That makes me sad," she said after a pause. "You should be able to come here without concerns for your safety. I don't worry. Honestly, things happen. But we're not small like Switzerland. We have a huge population and a great deal of land. The threat is spread wide. I feel like you're safe here. But I understand the pressures of family. And it's sweet that they would go to such lengths to keep you safe. Will they constantly be with you, though? I mean, I… huh." She laughed nervously.

"Tell me." Todor managed to sound both worried and protective. Prescott would guess from this conversation that Todor and Cammy Burke were at the beginnings of a romantic relationship but that Todor was already invested, and Cammy was warming to the idea. If he was acting a role set out for him by the Prokhorov crime family, Todor was doing a believable job.

"I don't want this arrangement to make you nervous," Todor said. "It's honestly my overzealous family."

"I just…Perhaps I misunderstood when you said you wanted to enjoy each other's company. In that moment, I imagined our being alone." Her voice wavered off.

"This will not interrupt our personal time, I assure you. This is wrong word. Private time. Our intimate moments?" he scrambled for a phrase.

"It's okay." She chuckled, obviously charmed. "It will all work out the way it's supposed to. I've never had a security team with me before. This will be an adventure. What time shall I be ready?"

Michaels tapped the remote control, and the audio file stopped. "The conversation continues with their plans," he explained. "It's all here. If you listen through, you'll hear that Todor tells Cammy he will be in D.C. for ten days. But Todor's hotel reservations are through this Sunday morning, and he has a ticket to return to Geneva, leaving out of Dulles Sunday evening."

"Any idea why?" Griffin asked.

"Guessing, though I don't want to lead your thought processes, Todor has a goal he plans to accomplish in America by Sunday morning, but it's expeditious to make Cammy think that they will have more time together. He's playing her. Hence a flag."

"Do you have any background on their relationship in the file?" Finley asked.

"Yes, actually. There are other interactions in the file, including conversations collected by our East European field office, which is tracking communications made by Sergei Prokhorov. Succinctly, Cammy Burke took a vacation to Switzerland, traveling alone. Sergei Prokhorov targeted her about a week before her trip. From the correspondence between Sergei and Todor, we've determined that Todor Bilov was instructed to find Cammy, strike up a conversation, and lay the groundwork for a romantic relationship. He was not to physically act on the relationship yet. They wanted Cammy Burke to be nurtured into a deeply felt connection. If he was successful, Todor would get further instructions. This trip to

America is Todor's further instructions. We believe that they are trying to develop Cammy Burke as a double agent. A Pentagon mole."

"You said that Cammy Burke works with special operators in her role in human resources at the Pentagon. Is there any reason to believe that the Prokhorov's have targeted that population?" Prescott asked.

Michaels shook his head. "I don't know."

"Todor's last name is Bilov, though, not Prokhorov?" Kennedy asked.

"Right," Michaels said. "From what records we can locate, Todor's mother was probably three months pregnant when Todor's biological father died." Michaels glanced over to his computer screen and shuffled the knot of his tie around, looking stressed. Michaels was much more comfortable in his cubicle, running through his intelligence feed, and less comfortable in settings interacting with people. "The mother remarried almost immediately. Baby Todor took his stepfather's last name, Bilov. Todor's biological father was Martin Prokhorov. Sergei Prokhorov's youngest brother. Todor's lineage is in the file."

"Okay," Frost said. "Long story short, big bad family leader Sergei Prokhorov has a nephew, Todor. Todor is assigned to develop Cammy Burke as an asset. We assume she's wanted by the family and worth the focus, time, and attention because of her position at the Pentagon. Did you find any other lifestyle or familial connections that would make us think anything other than a desire to get information out of the Pentagon in general, and special forces family life documentation in particular?"

"No, ma'am. That's it in a nutshell. Cammy Burke leads a simple life. From her purchase history and accounts, she knits, watches television, and reads. Yoga. Coffee. Outside of work, that's about it."

"Her age?" Prescott asked.

"Thirty-six. Single, of course. But she's never married. No children. No family that we can find. Friendships seem to be on-line. Searching through social media platforms, she doesn't socialize in person very often."

"That's a profile that we'd likely target. Nobody's going to be watching Cammy's back," Finley said. "And Todor? What about him?"

"Todor is forty-three," Michaels said. "He's also childless and never married. He told Cammy that this is one of his big regrets. Something he'd like to rectify."

"Of course, it is." Sarcasm rolled off Griffin's tongue. "I bet Cammy Burke ate that up with a spoon."

"Yes, ma'am."

"This is good information, Michaels," Frost said. "We appreciate your bringing it to our attention. We'll follow up. Do you have photographs of these two?"

"Oh, uhm," Michaels fumbled. "Yes, here." He maneuvered through his files, opening a gallery. "These are all from the field officer who tried to get eyes on the situation, in case… well, just in case."

Michaels brought up the picture of a man who was European chic. Tailored pants and a button-down shirt highlighted a fit body. Todor had meticulously slicked back his salt and pepper hair. He had the disposition of a mover and shaker. Monied and powerful.

The next photograph was of him laughing. His body language was comfortable, his countenance open and happy. The woman in the picture had the look of an athlete, long shapely legs, chiseled wasp waist, blonde hair that hung in waves down her back.

The third picture was of them hand in hand by the lake, her head resting against his shoulder.

In the fourth picture, the couple was front-facing.

Michaels pressed a button that made the focus zoom in on the couples' faces.

There was a collective intake of breath.

Everyone at the table, including Frost, leaned forward with renewed interest.

When Cammy's face came into focus, Prescott's heart stopped beating.

4

If the asset has surveillance, then the operation has gone bad.

~ Moscow Rules

FRIDAY

RAINE DECIDED to hold off on making Lucy's dinner.

There was something about this situation—possibly it was just the anxiety that Lucy was exuding—but… Raine had learned to trust her gut, and her gut said, *get ready*.

She decided to put Lucy in the second-floor hall bathroom and let her soak in the tub—hot water therapy did wonders for the psyche. And that would give Raine time to learn the lay of the land.

On this second search of the house, Raine processed through what she could do to harden her surroundings. Coming through the Army ranks, heading outside of the wire as a linguist, and later training and working with the special forces units to deal with the females they encountered—gaining trust and gathering intelligence —Raine had an eye for turning any location into a stronghold.

Upstairs in the master suite, the wooden floor, for example, could help. Raine looked at the floor-to-ceiling bookshelf to the left of the bathroom, set her shoulder against the side, and pushed to scoot the bulky piece a few inches over. Yes, that would work. If anyone burst onto the scene, Raine would put Lucy in the master bath and cover the door with the shelves. To that end, Raine threw a pile of extra pillows and blankets she'd grabbed from the closet into the tub. She'd bring up some non-perishable food in a minute.

Still in the master bedroom, Raine pulled the drape back and checked the windows. They looked out over the backyard with the heavy king-sized bed just to the side. The window was large enough that Raine could easily slip out, using a sheet tied to the bed's leg. But getting Lucy down a sheet…that would be tough. Raine would keep an eye out for one of those rope ladders folks purchased when they had bedrooms on the second floor. People typically got them once they had kids to save. Raine eyed the window again. *Maybe Lucy could squeeze through. That belly of hers…*

Raine moved a sturdy wooden chair next to the door, so she could wedge it under the knob. That might prevent someone from popping the lock like Raine had done on the kid's bedroom door earlier or kicking their way in. It would buy them some time to get Iniquus or the police on the scene.

Raine scanned one more time, visualizing herself quickly securing the room.

Yup. The master suite was the most protected. It was the place she'd keep Lucy once Lucy was out of her bath.

Raine would feed Lucy dinner in bed, let her watch some television before she fell asleep.

A quick search through the upstairs closets said that there was no escape ladder, but there was a fire extinguisher.

That might help.

It would sure be easier to plan if she had a scenario in her head, Raine thought as she moved the extinguisher to the master bedroom.

Downstairs, she turned on all the lights and checked the locks on the doors and windows, pulling the drapes shut.

Raine paused at the side of the front window. The sky was already dark. The clouds had moved across the silver strip of moon. She listened to a car rumble past the house and continue down the road. “Watch the paranoia meter,” she told herself under her breath, fully understanding how the sound of a parking car might send someone like Lucy scrambling up the stairs to wedge herself under Pete’s bed.

Goosebumps ran up Raine’s arms making the tiny hairs stand on end.

She sensed eyes were on the house. This was the bottom-dropping feeling Raine got over in Afghanistan just before an attack began.

And this time, she didn’t have any special operations forces on scene watching her six.

She had no idea how far away Strike Force was from this location. Did they move into the area when Raine sent her earlier heads-up text? Raine decided to touch base as soon as she got Lucy settled.

In the kitchen, Raine gathered the sharp knives and put them in the freezer, where she could grab them if need be but would keep them from becoming weapons of convenience if someone were to come in.

The house, to be honest, was easy.

Too many windows. Flimsy locks. Poor outdoor lighting. Tall bushes. Raine reminded herself that not everyone had lived a life that made them look at the world as preparation for the next big and bad that would descend on them.

She moved over to the stove and was reaching for the burner

knob to get the eggs cooking when her phone vibrated. The text read:

URGENT! Agh! Paisley, my kid is puking all over the place. Any way you could get me some Pedialyte and saltines?

That was from Strike Force. It meant she needed to get somewhere private and call in over a secure line.

She scrolled and tapped to bring up her phone app that encrypted her conversation end to end.

"Paisley here," she said, looking up at the ceiling. Water was running down the pipes. Lucy would be getting out of the tub.

"Deep here. You have a situation. Striker and Jack are headed your way on foot. They're five minutes out. A SWAT team is stacking up outside the house."

"This house?" If she had control of her voice timbre, surely that sentence would climb with shock. But such as it was, it didn't sound at all like Raine experienced the adrenaline dump that just rushed through her circuitry.

"Roger."

Raine scrolled to her clock app and pressed the stopwatch. The seconds began to spin forward. She brought the phone back to her ear. "Why? Was there information on the police scanner?"

"Not from SWAT. They keep that on a secured channel. Over the police scanner, we picked up our clues. They're closing the streets in the blocks surrounding yours. They're going door to door to move people out of the area."

"That means they expect bullets to be flying."

"Probably. They've sent out a vague description of you and Lucy."

Raine pivoted, sprinted through the living room, and took the stairs two at a time. "Wait. My description? Someone has eyes on this house then. Lucy's? They're saying watch out for a heavily pregnant woman?"

"Height, weight, hair color, and age are the BOLO—be on the lookout—descriptors that came over the scanner."

"Is SWAT trying to save us?" She opened the door to the hall bathroom. "I could go outside and have a chat with them after I get Lucy secured."

Lucy stood with one foot on the ledge of the tub, drying her leg with a pink towel. She stood, sucking in air, and pulled the expanse across her breasts, trying to hide her naked form.

"According to the BOLO," Deep said, "the blonde is armed and dangerous. They don't know the status of the other woman, possibly one of your victims. They're not giving out any more information."

Raine stooped to grab up Lucy's clothes, the phone pressed between her shoulder and ear. She focused on the woman's eyes. "Move. Follow me."

Lucy didn't move, just stood there, eyes wide, breath held behind pursed lips.

Her hands full, Raine rounded behind Lucy and gave her a push, pressing her shoulder into the younger woman's back to keep her moving along, steering her toward the master bath that Raine had designated as the safe room. All the while, she was describing where they'd be situated in the house to Deep. Striker and Jack would know where to go once they arrived on the scene.

"Striker plans to interface with the SWAT command and see if they can't preempt whatever's being planned. But prepare for it to get loud and smoky."

"Hanging up," she said and thrust the phone into her thigh pocket.

One last push moved naked Lucy into the bathroom.

Raine dropped the clothes. "We're about to be attacked."

Lucy's body convulsed.

"You are the mama bear. You will do whatever is necessary to save your baby. It's instinct."

Lucy's head nodded frantically.

"You will get dressed. You will leave this light off. It's going to be dark in just a minute, so look around and get an idea where everything is."

Her head twitched left and right.

"You will get the hand towel wet and wring it out. If it gets smoky, it's *not* a fire, but you need to put the towel over your mouth and nose so you don't breathe in the smoke. Say that out loud."

"Dressed, water on towel."

"Do you see the blankets and pillows in the bathtub? You will get into the tub, get your head below the lip, and wrap the pillows around your ears. There will be a very loud bang. Your head will ring. The more pillows around your head, the better."

"Pillows." Lucy bent and picked up her huge cotton pregnancy panties, dropped her towel, and stumbled her feet into the openings.

"You won't be able to get out of the door. I'm going to push the bookcase in front of it. As long as you are quiet, no one will know where you are. Can you do that for your baby? Stay silent?"

"Yes. Silent." She was yanking the straps of her bra up her arms, then threw the bra into the corner and crammed her head through the neck of her t-shirt. Her heavy breasts resting on the swell of her belly.

"Silent. I have help coming."

"Help, yes," Lucy said.

"One last glance around. You're about to be in the dark," Raine warned. "Don't turn on a light, not even a night light."

Raine flipped the switch on the way out the door, pulling the knob shut behind her.

She looked down at her phone's timer.

In two minutes, Strike Force would be on the scene. Chances were they could talk SWAT down.

With her back to the side of the bookcase, Raine squatted and pressed into her heels, exerting her thigh muscles, powering the bulk and weight across the door. She moved into the center of the bedroom to make sure the door jamb was effectively hidden. She pressed her cheek to the wall on the left, then the right, to make sure a vigilant officer wouldn't detect her ploy.

Raine glanced at the chair and decided that putting it in place or locking the door would make her look culpable. Even that fire extinguisher could be a problem.

Raine put the extinguisher under the bed. She yanked off her ankle holster with her gun and shoved them into the drawer in the bedside table, then grabbed a book from the nightstand and curled onto the mattress.

Her phone buzzed.

"Paisley here." She was breathing heavily from nerves and exertion.

"No joy. They're coming in. Get ready." The line went dead.

Raine pulled her earbuds from her pocket, slipped them into her ears, and plugged the end into her phone to make it look like she was listening to a podcast. These earbuds were the latest in specialized clandestine ear protection technology. They would protect her ears from the volume of the flashbang blast that she anticipated, but they would also allow the sound of human voices to be heard. The technology had been developed for those serving in the war when it was discovered that soldiers were failing their missions in hot zones filled with eardrum destroying explosions and bullet bursts because the soldiers couldn't hear each other's warnings.

Raine hoped the flashbang would only be thrown downstairs.

She scrambled off the bed and opened the bedroom door, so there would be no need for them to use the explosives up here. Quickly, she dove back into her place, curling up, hoping to look innocent and non-threatening. "Get ready," she called, her voice not able to get any louder than a conversational tone. "Silence now until I tell you otherwise. No matter what you hear out here, yelling, screaming, explosions—no matter *what* you hear—you will remain silent."

"Yes." Lucy's voice quivered out.

"Silence!"

Boom! The breacher's battering ram slammed against the front door, quickly followed by an explosion that was jarring even with the earbuds in. Raine hoped against hope that Lucy had had her head muffled with the pillows. In the bathroom behind the thickness of the books, Lucy would be better protected from the concussion of sound that traveled up the stairs and swelled with the smoke.

Raine cupped her hands over her ears and made a face like she was terrified and in shock. It didn't take much acting. She just reached down and found a seed of emotion already sprouted. "Come on, Striker," she muttered under her breath as heavy boots tramped up the stairs.

"Clear, clear," various voices rang as they progressed through the downstairs and others up here. They had a lot of boots on this mission.

A figure, terrifying in his black battle rattle, swung through the open door. His team coming up behind.

Rifles lifted, Raine was caught in the operators' sights.

She froze her movement.

One twitchy finger could put her permanently lights out.

A SWAT operator let his rifle swing from its strap as he moved to the bed and grabbed behind Raine's neck, gaining control over her head and, therefore, control of her body, forcing her off the mattress and down on the floor.

Raine made her body as compliant as possible.

The heavy hand pressed on her ear, driving the earbuds uncomfortably deep. Her cheek was constrained against the wooden floor, grinding her teeth into the inside of her flesh.

As she deliberately closed her eyes, so she wouldn't sneak a peek toward the bookshelf, Raine sent the mental command to Lucy, *"Keep your mouth shut!"*

5

Establish a distinctive and dynamic profile
~ Moscow Rules

FRIDAY

THE PICTURE of Cammy Burke was splashed across the big screen.

Prescott couldn't take his eyes off her. His breath was shallow in his chest, but he thought he was pulling off a stoic expression.

Frost shut the conference room door behind Michaels and walked slowly back to the head of the table. She pressed her knuckles onto the wooden surface and leaned her weight forward. Her gaze shifted, resting briefly on each of the agents sitting around the table. First Lisa Griffin, then Finley, Kennedy. Last and longest on Prescott.

"It looks like we might have a problem," she said. Smoothing the back of her pencil skirt, she took her seat. Her fingers intertwined, and she tapped her thumbs together. Pulling her eyes upward, she rested her gaze on the seam that brought the wall and ceiling together.

Quiet minutes followed.

"Okay, with that collective intake of breath when Michaels zoomed in on her image, I can tell you've all at least had a brush-by with this woman." She tipped her chin down. "Apparently, Cammy Burke is a known quantity. And now she's working in the Pentagon? We all know that's not her name, right?"

Heads nodded.

"Michaels *thinks* it's her name. That's significant," Finley said. "Research would have done a look-see into her Pentagon affiliation and checked her employment status to make sure it lined up with the chatter. That means Cammy Burke's cover is airtight, or Michaels would have more red flags waving."

Frost took a deep breath in, her mind obviously sifting and considering. "She'd have the contacts to make that happen. The game, though…" Frost got up and retrieved the remote control. She zoomed in on the woman's face and neck. With her brow pulled tight, Frost moved forward and squinted, then panned out again and walked back to her seat.

"It sounds like you've made up your mind that she's an adversary." Prescott's voice rumbled danger. He hadn't meant for it to. The picture up on the big screen had thrown him a curve. "And you'd be wrong." His emotions rising to the surface, Prescott fought the snarl that was forming on his lips.

Luckily, Finley pulled the attention away from him. "I agree with Prescott. You'd *have* to be wrong," he told Frost.

"Perhaps not an adversary. Maybe more of an obstacle. I'm not going to define her role right now." Frost took her seat and turned her focus from Prescott and Finley to the other side of the table where Kennedy sat. "You were the first to recognize this woman. You identified her by the sound of her voice alone. What can you tell me about Cammy Burke?"

Kennedy adjusted in his seat. "She had black hair when I met her in Brussels. There, I knew her as Clara Edwards."

The clock ticked loudly on the wall. Heads swung toward the photo on the screen.

"*That's* Clara Edwards?" Lisa Griffin let out a low whistle. "Well, that makes your last mission's boldness of action much more understandable."

Kennedy shot her a look.

Finley laughed out loud. "Seriously? That's Clara—we only have a few minutes to become comfortable with each other, so let me give you a hand job in the taxi on the way to our mission—Edwards?

"It wasn't like that. That's taking what happened and amplifying it in a way that wasn't... She... Look, she was right." Kennedy karate chopped the air as he spoke emphatically. "We made out in the taxi on the way to the mission. It worked out the way she anticipated it would. By the time we got on scene, we were comfortable with each other and seamless in playing the role of a couple. In a very short time, we were able to develop a connection that was read by our mark as our being in a romantic relationship. This allowed us to slide in front of Sergei's security force and meet our mission goals. Later, it helped us blend in with other couples as we attempted our escape. And we very nearly pulled it off."

"She abandoned you when you were under attack," Griffin countered.

"I had a laser dot on my chest. She did what she should have done. What was the use of her standing there and getting shot? Worse, what if those thugs hurt her to get me to comply with them? No, she ran and got away. She was gathering support and coming to my aid."

"And she stabbed that guy in the dick," Finley deadpanned.

Kennedy grinned widely. "There was that."

They all turned to take in Cammy Burke's softly curled hair, her demure dress, and her gentle smile.

"She looks much too ladylike to stab a guy in the dick," Griffin pointed out.

"That was just a few months ago," Frost said, leaning back, wrapping her fingers around the ends of her captain's chair armrests. "Okay, Kennedy, I assume, then, you were the last of us to interact with this woman. How was she?"

Kennedy blushed.

"Not like *that*." Frost batted her hand at him. "I don't need a blow by blow, as it were, on her snogging abilities. Backseat antics aside, how was she to work with?"

He blushed deeper. "I was glad to have her on my team. She'd be hell as an adversary. I remember thinking that at the time. She was professional, effective, nuanced, brave—perhaps farther toward the rash end of the bravery spectrum than I am. Resourceful. She manipulated the hell out of our target."

"What example of manipulation comes to mind first?" Frost asked.

"Okay." His focus drew inward for a moment. "All right, the goal of that mission was to make Sergei Prokhorov my asset. To that end, we had a stack of what he would call 'kompromat' photographs. The secondary goal of the mission was to gain access to his phone to download our new Internet-crawling spyware. All was going to plan. I had his phone open. The download was in progress. Clara had the pictures in her hand, leafing through them, picking out certain ones to show to Sergei, making snarky comments. It was keeping him distracted, keeping him from coming up with a plan, like calling his security over. It was a good partnership. Then she comes to this one photo." He sent a look first to Griffin, then to Frost. "Excuse me for being graphic."

Frost nodded.

"It was a close up of the man's penis and the young lady's mouth."

"His stepdaughter's mouth?" Frost clarified.

"Exactly." He cleared his throat. "When Clara held that image up for him, she had a look of pity in her eyes." He tapped a finger to the bottom of his nose. "A snarl of derision around her nostril. It was perfect. She said, 'Look how thin and scrawny it is. You have a *pathetic* dick.'"

Prescott snorted, despite himself.

Finley did too.

"It worked. Thc 'mat of old-man gray hair' was a second blow. Sergei was mortified, especially since Clara was saying that in front of me—a younger, fitter man." Kennedy reached for his water bottle. "It was like watching the guy take a knee to the groin." He spun the top and took a sip. "And for a moment, he lost his fight, which let me finish up with the download and started us out of there. We almost made it." He twisted the cap back in place and set the water in front of him.

"She wouldn't have been put into play with you unless she was a trusted partner." Prescott tried to get the target off her back.

"Or we wanted the same thing in that moment," Finley added.

"There's that." Prescott had to agree.

"She's not FBI, then?" Kennedy asked.

"No," Frost said. "She's not. I will tell you, though, the planning stages for this joint task force started right around three years ago. At that time, I tried to recruit her to the Bureau for the very reasons that Kennedy has been outlining. I became aware of her work from other operations where she showed up on the scene. I knew it would take some time to get her through Quantico and acclimated before she came on board with us. I was still developing our team, and I thought her fieldwork would be an asset to our endeavors. But she declined."

"So, *you* know who she is," Kennedy said.

"Up to a point. Enough that I made an overture." Frost shot a look Prescott's way. "When I approached her, I outlined how this task force would function outside of the normal FBI hierarchy and methods. That we'd be a lean and flexible team. She asked whom I had lined up so far. When I told her you were in charge, she said she doesn't work and play well with people named Damian Prescott. Since Prescott would be leading this band of merrymakers, she took a different path. *What* she's doing and for whom are the questions."

The muscles at Prescott's jaw tightened into knots. This was going to hit him very close to home. Prescott didn't want to share his personal life with the task force. It was still possible that he could maintain his privacy. But it wasn't looking good.

"I assumed you'd had a pretty bad run-in with her at some point in your career. You didn't get soft gloved by her like Kennedy did, did you?" She sent a sly look Kennedy's way.

"I…" Kennedy started.

"It's okay," Frost said. "Line of duty and all."

"If she didn't sign on with the FBI," Finley said, "certainly she's working for the United States, just another alphabet."

"*For* us? I don't know. *With* us?" Frost tipped her head from side to side. "She ran that mission with Kennedy. And she sent me a copy of her report. That's how we learned about Kennedy's special backseat talents."

"Come on! Could we move on from that? Talking about it is uncomfortable."

"Being used as a boy toy?" Griffin asked. They had been friends for decades. She was allowed to turn the screws on the poor guy.

Prescott had found the whole scenario funny. Up until now.

"It wasn't like that. It was a *tactic*," Kennedy growled. "And it *worked*."

"It's important that we know who it is we're looking at," Frost clarified. "I'm bringing up the backseat incident so we can better understand the personality and skillsets we'll be engaging with, or possibly against." Frost popped her eyebrows.

"The operator I knew as Clara Edwards is in this photo in the guise of a woman named Cammy Burke," Kennedy spoke slowly, choosing his words carefully. "Cammy, ostensibly, works for the Pentagon. I can tell you that this operator impressed the hell out of me. And apart from the dick stabbing, I'd roll with her." He held up his hands. "Bad choice of words. I'd *work* with her—I'd run a mission with her—any day." His gaze searched around the other faces. "Do you think she'd work with us on this? Maybe we could run over to the Pentagon and tap her on the shoulder."

"Hard to say, really," Frost said. "And probably not up to her. This woman's name is not Cammy Burke, and I was told that her affiliation is need-to-know. So far, we haven't needed to know, so we haven't been told. That includes me. And as to tapping her shoulder over at the Pentagon, I'm guessing you'd never find her there. Hmmm. I'm going to check if there is a real Cammy Burke on the Pentagon payroll, and her name is being borrowed. I can almost guarantee that's not the case. It would put a target on a civilian's back. But never say never. I'll let you know."

"From the picture, knowing that Todor is Sergei's nephew, it's possible that she's acting the role of dangle," Prescott offered. A dangle was someone who worked for a government and then *pretended* to turn to an enemy country to offer intelligence, acting as a double agent. But a dangle was a ploy to find out what the enemy government was interested in knowing.

It was a risky move. It could put an operator right in the middle of the lion's den.

"Becoming an actual spy often happened in the old USSR when people wanted to defect to the West. In the US, it was usually for money, but love could turn someone." Prescott gestured toward the photo and how the couple was sitting thigh to thigh. "Maybe she was playing that card…"

In the world of turncoats, there were four main reasons for anyone to betray their country. The FBI taught their new officers the acronym MICE: money, ideology, compromise, extortion. Though some would-be spies might choose espionage for self-importance, excitement, possibly even over a grudge.

Yes, if that's what Prescott saw in this photo with Todor—she was setting herself up for the dangerous role of dangle by pretending to get wooed by a dashing foreigner.

Prescott studied her face. It had been a very long time since he'd seen her look so relaxed and content.

He processed through what Michaels had shared about Cammy Burke. He'd said that Cammy liked knitting and television. That was antithetical to the woman he knew. But the character Cammy Burke, who lived a boring lonely life, would be the kind of vulnerable figure that could be preyed upon by the likes of Sergei Prokhorov and his nephew Todor to get to protected Pentagon information. Interesting that she chose to work in human resources. That had to be a big clue as to what was going on here.

"I agree, Prescott. It looks to me like a dangle," Frost said. "Let's put motive on the back burner for a moment. I'm still interested in learning about this woman." Frost turned to Griffin. "Moving around the table, you're next. Griffin, how do you know this woman?"

"Oh, nothing as exciting as Kennedy. I knew her as Oscar."

"Was that a last name?"

"No, ma'am, that was her first name. I'm not recalling her last name. It was about ten years ago. More."

"Good. Go on." Frost held the flat of her hand out to gesture at the picture of the woman with wind-pinked cheeks, smiling happily down at them.

"She looks like a woman I knew in my army days when I was training to work with the Rangers with cyber support. My guys were running into a lot of tribal groups who spoke dialects that were hard to communicate in, but a lot of the tribal elders spoke Russian from the previous war. The army sent me to language school. Oscar was there. She was a whiz with languages. She spoke, I don't know, four or five?"

"When I was with Clara, she was speaking flawless Russian. Her English was actually more strained," Kennedy said. "I thought she was speaking English as a second language."

Griffin lifted a brow. "Because?"

"Her American sounded like she had trained hard to clean up any foreign accents. Her speech ended up sounding mechanical, as you heard in the recording."

Frost turned to the other side of the table. "Is that how you know her, Finley?" Frost asked. "Did you meet her in the military?"

"Yes, but when I knew her, her name was Storm. Through the grapevine, I'd heard she'd died. I honestly thought she was KIA a long time ago, seven years maybe…"

Frost leaned forward. "Do you remember how?"

"Her convoy was attacked. Four of them were taken, prisoner. This was after I was out. It's rumor intelligence from one of my Ranger buddies. Seeing her photo's like seeing a ghost. Storm rolled with the Rangers most of the time. She went out with other army special operators' groups, Delta and Green Beret, so we know she was good at what she did. But those were some hairy missions. Like Griffin said, it was a long time ago that I was downrange with Storm, and I could be mistaken about identifying her."

"Let's assume she didn't die, and that *is* Storm. What did you think of her?"

"Professional. Prepared. Athletic. Ballsy," Finley said without hesitation.

Frost turned to Griffin.

"The same."

"Okay, personality-wise, it's all lining up. Same adjectives from Kennedy to Finley to Griffin. The kind of woman that would have been snatched up once she left the military service to be put into play on a different battlefield." Frost focused on Prescott. "And what name do you know her by?"

Prescott sat straight in his chair. He was going to get through this with the least possible personal revelations. "She's Raine Meyers."

"Raine, that's poetic," Kennedy said. "Is that her actual name or another nickname?"

Prescott held his body rigidly. "It's her actual name, Katerina Raine Meyers. Oscar Meyers was the name she got in boot camp. Later, when she started going out on missions with special forces, they rechristened her from Raine to Storm."

"Well, now." Griffin sat back and crossed her arms over her chest. "That sounded like a bit of sentimentality attached to it. And yet, she doesn't want to be on your team here at the FBI. Perhaps your backseat experience wasn't as good as Kennedy's was."

Damian clenched his teeth.

"How do you know her?" Frost asked.

"We went to the same high school." He shrugged to ward off more questions, but when Griffin raised her brows and tucked her chin, he could tell that didn't pass muster. "We started dating our junior and senior year."

She turned her chin the opposite way as if she knew that wasn't the whole story.

It was going to come out anyway... "We were eventually engaged to be married." Prescott's ribs compressed his lungs. *Man, he didn't want to get into this.*

"When did you see her last?" Frost asked.

"Seven years ago." He turned to Finley. "A Delta Force team went after the four captives. Raine sustained life-threatening injuries, but they were able to save her."

Finley was stoic except for his eyes. Having Raine back from the dead was probably quite the hit to his emotions. He and "Storm" had obviously been through some shit together.

Prescott turned back to Frost, who considered him with a worried brow. "Do you think that's going to affect the mission?"

"No."

"Prescott." Frost leaned forward. "Gut check. If Raine Meyers turns out to be a rogue player, could you take her down?"

6

Act innocent
~ Moscow Rules

FRIDAY

BALACLAVAS GUARDED THE SWAT GUYS' identities.

Once they dragged Raine up from the floor, the men treated her with kid gloves, like she might have a suicide vest on under her yoga tank, somehow.

During her pat-down, they discovered her cell phone in her thigh pocket. It was a phone dedicated to Raine's undercover persona, "Paisley," so everything would look on the up and up if they scrolled around. Even her texts to Lucy and Strike Force would work.

Raine sat on the wooden chair that she had set in place to brace the master bedroom door shut if someone breached the house.

When she stuck it next to the door, she hadn't considered this scenario.

Wriggling her wrists in their handcuffs, testing how tightly they'd been secured, Raine thought that if she were left alone in the room, and the SWAT guys didn't find her lock pick barrettes in her hair, she could get herself free, use her bedsheet method of escape out the window, and get her superior at the DIA to force the SWAT team to stand down.

Raine wasn't going to let go of her cover story until there were no more rifles poised and ready.

Even then. She didn't want to get her name into the system.

Since Raine didn't know what was going on, she didn't know if she was going to land in a jail cell tonight or not.

Bad timing for Murphy's law.

She had a party tomorrow night where she needed to set her hook in her mark Todor Bilov's psyche and start to reel him in. She'd been chasing after the Prokhorov's for years now. When she helped the FBI get their spyware crawling around Sergei's computer networks last fall, the data they pulled helped her solve the puzzle of who was targeting military families on social media.

The oligarch-funded bot farms had been testing the waters with simple scenarios. It looked like the Prokhorov family felt secure enough with their strategy to go after American special ops now.

Todor was Raine's ticket into the right circles, the right computer systems, and the best way to stop their attacks. *She hoped.*

But all that was contingent on her success tomorrow night.

This SWAT fiasco needed to get wrapped up.

Raine sent a mental message to Lucy. *Be calm. Stay silent. I've got this.*

"Name?" big bad SWAT guy barked at her.

"Paisley Moorhead," she said.

The name was obnoxious, and she'd picked it purposefully. She was hiding in plain sight. Who would be stupid enough to choose such an outrageous name? If someone were developing an undercover name, they'd pick something banal—Mary or Sue, and a common last name, Anderson, or Parker. Pick a name like Paisley Moorhead, and people didn't doubt its authenticity.

It was the same idea when she made up the character of Cammy Burke and had the DIA get her fake identity established at the Pentagon. Recognizable and common, but not too bland.

Strike Force was fully apprised of her Paisley guise. It had been decided that if, for any reason, they needed a connection to put Iniquus boots in play, Jack would act out the role of her boyfriend. Probing questions would find they were fairly new at the relationship, so she and Jack didn't have a lot of details about each other's lives. They were trying to keep things casual.

Raine wondered if Jack and Striker were outside, trying to talk their way in and if her story was going to match up to theirs.

This whole scene was ridiculous. Raine had stopped by the house to talk about next steps for Lucy.

It wasn't an op.

Raine wasn't wearing a wire.

With no comms, she and her Strike Force team would be winging it.

A second balaclava dude, off to the side, pulled her credit cards and driver's license, along with her work ID badge for the Department of Defense from the back sleeve on her cell phone—that DoD badge should be her get out of jail free card. "The name Paisley Moorhead checks out," he said without giving SWAT guy any more information like that Paisley had a top-secret level security clearance designated on her badge.

Should she bring it up?

"Where have you been tonight?" SWAT guy glowered at her.

"Here." Raine wasn't able to get her voice to tremble to make SWAT guy think his intimidation tactics were working, so she worked to show it with her eyes. Situations like this, when she wanted to convey an emotion, she had to use facial expressions because she couldn't give her voice nuance. It sometimes made dangerous situations trickier to navigate. Certainly, it made it harder for her to talk her way out of things.

"Here doing what?" SWAT guy asked.

"Uhm. I was making dinner for my boyfriend and me when I felt sick to my stomach. I came up to the bedroom to lie down for a minute to see if it would pass."

"Where's Lucy?"

How in the world would SWAT know the name Lucy? Maybe it was part of the phone call that got the SWAT team mobilized?

Raine forced her eyes away from the bookcase over to the guy with his rifle trained on her. She licked her lips and stared.

She used that moment to scan through the house in her mind's eye. All of Lucy's belongings were in the guest bedroom closet. It suddenly dawned on Raine; they'd found the coffee cups downstairs. Raine had left them on the front table when she was searching the house for Lucy after she'd broken in.

SWAT guy followed her eyes to the rifle, lifted his hand in a patting motion, and Rifle guy dropped his barrel.

Raine turned back to SWAT guy. "What?"

"Where's Lucy?"

"She was supposed to meet me for coffee, but she didn't show."

"You bought her a coffee anyway?"

Bingo, the cups. Raine would have to remember this lesson. "Whoever gets there first always buys the coffees."

"And you brought them home without drinking them?"

"Is Lucy in some kind of trouble? Why are you here?"

"The coffee. Why did you bring them to this house full?"

"I was waiting in my car for Lucy. She didn't show. Her meeting was probably running late. No biggie. I brought the cups in the house to throw them away. I put them down, and I forgot about them. My stomach wasn't feeling good. I thought maybe eat something. Then I thought no, better not. Then I laid down. Then this." She took a moment to put those details on a mental map so if they asked her to repeat the sequence, she'd have the images all lined up.

SWAT guy was reaching for her ID from the guy who held them in his hand. SWAT guy read over the DoD badge. He compared the photo to Raine's face. Raine had had that photo taken on Monday, so it should match up, even if she wasn't wearing makeup now and her hair was disheveled.

Maybe this would be over soon, and she could get some of her own questions answered.

Raine thought maybe she felt the seed of nausea growing in her stomach. It would be cool if she could vomit on the guy's boots. She focused on the sensation to see if she couldn't bring something up. All she got was a burp. "Excuse me," she said.

"This isn't your house." SWAT guy said.

"No, I'm housesitting."

"You work at the Department of Defense?"

"Yes." She burped again. This one was moister. "Blech. Ugh."

Balaclava guy's head was on a swivel, then he stalked toward a wastebasket.

"What do you do there?"

Raine panted, trying to work up some bile before the guy made it over with the trash can. "Analysis."

"And your friend who owns this house, what's her name?"

Poo. Balaclava wedged the can between her thighs.

"Martha Donaldson."

"And how do you know each other?"

"Yoga class."

"When will she be back in town?"

Oh good. Here it came. Raine leaned forward and coughed and retched into the can. She sat up with a little spew dangling from her chin. With her hands restrained, she had to leave it dangling. Great visual. "Next week." She coughed again. "Ugh. She's at her mom's house. Her mom had to have surgery."

Balaclava pulled a Kleenex from the box, wiped her mouth, and tossed the tissue into the can. It smelled horrible, which was excellent. It roiled her stomach more.

"Thank you," she gasped.

"Call her on speakerphone," SWAT guy said, then looked toward the door.

Raine started to turn, but Balaclava snapped his fingers loudly to tell her that wasn't allowed.

"All clear, no sign of a disturbance," someone said from behind her back.

Raine held her head straight forward. She didn't need to give these guys a reason to think she was a threat.

SWAT guy focused back on Raine. "Is Martha Donaldson in your contacts? We need to call her."

"Yes, the phone has a fingerprint biometric security. Do I have to be cuffed? Don't you need to arrest me to restrain me?"

SWAT guy nodded, and someone came up behind Raine. She could feel them working to release her wrists. Good. This situation was setting off warning signals for Raine. Ever since she'd been captured and held prisoner, she didn't do well under these kinds of circumstances. It was triggering her in ways that made her brain fizzle and snap. This was no time for her brain to go sideways.

SWAT guy held out her phone then walked around where he could watch her screen.

She got past the security and pulled up her contacts. Scrolling down, she tapped on Martha Donaldson's name. It had the picture of the homeowner and this address, even Martha's actual phone number. But Paisley's contact list was an app that let her press a number, and it would dial through to an alternate.

A female voice answered. It was Lynx at Iniquus. Surely, she'd been given a heads up. "Hey, Paisley," Lynx said, sounding tired.

"I'm glad you called. I needed to let you know that I'm expecting a package tomorrow. It's our weekly subscription meal box. It was too late to cancel when mom took a turn. It's going to have perishables in it. Can you make sure to get that put away when you get in? You're welcome to eat the food."

"I…I don't know that I'll be here to do that for you," Raine stammered.

"Oh? Are you okay? You don't sound like yourself."

"You're on speakerphone. I'm at your house, and I'm surrounded by a SWAT team."

"What?" Lynx shrilled. "Are you okay? What happened? Oh, my God. John," she called using the real Martha's real husband's name. "John, Paisley's on the phone, and she says there's a SWAT team in the house."

A man's voice came over the phone with a slight Bronx accent. It was their comms guy, Deep. "Paisley, are you hurt? What's happening?"

"I…I don't know. I was lying on the bed listening to a podcast then there was an explosion. I think they might have broken down your doors."

"My doors? What's going on?" Deep stormed. "Are they going to fix them?"

From a distance, Lynx said, "Ask her if she's okay. She didn't say if she was hurt."

Raine imagined Lynx leaning over Deep's shoulder. Raine was giddy with how well this was flowing. She almost believed the scene herself. "They've manhandled me. I'm probably covered in bruises. I'm scared. Whew! I'm shaking. They haven't told me why they're here."

"Is there someone there that can explain this to us?" Deep asked.

SWAT guy reached for the phone and held it closer to his mouth. "Mr. and Mrs. Donaldson, this is James Talbott, DCPD SWAT. We received a phone call from a woman saying that she shot and killed her husband and one of her children. She told our 9-1-1 operator that the voice in her head said she had to kill her other two children, and she didn't want to do that, but the voice was insisting. We came into your house to save the children."

"Children are at risk, and you're at my house? You have the wrong address! You have to go find them. You have to save them." Lynx's voice was frantic.

"The phone call originated from your home phone number. And two neighbors called to say they heard shots fired. They indicated that the blasts had come from this house."

"My husband and my only child are with me. We're in Florida. It's too early for my neighbors to be home. They all work late. My neighborhood is pretty empty until seven-thirty—eight at night. Which neighbors were these?"

"Ma'am, when we recorded the call, our 9-1-1 dispatcher said she heard screaming children in the background. And it came from your address."

"There's a computer glitch," Lynx yelled with all the emotion that Raine wished she could work into her voice. "Children are in danger. You *have* to find them."

"Did you break down my doors?" Deep asked.

"We breached the doors to gain access," SWAT guy said, standing there, one hand on his hip, looking like he wanted to rip someone's head off.

He was probably getting over-heated in that balaclava.

Meh, why not add some fuel to this fire. "And there was a bomb that exploded. Your house is full of smoke," Raine said, starting to cry. *Excellent.* Raine was so proud of this performance.

"That was flashbang, ma'am, not a bomb. It helps us to gain control of a situation without anyone getting hurt."

"I was hurt," Raine sobbed.

"Who's going to pay for the damage?" Deep demanded.

"Don't worry about that right now," Lynx yelled. "I need those kids to be safe. You need to do that now." She said it as a command as if everyone should just pack up and head out the door on a kid-in-danger search.

Raine was having fun with this. Maybe too much fun. She ducked her head and breathed in the smell of vomit, so she could adjust her facial expression.

"Paisley, where are you going to be?" Lynx asked. "You'll have to go home. You can't house sit for me. It's unsafe."

"But your things." She wrapped a hand around her throat as she cast her eyes around the room. "The doors were broken."

SWAT guy nodded his head as a signal, and the team filed out of the room. "The police will make sure the site is contained." He pulled a business card from the thigh pocket of his tactical pants and handed it to Raine. "I've given Miss Moorhead our contact information."

Raine clutched the trash bin in one hand and the card in the other as she stood.

SWAT guy ended the phone call and handed her the phone.

There was an awkward shuffling of feet as the last of the SWAT team gathered in the hall, then descended the stairs.

Raine sidestepped over to the bookcase and called softly, "Hang tight, Lucy, this is almost over."

A quivering, "All right" sifted out from behind the books.

7

Know the terrain.
~Moscow Rules

Friday

Frost deposited her purse in the bottom drawer of her desk. "I've requested information about the operator functioning under the names Clara Edwards and Cammy Burke. I told them I wanted to understand any role she's playing in Washington D.C. tomorrow at the event listed in the Todor Bilov file. I didn't let on we know her real-world identity."

Back from their dinner break, Griffin, Finley, and Kennedy were settling into the chairs around Frost's meeting table. Prescott had his head in the office fridge under Frost's credenza.

"I'm really just interested to know if she's working with our government," Frost said, making her way to join them at the table.

"If so, we want to be careful not to step on her toes or project a spotlight on her while we gather our intelligence."

Prescott sauntered over with his arm full of water bottles. He set them in front of each of his teammates. Prescott was antsy and ready to get a play in motion. It looked like tonight would be long, what with planning logistics and getting their game prep in place on a short deadline.

Lisa Griffin was looking down at her chest, brushing at the stray crumbs that clung to her sweater. "Which suggests the possibility that Raine, as Cammy, might not be working with our government."

"We'd want to be careful not to blow her cover even if she's not with the U.S.," Kennedy said. "She could be working for an ally. Interpol, for example, would make sense."

"Either way, we still need eyes and ears on Todor Bilov." Frost pulled out a chair next to Griffin and sat. "To that end, I've decided to place an undercover couple at the party." She slid her water bottle to the side and picked up a pen. "I want to keep this locked tight. I'm against bringing in agents that aren't already on our joint task force. And the rest of our team is engaged." Her gaze went from one face to the next as she considered. "It's unfortunate that Raine Meyers knows all of us." She focused on Griffin. "You're the furthest out time-wise. See what you can do with your makeup to change your bone structure. Perhaps colored contact lenses, arranging your hair in a way that Meyers wouldn't have seen when you were in language school. Do you have a plain-looking formal dress you could wear? Something that would help you blend in?"

"Yes, ma'am."

"Finley." She focused on him for a long minute. "It's pretty soon after your car accident to put you in the field," Frost said.

Finley had been transporting two prisoners from West Virginia to Washington D.C. in a snowstorm when his car careened off a cliff. He had spent three days hiking back to civilization with a head trauma. He'd lost a lot of weight during that misadventure that he hadn't put back on, leaving his face gaunt. His skin was the normal Washington D.C. winter pale. Prescott thought that Finley wouldn't look like the Ranger Raine might have seen who'd been baked in the Afghanistan sun and worked out for hours a day to burn away the boredom. Prescott thought Finley was probably safe from being recognized.

Finley shrugged. "We're just going to sit near Cammy and Todor and try to listen in on their communications, right? It's not like things are going to devolve into a fistfight. I can certainly sit and eat the awards dinner chicken next to the guy."

Frost drummed her fingers on the table, considering. "Prescott, you're a definite no go. Kennedy…too soon. Finley," she spun back his way, "do you think she'd recognize you?"

"Hard to say. I was one of hundreds of guys all dressed in the same clothes with the same haircut. Though my haircut is kind of similar." He petted a hand over the bristle that was growing back after his head was shaved for surgery. "Storm was sometimes the only woman on base. I'm sure we'd all recognize her. She wouldn't have much reason to remember me. Granted, she went out with my Ranger unit. But again, I was one in the herd. If I'm wearing black tie, I'm out of my soldier clothing and on a different kind of turf. That usually trips people up."

"All right. Finley and Griffin are the indoors couple. Our goal is to get eyes and ears on Todor and Cammy. Most important are the ears. Surveillance will be monitored by the outside team, Prescott and Kennedy. Kennedy will be the chauffer so they can be deposited in a timely fashion. Prescott will trail the couple as they move from Cammy's apartment to the venue and then to their next destination."

"Yes, ma'am," they said in unison.

It was a good plan for Prescott to have physical distance from the scene, though he wouldn't admit such a thing to Frost.

This was going to be the first time he'd seen Raine in the flesh in seven years. He wasn't sure what his reaction was going to be. Nothing good would be his prediction.

While Prescott had dated some amazing women over the years, Raine was the only woman he'd ever loved. She'd truly understood that his job pulled him out of country and downrange with no notice and with no time frame. Her position pulled her away from the home front, too. They'd always had a long-distance relationship, and it had *never* mattered. They were always safe at home in each other's hearts.

They had been great together up until the moment when things blew apart.

In Raine's mind, Prescott had done the one thing he knew Raine would not tolerate in her life.

To her, it was the worst kind of betrayal.

Seeing the picture of her smiling at Todor Bilov, looking so happy, Prescott was right back in the emotions of the night that ended his relationship with Raine.

Angry as hell, he'd stalked up the side path to his buddy Eric's house. He'd stopped dead in his tracks at the kitchen door. Through the window, he saw Eric with his arms wrapped tightly around Raine. Her head rested on his chest as he smoothed a hand down her back and pressed a long kiss into her hair. When Raine lifted her head, Eric cupped her face, saying something to her and stroking his thumbs over her cheeks.

Prescott hadn't even known she was back in the states. He thought Raine was still deployed in northern Afghanistan.

The anger that had propelled him to Eric's house, to begin with, became rage.

Oh hell no, not my fiancée, was Prescott's only thought.

From that point, Prescott had no idea how he got in the house. No idea how he separated the two. Prescott couldn't remember chambering a punch, but he felt the impact as his knuckles cracked across Eric's jaw. Eric's head jerked left, and his ex-friend dropped, unconscious at Prescott's feet.

The surprise and fury in Raine's eyes had startled Prescott back to his senses.

"Raine," he'd gasped, realizing what he'd done.

She answered by yanking off her engagement ring and chucking it at his face. He stood immobile as it bounced off his cheek and skittered across the floor.

Raine pushed past him and moved out into the night.

Her tires squealed as she raced down the driveway.

AND THAT WAS the last he'd seen of Raine Meyers.

Until today and her picture with Todor.

"Here are the steps that need to be taken." Frost's voice slid back into Prescott's consciousness.

Prescott wondered what he'd missed while his brain was rifling through his memories. He willed himself to stay focused.

Frost pressed her fingertips against the polished wood of the conference table. "I want everyone to go and take a tour of Todor's hotel, get a good lay of the land. Same with the awards dinner location in the Elysium. I also want you to drive the various routes between the two. Consider the possibility that they will go to Cammy Burke's listed address, though that's a more complicated cover for Raine to develop, so I'm assuming that's not where they'll end up. I'm particularly interested in Todor's hotel choice." She tapped a button on her phone, and a map showed up on the widescreen television.

They turned to look.

"He's in a five-star, here." Frost walked over so she could point out a location. "But there are two other accommodations of equal quality mere blocks from the dinner." She turned to face them. "Why would he stay on the other side of the city, especially if he only plans to fly in for two nights and the main event is seeming to take Cammy to this awards dinner." She turned and tapped the screen near the site of the event. Frost drew her fingers slightly south toward the Pentagon. "For reference, Cammy Burke's address is around here. His hotel and her apartment are about equidistant to the party. I feel sure this is not a logistical mistake on Todor's part. Let's make sure that we've mapped out the area."

Pens scratched notes onto pads.

"Griffin and Finley, I would love it if at some point during the banquet, Todor happened to leave his phone out, and you got hold of it to download spyware. Let's get that covered with a warrant. Barring easy access to his cell phone, I'd like you to contrive a way to drop a GPS in his pocket. Make sure to pick a reasonable design, perhaps an extra tuxedo button. And even better, let's get a bug on him, as well. Todor might have wanted that thirty-minute car ride from party to hotel, so he could make a proffer to Cammy. We want to know what the Prokhorovs are after."

"The first ask is rarely what they're looking for," Prescott pointed out.

"True." Frost rested her chin in the web between her thumb and forefinger as she considered him for a moment. She dropped her hand. "It's still interesting information to have. If we end up picking this Todor up or want to develop him as an asset, the way we did with his uncle, any piece of information might end up being the wedge piece that puts him under our control."

Frost waited while the agents jotted their notes, then said, "I have contacts in hospitality at the Elysium. I'll write down their names before you head out, hand them my card." She flicked a finger toward her desk, where a small black container held a stack of her business cards. "Check and see if this event is going to have table assignments. If so, I want you two, Finley and Griffin, sitting at a different table with your backs to Todor and Cammy. If the event doesn't have a seating chart, you're going to have to trail the couple to their table and do your best. Whoever is taking care of the warrant situation, I'd like you to add a camera and audio in Todor's hotel room. We know from Michaels' file where Todor is staying and the room number. According to Michaels, Todor got into town today, so placing the bugs might be tricky. Once you have the warrants in hand, send a technical team over to plant the electronics under the guise of housekeeping."

"I'll fill out the paperwork," Kennedy said. "What should I list as our intercept goals?"

"I want to see Todor get ready for the party. We need to know if he's wearing comms or if he's wearing a weapon. The intercept goal would be to observe if espionage plans were being made or documents are being passed. Our special forces community is at risk by Cammy Burke's access to personnel files. To that end, I'd like to see if he brings Cammy Burke back to his room."

Prescott absolutely did *not* want to monitor the couple back in the hotel room. After Raine's backseat operator tactics with Kennedy, he imagined Raine might do whatever she deemed necessary to succeed at her mission.

Watching her make love to Todor or any man would be hell.

He didn't even want to think about it. As Prescott pressed those thoughts to the side, his mind flashed to images of Raine's body underneath him the last time she was in his arms. Her breast cupped in his hand. Her eyelids half-open, sinking into the sensations as he slid in and out of her. Sweat along her hairline. The moan of his name on her lips. She'd arched as she reached for her orgasm, pressing her stomach against his, her muscles squeezing his di—

"Prescott." Frost jarred him back to the meeting room. "You

have a good relationship with Judge Silverman, why don't you take the warrant tasks off Kennedy's hands. I want you to handle them."

"On it." He bent his head to scribble on his legal pad, hiding his panting breath and the thrum of his heart.

Shit.

He still loved her.

This assignment was going to be hell.

8

Build in opportunity.
~ Moscow Rules

Saturday

"Does anyone want to tell me what last night was all about?" Raine was alone in the bathroom at the apartment rented under the Cammy Burke name, getting ready for tonight's event with Todor Bilov.

A wet toothbrush, some powder residue left on her sink, the toilet paper almost ready for a change, tampon wrappers in the wastebasket, a new issue of a crafting magazine folded back to a Valentine's knitting project and left near the tub, Raine was staging the apartment to look neat but lived in.

Though she'd try her best to keep Todor away from here, if it started to look fishy that he wasn't invited in, she needed the space to support her cover.

Raine's makeup case rested next to her work phone with its end-to-end voice encryption app running.

She was dialed into the Strike Force war room at Iniquus Headquarters and had switched to speakerphone, getting an update while she put on her make-up.

With a blush brush in hand, Raine leaned toward her mirror. "Someone pulled off one hell of a feat, from what the SWAT officer was saying about the phone calls to 9-1-1." She dusted blush over her cheek. "I've seen SWATting written up in the paper. But reading about it in the abstract and experiencing it real-world are very different animals." She swept her brush over the compressed powder, gathering blusher for the other cheek. "Thanks for the heads up, by the way. It kept my gun in its holster and my finger off the trigger."

"Jack here. Glad to be of service. That was a first for us. SWATting, thankfully, is rare. Last night was more dangerous than we'd originally suspected."

The night before, after the SWAT team left the house, Jack and Striker got Lucy out of her hiding place in the master bathroom.

Jack—a giant of a man, probably six foot five, and built like a Superman action figure with black hair and husky blue eyes—had stayed at the Donaldson house to handle security.

Meanwhile, Striker drove Lucy to Iniquus Headquarters.

Striker, Raine already knew. She'd been lent out to his team, back when he was a SEAL operator. On those missions, her task was to help with the women's interrogation and intelligence gathering. She and Striker had hit it off from the get-go.

At the time, Raine had been engaged to Damian.

And now Striker was engaged to Lynx.

Ah, well…

Raine's love life had, by necessity, always run secondary to duty and survival. Few men could understand her circumstances. Which explained why Raine hadn't been in a relationship-relationship—the deep kind, the interesting kind, the kind that made her *feel* the whole range of human emotion—since she'd ended her engagement to Damian Prescott, and that had been…a really long time ago.

Her job description and lifestyle—the secrecy and sudden unexplainable disappearances—didn't lend itself to domestic bliss.

True, working undercover with men like Todor had its moments —the fine dining and interesting conversations… But Raine kept herself vacuum-sealed against any emotional entanglement with her targets.

Todor made that policy particularly easy.

"Did you have any trouble getting home last night?" Jack's voice refocused her.

"No, it was fine. I drove the minivan to the nearest Metro station and got lost in the crowd. On and off the various trains, I took a Lyft back here to the Cammy Burke apartment. If anyone was following me, I'm pretty sure I was able to shake them," Raine said, digging through her bag for her mascara. "I'm sorry, you started with the SWAT fiasco. First, I'd like to know about Lucy. How did she do last night?"

"Striker speaking. I brought Lucy back to Headquarters. We have a full clinic here. The medical team did a thorough workup. Lucy was understandably agitated. They gave her some medication to help her relax and bring her blood pressure down. She's doing better now. Lucy and baby are fine."

"Whew, that's good to hear."

"We've settled her into a safe house until next steps can be decided."

Raine paused, mascara wand in hand. "Striker, I don't think Lucy should be alone."

"Agreed," Striker said. "We placed her in a support house. Sort of a half-way house for our clients who need to lay low but shouldn't be on their own. Typically this means minors who've witnessed crimes. There's a house mother who runs it. We thought

Lucy could use the extra care. The only drawback is it's a couple hours outside of D.C."

"Is someone contacting Lucy's husband?" Raine leaned over the sink to get closer to the mirror to apply the mascara and opened her mouth, so her eyes held wide.

"Lynx here. The DIA has a meeting planned for Monday at the Pentagon. They're going to request that Sergeant McDonald be brought home until this is resolved or other decisions can be made."

Raine slid the wand in and out of the container to load the mascara brush. "That means they're winning. They're taking a Delta Force operator out of the field. Not to say I disagree with the DIA's plan. I'm frustrated, is all. I don't know how Lucy ended up in D.C. She was at Fort Bragg when I first talked to her on the phone. Next thing I knew, she called to say she was up here, trying to hide. I told her I'd be right over. An hour later and BOOM! Fireworks." Raine leaned forward again and stroked mascara onto her lashes.

"I have information on that from my conversation with her last night," Lynx said. "Lucy realized that her husband probably wouldn't be coming home before he had to sign his re-up contract with the Deltas. She'd tried a balancing act over the phone to wherever it was that he was calling base. She says she's not even sure what continent he's on. She worked to convince him not to sign the contract and to come home as soon as his stint was up. At the same time, she was trying not to make him angry or worried about the home front, lest she become a distraction, putting lives at risk with his team. She decided that to protect her husband and her baby, she needed to go into hiding. She can't figure out how anyone would know that she was at Martha's house. Lucy said that she didn't tell anyone she was leaving."

"GPS on her car? Tracker on her phone?" Raine suggested.

"Negative. We checked for both," Lynx said.

Raine hadn't given Lucy enough credit. "That was kind of

badass, being eight months pregnant and trying to keep everyone alive in the face of terrorist threats." Raine threw the mascara into the bag and picked out her rose-colored eight-hour lipstick, what she thought of as "lady-like but still sexy."

"Lucy's in a tenuous position," Lynx said. "Lucy told me she thought it was a gift from God when her friend Martha said she was going to Florida for her mother's emergency surgery. Lucy knew you were up here, and she had hoped you could figure out how to keep her safe."

"Well, thanks to you guys," Raine said, "she made it through the SWATting—huh, I was going to call it a prank, but that's far from the truth. Jack, go back a minute. When I first came on the line, you said, 'Last night was more dangerous than we'd originally suspected.' Can you elaborate on that?"

"SWATting, in general, *is* a high-stakes prank," he said. "It's dangerous for police. You, for example, might well have shot someone blowing through the door dressed in black. And since you use the triple tap—one round to the head, two rounds center mass—that could have gone down very badly for all concerned."

"Fair chance," Raine agreed.

"People have been killed by SWAT responding to fake reports. Police have adrenaline-like all mortals do."

"I'd say someone was probably counting on that." Raine was half-focused on getting a good outline with her lip color before she filled her lips in. "Three corroborative calls."

"SWATting has become complex as it evolves. This isn't the first time that a group has used spoofing technology to make it sound like the call is coming from a certain house. And you're right, the police said three calls—one from inside the Donaldson's house, and two from the neighbors, all describing the same high-risk scenario. That meant no time to play around, just jumping in to save the kids."

"Exactly." Raine held her lips as still as possible for the lipstick to dry.

"Here's the kicker," Jack said. "Another police call went out about a half-hour after we left the house. A woman said that someone broke into her apartment, tied her to a chair, and blindfolded her. A single male, from what she could tell the 9-1-1 operator. Other than that, she had no other information. A neighbor saw her door open and peeked in. Seeing the woman tied up, he asked if she was okay."

"If she was okay?" Raine wrinkled her brow.

"Some people like that kind of play. It wasn't apparent that she was a crime victim versus enjoying a bondage scenario."

"Oh..."

"Nothing was taken. Nothing was moved."

"That's odd." Raine zipped the case and put it away in her middle drawer, pulling out a barrette and hairbrush.

"Let me add that as she was getting tied, the woman saw a rifle on her couch."

"Sniper rifle?" Raine asked, pulling her brush through her hair.

"It wouldn't have to be. A .223 bullet can travel six hundred yards and stay on target. Striker and I went to knock on her door and look out her window."

"Crap."

"As the crow flies, our instruments registered a clear shot to the Donaldson's house at four hundred yards. If you or Lucy had come out on the front lawn or positioned in the picture window in the living room, you would have been in his scope."

Raine's skin became humid as a sudden burst of adrenaline shot through her system. She peeled off her robe and stood there in her panties with a thigh holster already in place. "SWAT would have been blamed if it was a .223 bullet."

"It's possible. I don't know."

"What time did the sniper get there?" Raine asked.

"The victim said she'd just gotten home. She pinned a time to about twenty minutes before you arrived on the scene. That's how the caller had your vague physical description."

"Striker, it was a good plan to walk Lucy through the backyard and to the street behind. It looks like you saved the day. I'm glad I walked out with the SWAT team. We all got home safe. I'm putting on my bra, by the way."

"Deep here. I'm bringing up the computer program, so we can test your connection."

"You and Lynx were perfect on the phone last night." She bent over as she attached the clasp and jiggled her breasts into the cups. "I totally believed you guys were Martha and John Donaldson." Raine stood. "Where is the on/off button on the bra?"

"As a safety feature, you don't have one. My computer monitors it. When the mission is over, you need to call me to disconnect."

"All right. Is it on? Testing. Testing."

"I've got you loud and clear," Deep said.

Raine had never worn a bra with the communications system integrated with the underwire before. But if they could hear her past her boobs, it was fine with her. While the sounds around her were picked up and fed back to Deep's computer system to analyze and clear of ambient noise, Raine would hear Deep through little earbuds that she was dropping into her ear canals and would fish out later with a magnetic wand. "Can you test the earbud comms?"

Softly, she heard Deep say, "If you can hear me say cheese."

"Cheese." Iniquus had also provided her with a cocktail ring that hid a GPS in case things got crazy tonight. And the broach on her dress hid a camera.

"Let me pull on the dress and test the camera connection."

"Whenever you're ready." It was Deep's voice in her ear.

The dress was an Iniquus loaner. It was a one-shouldered Grecian style that was held secure in the bodice, so she could move athletically without fear of mishap. It was also able to support the weight of the camera broach. The skirt crisscrossed at the waist and draped romantically over her hips.

More important than the graceful movement of the fabric, if need be, Raine could tug back one side with her left hand while reaching for her thigh holster with her right. But when she sat, there was no risk of the sides parting and exposing her weapon.

The gun they lent her was tiny. She'd been warned that it had a hell of a kick, that it was going to kill her trigger finger, and she only had six bullets. But hey, it was invisible under a dress that would make people believe that a weapon wasn't possible.

With her gun now securely in the thigh holster, Raine stepped into the dress and zipped everything in place.

She reached to her shoulder to adjust the broach. "I'm dressed."

"I'm turning the camera on… I have a clear picture of you looking in your mirror." Deep was back in her ear. "A warning, the camera can't be turned off from your end. If you need to use the lady's room, we suggest that you keep the camera pointing toward the door, so don't lean over. Alternatively, you can put your hand over the broach."

"Copy."

Raine tipped her head back and inspected her neck where she'd used specialized makeup to hide her scars. Assuring herself that she'd done a good job, Raine added two elements of her own to her security equipment, a white sapphire cuff bracelet that hid a blade that could loop over her knuckle if she was throwing punches. Punch throwing was low on her expectation's list, but then again, Raine hadn't expected to get SWATted yesterday.

The other was a matching barrette that hid the lock picking tools that Raine never left home without. Raine took a moment to swoop up one side of her hair and pin the curl back behind her ear. She turned to inspect and thought she looked old-school glamorous.

"Striker here. Todor's car should be outside in five minutes. He's on the highway just north of you. We have eyes in the sky and a clear night. If anything separates you from the car, we'll be tracking your ring. So please do everything you can to keep it on you one way or another."

"Roger."

"Raine, we'll be in place. We won't interfere, but we have your back," Lynx said. "Good luck tonight."

"Thanks, Lynx." Raine turned and cut off the bathroom light. "I have a feeling I'm gonna need it."

9

Avoid static lookouts
~ Moscow Rules

Saturday

Prescott sat in the back seat of the town car behind heavily tinted windows with a computer, monitoring Griffin and Finley inside the event.

Kennedy sat in the driver's seat, with a chauffer's hat on his head, in charge of putting bookmarks on the comms feeds.

Audio samples of Todor and Cammy Burke's voices were tagged in the AI—artificial intelligence—system, as well as samples from Finley and Griffin. The program would target and amplify those voices while muting the others unless the outside agents overrode the system to listen more widely.

While the event had open seating, Finley and Griffin must have been able to position themselves close by. Every once in a while, one of them would turn enough that their glasses cameras picked up their targets.

Of added benefit, Griffin had gotten close enough to Todor that she was able to drop the bug in his pocket. If it stayed there, they'd be golden.

It was the bug that was picking up the conversation between Cammy and Todor now.

The FBI team might get what they needed: the reason for Raine Meyers to be involved with Todor and the reason why Todor was pursuing Cammy Burke.

Prescott had started his evening at the Cammy Burke high rise. He watched Raine emerge from the lobby on Todor's arm. A black fur stole draped across her back; her dress glamorous. Prescott was getting used to seeing her as a blonde. When they had been together, she had sable brown hair.

To him, she was gorgeous either way.

Through his binoculars, Prescott had to watch the gentle smile that Cammy sent toward Todor as they stepped into the drive.

It's an act. She's on a mission, he reminded himself.

It was hard to believe that this many years later, the floodgates of memories and emotions of their past relationship could open and swamp his system.

If he couldn't wrestle this down, Prescott was going to have to pull himself off the case. He obviously wasn't clear thinking when it came to Raine, and he wasn't going to jeopardize his teammates and their mission because he'd been jilted.

Jilted with good reason, he reminded himself.

Todor's close protection element opened the passenger's car door. Todor helped Raine in before rounding the car and finding his own seat in the back next to her.

The chauffeur stood poised by the driver's side.

When the couple was settled in the interior, both security professionals' gazes swept the area. They climbed in and drove away.

Prescott's job was to warn Finley and Griffin of their target's proximity. That way, his teammates could get out of their car, driven by Kennedy, just ahead of Todor and Cammy. It was always better to be in the front rather than coming up behind when surveilling someone. It made people less suspicious that they were being watched.

Once everyone had gone inside, Prescott parked the car, texted the GPS coordinates to Finley, put the keys in the console, and walked to Kennedy's car.

And there they sat. And sat. And sat.

Nothing of any interest was going on.

"How was your flight?"

"What knitting project are you working on now?" And on and on with mostly banalities.

Granted, they were at an awards dinner, and they were speaking behind claps and in between presenters.

The program seemed to be winding down, now maybe they'd hear something with significance.

Spinning off the theme of the last presenter's remarks, Todor said, "I read an interesting article about sleep deprivation causing one's brain to eat itself."

"Eating itself?" Raine paused. "Well, that would explain a lot," she added quietly.

"Why do you say that? Are you not sleeping well?"

"Actually, no. And it's left me feeling dull. I'm sorry if my conversation isn't scintillating tonight."

Prescott imagined a sad smile accompanied her words and could imagine her leaning forward just a bit, sliding her hand into Todor's, making him feel like the protector. Bold. And manly. Winding him around her finger.

"She's leading him somewhere," Kennedy said.

Prescott nodded.

"What you call this, mind chattering? Monkey mind? Is something going on at your work?"

There was a long pause. "Yes, actually. I'm rather concerned about a rash of phone calls I've been getting about contract termination dates."

"You work human resources at Pentagon." There was a question in his inflection. "You do nice things for people, yes? Make sure they have services, yes? The special forces and their families?"

Prescott leaned forward. Intent. Human resources for special forces and their families wasn't really a thing. Special Operations Forces, and the termination dates of contracts, this was getting interesting.

Kennedy gave him a thumbs up.

Keep talking, Raine.

"Yes. Normally. Well, yes… I shouldn't talk about this. I'm sorry, can we change the subject?"

Kennedy had laughter in his eyes when he looked over the seat at Prescott. "She's a pro."

Silence, then a mumble in Russian came over the comms.

Todor responded.

"Did he say twenty minutes?" Prescott asked.

"That's what I heard." Kennedy tapped the computer to mark that communication.

"Is everything okay?" Raine asked.

"I signaled my security man to tell driver we should leave in twenty minutes. It looks like speeches are done. Dessert and one dance for politeness sake, and then we go." A kissing sound. "Thank you for putting up with this. If you are tired, this must be excruciating. It is difficult for me to stay awake during speeches, and I am passionate about topic of literacy." He chuckled.

"It's your night. Whatever you want is fine."

"Your eyes keep looking over to my security man. You don't like my security."

"It's not them. It's that I don't like the *idea* of them. It makes me feel like something…that *you* might be in danger."

"I wish Griffin or Finley would turn around so I could see this playing out," Kennedy said.

"Agreed. I'm getting tired of staring at the floral arrangement," Prescott said. "Frost ordered them to keep their backs to Raine." Stakeouts had never been Prescott's thing. Deltas, CIRG, that was all high adrenaline action. Even his newest position as special agent in charge of their joint task force meant he was busy with the strategy even if he was less likely to be in the mix of things.

Sitting in a freezing cold car on a dreary January night, listening to nothing of importance was brutal.

"The reason for security," Todor said, "is that it should make you feel safe. You surprise me. You're very strong woman. I see in your eyes. When have you ever felt vulnerable? I don't mean 'maybe he will break my heart' vulnerable. But a real life or death fear?"

"I've been afraid and vulnerable before. I remember vividly this one time. I was in college. I spent the summer studying Italian in Perugia. I lived in a *pensione* on *Rue de Rosa.*

"Every day, I walked to school and ate at the students' cafeteria. I saw the same people there, and they grew familiar to me. I didn't speak Italian well enough to have a conversation with them, but I tried to look friendly.

"One day, one of the boys who I had said hello to a few times was outside the dining hall on his moped when I left to go home. He asked me if I wanted a ride. And I said yes."

"Oh," Todor exhaled. "This boy, you felt friendly toward him… Except this boy proceeded to frighten you."

"He did. Yes. Scarred me for life." Her laughter was a perfect amalgam of femininity and vulnerability. It was like a virility shot, the kind of laughter that made a man feel like a man.

Finley turned his gaze on the couple. He must have been spun around by the sound of that laugh, too.

And there it was; Todor held her hand to his lips, but his head turned as his gaze took in the room. Instinctual. He probably wasn't even aware that he was doing it, scanning to make sure that no other man had his eyes or intentions on Raine.

Prescott knew all too well what it felt like when his chest expanded with territoriality. Not that he considered himself to be a caveman. Raine could very well take care of herself. But that hasn't stopped his instincts. They were baked into a code as old as time. And Prescott saw it on this guy's face. He was guarding her.

Raine was playing with fire.

Prescott wondered if she knew that and was using it—if she thought this was a game.

A man in protective mode, especially one with the political and financial means to be deadly, was just that. Deadly. From the look on his face, Todor's ego was on the line.

Again, old DNA. It made a man fight for the win.

Finley swung his face toward the security guy, losing Raine's image, and Prescott was ticked.

They were back to audio-only.

"Please, tell me," Todor said, low and slow.

Prescott and Kennedy both braced to hear this conversation. Prescott was sure that all four of the men listening had already mapped the trajectory of her story in their minds. What man wouldn't, when a conversation turned like this?

"We were in school at the center of Perugia. I thought it was fine," Raine started. "But quickly, things started turning badly. He was driving like a crazy person. I thought perhaps this guy was trying to show off for me. He was racing up and down the cathedral steps. People who were lounging there were jumping up and stumbling to the side, trying to get out of his way, raising their fists and yelling. I was horrified by the desecration of a holy place. And I was scared. I wasn't wearing a helmet, and I could easily visualize being thrown and rolling down the side of the very high hill. I remember searching my mind for a word, *any* word, that I could say in Italian that would make this guy slow, or better, to stop, so I could get off. And finally, I just said the only thing that would come to my mind. 'Piano!'"

"What? Piano?"

Griffin turned her head that way, and Prescott got a flashing glimpse of Todor throwing back his head and laughing. And Raine's sweet lips smiling back at him. Then Griffin was back to watching the centerpiece.

"You laugh," Raine said, "but it really was genius. Piano in Italian means soft, slow, quiet. He understood and not only slowed down but stopped driving on the stairs."

"Ah," Todor exhaled his relief.

They all did.

It was a funny little story about fear from an overzealous motorbike ride.

"And then he drove down the road, past the turnoff to my *pensione*, he was talking—something about his veterinary school and pointing at things. It felt off. And I was scared again. But in a different way. We were now far from anyone." Her voice grew quiet. Her words came slower. "There were no houses, no cars, no people. I was dressed in a sundress and flip flops. Uhm that is a sandal."

"Yes."

"He stopped in a parking lot that was surrounded on three sides by tall rock walls. I looked around, and I thought, how could I be so stupid as to get on a bike with a stranger? There I was. Nowhere to run. No one to hear me cry out. He wasn't a big guy. But he was bigger than me—and muscular. I thought, now I was going to be raped, and there was nothing I could do. I couldn't even steal the motorbike and make an escape. I didn't know how it worked. I was horrified that I'd let myself get into that situation. And then I thought after he raped me, I could identify him. He would probably need to kill me."

"Oh, my darling, this story is terrible. Did he…? Were you…?

"No. Surprisingly, no. It was so innocent. I saw the situation through American glasses. What could happen very easily to an American woman. No, we were in Perugia, very Catholic. The girls were virgins when they wed. I'm sure rape happened. It happens everywhere. But no. He had taken me there because he wanted to teach me how to ride a moped."

Another flick of Griffin's glasses showed Raine looking ruefully at Todor. "But your question was when had I felt real life or death fear. And I felt it—the complete vulnerability of being a woman—at that moment. It was a terrible feeling. Oh, look! Dessert is here. And they've brought Bacci!"

"I'm not familiar with this chocolate. It is good?"

"It's made in Perugia. I must be psychic to be telling you a story—my story about motorcycles and fear when I lived in Perugia—and then be brought a dish of Perugia's famous chocolates."

"Women's intuition. You say this, yes?"

"Men do when they're poking fun."

"I don't poke you."

"Mmm. Well, you haven't *yet*," Raine answered.

Prescott felt his stomach drop.

"This is a phrase I don't know," Todor said.

"Never mind. The waitress is asking about coffee, should we? I don't know what you have planned…"

"No, coffees, but thank you," Todor said loudly.

"What was that story about?" Kennedy asked. "It's got to be a strategy."

"She's a vulnerable female who is frightened by the power of men," Prescott said. "She's not able to protect herself in the big bad world and is looking for a knight in shining armor. It was a great story, you have to admit. It's the kind of story that makes a man feel like he could step in and save her from her dragons. I'd say she's got him right where she wants him."

"Her next move?"

After the poking comment, Prescott didn't want to guess. "I'd say a few more 'I need a big strong capable man' tales of woe sprinkled lightly and sit back and wait for them to request a favor. Something small."

"Dance?" Todor's voice rose from the computer speaker.

"Thank you," Raine responded.

"And will she comply?" Kennedy asked.

"I think she'll give them something innocuous, so they believe she's trying. What I imagine she needs is the same thing our task force needs, to figure out what the heck the Prokhorovs are up to now."

The camera lens on Griffin's glasses settled on Todor and Raine walking away from the table arm in arm.

Behind Todor's back, Raine was flashing them the bird.

"Well," Griffin said. "So much for wearing disguises and lying low. Cammy Burke made us."

10

Technology will always let you down.
~Moscow Rules

Saturday

Raine shivered in the backseat of the car despite her faux fur wrap and the blasting heater.

Next to her, Todor was sending a text. She could guess what he was tapping out.

Here we go, she thought—*gut-check time.*

As if her next moves in this life and death charade weren't tenuous enough, now she had another worry.

Two faces from her military past had shown up at the event tonight. At first, she thought she was mistaken. A girl that Raine could swear she'd helped study for her Russian exam and who had flirted with her. Pretty girl, nice, hugely smart, but Raine wasn't interested in dating women. Or anyone other than Damian. At that time, Raine *knew* he was the love of her life. Her one and only.

The thoughts of youth and innocence.

Lisa… Mary Lisa? Something like that.

Then there was the guy escorting her. He looked pretty bad. Like he'd been sick and hadn't recovered. In her memory, he stuck out as the Ranger who had lifted her by her pack and thrown her in the back of his truck, crawling in beside her as they drove like bats from hell away from the firepower. *You don't forget a face that saves you.*

Why were they together posing as a couple?

Why were they at a literacy event?

Why did they stick so close to her?

The DIA didn't send them to watch her six; they'd paid Iniquus to do that. And Iniquus was a lot more subtle. She'd spotted Blaze and Striker over by the bar, taking turns with their back to her so the other could keep watch. Nice tactic.

Whatever these two were up to put her op in danger. So she'd warned them off with a solid middle finger.

Raine was nervous enough about what was going to go down. Last night and the SWAT force had been bad. Finding out the bad guys had a sniper was worse. Raine needed to calm her nervous system down, or she'd be reacting by reflex instead of stratagem.

Combat breathing in the backseat seemed like the wrong thing to do. What she needed was a laugh, genuine or not.

"What are you looking at?" she asked, lifting her chin toward his phone.

"My friend, he send me cat video. I open because I think important. Just cat riding skateboard wearing bear costume."

Raine tipped her head. "You know, Todor Bilov, sounds a bit like Teddy Bear. Maybe I should call you that as a nickname."

"This is a pejorative, no? It say that I am fat man, unfit man."

"You?" Raine scoffed.

"It say I am made of fluff-stuff inside. I am not a man with iron will." He made a fist, flexing his bicep, and grinned at her.

She leaned back. "Psh. As if."

"What does this mean to you then, Teddy Bear?"

"When I was a child, and I was afraid," Raine reached deep to find a seed of warmth and tried to bring that emotion genuinely to her eyes, a bit of sentimentality, "I'd hug my Teddy Bear and feel safe. I found him comforting. He guarded me against my nightmares." She smiled and opened her hand on the seat between them so he would lace his fingers with hers.

Raine knew he was acting as much as she was. But they'd both have to keep playing each other for fools. If she did a good job, he'd never know the truth of the situation. "I like your name, Todor. What does it mean? Do you know?"

"It comes from the Greek Theodoros."

"See? Teddy!"

"Which means gift from God."

"Your mother picked a good name for you." She watched his face in the flicker of lights as they passed through the Washington D.C. streets. They were headed in the direction of his hotel.

He'd asked her to join him for a nightcap there before he signaled the driver where to go. Of course, she'd said yes.

That had been the trajectory all along, and Iniquus was in place.

Raine tried to soothe her nerves. "At the dinner tonight, you asked me if I had ever felt vulnerable, and I shared my Italian piano story. I can't imagine you ever feeling vulnerable." She petted her free hand down his arm. "You're so steady and strong—your body, your mind. I wonder what it must be like to feel secure. To know that whatever you need to do to survive, you can do it. And if you can't, that you have the family there to make sure you're fine." She lifted her free hand to gesture toward their driver and the guy sitting shotgun.

Neither of them seemed to speak English, and she'd be darned if she was going to let them know that she spoke Russian and could follow everything they'd been saying. That they weren't speaking Bulgarian went on her interest list.

Todor turned to her as much as his seatbelt would allow. "And yet this is not true. Money and good family doesn't cover all possibilities. Though I admit, they have paved way to wonderful and fulfilling life for me. But I was not always so sure I would be allowed to live it."

"What does that mean, Todor?"

"When I was in university, I was diagnosed with Hodgkin's Lymphoma."

"Cancer?" Raine put her hand to her heart.

"Doctors say I had eighty percent chance of survival, but all I could think was I was going to be part of twenty percent, the two in ten, who die. It took up my every thought. I was terrified to die. As you can see," he paused to smile, "this did not come to pass. I was indeed one of majority who survive my diagnosis."

"Todor," Raine gasped.

"But my studies, they suffer. I became overwhelmed with anxiety. My—how you say? —mental health was as debilitating now as my physical health be while I have treatment."

"How did you get well again? You seem to be much better."

"Yes. There was trial with psychedelic drugs to treat anxiety."

She shuffled around in her seat so she could look at him face to face. "Here in America, those are against the law."

"I was in Europe at time. Thankfully."

He waited for her to nod, then he continued. "They say there are a few people, very few, that can't handle the psychedelic drug. That it pushes them into schizophrenia or psychosis."

Okay, this was all very familiar. Raine had just watched this in a documentary on one of her subscription channels. It was a worthy story, but Todor really should have chosen something that Cammy wouldn't have gone home and researched. This one would show up in a basic search. A real Cammy would start to ask questions. Cover blown—or at least doubts sown. This was Todor's first tradecraft mistake.

"But I was so miserable. I thought I can't live this way. I was trouble functioning. I almost, almost think if I had died that this might be preferable to be debilitation with anxiety. You say this or debilitated?"

"Yes," she whispered. "Debilitated."

"I had engulfing fear that cancer come back. I was willing to take risk and do drug."

"You were part of a medical experimentation group? In history class, I read about the era when dropping acid was a big thing and that people experienced bad trips. What happened? What was that like?"

"I had to go meet with this man who didn't call himself my therapist. He called himself my guide. In this role, he was supposed to keep me from having this bad trip."

"So that's possible?"

"Intention, he say, is paramount. The substance was psilocybin from mushroom. Magic mushroom, I think, is American phrase."

"Maybe. I don't really know." Raine fought to keep her muscles loose. They'd driven halfway into the tunnel and had rolled to a standstill.

Cars all around them were coming to a stop.

Todor's volume went up as if he were trying to hold her attention. "I tell you. This was amazing experience. There were colors I could hear as music and taste like gourmet foods. These colors came in and displaced my fears."

Todor's fingers tensed around hers. The muscles around his eyes hardened.

Raine's heart pounded, and she had to remind herself to breathe and not look out the back window. *Focus on Todor's eyes.*

"When this happened." He licked at his lips as if his mouth went dry. "I was filled with feelings of euphoria. When the psilocybin left my system, all anxiety that had been paralyzing me was gone too. To me, I had experienced the other side. Death. It was quite nice."

He paused.

Raine could hear her blood pounding in her ears.

The cars in the tunnel were inching up, packing tightly together like sardines in a can. It was a bad thing to do. One big impact from the rear would shove them into each other. If she were the driver, she'd have left a space to serve as a safety cushion.

Louder still, Todor said, "I remember being with my grandmother when she was dying, and the nurse woke her up to take a scheduled pill. My grandmother said, 'Oh, bliss. I want to be there.'"

Beads of sweat formed on his forehead and upper lip.

He released her hand and reached into his pocket for a handkerchief, which he used to mop his brow. He covered the move by saying to the driver in Russian and then in English for her sake, "Can you turn down the heat please? It's quite warm," though it was cool inside the car.

Todor turned back to her. "When Baba was fully awake, I ask her about that, and she say she was leaving body more and more, getting ready for journey home. Baba was not religious person. She was practical person. She think that when she die, she will decay, that is all. Life was just now. And when I was told that dying was my potential, I believe this too." He swiped his palms down his thighs, then rubbed them with his handkerchief. "When I die, I simply stop. I had discounted that moment when Baba was sharing with me. I forget about it until that moment with the drug. I feel like I experienced what it is to die. What she was telling me was on the other side."

He was trying to plant the seeds of death and dying by telling this story, to make her think about the fragility of life.

Tradecraft.

What she wanted to plant in return were the seeds of a bourgeoning traditional love relationship, where the woman was the delicate flower and the man the sturdy tree.

It was a game.

This was a game.

"Euphoria," she said.

"And peace. And while I do not want to die. I want to be here living my life. I, too, am no longer afraid."

"GPS has lost signal." The car's navigational system said.

Raine frowned. "That's unusual in this tunnel." She reached for Todor's phone that he had placed on the seat between them. "It says you have no bars."

"What does this mean?"

"I don't know. I've never lost GPS or cell reception in this tunnel before."

The sound of motorcycle engines swarmed from behind them.

Raine's fingers desperately wanted to inch her skirt to the side, to get her gun into her palm.

Todor swallowed hard. His body stiffened, though Raine knew he was fighting against it. She needed some way to not look at him. Her acting skills were failing her. She popped open her clutch and pulled out her compact and lip gloss. Placed there for this very reason, Raine opened the compact and angled it to see out the back window, pretending to fuss with her hair.

Her bracelet slid up her arm. She could put her middle finger through the decorative circle, pull outward, and a two-inch-long, razor-sharp blade would stick out of her fist. Or, she could open the door and jog over to the maintenance walk and crawl up the side and under the rail and run. But duty to country kept her in her seat, pulling off the top of her lip gloss, pretending to primp.

The assailants were here.

A bang and a fragmenting crack sounded.

Both the driver's and Todor's windows burst with splintering glass. She'd had her mirror up so she could raise her elbow to protect her face. Just before the explosion of shards, she saw Todor and the driver both duck down to protect themselves.

Hands holding stun guns reached through the open windows.

She used the noise to unclasp her seatbelt and unlock her door.

They stunned Todor—One Mississippi, two.

Good, that wasn't bad.

The driver took a slightly longer hit. But he wouldn't be medicated.

Todor and the driver's involuntary screams, though, lit Raine on fire. She squeezed her hands around her thighs and begged herself not to react with violence.

This was far worse than the SWAT team last night.

Man, she needed just a little downtime before her nervous system took these hits.

A hand came through Todor's window, and a syringe went into his neck.

The door popped open.

A man in a black helmet pulled Todor from the seat and over to a waiting motorcycle.

Another man was revving his engine. The sound echoing through the tunnel was menacing—a warning. Stay in your cars.

Slumped over, Todor was wedged between the backrest on the motorcycle built for two and the driver. His body draped onto the motorcycle driver and somehow attached with a harnessing system.

From her position, pressed against her door, Raine could see little of the mechanics of the process. The rhythm and coordination of their movements spoke to their practice and meticulous preparation. That the team was this skilled needed to be noted in her reports.

What kind of family would come up with this kind of scenario to sell a scheme?

Biological family, that was.

Raine could easily see her military or DIA family planning such a thing.

As Todor was transported forward. Raine glanced toward the CPSs—close protection specialists—in the front seat. The driver slumped against the steering wheel. The one riding shotgun had his hands in the air.

Through the front window, Raine saw the rifle barrel aimed at his chest, keeping him in place.

Raine's brain screamed, "Run!"

She set her jaw. Two seconds. She could do this.

A black motorcycle helmet pushed into the back seat.

Raine's scream was an illusion, more of an *agh* than anything else. Her vocal cords wouldn't allow her to shrill or get much in the way of volume.

The stun gun hit the CPS in the neck.

One Mississippi, two Mississippi, three… Okay, that was overly zealous. Maybe the black helmet guy was having trouble managing adrenaline.

Since she was smaller than the CPS, hopefully, black helmet would be able to get his finger off the trigger sooner.

Raine laced her fingers into the door latch. She could still run, except for that rifle barrel.

And now, her turn.

The bright torture of electricity shot through her system. One Mississippi. Two Mississippi. Three Mississippi. Four... were they *trying* to kill her?

She'd fight, but she was unable to make a voluntary movement.

The weight of her arm dragged the door handle down.

The sheer bulk of her collapsing body pressed against the door, and it swung wide. She tumbled to the ground. Her head smacked against the blacktop.

A shot rang through the tunnel.

If she'd been hit, she couldn't feel it past the riot of her body's reactions.

Her nervous system was screaming.

A heavy weight draped over her. She was aware enough to know that someone had thrown their body over hers protectively—a soldier's move. A last-minute hail Mary when a buddy was shot and bullets strafed the area.

Her lids half-open, in her delusional mind, she saw Damian's face. Beautiful, wonderful Damian. Strong, steady Damian. She dreamed that his brown eyes, normally filled with warmth, were now filled with fear and concern, and love.

It was just the way she wanted to be looked at in that moment.

Someone who knew her.

Someone who gave a damn about her.

Someone who might forgive her for throwing their relationship away when she just couldn't cope anymore with anything.

Raine's breathing was laborious and painful.

Everything about this moment was excruciating.

Something about that elongated zap seemed to be the final swing of the hammer.

She couldn't do this job anymore.

She was done.

And with that, she closed her eyes and slipped away.

11

Be non-threatening.
~ Moscow Rules

Saturday

Prescott and Kennedy had been two cars back, trapped in the traffic jam in the tunnel with no reception, following the GPS and bug the inside team had planted on Todor at the beginning of the night.

Their comms hadn't picked up signal since Raine had been teasing Todor about calling him teddy bear.

"I don't like this," Prescott had muttered as the roar of motorcycles came up the tight alleys between the rows of stopped cars. He'd spun his head as he counted them in the dim light.

Six, at least. Eight…

He'd pulled his gun and reached for the door handle.

"Steady," Kennedy said. "Let her be a professional. She hears them coming, too. She's not going to risk her life for this op. That wouldn't serve anyone. She'd get out if she thought she needed to. She's skilled."

Prescott had checked himself.

He wouldn't go running in like a lovesick schoolboy.

This was more than stupid; it was dangerous.

He'd pull himself off the case as soon as he got back to the debrief.

"I was there with her in Brussels. I've seen her in action." Kennedy had reassured his teammate. "She's cool under pressure, a chess player, skilled as hell." Kennedy had the voice of someone talking him off a ledge. "Trust her."

He trusted her. He didn't trust the situation. Every single person in this tunnel was stuck. Mothers and kids. The elderly and enfeebled. As the motorcycles vaulted past his window, he saw they all had pistols strapped to their thighs.

One thing for sure, Prescott didn't want shots fired in the tunnel.

He'd jammed his Glock back in its holster.

Sitting there had been antithetical to every instinct roaring through Prescott's system, commanding him to act and save Raine.

In his mind, the possessive *his* hid just behind her name.

That was a hell of a thought.

And he'd have to deal with it. Later.

He'd watched as the black-clad motorcyclists swarmed the car, broke the glass. There were too many players, too much confusion to make sense of the action from his angle.

Clutching the steering wheel, Kennedy chanted his mantra, "Steady. Steady. Steady. We can't have a gunfight in here." Probably as much for Prescott's sake as for his own.

This op was orchestrated.

Someone probably stopped traffic up at the top of the tunnel.

Nowhere to run.

Nowhere to hide.

And motorcycles.

Prescott had kept it together while the men pulled Todor limply from the car. With no working comms, he and Kennedy couldn't even move assets into place to see what happened, but they'd be able to track the GPS once they were out of the tunnel, as long as Todor kept his jacket on.

Prescott tried to imagine what they'd do to save Raine if she was taken to a different location than Todor was. The FBI didn't have warrants to track her. Hence, no GPS was planted.

Maybe Frost had figured out Raine's affiliation.

Did Raine's organization have a wire on her?

That thought had sent fear racing through his system. The bad guys finding Raine wired up, and probably with hidden weapons? That scenario could only play out badly.

Kennedy popped his door. "They're leaving."

With that green light. Prescott dove out the passenger's side, running with his head low toward Todor's car.

He had watched as Raine spilled to the ground. Her feet still inside the vehicle. Her head smacking the pavement. Her chest heaving as she sought air.

And now he was on top of her, looking into her dazed eyes as a bullet whizzed overhead.

"Sir, are you all right?" Kennedy must have headed to the driver. "I have first aid training. I'm going to help you."

His saying that reminded Prescott that he had to preserve Raine's cover. He had no idea who might be watching and what plans might be in play.

Outing Raine could be deadly.

As the sound of motorcycle engines drifted off into the distance, Prescott clambered off Raine, placing his fingers on her neck to check for a heartbeat. "Miss, are you all right?"

He slapped her cheeks lightly to rouse her, but her face remained slack.

Her dress with its high slits had swept to the side, revealing black lace panties with a little blue ribbon. He could see the curl of her pubic hair, and even here, even now, it had the same effect on him that it always did.

Brushing his hand down the fabric of her dress to cover her, he aimed to protect her modesty and give himself some relief.

A hand on his shoulder spun Prescott around. "I'm a nurse," a middle-aged woman said.

Prescott hoped it was true. She was in scrubs. But she could be a plant. He'd watch her every move.

"I saw the man use a stun gun on her and the driver," she said as she crouched by Raine's side. "I saw sparks, anyway."

"This guy has stun gun burn marks on his neck," Kennedy called through the open door. "Conscious. He doesn't have control yet. He has a gun in a shoulder holster."

Prescott had seen Raine's thigh holster. She'd had the ability to shoot her way out of the situation. She could have escaped with her skillset. When she was attacked, Todor was already pulled from the car. She wasn't protecting him. She must have been protecting the mission.

The nurse looked over her shoulder toward Kennedy with a startled look.

"He was their driver." Prescott hoped he could keep her calm so she'd focus on Raine. "I bet he was also supposed to be their security guard."

"He didn't do a very good job of that, did he?" she deadpanned.

"I'm checking the other guy," Kennedy called.

"Under the circumstances, what he did was probably best," Prescott said. "If the kidnappers started shooting in the tunnel, ricochet might have killed people, including the guy they were kidnapping."

"Are you police?" she asked, looking at her watch while she held Raine's pulse.

"Avid reader. Is she okay?"

"It's going to take a while to regain her muscle control." She laid Raine's arm across her stomach. "Her vitals seem stable. We need to get her warm. There's not much else to be done. I have something with carbs and electrolytes in my car that might help her restore glycogen to her muscles, but it'll be a while before I can give her anything. A trip to the hospital is probably in order. He zapped her for an aggressively long time."

"Hey," Kennedy called. "I'm going to jog out of here to find phone reception and get rescue headed this way. This guy's not looking good, either." Without waiting for Prescott to respond, Kennedy took off running.

Prescott came to a knee and curled his toes under, sliding his hands under Raine. "I'll move her to my car where there's heat. You're right. The pavement's too cold to leave her here. The night air…"

"Hypothermia," the nurse said with a nod. "My car's right here." She opened the side minivan door. One of the passenger captain's chairs had been removed, leaving a gaping space on the floorboard, a perfect place for Raine to be comfortable. The nurse reached onto the backbench and pulled out a folded sleeping bag, and laid it down. "Okay. I've got her head." She rounded Prescott and got her hands into position. "On three. One. Two. Three."

He pressed to standing and rolled Raine toward his chest. The last time he'd carried her like this, she'd fallen asleep holding his hand under the stars on a trip to Egypt.

That whole trip, she'd been having nightmares and trouble sleeping. He hadn't wanted her to wake up enough to walk into the hotel. "Hush," he'd said that night as he'd scooped her up. "Just sleep. I've got you." He'd loved the feel of her nestling against him as he carried her in. Trust. Comfort. It was a perfect memory.

Raine didn't have the muscle control to nestle this time. She had to allow herself to be lifted and carried whether she wanted to or not.

"I've got you," he said. Prescott thought about the story she'd just told back at the dinner of feeling vulnerable. He hoped that before her eyes closed that Raine had seen it was him. And that she knew he would keep her safe.

He *would.*

So much for his decision to remove himself from this op.

Now, he was all in.

12

Maintain a natural pace
~Moscow Rules

Saturday

Raine waited in the hospital lobby, hoping Todor would hurry up and rouse himself from the medication the motorcycle guy had shot into his system so he could get released and they could leave.

The sooner, the better.

Todor's ambulance, and hers, had arrived here at Suburban Hospital at about the same time. He'd been "found by a stranger on the side of the road after he'd dropped from the back of the motorcycle." Or so he was told. He didn't know why. He'd been unconscious, after all.

That, according to their intelligence, was the story Todor planned to feed her later.

They must think I'm an idiot.

Okay, maybe not idiot, gullible. And that was what Raine had been reaching for with her fictitious role—Cammy Burke: lonely, romantic, trusting.

It was a little insulting that they hadn't given this event more thought.

Raine unclasped her barrette, combed her fingers through her hair, and slid it back in place.

As far as scenarios went, this one must have been planned by someone who didn't read fiction and didn't understand a good plot arc. It would have been better if Todor had roused from his medicine, punched his captor in the face with a lucky swing that put the bad guy out, and he escaped barefoot into the night.

But that would have dragged things out longer than their time table afforded. They needed Cammy's survival hormones still humming through her body the next time she spoke with Todor.

To that end, they probably dosed Todor a little too heavily; Raine was already bored.

This was their big test: Would she stick with him or go shrieking into the night?

Cammy Burke had made it easy for them. They thought they were just locking down that necessary love-connection-hormone-filter, then their op would be golden.

They were right. Cammy Burke would only care about the outcome. They were all going home, none the worse for wear.

Cammy Burke wouldn't wonder too much about the scene beyond the pablum they'd feed her.

Raine would have to clamp down on the sarcasm and disdain of her inner voice. It could pop out at any time in vocabulary choice, which was poor tradecraft. She guessed there were times when not having a normal vocal range could be helpful…

Still, she'd be careful to steer her conversation away from anything that would ask for an explanation beyond, "How did you get away? Who were these people? Are you in danger?"

There was an older woman in stained bedroom slippers who had tipped back in her chair, lightly snoring with an opened magazine over her face.

Raine wasn't convinced this wasn't a plant sent to monitor her. She'd stay in character.

She should probably pace.

Yes, pacing felt like the thing Cammy would do. A little hand wringing, maybe.

Raine's muscles were sore from being stunned, but other than that, she was okay. Moving felt better. It was too cold to sit still in a one-shouldered evening gown. Her fake fur stole must have slid off in the car back in the tunnel.

She glanced over at the old woman who was subtly tracking Raine's movements.

Granny would probably be making a report to Sergei Prokhorov at the end of the night.

The FBI would be making a report, too. Raine would have to get word to her supervisor, Hasan, so he could tell the FBI they weren't being helpful. They needed to get out of her way.

Damian was somehow in the mix…well, that was a distraction she'd allow herself to process once Todor was dropped at the airport for his Sunday afternoon flight back to Geneva.

It should probably have made her feel better knowing an FBI team was on hand. And if she'd been working solo, she might have appreciated them, but Iniquus had her back.

Iniquus positioned a nurse, traveling right beside Todor's car. She had had some magic drink that helped Raine regain control of her muscles fast.

Somewhere in the tunnel, not too many cars away, Gator and Jack had been on motorcycles, able to follow the attackers' bikes in case, somehow, she got scooped up in the event. Or things got more violent than had been anticipated. Without radio frequency in the tunnel, one of them needed to ride ahead to coordinate next steps and get an ambulance in.

Iniquus has mad resources. Skilled as hell. Smooth operators.

This offered no guarantee that things would turn out okay. But at least Raine could cross incompetence off her list of worries.

Many years ago, when she was newly recovered from her near-death episode in the terrorist camp, and she'd declined a new contract with Uncle Sam, Raine had considered applying to Iniquus. Granted, they hired special forces who had retired from service and preferred tier one operators. But at the time, there were no women in those positions.

Raine had rolled out on her fair share of military special ops missions. She'd trained on the fly, learning from the best of the best. The men she worked with needed her to be a full-tilt asset with limited liabilities.

While she did most of what the men did, not having the opportunity to go through their specialized schools, she didn't get their patches for her uniform.

Raine never did her work for ego and ribbons. It had been about the desire to get the job done. Keep everyone safe. And go home.

Since the day she'd signed with the Army as an eighteen-year-old reservist, Raine had found the going home part was the hardest part of her job.

Had the time come? Yes. Her decision was made back in the tunnel.

Maybe Iniquus was hiring strategists… Maybe she was ready to settle down.

This last shocking experience—Raine chuckled at the pun—made her realize she was no longer going to do boots on the ground. She didn't want anything to do with fieldwork anymore.

Okay, she had a trajectory—a new job.

But first, she needed to protect the Delta Force wives.

Raine owed Delta Force her life. She'd even the score by seeing this mission through, then she'd hand in her resignation.

Raine was serious.

This part of her life was soon done.

Reaching up, Raine adjusted the underwire of her bra comms as she heard Deep in her ear. “Be advised target getting ready for release.”

“About darned time,” she grumbled under her breath.

She got a chuckle from Deep by way of reply.

Raine worked to replace the smile that had snuck onto her cheeks with a Cammy Burke distraught expression.

She pulled her hair to the side to reveal the bandage that covered the burn mark on her shoulder. She hadn’t really needed it, but it made for good theater.

On paper, getting stunned was fine—two or three seconds of zap, then fifteen minutes of disability. Raine had been Tasered in training. It wasn’t like she’d never felt that level of shock before. Gator had tried to warn her. But she was big bad Storm Meyers; why should she listen?

For heaven's sake. She did a mental eye roll.

Well, it was the periodic reminder that Raine needed to check her ego at the door.

No more big and bad for her. No more “Storm damage!” Her next job would not only be calm, but she’d work regular business hours, Raine promised herself, pivoting at the end of the corridor and starting back in the other direction.

Or not.

She could retire and read books, paint watercolors, and see the fun parts of the world instead of its dark underbelly.

Speaking of dark underbellies…

The old lady lifted a corner of the magazine, got Raine back in her view, and replaced the magazine on her face.

Mmmhmm. A Prokhorov babysitter.

Raine upped her level of angst two notches for show.

It wasn’t that hard to do.

With Todor roused, this next step put her whole op on the line. If she succeeded at her job of dangle, she'd be in her best possible position to find their computer systems. If she failed…

She wasn't the only one feeling the pressure.

This case had the Pentagon and DIA rattled, with good reason. The Prokhorov family liked to try out their schemes on a smaller scale and watch to see what happened next.

The crime family didn't start with Delta Force. They'd tested the waters last June and apparently liked how that felt.

Raine had been working this case for almost nine months. She'd gotten involved in the Twitter threats last summer. A group who said that they were connected to ISIS hacked into the Military Spouses Support Twitter and Facebook accounts using those platforms as vehicles to threaten the community by replacing the women's icon pictures with an ISIS black flag, and sending the individuals terrifying direct messages using their full names instead of their social media handles.

With that success, the hackers moved on to attack the US Central Command's YouTube and Twitter accounts.

There, they put in the military spouses' full names along with the message: **You aren't safe. ISIS is in your computers and cell phones. We are everywhere.**

And to the women: **We know everything about you, about your husband, and your children. You will see no mercy.**

Or: **While your husbands fight and kill in our country, we will do the same in yours. We are coming for you.**

Nobody was harmed.

Neither attack connected to ISIS. It was developed by Dancing Bear, a Russian cyberespionage group affiliated with the bot farms in Bulgaria run by Sergei Prokhorov.

Unlike the cyber-attacks that happened publicly over social media, this attack on the Delta Force was found in the Unit wives' personal emails. The explicit messages included recent pictures of the women and their children that someone had taken without their knowledge. They were told, "You can run, but you cannot hide. We know everything about everything. Here's an example:" And then there were recent pictures of their families and best friends with their home addresses, phone numbers, emails, and passwords.

No safe-havens. Everyone they cared about was exposed and at risk.

The communications were ostensibly sent from someone they frequently corresponded with, so they were opened without hesitation. Ten minutes after the message was read from their computer, that message disappeared, and the wives were left feeling frightened, violated, and gaslighted.

What they had seen with their own eyes *wasn't* there.

They'd had no time to think of screenshots or forwarding. There had been only enough time to read, reread, and deal with the adrenaline.

Then *poof*.

The information was consistent over each woman that the DIA had interviewed. And each wife interviewed had decided to pressure their husbands not to sign a new contract.

If this psychological terror attack was successful, the terrorists didn't need to physically attack and kill our special ops forces. The military would lose Delta Force tier one operators—who not only had the expensive training under their belts but also a minimum of six years' experience and leadership—through attrition.

If anything were to happen to a Unit wife—besides the horror of the attack itself—it would stomp morale into the dirt.

The Delta operators trusted their families were safe and cared for while their team was downrange. This confidence allowed them to focus. To be successful.

So there was that.

That was the tip of the spear. There was also the shaft.

The person or persons who held this weapon could thrust it out, again and again.

With a surreptitious glance at granny, Raine kept moving up and down the hallway.

Could Granny be an FBI special agent?

After the "ISIS" Twitter and Facebook threats went out, the FBI opened a case file at the same time the DIA did. Raine had teamed up with one of them on the Brussels mission that ended with mixed results. They got what they wanted, but the FBI attaché was captured and had a rough go of it.

Oh, look. Granny was awake and texting.

Raine bet that Todor was going to come through the door any minute now.

She turned for another pass up the hall, when sure enough, Todor stalked through the swinging doors toward her.

His tuxedo shirt unbuttoned at the top, his bow tie hanging undone, his jacket was draped over a finger, hanging down his back like a nineteen fifty's movie heartthrob.

He probably styled himself in the mirror to sweep her off her feet.

Okay, here I go, getting swept! Deep breath and...

"There you are," she exhaled and rushed into Todor's outstretched arms. She let the stress of the day move through her body, leaving her trembling and tearful, just the way she should be.

Todor wrapped her tightly into his arms and kissed her hair.

Her cheek pressed to his chest; she heard his galloping heartbeat. Yeah, he was worried that he had failed, and she'd say "have a nice life" and go home. Crunch time for him, too.

He reached for her chin and tipped her head back. "Did they hurt you?"

Raine pulled up the seed she'd saved from the moment that Black Helmet pushed into her space, trapping her and making her claustrophobic. "It was horrible. I was so scared for you."

His fingers traced over the white bandage square on her shoulder.

"They used a stun gun on me, but there was a nurse in the car next to us." She petted her hands over his arms and chest. "What happened? What did they do to you?"

"Come, you're exhausted." He wrapped his coat around Raine's bare shoulders. "Let me take you to your apartment. I'll tell you on the way."

Raine didn't move. She stood there looking up at him with a frown.

"What is it?"

She shook her head and looked to the side and up as she sniffed air into her lungs.

"You are frightened to go home?"

Raine blinked to loosen a tear from her lashes and felt gratified as it drifted down her cheek.

Todor stroked it away with a gentle finger. "Would you feel less frightened if you stayed with me?"

She nodded and let out an exhale of relief.

"You were attacked because you were with me." The incredulity in his voice was more satisfied than concerned. Todor believed he was winning with this stupid old-school KGB plan of his.

Ha! She'd set her hook. Now line. Soon, the sinker.

Raine swallowed and hitched her breath, doing her best to play the "distraught female, realizing she was in love." It was something she didn't have a seed for. For inspiration, she had to turn to the rom-com movies she'd seen.

"I suppose at my hotel there is more security." Todor paused as if weighing this plan, but he was really battling away a victory smile. "Yes, I take you there with me."

Raine slipped her hand into the crook of his arm and laid her ear against his shoulder while she surreptitiously moved Todor's hotel keycard, which Iniquus had brought back to her, back into the breast pocket of his jacket. "Thank you."

"Well played," Deep's voice was in her ear. "We've got eyes on you."

Raine reminded herself that any glint of her own feelings of victory needed to be tucked away.

She still had work to do.

13

> Select a [surveillance site], so you can overlook the scene.
> ~ Moscow Rules

Sunday, early hours of the morning

The FBI joint task force members, Frost, Prescott, and Kennedy, stepped out of their cars in front of Iniquus Headquarters.

Kennedy had stopped in to check on Raine as Cammy Burke at Suburban Hospital. He hadn't tried to take a statement. Lying to an FBI special agent was against federal law, and they had made sure they didn't put Raine in that position. Kennedy hadn't even introduced himself with credentials, but Kennedy thought it would be a good idea for Raine to see him, so she'd know she was operating next to a past ally.

Prescott had stayed out of sight.

Iniquus, no doubt, was monitoring Raine's comms. That would

explain why Prescott and Kennedy found Striker, casually leaning a shoulder into the wall, outside of Cammy's cubicle.

Striker had pushed off the wall and bent close to their ears. "When you finish up here, can you come to Iniquus for a meeting? Since we all seem to be holding cards from the same deck, maybe we should know if we're playing the same game."

Prescott had dialed it in to Frost.

And now, here they all were, standing in the brittle winter night air in the glow of the Iniquus Headquarters' lights.

"We're meeting with the DIA as well as Strike Force," Frost said as she joined the two men. "A warning, other than Prescott's personal relationship and her military career relationships with Griffin and Finley, the only thing we know about Raine Meyers in the last seven years is what Kennedy learned on his mission in Brussels."

The two men stood stoic, waiting to see where this was going.

She faced Kennedy. "According to Clara Edwards' report, and you don't need to verify this, you picked her up at the hotel, she suggested you get physical to break down barriers between you two so that when you arrived, you'd be relaxed and comfortable in each other's arms."

Prescott thought Kennedy did an admirable job about not rolling his eyes. Prescott didn't want to go over that part of the mission again either.

"Interesting technique." Frost tapped her foot. Standing there in her skirt and high heels, she must have been uncomfortable. Prescott looked toward the door and gestured to get them moving.

Frost ignored him.

"It worked," Kennedy muttered.

"Hear me out. This is the piece I want in the fronts of your minds when we go in there. When you picked her up that night, she *decided* you needed to change your energy around her. She figured out a way to do it and *made* it work. From that, it can be surmised that she's a psychological tactician. She'll use what she has available to get to her ends. We don't understand her ends." She looked from Kennedy to Prescott. "As we go in, if she's here, this is something to keep in mind as we make decisions about what we share and how we emote."

"She's no Femme Nikita," Prescott said with a laugh. Raine being *that* devious was absurd. It was a lot more likely that Raine got in the cab, found Rowan Kennedy to be a handsome guy, and thought, *why not*? How she wrote the incident into her report was probably the manipulation.

Frost tipped her head, her eyes narrowing as she tried to read him. Prescott hoped all she'd read on his face was that he was damned tired and freezing cold. He'd like to go in.

"After throwing yourself bodily on top of her during the tunnel incident, do you have reservations about your ability to maintain your objectivity? Who she was when you knew her may very well not be the person she is now. She was captured. That has consequences."

"Objectivity, on my part, isn't a problem," Prescott said, thinking Frost was typically more collegial than this. Whatever was happening on this case seemed to have her more worried than usual. "I can't speak to anything that happened to Meyers during that event."

"Event?" Frost quirked a precisely plucked brow.

Kennedy did a double step to snatch the handle and hold the atrium door open for Frost.

Prescott was thankful Kennedy had given him a reprieve from responding.

"Event" had been the term Prescott used to distance himself from his thoughts about Raine's capture. Distancing himself from the sheer horror of his imagination.

He pressed the air out of his lungs. Pushed and pushed the breath and the thoughts from his system.

The idea that anyone had touched Raine. Had put a blade to her throat and slid the edge through the flesh of her neck. Had sliced through her windpipe, trying to take her life.

She'd be dead today except for his brothers on his Delta Force team Echo, while *he* wasn't there.

Prescott would have been there with Echo had he signed his re-up.

Instead, he'd come home to work for the FBI.

That thought killed him.

He'd failed her before. And no matter what it cost him. He wasn't going to fail her again.

They walked to the elevator bank and into an open car. Damian tapped the button to take them to the Strike Force war room. He'd been here for enough cases now that he felt comfortable in his surroundings.

They rode in silence.

When the door slid open, Prescott stepped out and gestured toward the door that stood open for them.

Inside the war room, Striker leaned over Deep's computer at the front of the room. He stood when he saw them come in. "Can you shut the door behind you?"

Prescott pulled the door closed.

Striker joined them at the front of the room. "FBI Joint Task Force—Deputy Assistant Amanda Frost, Special Agent in Charge Damian Prescott, East European Attaché Rowan Kennedy. I believe you all know me and my colleague, Deep, who will be providing us with support tonight."

They murmured and nodded their greetings.

Striker opened his hand to the man who had stood and walked toward them. "From the DIA, we have Javeed Hasan."

There was a pause for handshakes, then Striker said, "It's a late night. Please make yourselves comfortable. Catering has brought food." He gestured toward a long table at the back of the room that had fresh fruit and sandwiches. "There's water and energy drinks in the fridge, coffee in the pot. Bathrooms are the door in the back, right corner of the room." He turned to Hasan, "Would you like to begin?"

Hasan didn't look like a DIA agent. He was in jeans and a black turtle neck with comfortable looking loafers on his feet. It was Saturday night, maybe they'd pulled the guy off his couch, and he had been three beers into his movie.

Hasan scratched at his five o'clock shadow, then gestured to the three who were settling into seats. "Is this your whole team?"

"We have two agents associated with our mission still on-site at the hospital."

Hasan nodded. "Can you tell me who you're surveilling?"

"Todor Bilov," Frost said. "I've been apprised that the same covert operator who played the role of Clara Edwards in Brussels is the woman who is playing the role of Cammy Burke tonight as his date. A question, Cammy Burke is not a real person. It is a fabricated cover developed for your officer?"

"Exactly." Hasan pointed at Kennedy and got a smirk on his face. "You were the FBI operator in Brussels?"

Kennedy rubbed his fingers into his eyes. Prescott thought he was regretting that whole Brussels taxi scene.

Hasan picked up his coffee and moved it to the table in front of the FBI agents, finding a seat across from them. "Our operator in the field tonight is Raine Meyers. I only tell you her name because she recognized Lisa Griffin and Steve Finley at the party, and of course, Damian." He lifted a hand in Prescott's direction. "Right now, Raine is operating under her cover identity, Cammy Burke. On paper, Burke is a civilian with the Pentagon. Burke is listed as a human resources specialist, according to DoD records."

"Raine is developing an asset, Todor Bilov, by allowing Bilov to develop her?" Prescott asked.

Hasan touched his nose then pointed at him.

"Does she know who attacked their car in the tunnel?" Kennedy asked.

"Yes, it was Todor's people. She was aware that this was going to happen. It didn't quite follow their planning, but close enough." He nodded toward Striker and Deep. "That's why we had Iniquus on-site, both to keep an eye on what happened with Todor and to protect Cammy, as Cammy would not have security skills to whip out in a circumstance like that. Raine had to sit on her hands and let things unfold."

Striker lifted his chin toward Damian. "Prescott, you stepped in as our nurse began her task of supporting Cammy Burke. Two Iniquus operators were in the tunnel on motorcycles as back up. It was complicated without comms. It was Gator's job to drive out behind the attackers, getting clear of the Prokhorov's jammers to make a call for an ambulance for Raine and to let our outside team members know to be ready for their next steps. Jack stayed on-site to provide close protection." Hasan's focus landed on Prescott. "Good thing Jack recognized you, Damian, as you jumped into the scene. That might not have ended pretty."

Frost crossed her legs. "I'm sorry if we stepped on any toes." She leaned forward. "Of course, we had no idea who Raine Myers was working with, or we would have coordinated. Thank you for responding promptly to my inquiry about which agent had played the role of Clara Edwards."

Kennedy focused on Hasan. "Clarification. That was Todor's crew attacking him? They stunned him, drugged him, and dropped him by the side of the road?"

"His watcher was waiting to call an ambulance just down the street from the tunnel," Hasan said.

"To what end did they develop that plan?" Prescott asked.

"An old Russian spycraft ruse." Hasan leaned back in his chair and rested an ankle across his thigh. "The science behind it says that if adrenaline is running through the body because of fear, that if there is a male and female subject in danger, they will intensify their connection. Todor was instructed to get Cammy on his hook romantically, so she was an ongoing asset—mole within the Pentagon. He knew already that she was a little gullible. She had some conspiracy theories that she ascribed to. And she was a bit of a Russophile with lots of Russian art and literature books on her Kindle. Romance novels of the virile men of Eastern Europe."

"She laid the groundwork to make herself vulnerable." Frost nodded.

"Yes, but we were grateful that Todor was given a short timeline to get her on board. We think they either lost an asset, or they need a specific piece of information, or, who knows, maybe there is some external pressure on them. We don't know exactly what it is. We have a guess that I'll go over with you as we talk this through. Todor flew into D.C. this weekend explicitly to woo Cammy. If Raine is able to pull this off, then the next move we expect him to make is an ask. Something small that she can do for him. Something that he'll convince her will help him stay safe from the bad guys who tried to get to him."

Frost's phone buzzed as a text dropped into her inbox. "This is my agent, Lisa Griffin." She read the text. "She says that Todor's GPS is leaving the hospital."

Deep clicked at his computer. "I have Cammy Burke's GPS leaving the hospital, too. She's wired. I'm taping their conversation, and the computer is monitoring her for any danger close words. It will send me an alarm if there's trouble. We expect them to head to his hotel."

The group turned back to face each other.

Frost turned her phone over in her lap, then said slowly with carefully measured words, "Our task force with the FBI requires us to pursue the Prokhorov family. My superiors have indicated to me that they have been sharing the information that we've obtained from the joint DIA/FBI venture in Brussels with one another. The

FBI will not stop following all links to this family. They are just too dangerous. However, since we seem to have a shared interest," she paused with a tilt of her head, "I don't see how it would profit either of us to elbow each other out of the way."

Hasan laced his fingers and pressed his steepled index fingers under his chin.

Frost smiled as she sat back. "Why is the DIA concerned about the Prokhorovs? The family deals in psychological ops against the U.S. and asymmetrical cyber-attacks. Has the family targeted our military now?"

By way of response, Hasan turned to Deep. "If you'll bring up the AC-661 video file, please."

Deep turned his attention to the computer screen.

Hasan smiled at Frost. "I want you to see a video that was captured on the day Todor made the phone call telling Cammy Burke he was heading for Washington D.C."

A screen came down from the ceiling. They all swiveled in that direction.

Prescott had no idea what might be recorded in this video. His body braced.

14

Betrayal may come from within.
~ Moscow Rules

Sunday, early hours of the morning

“Let me set this video up for you,” Hasan said. “At the time Cammy Burke was finishing up her role in Switzerland, I rerouted her to Brussels as Clara Edwards. Proximity wise, Raine was the closest U.S. agent who knew the players and could speak Russian with the level of ease that was required to compromise Sergei Prokhorov. As you know,” he turned toward Kennedy, “that mission was a last-minute attempt to catch Sergei while he was vulnerable. The FBI contacted the CIA, the CIA contacted the DIA, and so it goes. Cammy Burke had been in Geneva meeting and falling in love with Todor Bilov.”

Kennedy furrowed his brow. “Helping with the Brussels mission, being in such close proximity to Sergei, surely compromised Raine's mission as Cammy. The Prokhorovs must have pictures of Cammy Burke and Clara Edwards and know they're the same woman. With advanced computer recognition software, a change of hair color alone wouldn't help."

"Oh, we're absolutely positive they have photographs of both Cammy and Clara," Hasan said. "The Prokhorovs fine-tooth combed through the Cammy Burke cover, making sure she wasn't a dangle. We had Raine as Cammy Burke get on a government plane back to Washington, then she exited before take-off to don another cover, Clara Edwards. Clara Edwards wore theatrical facial prosthetics that were developed to change Raine's features just enough that she was unrecognizable by artificial intelligence. Tiny changes, imperceptible to any person who was near her, precisely chosen to confuse the programs." He looked at Frost. "Raine Meyers' minor in university was film acting. Did you know this?" He spun to Prescott. "Well, you did, of course, Damian. A very helpful minor to have in the spy business."

When Prescott didn't respond, Hasan slapped his hand to his thigh. "So that's all clean. Long story short, over the summer, we targeted Todor Bilov as our way into the family. To that end, we made sure that the Prokhorov family was aware of Cammy and her special Pentagon access. We developed mutual friends on social media. Slowly and innocently, we got the two chatting. Our sock puppets interacted with Cammy, goading her to go ahead and be brave, take her bucket list solo trip to Geneva. Magical things could happen there." He paused as a grin spread across his face. "Cammy Burke booked a hotel a few blocks from Todor's apartment near the city center. It all looked very innocent. She had no idea that Todor lived in Geneva. He had listed Prague as his home. Very quickly, Todor got the call that he had a task to perform for the family."

"Is his life in Switzerland a cover for other things he does for the Prokhorovs?" Prescott asked. He was sure there was a lot more to this than the few sentences of explanation—a team who had spent days, weeks, months in preparation.

"No, he is what he says he is on paper. But when your Uncle Sergei tells you to do something, and he's been paying your bills your whole life, you do it. Todor, as it turns out, has a good reason why he stays away from his family. Cammy was able to get surveillance into his apartment. We already had spyware on his phone and computer from the apps he has downloaded." Hasan raised his hand to the screen, and Deep clicked something on his computer.

The room dimmed, and the video began.

"As far as women go, she's lovely." Todor was lounging on a couch with another man reclining, his head in Todor's lap. Todor stroked his fingers through the man's hair. "She's intelligent enough to have interesting conversations, not so intelligent that she thinks she's my equal. Physically fit to make her pleasing to look at, a nice sense of style. If I were the kind of man to have a relationship with a woman, I might pick her."

"A man as handsome as you won't have any problems wooing her."

The two men, Todor Bilov and, by appearances, his boyfriend, was speaking in French. It was one of the languages that Prescott spoke, but Todor's accent was thick. Prescott was glad for the translation at the bottom of the video.

Hasan held up his hand, and Deep hit pause.

"His name is Frédéric Marquette from Paris, France," Hasan said. "Todor and Frédéric have been living together for three years. Frédéric is in the hospitality business." Hasan lowered his hand, and the video began again.

"She seems grateful for whatever attention I give her. She laps it up like a kitten with a bowl of milk. She was deprived of love growing up, poor little thing. This deprivation makes her an easy mark for any man with bad intentions." Todor lifted and dropped his brow several times in a show of an old-timey ne'er-do-well.

"She told you this?"

"She told me stories in passing. She said that when she was a little girl, her mother would give the clothes that they could no longer wear away to a charity."

"Yes?"

"And that before the clothes were given away, her mother would clip off all the buttons and put those buttons in a button jar, so if she ever needed a button to mend their clothes, that she'd have a supply."

"She gave poor people clothes with no buttons? How would that help anyone?"

Todor shook his head.

"That's… fairly evil, *n'est-ce pas*? Clothing without buttons is simply crazy."

"When I asked Cammy if her mother found the button jar helpful, Cammy said that she never saw her mother sew on button or repair clothes in any way. This answer didn't surprise me. Cammy told me that she and her brothers were uncared-for children. She said that at that time, other adults in her life—her teachers and priests—replicated her parents' sentiments and didn't care for her either. She said this with shrug. She say it taught her to depend on herself, and this was good thing. But I know this is lie she tell herself. She wishes someone to step in and love her. Tell her she good girl and coddle her."

"This is why you think of her as a kitten to be saved and petted."

The war room at Iniquus smiled and chuckled. There was a "well done, Raine!" vibe going on. But Prescott knew that, while she was manipulating Todor by telling him that tale, it was a true story. Raine never spoke of her family outside of Prescott and a few other dear friends. This op must mean something special to her if she was exposing what she hid under her protective armor. Prescott wished Hasan would just spell it all out.

"But you don't have bad intentions. I mean, nothing bad is going to happen to her, is it?" Frédéric asked.

"No, nothing. Before I agree to do what Uncle wishes, of course, I asked these kinds of questions. Anything my little Cammy does will be of her own volition with maybe little help from my uncle's tactics. Wait, I take that back, she will be frightened, and she will have a little tiny shock."

"Emotional shock?" Frédéric tipped his chin, so their gazes connected.

"No, electrical. Nothing that will truly hurt her. A shock and fright. After that, then it will only be me gently prodding her to do what is wanted. She is perfectly safe."

"And you believe this is true?"

"Since I wasn't given a choice in the matter, I've decided to believe it."

Frédéric nodded with a frown. He accepted Todor's placating kisses.

"But you have to pretend to be in love with her. Can you get yourself hard for her?"

"Maybe if I close my eyes and picture you." Todor bent with a smile.

Frédéric turned his head to deny Todor more kisses. "Anatomically, this would be a difficult thing to imagine."

"I think you're feeling jealous. Maybe I should pet you like a kitten." Todor's hand slid down to wrap Frédéric's dick, now tenting his loose cotton pants.

Frédéric shut his eyes and reached down to yank the pull string holding the pants around his waist. "Do you think she would continue to see you as a boyfriend if there was no sex?" He blinked his eyes open and focused on Todor. "I wouldn't continue to see you as a boyfriend if there was no sex."

Todor laughed. "She's too kind of a person to say, 'well that's it then' and walk out the door. She would stick with me long enough that I wouldn't think that her leaving a possible love relationship was about my not getting her off. Besides, I have a plan that will keep her from being in the mood for lovemaking Saturday night, and I leave again Sunday. The window is very small."

Frédéric closed his eyes, obviously appreciating the sensations of Todor's hand job.

Prescott wished the angle was a little different, so that wasn't the focal point on the large screen.

"From a single night in Washington, you can progress your relationship enough that she'll do as you ask?"

"There's a time-tested formulation that was explained to me. This will make my little Cammy feel as though she's in love with me even if she is not. First, a personally difficult story. Next, a big dose of fear, followed by whispers baring our souls in the dark."

"Pillow talk often leads to screwing around. At least for us, it does." He shifted further up in Todor's lap. "Do that thing I like with your palm on the tip."

Todor adjusted his movements. "She will have just been through harrowing experience. I'm not such a cad that I would take advantage of her shaken countenance. No, I will hold and soothe her like she is a child. She will like this, being cared for with nothing asked of her in return."

"But the next day…" Frédéric said on a moan. "Yes, just like…that."

"The next day, I will be on a plane back here to you, my love. Once I'm here, I'll call her to let her know I have arrived at the airport. Following, I train her with a phone call every day for three days, then I will not call her for three days."

"This is specific."

"Like I say, this is time-tested psychological formula. After days of hearing nothing, I ask for small favor, something that she will see as doable. But then, this is trap. I will ask for second thing. She will say no because it will be obvious that this is espionage. But I will persuade her. And once she's done that thing, I have my kompromat. She will be my little mole inside of Pentagon, and I can get what data I need on special forces families with no more, as Americans say, 'skin in game.'"

"I don't understand what your uncle wants with a paper pusher at the Pentagon. You said she did things like arranged insurance and such. Here." He lifted his hips and slid his pants down to his thighs. "Would you massage my balls?"

Again, Todor adjusted to comply. "Russia cannot beat the United States with military weapons. The Kremlin realized this. Years ago, they switch from putting military money into bullets and start putting it more into psychology and computers. Thus, my Uncle Sergei and money that freely flows his way for his asymmetrical threats to the U.S. My uncle was instructed by Kremlin to find a way to destroy United States action movie heroes, their Special Operators. If you cut head from serpent, body dies. I don't know Uncle's plan, but Cammy Burke has information my uncle needs. When I please Uncle Sergei, he continues to pay my expenses. We can't live our lifestyle on monies earned at a charity."

Frédéric reached up to cup Todor's cheek. "You are so sexy with that glint of power in your eye."

The video ended.

"I turn the image off here because it becomes quite graphic," Hasan said, "if you'd like a copy of the whole event, you're welcome to view it. What I wanted you to see here was that the Prokhorovs targeted a fictitious Cammy Burke, they planned to entrap her and use her as an asset, and that the family has an asymmetric plan targeting our special forces. The Delta Forces, to be specific. I'll share more about that momentarily." Hasan looked over at Prescott. "You were in the Unit before you moved to CIRG, living down at Fort Bragg, is that right?"

"Yes," Prescott said.

Hasan nodded his head, cogs whirring. After a long moment of silence, he turned to Frost. "In this same video, Todor goes on to explain the whole motorcycle stupidity that has, in Todor's eyes, proceeded as planned tonight. This video," he wagged his hand toward the screen, "is now our kompromat for Todor Bilov. He's ours, both from his illicit relationship—illicit in the eyes of Russia, at least—as well as his sharing secret mission-relevant information with a foreign national, Frédéric being French."

"It was a farce. That whole motorcycle incident was staged by *him*?" Frost laid her hands on the table. "That's some chutzpah."

"It was. And had we not known it was going to happen, people would have died tonight." Hasan sipped some coffee, giving the FBI agents a moment to process.

After a moment, he continued, "For everyone's sake, I'm glad we had the information affording us the opportunity to take countermeasures." He raised his mug toward Striker. "We hired Iniquus to provide Cammy Burke with security. We needed to make sure we didn't have any DIA operators involved, no names, no faces, no way to dismantle the cover that Raine's been building for years and trotted out for this case."

Striker was sitting on the table to their left. "Since we had the script, we were able to position our operators in advance. Lynx and Blaze were walking near the corner where Todor was to be dropped onto the sidewalk. The operators came onto the scene as one of Todor's team called the ambulance. Lynx flashed her EMT badge his way, then set about checking Todor. She took his key card, which was still in its paper sleeve with the room number written on it. The DIA has surveillance warrants, so we bugged his hotel room. Audio and visual. We're waiting for Cammy Burke to find a way to Todor's hotel room and allow him to pet her like a kitten, psychologically speaking."

Frost was nodding along as if keeping beat with a song. "We

have the room bugged as well. Though we were given warrants for audio, not visual since we're fishing and didn't have a specific threat."

"We swept Todor's suite when our technicians went in," Deep said. "There were two types of bugging devices that we found. We assumed that one type was placed by Todor since it was not professionally mounted. We weren't sure who the other bugs belonged to. Mystery solved. We left all of them in place. Ours is the only visual recorder."

"Blaze and Lynx are in the room across the hall. Raine has a code word, and they have a key," Striker said. "But they're monitoring the feed along with us."

"We have Finley in the room next door monitoring," Frost said. "Lisa Griffin is joining him there. I'll let them know Iniquus is on the scene."

"While we're waiting for Todor and Cammy to get to the hotel room," Hasan said, "let's continue. We all know that there is an ongoing threat. The DIA works closely with the head of the Insider Threat Human Resources Team and the Insider Threat Mitigation Division. If you're not familiar, the InTM program works to detect, mitigate, and deter threats to information about personnel and resources. In the position we crafted for Cammy at the Pentagon, she is the liaison between the threats program and the human resources division. This gives her access to everything the United States military would know about the Prokhorov threats and what they're doing to mitigate them. If the Prokhorovs know what's happening on the inside—like we knew about Todor and his schemes—then they can counteract them, just like we did tonight with the motorcycle scheme."

"And you know the specifics of these threats? How they wish to affect attrition?" Frost asked.

"Yes," Hasan replied. "Thanks to Iniquus, who brought the information to our attention recently, the DIA now has a better idea of the next asymmetrical warfare steps that the Prokhorovs are taking. If you'll remember last June—"

"Sir," Deep interrupted, "you asked me to let you know when Todor and Cammy got to his room."

Prescott's gut clenched. If the FBI and DIA were following, surely Todor had back up and watchers on hand. Raine would only have weapons of opportunity. That set off Prescott's protective instincts.

He stood to go to the food table, so he could regroup.

Normally cool under fire, Prescott had to admit that seeing Raine vulnerable on the blacktop earlier that night messed with him. He needed to stay professionally focused. The last thing he wanted was to get booted from this case.

"All's well?" Hasan asked, looking toward Deep.

"They didn't speak in the car. I'm following the GPS and ambient noises. They just got off the elevator."

"Okay, good. Can you bring up that feed on the screen?"

15

Keep any asset separated from you by time and distance
– Moscow Rules

SUNDAY, EARLY HOURS OF THE MORNING

ON THE SCREEN, they watched Todor standing behind Raine. He slid his jacket from her shoulders, dipped his head, and kissed her neck. "I am so proud of how strong and brave you were tonight. You amaze me."

"You have someone in the hotel as backup?" Prescott asked, realizing too late that they'd just been over this. *Head in the game.*

"Affirmative," Deep said. "Across the hall."

Todor laid the coat over the chair and turned. "You were beautiful tonight at party." He reached out and petted his hand over her hair, took hold of her chin, and tipped her head back, so their gazes met. "You're even more beautiful now."

Raine lowered her lashes and let a little frown play across her lips. Was she blushing at the compliment? Or maybe she was blushing because she knew she had an audience for this. She knew, at least, Iniquus was eyes on. Unless Deep told her through comms, she wouldn't know the FBI was in on this show.

Raine turned and stepped farther into the room, sending a long glance at the king-sized bed.

"I hoped you would invite me to your home tonight. This hope is very forward of me. I wanted very much to make love to you." He coughed and cleared his throat. "The events of tonight conspired against these intentions."

She turned back to him with sad eyes. "I'd planned to invite you. I'd hoped you'd stay the night and that things would progress in our relationship. But, to be truthful, I need some time to recover." She paused as she touched the bandage on her arm. "I'm really tired. I'm not up to making love. Can we go to bed? Would you hold me?"

"Yes, come." He reached in his drawer and pulled out a pajama top to hand to her. "Won't you make yourself comfortable?"

Hugging the top to her, Raine made her way into the bathroom to change.

"Sorry to leave this up," Deep said. "but I need to see if she signals me."

"Where's her gun?" Prescott asked.

"We took it off her in the nurse's van." Deep touched a button. "Take your dress and bra into the bedroom with you. I'd like to have back up comms, see if you can't angle the brooch in a way that might capture something besides the ceiling."

She gave him a thumbs up.

"Her brooch has a camera," Striker clarified.

"Why is she considering her bracelet?" Kennedy asked as Raine stalled over removing the jewelry. "She wore that same bracelet when we were on the Brussels mission."

"It's a knife, her only weapon." Deep pressed the button again. "Backup is two steps away. I'm with you. I won't leave you. The decision is yours."

She nodded and unclasped the bracelet. She pulled off her heels and stood barefooted as she unzipped the side of her dress. Letting it slip to the ground, she stepped out of the pool of fabric. She unclasped her bra and dropped it to the floor.

Frost and Kennedy were looking at their shoes.

Hasan was looking at his mug.

Striker was looking at the door.

And Prescott was staring at Raine's tight body, the little black lace panties that she, thank god, left on.

The last time he'd seen her in a bathroom dressed like that, she'd leaned over the sink, tipping her hips up at him. She'd watched him in the mirror as he slipped his fingers into the sides of her panties and oh so slowly slid the silk down her thighs. He'd left a trail of kisses up her spine before he'd nuzzled at her neck.

Already wet, she'd looked over her shoulder. "Hurry, Damian, stop teasing me. I want it fast and hard." She'd wiggled her ass at him, and he happily complied with her command.

Until he was thirty years old, Raine had been the only woman he'd made love to. He'd felt like he was cheating on her with every other woman he'd slept with since their breakup.

It had been a while since he'd even thought of taking a woman to his bed.

Prescott's body was reacting; he scooted a little closer to the table.

Luckily, Raine pulled the blue pajama shirt over her. When it was buttoned, she was covered to mid-thigh.

She leaned in toward the mirror and inspected her neck.

Deep pressed the button. "I have you on the big screen, and I can't see the scars. The makeup still covers them."

Raine sent one more look to the bathroom mirror. It was a "Welp, here goes nothing" look.

Deep pressed the button. "You've got this."

She pattered back out to the bedroom, where she carefully placed her bra on the chair then draped her dress, so the brooch took in the bed.

Todor stood there bare-chested, dressed in the bottoms of those pajamas. "Come here, Kitten."

Prescott thought he had read the guy's face correctly back at the dinner. When Todor had surveyed the party goers, he felt a sense of ownership over Cammy Burke. Prescott had misinterpreted the underlying emotion. It wasn't about love; it was about the power of owning someone's emotions to get his needs met. Todor wasn't scanning for possible suitors to rival him, but to see if she had any other eyes which were interested in the connection he was making with a high-status Pentagon employee. Luckily, Todor didn't have the training to spot the eyes looking his way.

Todor and Cammy slid into bed from opposite sides.

When Raine pulled the covers up to her chin, Todor tapped the lights off.

Bathed in the eerie green light of the night vision camera, the two wiggled and squirmed in to spoon.

Prescott's chest expanded. His nostrils flared. That *that* man would touch Raine set off something dark in his system—primal. Prescott packed that reaction deep in his gut.

Raine had worked her way into the high-level, high-stakes intelligence game.

More than capable of playing this dangerous charade, she had the confidence of every single person in this war room.

But an operation was more than a single person. It was a team sport

Prescott needed to make sure he made the cut and stayed on the team, so he could be there to help keep Raine safe, just like he should have been back when his old team rescued her from ISIS.

Game face on, Prescott knew without turning his head, Hasan was watching him.

16

Deception
~Moscow Rules

Sunday morning early hours

She slid under the covers. "I told you motorcycles were scary."

He chuckled as he turned out the light.

Bathed in the dim red glow of the clock radio, she wriggled back into Todor's arms. "That was unnerving, though. I was thinking about the motorcycle, and then *that* happened."

"You were thinking about Perugia because I asked you for a story. And that was a vivid memory."

"True. And so much better than thinking that I had suddenly developed psychic powers." She punched at the pillow, then rolled her long hair and tucked it under her neck so it wouldn't go up Todor's nose. He wasn't used to going to bed next to someone with long hair; she'd manage it for him. "Every single story that popped into my mind, I might start interpreting as a premonition." She reached for his hand and pulled it across her waist. "Can you imagine the horror of living that way? I'd never leave the house. Or my bed. I'd just lay in my bed until I died of thirst… Or needed to use the bathroom."

"I've read articles about bathrooms being one of most dangerous places in everyday life," Todor murmured. "Slips in bathtub."

"Or perhaps it's a shaving accident. You never know. A cut could get infected. I could go down via blood poisoning." She smiled as she said it to change the sound of her voice.

He pressed his lips against her shoulder. "Blood poisoning is rare. I think you're safe."

"Are you?" Raine flipped to her other side and posted a hand under her head. "Safe, that is. My god, Todor." She exhaled forcefully. "I was terrified for you." A sob stuttered her voice. She pushed to sitting and crossed her legs in front of her, pulling the blanket across her lap. "During the attack, I tried to get out of the car to go get help, but I collapsed. There was a nurse there who checked on me and your no-good security guys. I won't even ask why they *allowed* that to happen to you. I hope they aren't getting paid for failing at their jobs." As best she could, Raine ratcheted up the volume of her voice along with her indignation. "There was also a man who helped me. I think you need to know this. He identified himself to the police as an FBI agent. He didn't mean for me to know. He showed his badge to the police officer, not to me. And an FBI guy was asking me some questions at the hospital. I didn't like that. I wasn't sure what to say." She rubbed her hand up and down his thigh. "I felt like I needed to protect you from him."

A silence held between them.

"It seems curious that they happened to be right there," she whispered. "Was that a coincidence?" Raine was going to use the sudden appearance of Rowan Kennedy to her advantage. She'd show Todor that she was on his side, and she'd process about

Damian being on the scene in the tunnel later when she could focus her brain on that situation.

Raine hadn't seen Damian since that night in Eric's kitchen.

"Doubtful." Todor sighed. Pulling himself up to sitting, he pressed his back against the headboard. "Are you sure FBI and not CIA?" He clicked the bedside light on.

"I saw a flash of his badge, but yes, I think FBI. Why would the CIA be interested in you?"

"Because of my family." He touched his heart.

Raine reached for a pillow and hugged it to her. *What kind of cockamamie story was he about to hand her?* "You told me your parents had both died, and you don't have any family."

"My parents have. They're dead. They died in a car accident when I was in college."

Uhm, nope. They held eye contact. "I don't understand, and I think it's probably best that I don't. Just… Are you in danger?" She paused, but he said nothing. "Obviously, you are. Why? Do I want to know?" She clutched the pillow tighter. "Maybe it's better if I don't." She turned to look at her dress. "Maybe it's best if I left." She reached a leg out from under the sheet, knowing that he'd stop her. It was imperative to her mission that he wanted her Pentagon access. She needed to know what he was fishing for and how it all fit into the threats on the Delta Force wives and the attack on Lucy McDonald. But to stay without his insistence would look suspicious.

"Cammy."

She stilled, then turned back to her position with the pillow in her lap.

"I knew when I came here that I would be under the eye of the American intelligence community. This was good thing. I believe because FBI was surveilling me, I was rescued." He covered her hand with his. "And they protected you."

She opened her mouth and exhaled, looking down with a little frown of concentration.

"Rescue operation was quick, men operating were best of best. It was surgical. I'm *lucky* they are watching me," he reiterated.

Raine knew for a fact that's not what had happened at all. He had been dropped from the back of the bike, and his buddy had been standing there and phoned 9-1-1. That guy left as soon as the ambulance got there. Deep had given her a blow by blow in her ear comms.

So far, though, Todor's rendition was convincing. She wondered if he cooked this up on their ride to the hotel or if this was a prefabricated story.

"I understand why FBI would watch me. I can guess what kidnappers wanted. But I don't have what these people think."

Her lips barely moved; her voice was almost inaudible. "What do they think you have?"

"You know, all over the world, United States has reputation for being land of milk and honey. And America is right to be proud, to stand tall on world stage. But they must fight against people with dark souls. Sometimes, only way to fight is, how you say? Fight fire with fire."

"Does this have to do with you and your charitable outreach? Are you doing intelligence for your own country? I thought—you told me you run a literacy foundation. I believed you."

"Believed. This is a past tense verb?"

"Yes. It is a past tense verb, but I didn't mean to say it that way. I meant to say believe. I *believe* you when you tell me things."

"Step by step, okay?"

"Okay, first step, Todor, I need you to know that I care for you. Tonight when you were attacked, I realized how much. How —" She swallowed, blinked back tears, gasped, clutching at her chest.

He reached out to lace his fingers into hers. "I need you to listen. Tell me if I'm too complex. I need you to understand history in order for you to understand present situation."

She nodded.

"Come. Let me hold you in my arms while I tell you story."

Another flick of her gaze toward her dress. A shift of her focus to the door. She could feel Todor tensing, scared that she would leave, and he'd have blown his op. It was rewarding, but she tamped down a victory dance. Victory was still a distant goal. Finally, her eyes rested on his. Their gazes caught. She held her breath, then sighed.

A lot of sighing going on, too much?

"That's my girl. Come." He held his arm wide and lifted the sheet with his other hand.

After Raine snuggled in by his side, he took time to tuck the covers around her, to tenderly brush the hair from her eyes. He touched his lips against her forehead and pressed a kiss there while he breathed in and out.

Her hand on his chest, his heart raced. She'd scared him. She pursed her lips together to keep them from curving into a Cheshire smile. Raine could tell he was going to spin one hell of a yarn. Prefabricated, she decided.

"All right, a story. Many decades ago. Sometime in mid-nineteen-fifty's, there was scientist here in America who experimented on seven black prison inmates."

She turned her head up, and he dropped a kiss into her hair—patted her—telling her without words that he wanted her to settle into his story and listen.

"Doctor gave them doses of LSD. Two had a single dose, two a double, two a triple, and one poor man was given a quadruple dose. Now, LSD was discovered by Swiss chemist Albert Hofmann earlier, but there was the war. World War II. It wasn't until later that psychedelic properties of LSD were discovered in his self-experimentation."

"Does this have to do with your magic mushrooms for your anxiety when you recovered from cancer?"

"Yes, because of *who* I am, I got to be part of study of mushrooms."

"Who you are? I—"

"Let me work my way forward, yes?"

"Yes. Sorry."

He patted her thigh, accepting her apology. "Hoffman, he wrote in his journal '... Little by little, I could begin to enjoy unprecedented colors and plays of shapes that persisted behind my closed eyes...' This is what happened in my experience. But that was when Hoffman was taken only 250 micrograms of the formulation. I can't imagine what it was like for men in Kentucky prison. Those seven men received LSD doses for seventy-seven days straight."

Raine gasped. "Did they go mad?"

"No one knows. It's assumed they die."

"Surely, the authorities…"

"It was authorities who conduct the tests. You must remember, black prisoners had same consequence to those people as lab mice do today. It was different time. This was time of Jim Crow in United States."

"You know a lot about American history. I'd say even more than—"

"Kitten, I need you to listen to my story," he reprimanded.

She nodded against his chest and was quiet.

"The seven men probably die and never knew that they were lab mice in secret program that CIA was running to develop mind control."

"What?" She flung her head back. "You're kidding."

Todor put his finger to his lips, and she curled back down obediently.

"CIA based its mind control program out of Fort Detrick, fifty mile away from Washington D.C. in Maryland. Easy enough for

Langley to stay in close control. That wasn't only clandestine science that was happening at Fort Detrick. Your Army used this base to plan germ warfare. The Army and CIA both working on chemical and mind-control weaponry."

"You're sure of this? Is it happening now?"

"Not now, no. Not bad things, anyway. Now, they do good works developing protection against things—plague, crop fungus. You might have read about work on Ebola."

Raine shook her head "no" but remained silent.

"CIA hasn't disclosed everything. In nineteen seventy's, they destroyed most of their records. We know quite a lot because of congressional hearing."

"But the US stands against bioweaponry and chemical weapons," Raine whispered.

"Context though, Cammy, this was happening during war. Japan was engaged in germ warfare in China, and America was afraid not to have like weaponry, so they hire a biochemist who had escaped Nazis to come and survive in America. He was working as professor of biochemistry, and he was thrilled to have some means to show his appreciation to new country. He come work at Fort Detrick, the Army Biological Warfare Laboratories. Now, America had new war, Cold War."

"Okay…? What has this to do with you. This is all a long time ago. You were a baby in the nineteen seventies."

"Tiny steps to understand, yes? Cold War. Two odd events happened. One, Hungarian Roman Catholic cardinal, was tried for treason. At trial, cardinal appeared disoriented, his voice flat, and he confessed to all crimes. There was no evidence that he committed any crimes. The second odd thing happen after the Korean War. They found stack of signed statements made by American POWs who make confessions of war crimes. CIA think they understand why. They say Communists had developed brainwashing."

Raine laughed.

"I'm not kidding. They figured only way these things had happened was through brainwashing or maybe drug-enabled mind control. Of course, if Communists had these techniques, Americans must get them, too. And they have perfect place to work on problem."

"Fort Detrick."

"Exactly. Your CIA officers in Europe and Asia captured enemy agents, and they want to interrogate prisoners using some chemical means to expose their secrets."

"Not my CIA officers, I wasn't born yet."

"Excuse my poor English."

"Your English is excellent. I'm just making the point. I don't condone *any* of this. And you're talking about truth serum here, right?"

"Many things. They tried many things, including ways in which to use chemicals to induce people to do things that was not of their own volition. First mind control project was called Bluebird. Then Artichoke."

"What?"

"And lastly, it was called MK-ULTRA. It was because of MK-ULTRA that there was formalized alliance between U.S. military and CIA."

She petted her hand rhythmically over his chest. "Did this program stop?"

"Scientists outside of Fort Detrick have suspicions. They were, how do you say? Whistleblowers?"

"Yes, Whistleblowers are people who see wrongdoing on the inside of an institution and bring it to the right authorities' attention."

He picked up her hand and kissed her palm, then held it against his heart. "When person blows whistle, they pack up everything at the Fort Detrick and destroy. But they were missing fifty-five micrograms of poison in six vials. Each vial could kill tens of thousands of people. Perfect for terrorism. They never locate this."

"How do you know this? It sounds like something out of fiction…like the Bourne character in the Robert Ludlum series."

"It was declassified, for one. For another, the scientist who escape Nazis to come live in America? That was my Great Uncle Hans Bilov. My uncle is responsible for experimenting on the Kentucky prisoners and later for working on all projects ending with MK-Ultra. Also, I study this in school, at university. My family have brain for science. We tend to study chemistry. I have my doctorate in pharmacy, for example."

She sat up. "I thought… I assumed…you work for a charitable nonprofit. I thought you were a Ph.D. in literacy or…not for profit management." Okay, the PharmD she knew about. So that part, at least, was right.

He covered her hand. "When I try getting job in field of pharmaceuticals, I was unsuccessful, though I have excellent credentials. But my name is known as being associated with Hans Bilov. They would be too afraid to hire me, of bringing attention and possibly ire of CIA. What if *I* had formulations in a vault somewhere, or maybe knew where was vials?"

"Do you?" she exhaled.

"No, Cammy! But my being in Washington D.C., so close to Fort Detrick, this must have made FBI worried. I think this is reason for men on motorcycles. They must think I know where these vials is. If they existed, they would be perfect chemical agent for terror. But I do not know. There is no secret for me to hide."

"That's why your family insisted on your having security here? It isn't the gun violence. They were protecting you from the CIA?"

"Yes. No. I don't know. My family tell me take precautions, so I do. But FBI men save me and let me go." He tipped her head, so their gazes met. "Look, my family name, Bilov, pave way for me in psychedelic study, which save my life. I'm not sorry for this. In my part of world, we are very old people. Family connections, *family* is everything. We've learned through centuries it's not wise to be trusting of others. Family trust, yes. Outside family," he made chopping motions, "trust is earned slowly. Once earned, then you're embraced by all."

"You're telling me this story. Does that mean you trust me?"

"Yes, Kitten." He brushed at her hair. "I do."

And Raine knew that, while the story about Fort Detrick and mind control drugs was factually true, the scientist's name hadn't been Hans Bilov. And this guy certainly hadn't been Todor's uncle. *Nice try there, bub.* Man, he thought she was gullible.

17

Don't harass the opposition
~Moscow Rules

Sunday

"Nice digs." Lisa Griffin swung through the Strike Force war room door and stopped. She turned to the man in an Iniquus uniform—charcoal-gray camo pants and dark gray compression shirt—showing off the Iniquus philosophy: Train hard. Be ready. "Thanks for the escort."

When the door closed, she strode into the room, her gaze on Frost. "Exciting night. Lot's doing. Well, there was. From the snoring Finley and I were listening to when we left the hotel, Todor's asleep. I don't know, that could be Cammy. I shouldn't judge."

Kennedy pointed at the screen lit up in green night vision. Todor lay on his back with his mouth hanging open, Raine on her back, twiddling her thumbs.

"Counting sheep usually helps." Griffin turned from the screen to the others in the room. "Finley's right behind me. He saw one of the Panther Force on the way up and stopped for a second to pass him some information about Anna. She's going to be running a Zoric family errand this week in Slovakia."

Finley's girlfriend, Anna, went by the name of Zelda Fitzgerald. She was with the Asymmetric Warfare Group. The AWG was a special mission unit that worked with the Army and joint forces. Their task was to identify new ways that the U.S. might be attacked and come up with solutions.

"Best wishes to her," Kennedy said. "I'm headed back to Eastern Europe myself next week. Small world. Interesting times."

Finley came through the door and lifted his hand in salute. His head on a swivel. "Everyone's pushed back in their chairs, catering has the table supplied, I guess we don't think this is the end of things for tonight." He stepped forward and knocked his knuckles on the table. "Now that Todor's done what he came here to do, is there something we've discovered that we need to pursue?" Finley's gaze rested on Hasan.

"That's possible. I'm Javeed Hasan." He leaned forward with a hand outstretched for a shake. "I work with Raine Meyers at the DIA."

"Good to meet you. Steve Finley, FBI, domestic terror."

"Lisa Griffin, FBI, cyber."

As Hasan reached out to shake hands with Griffin, Finley looked toward Frost. "DIA, huh? So this has a military component?"

"There's a military component," Frost said. "The DIA believes that Todor's trip to visit with Cammy Burke is to gather information about another case they're investigating."

"Does this have to do with the psychedelic mushrooms and CIA brainwashing story Todor just got done feeding her?" Lisa snorted as she pulled out a chair next to Prescott and sat.

"Interesting story," Prescott said. "It's easy to look up that data. The information was thin but basically accurate. That all would give credence to his story. Not many people know about the research at Fort Detrick. He tied it into his story from the back of the car and taking mushrooms. That was nice and neat. Two ways I'd read that —One, Todor tried to figure out a good story to go along with a really strange kidnapping plot, and he landed on this and thought Cammy was incurious and wouldn't do an Internet search. Two, the Prokhorovs thought Cammy Burke was a dangle, and they wanted to out her by handing her this bizarre story to see if she'd go along with it and play dumb."

"It's the first one," Hasan said. "Well, close. It was something the boyfriend Frédéric was researching. When Todor was telling the story, I remembered seeing that on his computer history, both the trials into treating anxiety, the use with cancer survivors, and the dark background history with the CIA and Fort Detrick. Interestingly, Griffin," he turned her way, "you mentioned the Zorics. The Slovakian Zoric family was Todor's support. They provided both the close protection and the motorcycle riders."

"Why?" Finley asked.

Hasan gave a one-shouldered shrug. "The Zoric family has infrastructure here. The Prokhorovs work the cyber threat angle from the relative safety of Bulgaria."

"Those families don't usually work and play well together," Finley said.

"True." Hasan nodded. "And probably the reason Todor got an extra dose of meds. But if the right person made an ask, differences can be put aside."

"Amateur show." Finley took a seat near Striker.

"To be fair," Griffin said. "Todor isn't a real spy. He's just kinda doing his uncle a solid, is what I think. Is there still coffee around here?" She got up and looked at the table, then spun back and pointed at Finley.

"Black, thanks." Finley turned his head to take in all the players. "My point being. The Prokhorovs didn't send in one of their best. I can't imagine that what they're doing is significant. Or maybe it *is* significant, but it's not a high priority. Would I be reading the situation correctly?"

"If I may," Hasan began. "The situation is quite dangerous. From what intelligence we've gathered, they're using Todor because he was in the right place at the right time and had already built rapport with Cammy. Raine did that intentionally. Todor is the asset she's been developing."

Hasan took a moment to catch the FBI agents up on the threats to the Delta Force operators' wives.

"This could devastate our programs," Finley said. "People start dropping out, morale plunges. It's strategic, to be sure, and just the kind of thing the Prokhorovs traffic in. The Russians figured it out. They weren't going to win with bullets, so they went after our brains."

"Americans are easy marks for disinformation and propaganda. Over in Russia, the government practiced their psyops—psychological operations—on their own people," Kennedy said. "As the Russian people realized what was happening, they became inured to it and built up immunity. The United States hasn't yet been damaged enough to develop the kinds of psychological calluses that the Russian citizens have. In this case, we can't return the attack. We actually have very little we can fight with. Publicly exposing them is about it. Maybe figure charges and put some folks in prison." He gestured toward Finley. "Finley's team put a whole group of Zorics behind bars last year, but it hasn't seemed to slow down the family's U.S. operations."

Frost nodded. "Threats, isolation, economic sanctions. But that's all political and dependent on election cycles. The Russians have been around for a very long time, while we are in our adolescence as a nation. They've learned to keep their heads while we're champing at our bits."

Hasan leaned back in his chair and laced his hands behind his head. "I'm preaching to the choir here. Sorry to dummy this down when you're all professionals. But sometimes, a sweep across the horizon is helpful to get one's bearings. Setting morale aside, repopulating special operations forces isn't an easy task. Only thirty percent of the kids coming out of high school qualify for a military career: lack of health, poor education, criminal records, and weight. The pool to draw from to develop special operators is growing smaller. Once operators are recruited and trained, it's imperative to the ongoing success of our teams that they re-up. Malcolm Gladwell wrote about the reasons in his book *Blink*. Gladwell talked about the idea of applying knowledge filters that, in the blink of an eye, can home in on the few factors with real situational meaning, culling through the myriad variables and possibilities. That's not learned. It's earned. Out on task, on the battlefield, under fire—those skills are burnished into our soldiers. Their training is one step, their action and experience are another, and that's how we move on down the road. That's how trust is built on the teams. You start peeling operators out of the ranks and try to build new teams over and over? We'll be limping instead of sprinting."

"We need to figure out how they got to the Delta Force wives," Griffin said. "Delta Force is one of the most secretive of the special forces units. Delta Force is black ops. They're wiped from public view. The unit's very existence is veiled in secrecy. Outside of a newsworthy operation or an operational death, there's a facade that no one could breach."

"But someone kicked in that door," Prescott said.

"Quite literally." Hasan raised his brows. "One of the threatened wives, Lucy McDonald—eight months pregnant, married to Sergeant Arthur "Dice" McDonald, Echo—was attacked Friday in

D.C., she was trying to hide at a friend's house. She was SWATted, and the bad guy had a sniper sight trained on the front of the house."

"What?" The FBI leaned forward in their seats.

"Was Lucy hurt?" Frost asked.

"She was assessed by our doctors after her rescue," Striker replied. "Both mother and fetus were checked out. We've moved Lucy to a safe location. Her husband is being brought home from the field."

"Already, they're effective. Echo is a man down," Prescott said. Targeting Delta, like targeting Raine, was putting *his* family in the crosshairs. "There's more to this story," Prescott said.

"Raine Meyers was on the scene of the attack in a different undercover role as Paisley Moorhead. Paisley Moorhead was the contact we offered to the Delta Force wives who have received threats as a link for DIA support. Iniquus, as you know, is on this case, they were Paisley's back up. They all kept the wife, Lucy, safe."

"Raine seems to be running in a lot of races," Kennedy said.

"We're pretty sure it's the same race," Hasan countered. "The DIA is going after this from different angles. Originally, Raine's angle was to be the dangle that got her into the inner working of the Prokhorov family and discover their computer servers so they can be destroyed. It's too long of an action. With a pregnant wife being attacked, we need to get this part of the puzzle solved now. Raine is trying to find the most efficient way to shut this threat down."

Frost turned to Griffin. "What are you thinking about all this?"

"If a terrorist could get to the Deltas, everyone's eventually fair game. Russia likes to try things first on a small scale before they hit their real targets. Last June, there was that Twitter account hack targeting military wives with threats."

Everyone nodded.

"My first thought," Griffin said, "is that the Prokhorovs have that computer system and have developed very sophisticated artificial intelligence, AI. They've been buying data from phone and computer apps that are giving them untold amounts of data points on American's daily lives. With AI software, finding the Deltas might be easier to hunt down than other special operations units. I bet that's why the Prokhorovs picked them."

"How's that?" Frost asked.

"The Deltas operate out of Fort Bragg. They aren't stationed at different posts like the Green Berets, for example."

"More?" Hasan said.

"Okay. On the cyber side of the FBI, we know that the Prokhorovs have developed a system that is like the TIA system that DARPA—our military scientific researchers were developing."

"TIA, what does that stand for? I'm not familiar with this," Frost said.

"TIA is basically Big Brother. Total Information Awareness. Right after 9-11, DARPA envisioned a system that pulled together as much information as they could about people. A virtual dragnet. They got the idea because there were intersections between all the 9-11 terrorists. It was found through analysis of known data that with seven clicks, all nineteen terrorists could have been linked together. Two of the men were on the CIA terrorist watch list. They were connected through physical addresses that were given. Five of the terrorists gave the same phone number to the reservation agent when they were buying their plane tickets. It was all right there. Right there! The towers would have been stopped. The war would never have happened. All the dead. All the maiming and damage. All the families torn apart, the kids who grew up without their parents. The first responders dying of horrific chronic illnesses years later. All of it could have been stopped. *That* would be the good use. But the world doesn't work like that. If things can be used for good, we must imagine their mirror image. Using the tools for evil."

Hasan leaned forward to rest his forearms on his thighs and lace his fingers, hard focused on Griffin. "Homeland Security operates a sophisticated targeting system called ATS—Automatic Targeting System—it assesses comparative risks of arriving passengers. They use this system to decide whom they stop to talk to or whom they let pass on through. They can't tell the public about their success rate because that might give away how analysis is done. But we know that it thwarted a guy out of Kosovo from getting into our country. He wasn't on anyone's radar—a cleanskin in the vernacular—he got turned around and sent home. A little over a year later, they found the stump of his arm chained to a steering wheel that had been part of a suicide car bomb that killed over a hundred people. His thumbprint was used to identify him. Thanks to the ATS program, he wasn't in the U.S. creating havoc."

"Which is probably a good use of AI, but not the dragnet that DARPA proposed with TIA," Griffin said. "TIA was considered to be ethically and constitutionally unacceptable, which is why it doesn't exist."

"The Prokhorovs don't have to deal with these kinds of ethical issues," Frost said. "If they had a TIA system, apply that to this situation."

"All right." Griffin tipped her head back and stared at the ceiling. "Stream of consciousness—not ready for public consumption thoughts?"

"We'll take that," Hasan said.

"Thinking about the Delta Forces all housed at Fort Bragg makes this kind of easy, doesn't it?" Lisa posed the rhetorical question. "Think of all the records that can be culled—medical history, prescriptions, travel, banking, purchasing habits, phone calls, web surfing, family and friends, social platforms, and on and on. If the Prokhorov's had an AI program set up, and they were looking for those who lived at Fort Bragg, and they checked the age and gender, then they checked back to past assignments."

"Deltas pull from all branches of the military and all special operations forces but mainly from Rangers," Prescott said. "If the AI tracked a man from, say, Fort Benning—where some Ranger units are stationed—and he moved to Fort Bragg, the software might look into that closer. If the wives suddenly went radio silent about their husbands on social media… I can see that. An AI program finding them and their private information. That's similar to what happened to the military families on Twitter last June." He paused. "Someone is obviously boots on the ground, though. An assailant could pull a SWATting ploy from anywhere in the world, rerouting the phones through the Darknet. But you said there was a sniper. That's a whole different level of concern."

"If data collection was how they narrowed in on the victims, that proves the point about the dangers of TIA," Griffin said. "In the end, TIA didn't balance damage to Americans versus security from terror. In fact, there was an argument that said having a TIA system would endanger people."

Hasan lifted his chin and pressed his lips, considering. "Given the Prokhorov family's specialty in cyber warfare, I think Griffin probably hit on it. If accurate, they assigned the computer the task of identifying people at Fort Bragg and worked backward through their histories to cull out Delta Force. Of the Tier One operators, the SEALs would be harder to target than the Deltas. I'm guessing that since the SEALs are on opposite sides of the country, their teams might not take the same punch as those who are in close concentration."

"We're throwing out the idea of a mole?" Finley asked.

"Mole is possible," Hasan said. "But not probable. There are so few people that could access that information. The DIA is actively looking at each and every one of them."

"And Raine's role?" Prescott asked.

"First, she's playing the role of Cammy Burke. Her mission is to discover what the Prokhorovs want from her, and when that drain is dry, then to use the kompromat to get Todor to marry her."

Prescott looked at his shoes. "That sounds extreme."

"With fake papers, so she and Todor can go visit the family and find out what's what."

"Into the lion's den?" Kennedy asked. "That's ballsy."

"But that plan takes time," Hasan said. "The first physical attack on the wives was attempted and only failed because of Raine's quick thinking. We don't have any more time to work behind the scenes. When it comes to protecting the Delta Force wives, we need action."

The room stilled as everyone contemplated the fallout.

Hasan said, "Our goal is to neutralize this threat and decide next steps."

"Todor's waking up," Deep said from behind his computer.

They raised their gazes to see Todor in his pajama bottoms, pulling the hotel room drape open. The camera image went from night vision green to natural ambient light.

"Listen," Hasan said. "I've been thinking about how to handle the Delta Force crisis. I think I've hit on an idea. It would require a joint DIA-FBI mission." Hasan turned to Prescott. "Sound like fun?"

18

Don't look back
~Moscow Rules

Sunday

"I'm going to go get some fresh air while we're waiting," Prescott said.

Striker had suggested that everyone take a break. They had a nap room two floors down, set up with sleeping pods for the convenience of Headquarter visitors. Hasan and the FBI team could at least get a little shut-eye to clear their heads for when Raine got in.

Raine was in the Lyft, seeing Todor off to the airport.

Raine was probably as exhausted as anyone. More so. No one else had their nervous system lit on fire.

Prescott pushed through the atrium door and out into the early afternoon sun. The day was warm for January. The air still. The sky shone bright and cloudless blue. It should be an invigorating day, one where he thanked God for the beauty around him as he paused to breathe deeply. He circled the building to the north side, where they had chairs set under the ancient oak trees.

As he sat, Prescott watched a squirrel race up the trunk and chitter along the bare limb.

Raine.

He pulled out his phone and tapped on a gallery file, scrolling to the last picture he had of them together. It was taken seven years ago, and somehow, Raine was even more beautiful now. Wisdom and intelligence in her eyes. Compassion in the set of her mouth.

Every picture of her up on the screen as Cammy Burke, every second of video with her flash of lashes and the tip of her head... they drew him back in time.

Prescott and Raine had been together since high school. They'd decided to be casual about their relationship as they headed off to different universities. It had worked for them when it didn't work for other couples he knew trying to stay together after high school graduation.

Raine had called him sobbing freshman year, the Twin Towers had fallen, and she had to help. She'd joined the reserves. She hoped he wouldn't be mad.

Prescott had been sitting by the phone, trying to figure out how to tell her he had just signed on as a reservist.

They always seemed in sync.

Love was their glue when nothing else held them together. Especially not geographical proximity. Through their university degrees and reserve requirements, into their full-time military careers, their unassailable bond gave them a solid base to depend upon.

They got engaged over Skype.

Damian's mom helped him get Raine's ring—a simple titanium band—and mailed it to him. Prescott carried that ring into battle and through boredom. He kept it with him for months before he was able to bribe a guy to let him on the convoy to the village where

Raine was developing intelligence. He was there long enough to take a knee and slip the band on her finger. He'd get her something fancier once they were home for good when a diamond wouldn't get caught on her combat gloves. Snag her up. Put her in danger.

Their plan had been to finish through their fifteen-years mark in conflict regions, God willing. They'd apply to finish out their last five at the same base while they started their family. Then they'd work on getting a house with the white picket fence and jobs in the alphabets once they'd hit their twenty-year mark and retired from the military. They'd live in peace—the American dream.

The plan was laid.

It was a good plan.

He scrolled to another picture. Raine was sleeping on a rock by the river, shaded by an overhanging limb. A smile played across her mouth as she dreamed.

He thought he'd get to watch her smile in her dreams until his last days on Earth. A bold thing to believe when you were a Delta operator, and your fiancée swam with the SEALs.

The clear trajectory of their life's goals got Prescott through many a hard-fought mission and many a night when he struggled against the odds because he wouldn't break faith with Raine. He'd fulfill their plan.

He turned to the next picture. It was Raine thoroughly pissed at him. Furious. And madder still because he'd pulled out his phone to capture her picture. He'd exalted at the fierceness in her eyes. The capacity of her body. She was *mesmerizing*. She was fire.

Prescott knew why Raine had thrown the ring at him when he punched Eric.

It was probably the one thing that Prescott could have done, in her eyes, that would be unforgivable and make loving him untenable.

After some time processing their breakup, Prescott thought it had been inevitable. They'd been a decades-long habit. They'd been touchstones at a distance. They had crazy good sex when they were together and great companionship. But for both of them, duty quickly turned their focus back into the headwinds, needing to get back to their units.

The military had been their focus since they were eighteen. They'd never had a chance to try on a normal kind of relationship.

He bet that neither one of them believed they'd both make it out of the war—that their engagement would end up in a walk down the aisle. It had felt good, though, knowing he'd belonged with someone, and there was something on his horizon, even if their marriage and peaceful future life were mirages.

A text dropped: **She's here.**

Time had spooled by while he was caught up in his reminiscence. Prescott took one more look at Raine's photograph, then closed the file.

Okay, Prescott thought, here we go. *Time to face the Storm.*

19

Anticipate your destination
~ Moscow Rules

Sunday

The Lyft driver wasn't allowed through the Iniquus gates.

Blaze climbed out of a charcoal-gray Jeep just on the other side of the barrier, ready to drive Raine up to Headquarters.

She pushed the door open on the Prius with a "Thank you," showed her Cammy Burke DoD credentials to the guard, and let a glorious Malinois sniff her over while her ride turned and headed back up the road.

"Thank you, ma'am." The guard handed her back her I.D. then pressed a button. "Your escort is waiting," he said as the heavy metal pickets slid soundlessly open.

Blaze stood at the bumper of his vehicle. Well past the six-foot-tall mark, Blaze had rusty auburn hair that liked to curl when it got any length to it. He was a retired SEAL and had been on the DEVGRU—SEAL Team Six—with Striker back in the day.

Blaze had a beautiful singing voice, rich and melodic, like warm caramels.

Raine wondered if he remembered them singing together around desert campfires when she still had a voice that had a vocal range. Raine sent him a tired smile of thanks when he popped her door open and helped her in.

Raine was still wearing the Iniquus evening gown and comms bra. Deep had told her that Lynx arranged for a change of clothes, something more comfortable. It saved her a trip home.

Right now, some carbs and a power drink would go a far pace in making the upcoming pow wow tolerable.

Raine got the importance of hot washes—debriefs right after a mission.

She'd prefer some sleep first.

The vehicle parked, they walked through the atrium, rode the elevator up, and walked down the hall.

Blaze held the Strike Force war room door wide for her.

When she passed into the room, everyone stood and clapped.

Raine ducked her head as the blood rushed to her face. She'd never liked recognition.

"There she is!" Hasan grinned. "Well done!"

"Thank you." Raine waved her hand, hoping everyone would sit down and go about their business. Lisa and Steve, Rowan Kennedy from the Brussels mission, Amanda Frost—great, it was her joint task force, huh? That explained Damian's being on hand in the tunnel.

About half of the Strike Force team was here. And Hasan was the only one from the DIA. That made sense, too. This mission was so dangerous. They had been trying to keep the footprint very small.

With the FBI in the mix, that had obviously changed.

As Kennedy shifted over, Raine spotted Damian at the back of the herd.

Damian. Seven years melted away.

Though she knew it was professionally and emotionally, the absolute wrong thing to do, all Raine wanted at that moment was to rush into Damian's arms because his arms were her resting spot.

Don't be stupid. That's self-sabotage. You might as well walk out into a minefield.

Raine tightened her muscles to stop any forward momentum.

Their gazes held, and Raine didn't know what to do next.

Luckily, Lynx sidled up beside her. "I bet you'd like to get changed." She lifted her hand toward a door at the back of the room. "I have some yoga wear ready. I thought you'd be more comfortable. And some sneakers. Your feet are probably killing you in those heels." They started companionably forward. "Have you eaten? Why don't you fix yourself a plate once you're changed?" she asked, pointing to the table of food.

There was something in Lynx's eye that told Raine that Lynx understood the situation and she was there for her in sisterhood and solidarity.

As that thought formed in Raine's head, Lynx said, "Whatever you need. Okay?"

"Yes, thank you."

ALONE, Raine sat on the padded chair in the bathroom dressing room, letting the thrum of her blood slow before she bent to tug her heels off. She had blisters across the tops of her toes.

Next to the chair were yoga leggings, a tank top, and a fleece jacket.

The tennis shoes, new in their box, were her size. Beside them sat a black bag with green tissue paper. Inside, Raine found a sports bra, panties, and a pair of ankle socks. The change would feel good.

Raine tugged off her clothes from last night and moved to the mirror to peel off the facial prosthetics that altered her bone structure. She used just enough glue and latex to confuse recognition programs and identify herself as Cammy Burke, but not enough to freak someone out if something came loose, and she had to pull off a chunk of her face.

Each of Raine's covers—Cammy Burke, Paisley Moorhead, and the others—had their own makeup routine, practiced, and perfected. It had to be the exact same each and every time—no room for mistakes.

Raine pulled a makeup-removing cloth from the plastic envelope and cleaned off the rest of her theater makeup, letting the scars on her neck show.

Part of her knew she was doing that because she wanted Damian to see. To what end? She wasn't sure. There was a niggle in her stomach that made her think she wanted revenge, but she couldn't think why. She was too tired to figure out why. She'd put that thought on a shelf to look at later. Or not. Maybe he'd just move on his way, and she wouldn't need to process any of her emotions.

With the ball gown hanging from the bathroom hook, along with the now-disconnected comms bra, Raine dressed in the new clothes, tied her shoes, and went to face the music.

When she emerged, the players were sitting in a circle.

She rested her hand on the chair next to Hasan that was left open. "Is this for me?"

"Please." He stood and held out his hand for a shake. "Congratulations. Job well done. Deep's been monitoring Todor's communications," Hasan said as Raine accepted his congratulatory handshake. "Your boy has reported back to Sergei. Everyone on the Prokhorov side is jazzed with their outcome."

Raine stretched her lips into a tired smile as she took her seat.

This felt more like an intervention than a debrief. She wondered whose grand idea it was to seat Damian exactly opposite her and Hasan. She turned her head to take in all the faces. "Hey, everyone. Thank you for your help. This feels like old home week, doesn't it?"

Lynx was to her right. *Solidarity.*

"Raine." Hasan took his seat and swiveled to face her. "I caught you up when you were on your way to Iniquus. You know where everything stands from this end, the ideas that we've considered." He spun and let his gaze take everyone in. "I believe we're all up to speed?" He watched them nod, then focused back on Raine. "You and I can evaluate the mission further when we're one on one. I'd like to hear your thoughts about how things went. How we can support you better in the future. As to right now, while we have the FBI and Iniquus available, I thought we might review possible next steps. To that end, I have a proposal I'd like to run past everyone."

The group shuffled in their seats, pulled out pads and pens.

Before everyone refocused on Hasan, Raine said, "This is going to take boots on the ground."

Eyes came up and rested on her.

Hasan had a way of presenting his ideas as if they were a done deal. She wanted to interject her own thoughts before he got rolling.

Hasan swiveled toward her.

"Let's set the Cammy Burke-Todor Bilov mission to the side for now." Raine ignored the others and spoke directly to Hasan. He was the one who would devise her next moves and order her into action. "We know that Todor will be cycling through his events list. I get three days of calls and three days of cold shoulder, then an ask. We know that ask will be a red herring. It's going to take time to unwrap all that. I want to focus on the fact that Lucy was attacked. They tried to put a sniper scope on a young, innocent, pregnant woman. We have to assume that given the opportunity, they would have pulled the trigger. Why else would they be there? More fear? More fear wasn't necessary. Lucy was so terrified, I thought she'd go into labor. Even without being shot, an early birth could have serious consequences for both mother and child."

She forced herself to speak slowly and clearly. Without vocal range, it was harder for people to understand Raine when her words rushed up on each other. "We know for a fact that there are women who are in harm's way at this very moment. The Delta Force contracts are being issued. We assume they'll be signed. Someone's going to die unless we shut this down."

"Agreed," Hasan said with a nod of his head.

Before he could say anything more, she added, "Someone on the inside was involved. They *had* to be. The identities and particulars of "the Unit" are too highly guarded. At least, I had thought so up until you shared with me Lisa's thoughts about artificial intelligence software like the proposed TIA system. Even then, obviously, this isn't a cyberattack by itself. There are people willing to kill. I think it best if I work with Iniquus to manage the Todor mission from afar. And I think that "Paisley Moorhead" needs to head down to Fort Bragg and stay at Lucy's house. I want to see what I can see."

Raine thought her best chance at getting a green light was to make the bid and hope the others would get behind her.

Hasan, on his own, was unlikely to go for it.

Raine couldn't protect the wives from D.C., and she couldn't protect them from a North Carolina apartment. She needed to be right there at Fort Bragg with eyes on to gather intelligence.

It was what she was trained to do.

"Without Lucy at her house, that would be tough," Hasan said. "We'd need permissions and paperwork. Your showing up like that... The tighter the circle, the better. We agree on that since we don't have facts on the table about the inner workings of this time bomb…"

"Except," Raine countered, "that the Prokhorovs need Cammy to spy on the effects of their Delta wives terror efforts."

"Do we know that's true?" Hasan asked. "Let's be careful with speculation. You're playing the Cammy Burke role to figure that out."

"Fine. Working theory. Obviously, I need more data." She held her hand up, pointing over to Deep. "I don't have to be in D.C. to take calls from Todor. Strike Force can reroute calls and make them look like they were answered anywhere on a GPS readout. He put an app on the Cammy Burke phone that makes it look like she runs her daily circuit: work, lunch, work, home, coffee shop, sometimes a movie. It's a preprogrammed maze Cammy appears to follow, so the Prokhorov's think she's a good little mouse." Raine leaned back in her chair to catch Deep's eye. "Right Deep?"

Deep looked over the top of his computer screen. "We can leave that program running and adjust as needed, rerouting any calls that come to the Cammy Burke phone to another phone. No problem."

Hasan sent her a smile. Raine knew that smile. It said they were on the same page, but with a twist.

Raine had learned to be suspicious of the twists. She'd follow through, though, if it kept the wives safe.

She shifted painfully. Every part of her ached.

Her body was wearing down from her years of jogging through rough terrain with a heavy pack, jumping out of planes, and fast-roping into the fray.

Once they eradicated the threat to the Delta wives, Raine promised herself she'd move on to a quieter life.

Thirty-six was too old for falling out of cars onto ice-cold pavements. She reached up and rubbed the sore spot on the back of her head.

She would admit it to herself; she was tired.

First things first, though, Raine had a debt to repay.

20

Pick the time and the place for action
~ Moscow Rules

Sunday

Hasan lifted his coffee cup. "Have any of you heard of Café Ground Zero?"

He paused for a moment as he took a sip.

Prescott bet everyone there in the Strike Force war room had read about this. They didn't answer because they wanted to know where Hasan was going with it.

When no one responded, Hasan pressed on. "Up at the Pentagon, where Cammy Burke works," he tipped his head Raine's way, "there's a hot dog stand smack dab in the center of the courtyard. It's rumored that back at the time of the USSR, the Kremlin had pointed two missiles directly at this hot dog stand. The story goes that the USSR was watching activity around the building. U.S.

military brass went to that location constantly. In and out, in and out. The USSR believed the hot dog stand was the planning center, or maybe the control bunker for the Pentagon. If that were true, the first thing the USSR wanted to do was send two ICBMs in to wipe it out." Hasan sat back, looking pleased with himself.

Everyone in the circle was lost.

"Are we the missiles or the hot dog stand in this metaphor?" Raine asked.

Prescott thought Raine looked exhausted and probably didn't have two shits to give at this point about missiles or hot dogs. She probably just wanted the mission up on the board, assignments distributed, and everyone moving on.

"Metaphor… I meant to get across the idea that standing on the outside looking in, you can't be sure what it is you're seeing. To know that the hot dog stand was a hot dog stand, the USSR needed boots on the ground. Otherwise, they were guessing, as Raine pointed out, about Fort Bragg." He rubbed his hands together then said, "I suggest we introduce a Delta operator who needs to re-up. Get surveillance on his wife and have her expose the terrorist." He spread his hands wide. *Tada.*

"No," Raine was emphatic. "Those wives don't have the training. You'd be sending a puppy in to fight a hyena pack."

"You know me better than that, Raine," Hasan rebuked. "I'd never put a civilian in harm's way."

"How are we going to do that?" Finley asked. "That's a tightly-knit group. Everyone knows everyone. You can't pick a player, insert them, and call them a Delta operator. The skillset is too specific and too difficult."

"They all know Prescott." Hasan nodded his way. "They call you Deimos, right? Son of Ares and Aphrodite, getting the genes that made you both deadly and good looking." He looked Raine's way and popped his eyebrows, then turned back to Prescott. "Deimos, the god of dread?"

Prescott didn't like the bite of condescension in the guy's tone. He'd heard it in bars by men who thought that with the right training, they could have been an operator. Prescott ignored guys like that. They usually thought they wanted to pick a fight. They had no idea how fast they'd be put on the ground. Prescott scratched his thumbnail along his jaw.

"Wait. You were a Delta operator?" Lynx asked. "I could have sworn… Sorry. I, for some reason, thought you were a Green Beret."

"Because you've run into me at events where I was hanging out with our mutual friends who are Green Berets. Same crowd, different branding."

"You're probably right," Lynx said.

"I think we can make it work," Hasan continued. "You're thirty-six. That's about the average age of a Delta operator, right?" Hasan asked. "Delta operators go where they're needed. They work with any branch of the military. They roll out with the CIA and the FBI. They're non-discriminatory when it comes to taking down the bad guy. What if Deimos was working a black op these last few years and needed to be FBI as part of his cover? You bounced with CIRG for years. Probably brushed past a bunch of your brothers in hot zones."

"I did. They know I was in the CIRG." If there was an undercover role of Delta operator getting ready to re-up, Prescott wanted it to be him. It was his duty. He was bound by the oaths he'd taken to his brothers. He wanted to be there to protect their families, just like they'd protected Raine.

Frost puckered her mouth, her eyes almost closed as she processed. That meant she was considering this as a viable option.

Prescott leaned forward, resting his forearms on his thighs, lacing his fingers together. "The DIA could rework my military file. It's plausible. And the best part is, every operator understands need to know. They don't need to know, and I can't say a word about it. I don't need to develop a cover story."

"If you show up in the Delta ranks, you won't just be training with them," Kennedy said. "You'd be deploying with a team."

"That puts everyone else on the mission in harm's way unless they're sending you over to distract the bad guy with your pretty self, *Deimos*." Finley winked.

Prescott snorted. "Yeah, well, I still train with CIRG. Like Hasan said, FBI's CIRG, CIA, and Delta—we all roll together."

"And no chest-thumping at all." Griffin laughed. "Pretty self…"

Prescott took the ribbing. He'd probably get teased about that like Kennedy caught it for his backseat caper. "Point being I can still bring the rain. I could plug back in." The moment that phrase left his lips, he regretted it. Freudian slip? He slid his poker face in place and set his gaze, so it wouldn't drift over to where Raine was sitting across from him.

Hasan looked at the ceiling.

Everyone stilled.

Hasan lowered his gaze to rest on Striker. "What's the word on Lucy's husband, Sergeant McDonald?"

"His team finished a mission. They're headed stateside. They'll pull him out of the ranks, and Iniquus will provide transport to reunite the family, maintaining the integrity of our safe house."

"Who leads that Delta team?" Hasan asked.

Striker opened his phone. "Josiah Landry goes by—"

"T-Rex," Prescott finished. "Echo. That was my team."

"Perfect!" Hasan slapped his hand on his thigh. "I love it when everything lines up neatly. It makes it seem preordained. They're a man down with McDonald gone."

"I suppose we can make that work." Frost turned to Prescott. "I'm assuming you've kept in touch with your brothers."

"Of course. And I have a *duty* to their wives and children." Prescott shot her a hardened gaze. "If there's a way in. I want it."

"I understand that, but it's not my point," Frost said, rubbing her eye. She blinked and focused. "They'd know if you were married. You would have invited them to your wedding. They would know about your wife. The point of you going is to make a place for an agent playing the wife's role, or there's no one for the terrorists to target. It's got to be someone you've at least mentioned in passing." Frost leaned forward. "Talk about bringing the Raine." She smiled. "You know Raine already, so you'd have back story. You said you'd been engaged, and you haven't seen her in seven years. That sighting seven years ago, was it after you joined CIRG?"

"Yes, ma'am," Prescott said.

"Raine was deployed with the military when you joined the FBI?" she pressed.

"Yes, ma'am." He didn't like talking about Raine as if she weren't sitting right there. He could feel the stress rising in waves off Raine. Prescott hoped he could divert attention long enough that she could figure out if she wanted to say, "No—our past relationship jeopardizes the mission," or whether she wanted to be in the fray even if it meant teaming up with him.

"I see," Frost said. "Your friends know that you broke off the engagement with Raine."

"I mentioned in passing she and I had gone our separate ways." His eyes flicked toward Raine and away. "I never mentioned any details."

"Do we need to know why it unfolded that way?" Hasan asked.

Yeah, he wasn't going to touch that question, so he deflected. "If we passed me off as a Delta operator who was assigned to a black op… it could be part of that." His gaze sought Raine's and held for a long moment while he tried to read her.

It used to be easy to do.

Now, he wasn't sure…

"That works," Kennedy said. "You would have tried to keep

Raine out of any fray by saying you'd broken up. Then you quietly got married just the two of you."

"We could arrange for it to look that way on paper," Hasan said. "Now that the black op is completed and you're back with your team, she can come out in the open."

"You both had lives here in D.C.," Frost said. "She might have lived separately to maintain your cover."

This time when he looked Raine's way, all he saw was the fatigue. It made him think of her story about being on the back of the careening motorbike in Perugia when she climbed on by choice, but then it became a nightmare.

Prescott held up his hands. "Before another word is said, I want to hear what Raine thinks of all this."

"I'm a disciplined soldier. I go where I'm told to go and do what I'm told to do, to the best of my ability."

Thing was, in the last forty-eight hours, she'd been through a SWAT event, saved Lucy McDonald, trapped Todor, been shocked, dropped to the road and sustained a head injury, and been sleep deprived. She looked miserable.

That he had anything to do with that kicked him in the gut.

"Let's sleep on it," Prescott suggested. "Let's talk about this Monday."

Hasan shook his head. "It's possible that there's someone inside the gates of Fort Bragg right now putting the Delta Force families at risk. We don't have time to soft-pedal this. Listen to Raine when she says she's a soldier and doesn't need coddling and believe her."

"I—that wasn't the intention of my suggestion," Prescott countered. "I think there are nuances that we need to consider. Time to let those concerns present themselves. We need to adapt to them."

"If the wives get wind of what happened to Lucy McDonald, they might decide to go into hiding, scattering around the country. We don't have the resources for that." Frost pressed to the edge of her chair. "This has the potential to flash at any moment. I'm with

Hasan. I think getting you down there and poised as an Echo operator so Raine can gather first-hand information is a solid plan."

"Consider this, the wives are only approached when the husbands are downrange. That means I won't be there to support Raine," Prescott said. "She'll be on her own."

"We have an Iniquus contract," Hasan countered. "She'll have Strike Force backup."

Prescott was looking at Hasan, but in his mind, Prescott was back in Eric's kitchen the moment after Raine had flung the engagement ring at him and had run out the door without a single word. He'd spun to see if Eric had come to, so he could go after Raine, but his gaze landed on a letter in Raine's handwriting, laying on the table.

Eric, please help me.

PRESCOTT'S PHONE had alarmed with a CIRG call out. He checked Eric's breathing, pocketed the letter, and jetted into action.

On the long flight to his mission in Africa, Prescott consumed that letter. It explained why Raine couldn't talk anymore. Her vocal cords had been severed when she was captured and nearly beheaded.

Beheaded. That word still winded him.

It took Prescott three weeks to get back from his deployment in Nigeria.

When he did, it was as if Raine disappeared from the face of the Earth.

Since they weren't married, no one with the military would give him any information. Her friends didn't know. His brothers in Echo couldn't say a single word. Missions were classified.

Echo force were the ones asking *him* for an update. He'd had to admit to them that he and Raine had essentially called it quits.

Everyone loved Raine. The team threatened to kick his ass if he'd hurt her, especially after what she'd been through.

Could he put his and Raine's history to the side for this mission?

Probably not completely.

If he didn't go, it would be someone else. The DIA would fill that space with another guy, and Raine would be deep undercover, trusting a stranger to play the role of husband.

"Prescott?" Hasan asked.

Prescott nodded. "I think we have a solid plan. If we can get it organized, it looks like I'll be rolling with my team and my wife, Raine."

21

Hide small operative motions in larger non-threatening motions.
~ Moscow rules

Sunday evening

Striker tapped a button on the wall, and a whiteboard appeared from behind the panel. "When are you thinking of putting this in place?" he asked.

"Move Prescott and Meyers down there Tuesday if we can all swing it," Hasan said.

"Short notice, but all hands on deck, we can make it happen." Striker picked up a marker. "Let's talk this through. Our intake information tells us that Raine Meyers should be a cleanskin for any players in this scenario." Striker referred to the term for someone who hasn't shown up on anyone's radar screen as a player. "She's here in D.C. on disability from the military, and she occupies her time doing watercolor illustrations for children's books. A career that will blend well with her mission face."

"You have published books available?" Frost asked.

"I have about two dozen now," Raine said. "Some are my actual art. Some were done by a DIA artist copying my style. I try to put out three a year to keep that cover going. I have a children's manuscript on my art table. I can bring that down and do some painting. Set up a studio in one of the rooms. It's a good conversation starter."

"You do art?" Prescott asked.

"I had a lot of art therapy while I was recovering." She touched her throat.

Prescott was trying hard not to react to Raine's scars. When his gaze settled on her neck, he imagined the point of the terrorist's dagger slicing through her flesh. It was a kick in the gut, and all Prescott wanted to do was grab Raine into his arms to become her sword and her shield.

"What was your hair color when you were in the military?" Lynx moved over to Striker and reached for his marker. She started columns across the top of the board: Personal Appearance, Backstory, Packing List, Threads to Tie Up.

"Sable brown," Prescott said.

"You went blonde for the role of Cammy Burke?" Kennedy asked. "You had black hair in Brussels."

"Each of my covers has her own makeup, facial prosthetics, clothing styles, and hair coloring. But I keep the length long to give myself options."

"Your makeup changed the shape of your face. I can see that now that you've removed your makeup," Kennedy said. "To be honest, I see two things that might still make you recognizable to Sergei. In the picture that we put up of you and Todor over at the FBI, I recognized you as Clara Edwards even with the changes that made you into Cammy Burke. It's that thing you do with your head."

Raine sent him a startled look. "The thing I do with my head?"

"Yes," Lisa and Finley said.

"Like a thinking tilt." Kennedy tipped his right ear toward his shoulder.

"Thinking tilt." She frowned. "Thanks for the warning. I'll work on thinking with my head straight up and down. And the other?"

He held his palm up, then did a little circle with it, like he didn't want to say the next thing. "Your voice."

"Yes, well." She pulled a leg up under her hip and leaned an elbow onto the back of Lynx's now empty chair. "There's little I can do about that other than smile shyly and keep my lips sealed. Using a softer voice sometimes hides my lack of vocal range. And animated hand gestures. Larger than normal body language moves." She skated a hand down her thigh. "Internationally, using an accent, so people think that flatness is language-based. But that's neither here nor there in this instance."

"You did that with me in the cab on the way to the museum when we were assigned together," Kennedy said. "I would have sworn you spoke English as a second language."

"We didn't talk much." Raine sent him a wink.

Prescott ducked his head to hide a chuckle. That was Raine's sense of humor right there—dry, maybe a little snarky, sometimes a little on the wicked side.

Kennedy blushed and cleared his throat, obviously regretting bringing it up. "We didn't. But your Russian seemed to me to be on point with the accent."

"My language skills aren't bad, or so I'm told by Russian nationals. They can all tell I'm not a Russian as a first-language speaker. Most of them guess that I'm from one of the smaller former USSR countries. When they ask where I'm from, I simply apologize for not speaking better Russian and ask them a question that turns the tables. Too bad I can't apply that trick in North Carolina, pretending Damian picked me up as a Russian bride from an online service."

"My loss." He narrowed his eyes at her. "I hear Russian brides are very grateful." He was rewarded with a snort of laughter. Different laughter. Flat laughter. Not the musical tones that he'd loved to hear. He couldn't get used to her new voice.

"Going deep undercover and pretending to be something you're not twenty-four/seven, day after day is a big ask," Frost said. "Given the history between the two of you, this might become complicated. We can assume it will become complicated." Frost had that scrutinizing gaze resting on him, and he wished she'd cut it out. "We depend on your professionalism, even if this feels awkward. I've been mulling this over, thinking that it might be better since the Delta operator role will be in and out of the scene if we don't just dip into our CIRG and grab another guy who's background fits the bill."

Prescott fought to keep his muscles loose. If he looked too dedicated to this mission, it might play against him.

"Prescott was on the team that McDonald is being pulled from. There may be chatter that we want to hear," Finley said. "And Prescott will already have the men's trust."

"A newlywed couple might be an easier play," Frost continued.

"There's a lot to learn," Kennedy said. "It's easy to make mistakes if strangers just met and are heading in to play that role. They'd need weeks of preparation to pull that off as authentic and not blow their cover. You're talking about getting agents in place within the next forty-eight hours."

"If I may," Lynx said. "People who are playing the role of a married couple often do it poorly. They're too loving. Too pink hearts and turtle doves. Prescott and Raine have a level of irritation that speaks of a solid relationship history. History shows in the eyes and micro-expressions and is picked up by the viewer's brain. If it's authentic, they're trusted. If it's inauthentic, it plants seeds of doubt and distrust, though they may not know why they feel that way. Microexpressions are involuntary and can't be replicated. The schadenfreude and passive-aggressiveness that develops in couples who are past the honeymoon stages aren't replicable."

"I'm being ordered to roll my eyes when Damian turns his back?" Raine wrinkled her nose and sent him a stink face.

"Yes. *That*. Can you handle that, Prescott?" Frost asked.

Prescott locked gazes with Raine, a little smile playing on his lips. "I serve my country and am willing to jump out of a plane into dangerous territory. I think I can handle this."

Raine didn't smile back. She got that feisty glint in her eye as she lifted a brow. "Handle *me,* you mean?"

"No one's going to handle you, Raine. I meant I can handle pretending to be your long-suffering husband. Especially since they'll need me to go downrange for this to work."

"I'll get to do all the wifely tasks."

"Some of the wife tasks, not *all.*" He held her gaze, so she knew exactly what he was saying.

"Good," Lynx said. "With that cleared up, we need a basic sketch of what's going on with your life trajectory. You're moving to Fort Bragg. But…you don't have children. We know your contract is due to re-up, in what, a month? What will you tell folks when they ask those pesky personal questions?"

"Life—I'm working from home, so this is an easy move for me," Raine said. "Damian plans to re-up. He misses the team. Damian's other mission came to an end suddenly. That's why we didn't have much time to contact everyone and tell them we were heading down to Fort Bragg."

"They know that I was deploying with CIRG," Prescott said. "We liked living in D.C. I might want to go back and work for the Pentagon, maybe the FBI eventually. In case we have anyone in common, I need to be able to tell them I was working out of FBI headquarters, and I made some good contacts."

"If someone has your FBI card?" Lynx asked.

"I tell them I can't talk about what I did." Prescott stretched out his legs and crossed them at the ankles. "Now that my re-up date is looming, I'd like to do one last contract. You asked about children." He searched out Raine. "It's the first thing the wives will ask you about. How about this, Raine? You hadn't wanted to be basically a single mom with me bouncing off for stretches of time whenever the phone rang. But now, with your biological clock ticking, man, that sounds like a…rude. I'm sorry." He felt the color rise in his face. "This might be the right time to try for a baby." He opened his hands to ask if this was a good storyline. "We're hoping to get pregnant?"

"Trying is easier when you're on the same continent, babe."

He saw something pass through her eyes. If he didn't know better, he'd say it was longing. Something that felt sad. Then he reminded himself she was getting into her role. This was her acting.

She shot a look over to Hasan. "If they keep sending Damian out when I'm ovulating, I swear to god."

The men went pink, which made her laugh. "You're willing to talk about taking out whole battalions of enemy combatants, and it's all good. Talk about a woman's fertility cycle, the awkwardness gets thick. It's backstory, gentlemen. Damian needs these thoughts in his head to be on the same page."

"Speaking of baby-making," Hasan said, "what's the solution there? You two will have to share the same bed."

"Unless he snores, in that case, he can take the couch," Raine replied. "He can sleep in the bed with me. Damian's not a shithead. He'd never touch a woman if she didn't want to be touched."

"Okay," Frost said. "This is a good conversation to have. We can find most interior surveillance apparatus."

"Iniquus can sweep as we move them in," Striker said. "Then

we'll place our own surveillance, audio-visual, so we'd know if anything new was planted and give Raine and Damian a heads up."

"Good," Frost said. "That will help but doesn't cover everything. Someone could do surveillance with telescoping camera lenses and audio augmentation from outside, so there would be no electronics to find. What's the solution?"

"It's winter," Raine said. "We can wrestle under the covers and make a lot of noise. Congratulate each other afterward for a job well done."

That was obviously sarcasm even without the requisite acerbic inflection. "We'll figure something out," Prescott said. "Let's not make it an issue."

"If you decide that you need to engage sexually for the assignment," Hasan said, "that needs to be reported. It changes the dynamic and will need monitoring and possibly counseling to keep perspective."

Raine gestured toward Kennedy. "Look, Rowan and I made out in a taxi. I didn't need counseling after. I'm a big girl. I understand my job."

Kennedy shifted around, a sour look on his face. He'd be living this down until the next embarrassing scenario took its place.

"You never saw Kennedy before," Hasan countered. "You could well anticipate never seeing Kennedy again. You have a deeper emotional connection with Damian. We're exploiting your past emotions. That makes this more complicated."

"If you say so," Raine said, crossing her arms over her chest.

"This is good," Lynx said. "Let's keep brainstorming this. I think Damian's cover is easy enough. Raine's is fine up until a point. We do have some problems with your past military experience."

"How do you mean?" Striker asked.

"The Delta wives are vulnerable where Raine would not be. She's operated with the best of the best under the same conditions as the Deltas do. If she walks in there as a super warrior, they might choose to bypass her when it comes to making the threats. And while I'm making that point, I think it needs to be a shorter period. I'd say two weeks, but that Damian will sign as soon as she gets the threat."

"Why?" Frost asked.

"Because Raine needs to fail to bring her husband to heel in order for them to move on her threat," Lynx said. "While I think of it, Hasan, do you have a list now of where each of the contract deadlines falls? I'll just note that on the board." She reached up and scrawled that under the "Packing List" column. "Raine will want to meet and get close to those women in a delineated way, so she's besties with the next possible victim and sticking close."

"Agreed," Raine said, "both the target list and the time frame."

"Let's fine-tune this piece. Do they know specifically why you and Raine broke off your engagement?" Lynx asked.

"Do they?" Raine spun to look at him. "Personally, up close, like you went out drinking and crying on their shoulders?"

"I kept my grief to myself," he said dryly.

Frost grinned. "Excellent. Everyone's going to think you've been married forever."

"They don't have details then that you need to overcome?" Lynx asked.

"None," Prescott said, crossing his arms over his chest.

"Back to Raine being a soldier up until seven years ago," Striker said. "They all know she was captured and injured. How about we give you a disability?" Striker said. "Short term memory loss. Distractibility. We make Raine weak and needy."

"Raine can handle the cover," Hasan said. "That she was away in rehab. Is that enough?"

"Prescott married her there," Finley said. "She's a delicate flower now, and Prescott's the big bad soldier boy that keeps her safe."

"Timid voice, shy eyes." Raine nodded. "I can do that."

"More," Frost said. "What does Raine *Prescott* wear? What does she listen to? How does she spend her day? Does she have a pet? What about her besides her acting abilities shows these vulnerable attributes?"

Prescott was startled to hear Frost put Raine's name with his family name. He'd always assumed Raine would keep Meyers. But then, they needed her to be tied to him. And they needed her to be under his protection. The more traditional, the more an outsider would read her in her role.

"Raine Prescott likes the house dark and quiet," Raine said. "She's uncomfortable around noise and people. I can't get information in busy places. I need one on ones, and I need them to pity me. I up that feeling of femininity with southern ladies' clothing. Nineteen-fifty's style fit and flare dresses that show just the right amount of cleavage to be ladylike and have the traditional 'my job is to be attractive for my husband' vibe. They would also showcase the scars at my throat."

"You can't lift weights and run," Hasan said. "Even at home, they could be monitoring your exercise abilities."

"If I didn't exercise, I couldn't explain my present physique. And I can't lose my physical abilities because I may need them on this mission," Raine countered.

"Yoga and jogging, then?" Lynx suggested.

"Yup, that'll work. My hobby is reading. My part-time job with watercolor illustrations keeps me busy. I love my husband, and his being in harm's way is hard on me. I liked it better when he was working on his last mission. At least it was mostly in the states. That's all I know about it. He had meetings, he'd fly out, and he'd come home—sometimes with cuts and bruises, nothing like when he was with the Deltas."

"Good," Frost said.

Hasan thumped his hands on his thighs. "I'm not convinced this is going to work."

The room stilled.

He stroked his thumb up and down his jawline, looking back and forth between Prescott and Raine. "It has to be Prescott who goes in. The operator is the hardest role to fill. It's possible that we can pull a different female DIA agent, so we have a representative from both intelligence communities, or that we can work with Iniquus, say, Lynx there, or Margot from Panther Force, she's ex-CIA."

Prescott would rather he go and leave Raine out than have Raine go and leave him out. Selfish as that was to think. "What are your reservations?" he asked.

"Striker is right. People at Fort Bragg knew Raine as Storm Meyers. The Delta Force family will remember her as a GI Jane."

"Some of them will also remember her from the terrorist rescue," Prescott said. "And having seen how bad it was. How close she came to death. It isn't a leap to think that she's a different person now. We all know strong operators brought low by their injuries. We use her experience to make her delicate and vulnerable. Physically and mentally."

When Prescott chanced a glance Raine's way, he read a thank you in her eyes.

"Why don't I come in functional?" Raine asked. "Not great, but okay. After I get a threat. Hopefully, I'll get a threat. Then, it can have a visible impact on me."

"All right," Frost said. "Prescott, you're going to be a big part of selling Raine as vulnerable. You're afraid that a wind might come up and blow her away. You're to *protect* her like she's an infant. Tuck her under your arm to shield her. Always hold her hand and send her looks that you're assessing her wellbeing."

"You're worried about her," Hasan said, "but you still have hope she'll pull out of this."

It seemed Hasan had changed his mind.

"I don't have any problems with that. Do you, Raine?" Prescott asked.

Their gazes caught. "Not a single one."

Lynx had her eye on Raine. Prescott had known Lynx through various contracts that the FBI signed with Iniquus. She had a rare gift for reading people like they were books. It was crazy how accurate she could be. How she could pull a word or phrase from their speech, add in their body language, and interpret what was seemingly invisible to everyone else. Dead on. Spooky good. He wondered what was churning in her mind. Something. Her gaze flicked to him. And she nodded in agreement like she heard his thoughts.

He'd like to sit her down with a scotch and pick her brain about all this.

But right now, he was exhausted. Prescott wanted to go home.

"Okay, then." Lynx snapped the cap on her pen. "I'm going to call this meeting to a close."

Everyone looked a little startled.

"We're all running on vapors. Raine hasn't slept in days. It's time everyone went home and hugged their loved ones, pet their dogs, kicked back with a book, and got some sleep. We'll be much more productive for it."

The general consensus was relief.

"Damian and Raine," Lynx said. "If we can meet here first thing in the morning. We can start to flesh out your domestic life. Pick your furniture and housewares, start packing the moving van. Iniquus has all that available. If you'd both bring thumb drives of pictures of the last decade. Especially those with you two in them. We need to populate your mission-dedicated phones and laptops."

And with that, everyone stood and started out.

Prescott walked across to Raine and reached for her hand. "You came in a Lyft, Mrs. Prescott. Can I give you a ride home?"

22

Float like a butterfly; sting like a bee.
~ Moscow Rules

Monday morning

Prescott rested his hands on the top of the steering wheel while Raine clambered into his black SUV outside her high rise. The more time they spent together, the better chance the stiffness would shake out of their relationship.

"When we get down to Bragg, I'd like you to wait for me to open your doors for you, please. Hold your chair. I'd like the opportunity to do the gentlemanly niceties."

"You're right," she said. "We should start practicing that now."

Raine was dressed in a pair of form-fitting jeans and a chunky turtleneck sweater. No makeup. Her hair was wound smoothly into a military-style bun. After she pulled her lap belt into place, he started through the parking lot.

"Who's going to be there this morning?" Raine asked, rubbing Chapstick on her lips and stowing it back in her bag.

"From my team, Kennedy and Griffin. They're our experts on asymmetrical warfare out of post-USSR countries."

"Lisa's a mad wizard with cyber." She pulled her eyeglass case from the bag and popped the lid. "I like Rowan Kennedy, though I only know him from that one op we ran together."

"I heard about it."

"By the watercooler?" She dropped her bag to the floor.

"No, in a debrief."

"What was your take away?"

"I formed an impression of Clara Edwards, not Raine Meyers. But I thought she was fierce as hell. That I'd like to run an op with her, but I'd be conscientious to protect my zipper." Prescott pulled to a stop at the top of the lot and waited for an opening in traffic.

He'd wanted this conversation. He wanted to know her thinking. When Prescott had read the report, he'd had the impression that the FBI was somehow behind the curve, and Clara Edwards had a lot more nuanced information about the event. She'd worked Kennedy like a Claymation figure to fit into the scene she constructed.

"We were briefed on how tactically skilled you were in emasculating the mark by describing his pathetic penis," he said. "And then you stabbed the other guy in the dick." Prescott pulled out and started down the road.

"If you only have one good thrust, it's important to make it count."

"Hard to imagine a guy being able to chase after you with a severed member."

"My thinking exactly." Raine turned her head toward the oncoming cars. "A girl's got to do what a girl's got to do," she said under her breath.

"I'm not disputing that. Just letting you know, you keep

targeting a man's penis, and you'll get a reputation." He slid to the left to get around the semi belching blue smoke.

"Oh, come on. I've only ever applied dick abuse on missions. And only when it serves the greater good."

Prescott turned her way, and she batted her lashes. "In my personal life, I'm very fond of penises."

He looked out the driver's side window when a grin spread across his face. *Yeah, I remember*.

Prescott wished he could rearrange his hard-on into a more comfortable position. He'd gotten a big heads up when Raine glanced down at his fly when she'd said she was fond of penises.

He bet she didn't realize she'd done that.

It was a split second, but it was enough to get memories of her flashing through his mind. The slick sheen of sweat and the tangle of sheets around her long legs, the way her breasts would grow heavy in his hands as she became excited, the tension of muscles around her eyes as she orgasmed.

Prescott purposefully distracted himself from his memories by recalling his colleague Steve Finley —the FBI cautionary poster boy of what happens when you go deep undercover and fall in love.

Finley lost his undercover role, lost his relationship with the woman, heck, almost got her killed. Emotions in the field were a no-go. Finley's job had been to pretend to fall in love. It's hard to keep emotions under control over time with someone who was truly lovable and not develop deeper feelings. And that woman, Lacey Stuart, had started off as a stranger.

Raine was far from being a stranger.

Even if their relationship was dead and gone, he still loved her. Always would.

Huh.

Wasn't that last thought a kick in the gut?

"You look like you're having a whole internal sparring match with yourself. Care to share?"

"Nope. Well, yeah. I guess we need to get this all out there. It affects our mission. Given our past, I think it's better if you don't tell me about your personal life and the penises it entails."

"This is a weird conversation."

"Granted. It's not one I could envision having with anyone else."

"Okay, of penises and missions then. We won't be having sex."

"I—"

"Sex is for my personal pleasure and not my job. I wear my ring for that purpose." She held out her right hand.

They'd pulled up to a four-way stop, so he reached over and inspected it. He was pretty sure it had a hidden compartment. "How does it work?"

She twisted the gem, and the top sprang open. A single tiny white tablet lay in the small space. She snapped it shut.

It was his turn to cross the intersection. His foot pressed the gas. "What? You drop that in their drink?"

"If the need arose."

"I hear the double entendre. What is it? If they found the pill and made you ingest it, could it hurt you?"

"No, if someone were to find it, I'd tell them exactly what it was. It's my ringworm pill."

"What?" he sent her a bewildered look.

"It's a medication for fungal infections like athlete's foot, jock itch, ringworm… Some clever doctors discovered another use. When men undergo penile operations—urethral reconstruction, for example—they give them this medication postoperatively. It keeps their erections at bay, so they don't pull out their stitches."

"I see. They can't get a woody and take you to bed. Have you tried this? It works?"

"It's not my intention to have sex with the bad guys. I never have, and I don't plan on it. It's better that I sympathize and pet their deflated egos anyway. Their fear of showing off their lack of prowess to other women, who might not be as caring, means they value their relationship with me. And yes, I've used this on men before. And yes, it's been effective."

Prescott had to admit, that pill and this talk took a weight off his chest that he'd felt since Kennedy told the team that Raine was also known as Clara Edwards.

"I'm trying to categorize the need for this conversation," Raine said. "Is this a jealousy thing? Is this you not wanting me to use my feminine wiles against a man as part of my job thing? Are you feeling protective of my virtue?" She slid her mirrored sunglasses into place; he wouldn't get to watch her eyes anymore.

Landmine's ahead. Watch your step.

"Men are pigs." He kept his eyes on the road.

"So you've always maintained."

"It's made me worried for your safety. A bullet. A dick. Anything. Everything. I'm not demeaning your capacity, and I never tried to shield you from danger. When we were together, the thought of you being hurt—abused… I was in the camps. I saw how the women were treated. I know what happens there. I was selfish. I didn't want you in those situations because *I* didn't want to feel what I knew I'd feel, what I *did* feel, and *have* felt." Prescott gestured toward her neck. He forced the next words out of his mouth. "It consumes me with guilt that you were in danger, and I wasn't by your side. I wasn't there to help you." Prescott's ribs constricted around his lungs and heart, squeezing down hard.

"That's quite the confession," Raine said. "And I understand the sentiment, because I've felt the same about you."

Prescott wished she had more vocal range so he could get the emotions behind her thoughts; her words sounded flat and unaffected.

They rode in silence through two street lights.

"When you've concluded this case, will you keep developing Todor?" he asked.

"I have to, don't I? He has the connections we need."

"How far will you take that?"

"However far my country needs me to take it." She'd shifted around in her seat, so she was facing him. "Your jealous streak is problematic."

"This isn't jealousy," Prescott all but growled. He turned his head to look her in the face. "I've *never* felt jealous or possessive. What I've felt was protective." He turned to look back out the windshield, maneuvering them through the early-morning bumper to bumper traffic. "That's different than jealousy. And it's all I've *ever* felt toward you."

"Never jealous? Not even once?"

In his peripheral vision, Damian caught the sneer forming on her lips.

"Not even when you broke Eric's jaw, and your *best* friend from growing up had to eat blender food for months because his mouth was wired shut? You could have killed him with the jealousy behind that punch."

"I won't discuss that," he said flatly. He'd promised Karen, Eric's then-wife, that he wouldn't tell anyone what led him to their kitchen that night.

The rest of the ride was in brooding silence.

Prescott pulled up to the guardhouse at Iniquus and handed his credentials through the window.

"Straight through the gate, sir, follow the road to the visitor's lot. It's marked. Do you know where to go from there, sir?"

"Yes. Thank you."

"Have a good day, Special Agent in Charge Prescott."

Prescott closed the window while the gate slid open.

"That's quite the mouthful, isn't it, Special Agent in Charge Prescott?"

Prescott drove up the road without answering.

Up until Friday, in his mind, Prescott had painted a picture of

Raine living a quiet life somewhere, doing community theater and singing. Doing the things that brought her joy after more than a decade serving her country. But since he'd learned she was in the field, playing with some of the most dangerous criminals in the world, his system iced with fear for her. He'd seen first-hand the atrocities the Prokhorovs were capable of.

He parked and turned to her. His face grim.

She preempted anything he might have said. "At some point today," she said matter-of-factly, "I'm going to strip down to my underwear. You're going to look at my body and all the new scars. You're going to habituate yourself to them. You will stare at them, and touch them, and get used to them as if you've seen them every day for most of the last seven years."

Their eyes held for a long moment.

Finally, he said, "I'll get your door for you."

23

Keep any asset separated from you by time and distance until it is time.

~ Moscow Rules

Monday morning

Just as Prescott was about to pop his door open, Raine's phone rang with a dedicated tone.

She answered on speakerphone. "Yes."

"Deep here. Todor's calling in. You're GPS reads as the parking lot at the Pentagon."

"Copy." She swiped to end the call. It rang with a different tone. "Hello?" She was suddenly breathless.

"Oh, my darling." Todor's voice rose from the phone she'd balanced on her knee. "I'm so glad you answer. Where are you? You sound winded."

"I just got to work."

"Do you have a moment to speak?"

"I can…" She looked around.

Prescott wanted to give her space to work, but opening the door would make noise. He touched the door handle and sent her a questioning look.

She shook her head "no." "Let me get back in the car. It's a little chilly standing out here." She opened the door, waited, and shut it again.

Prescott could see her shifting into character, becoming someone else.

Raine powered her seat back, so she was looking at the ceiling. She pulled the phone up to rest under her chin. She smiled. "Hi, I'm glad to hear your voice."

"How are you feeling today? Have you recovered? I sent you text message yesterday after my plane landed. It was so late. I didn't want to wake you if you'd been able to get some sleep."

"I still have a headache from the fall. Otherwise, I'm okay. I got your text saying that you got home safely. Thank you for that. I was glad to know you were all right. It's eight o'clock in the morning here. Early afternoon all ready for you. How is your day coming? Did you go to work?"

"I did this morning. I'm home right now."

"Were they surprised to see you?"

"Surprised?"

"You were supposed to be here in D.C. all week."

"Yes. This is true. I don't know that anyone keeps up with my schedule."

She'd rattled him. Caught him in his lie. Threw him off balance.

"I'm wondering where all this leaves us, Kitten. I want to make it clear to you I have only best intentions toward you and our relationship. Virtuous intentions. You are very dear to me. I want you in my life. I want more."

"I. Yes. Yes. I want more too."

"Do you trust me?"

Todor had plunged in too fast. He was checking boxes on some list someone had handed him. The KGB formula he'd been telling his boyfriend Frédéric about.

Raine put her hand over her forehead. "It's not a matter of trusting you, I don't think. The attack Saturday night wasn't your fault. It was very scary, though. To answer your question, yes, I actually think I still do. I trust you."

"Prove it."

Raine lifted her hand with the pillbox ring and looked at it.

Prescott wondered why she'd chosen to wear it today.

"How can I do that?" she asked.

"I need you to help me kill someone."

She gulped at the air.

Todor's laughter filled the cab. "Oh my god, you're precious. I'm sorry. That was my dark sense of humor. After last Saturday night, I'm in a dark mood."

Raine stayed silent.

Yeah, he thought he was being clever. And that didn't go to plan.

"Please erase that from your mind. I… I'm still a little shaken. What I thought I was going to say was, please tell me about you. I want to know you better. While I visited you, I told you one of my deepest darkest secrets. I feel exposed. You say this? Or, hmm, I feel imbalanced. Like you know about me, and I don't know about you."

"To be honest, there's very little to say. I don't have a story like yours."

She was letting him squirm. She was going to have to give him what he wanted to keep the play rolling out on schedule. Prescott looked out the side window so he didn't distract her from her concentration. It was interesting to listen to her work.

"Your family, for example," Todor said. "Tell me about them. There is a reason why you have not spoken of your family."

Prescott's muscles tensed. Raine's family life had been terrible.

"My parents had psychological problems, Todor. My father was a professor, my mother, a teacher. No one knew they had children. Even though there had been three of us."

"Your brother died in an accident?"

"When he was seventeen. Yes."

"And your other sibling?"

"Another brother. Older. He's in jail for a DUI where he killed someone. Alcoholism runs in my family. Self-medication for underlying craziness. Luckily, I think that I bypassed the crazy genes."

"Go back," Todor said. "How is it that no one knows that your parents had children? I can't understand this—how would they hide that they had children? *Why* would they?"

"I don't try to sort their craziness. This is too early in the morning for this conversation." The pace of her words became brisk and business-like. "Can I speak to you when I get home tonight?"

"I have now to speak. And I'm worried. Please don't hang up. Instead, tell me the rest of the story. I wish to know, so I can best protect you, take good care of you."

Prescott felt Raine's eyes on the back of his head. *Great, so Todor wants to protect her, too.*

"All right. I'll tell you." She paused for an overlong minute. "I didn't know that my parents hid the fact that they had children until I ran into the secretary for my mother's school just after my high school graduation. I mentioned that my mother had worked at that school most of her career. The secretary said, 'We must be talking about two different people. The teacher I knew by that name didn't have any children, though she always wanted kids of her own.' I showed her a picture of my mom, and yup, the same woman. They had worked together for twenty years. My mother told people she was childless."

"That must have hurt very much. In my country, people would

think they were a double agent, or something, to hide their child. Is this possible?"

"That my parents were spies? Sure, anything's possible. But it's doubtful. If they had been double agents or something, they would have gone to pains to make me unremarkable, and I was very remarkable as a child."

"You're remarkable woman now. But I get sense your being remarkable was bad thing then. Tell me this story."

She sighed.

"It's painful?"

She swallowed audibly.

"You do that a lot."

"What's that?" Raine asked.

"I hear you swallow. You swallow down your feelings. Swallow down your words. If you trusted me, you could tell me something deeply vulnerable. Why were you remarkable to people so much so that you know your parents weren't criminals or spies but mentally unstable?"

"Todor, those stories make me feel ashamed."

"Certainly not more than the shame I feel about my Great Uncle Hans and his terrible experiments on the prisoners. I open up about this shame with you. I trust you, and I want our relationship to be *more*."

Prescott knew that thinking about her family would probably bring back Raine's nightmares, and the dark mood. When they had been together, Prescott had gone out of his way not to ask questions. He'd listened if Raine wanted to share, but he never scratched at old scabs and made her bleed.

"Why are you ashamed of your family? You can trust me with your secrets. I will guard them in my heart," Todor pushed.

"I've told you some of this. When I was little, my parents never took us out in public. We children went to a private Catholic school, and we went to church. My parents didn't take us anywhere else.

My mother told me it was because she didn't want us to catch swine flu and die."

"What is this swine flu?"

"A made-up pandemic that my parents used to keep us out of the public view."

"How did you shop for clothes and things?

"We didn't. I went to a Catholic school. There, I was ashamed because of my clothes. My uniform skirt's hem always came down, and I stapled it back into place. I wasn't clean. My teeth weren't brushed, my hair greasy. I knew I needed to take care of it. I got distracted. More than that... I guess it all seemed like too much of a hassle. I was too tired. I didn't have the energy to parent myself as a six-year-old child."

"You were depressed."

"To the point of being suicidal. I remember very clearly that I was in fourth grade, and I just wanted it to be over. The only reason I didn't try to kill myself was that I was afraid to botch it and not die. I decided to wait until I was older and could make sure that I was successful. But we were talking about my clothes. Every year was the same. I had one uniform skirt, three blouses, three pairs of socks, and 3 pairs of underwear."

"That's not enough to get you through a five-day school week."

"Let alone a seven-day week. I wore the socks twice. I put on the underwear one way, then flipped them inside out and wore it the other. Things were washed once a week, so I had to put everything in the dirty pile on Friday in order to have something to wear on Monday."

"So what? You went how they say, you went commando?"

"Yes. All the time. I didn't want to do that with the uniform skirt. So on weekends, no underwear. This might seem okay, but it gets worse. My parents didn't buy any other clothes for us children besides our uniforms. The boys had several pairs of school pants, but I only had the one skirt, and it was in the wash. My grandmother would usually send me an outfit for my birthday and a dress at Christmas that I used for church. I would wear these for years."

"You didn't outgrow them?"

"Sure I did. I just kept putting them on, though. What choice did I have?"

"It is a shame that you didn't have pretty clothes. Grandmothers have old-fashioned style."

"No, that's not it. It's that the clothes my grandmother sent me were cheap—they weren't built to be worn as much as I wore them. The crotch would always rip out of the pants or the shorts. I'd be out playing with the neighborhood kids and forget to keep my knees together. Then they'd see that my pants were ripped, and I had no underwear. When that happened, they were always uncomfortable around me from then on. They'd never talked to me again. It was never a rumor at school. I was never teased about it. I guess it was so strange for them—they always had proper clothes, clean hair, brushed teeth, and their labia wasn't hanging out of their ripped and faded shorts. They just…they were… I…"

"Kitten, I'm sorry."

"The worst was this one time I went on a school field trip. We didn't wear our uniforms that day, and I had to wear my weekend pants. The teacher had already yelled at me for not having the decency to wear clothes that weren't stained and had pointed out that they were so short they could see my ankles. By afternoon and the ride home, I had forgotten about the rip in the pants, and my legs came open. The girl sitting across from me on the bus was furious. Like I'd flashed her my private parts on purpose. She was yelling and pointing. She got the male teacher involved."

"What did you do?"

Prescott could tell from Todor's voice that this wasn't at all what he'd anticipated. Raine was giving him a story that, to any normal human being, would sow seeds of compassion. Todor sounded like she'd caught him up. See where she'd come from? See how people had failed her? Genius. Yet, she'd pay the price for picking at old wounds.

"I acted like she was crazy. She was yelling, 'Spread your legs and show him.' I was like, 'Are you kidding me, you nut job? I'm not spreading my legs for the teacher.' The teacher freaked out. He couldn't tell me to spread my legs to show him that my pants weren't ripped and that I wasn't, in fact, showing my vulva to my classmate. What if what she was saying were true, he saw my girl parts, and he'd *ordered* me to show him? He'd be fired, probably brought up on charges. Luckily, that same day, another girl had gotten her first period and had blood all over her backside. I think that teacher had had about as much of pubescent anatomy as he could handle. He probably quit after that."

"Pubescent? How old were you?"

"I don't know. Fifth or sixth grade. That would make me about eleven?"

Prescott knew pieces about Raine's childhood. She always contended that she wasn't a good candidate to become a mother since she had no idea what a good mother did. Or a good wife, for that matter. Prescott had had to convince her on both counts: Marriage and motherhood, love and family, weren't out of her reach just because her parents had failed to be role models.

By the time Prescott met Raine in high school, her brothers had left for college, her father had disappeared, and her mother was certifiable.

At the time, Raine and her mother had lived on her mother's disability check. Raine had moved on to the public high school. She blended in without a hitch. She had an afterschool job to pay for her expenses, and pretty much took care of herself.

Prescott had never heard this particular story about her clothes before, but it fit the pattern. The things that went on in Raine's house were bizarre by most people's standards. Both parents had professional jobs. They made money; they just didn't spend it.

The reason Raine and her brothers had gone to a private school was that her parents were irrational about people of color. They wanted their children in an all-white school so they wouldn't bring home diseases spread by inferior races; her parents didn't want to get sick. This was particularly odd since they were both educators with people of color in their classrooms.

Raine abhorred her parents' beliefs.

Her parents' strange choices extended to every aspect of their lives. Raine had stories about the food she ate. There were only three meals that were ever served. Every single day until she started earning her own food money, Raine had been given oatmeal for breakfast, a bologna sandwich for lunch, and a pot roast for dinner that was cooked on a Monday and reheated, portioned, and served again and again until the next Monday and a new roast was made.

The oatmeal was cooked the night before, and her father would then spray for cockroaches. In the morning, the oatmeal—that had sat uncovered on the stove all night—was purple-gray slime and tasted of chemicals. Raine was convinced that her parents were slowly trying to poison and kill their children. She always expected to die an agonizing death as a kid.

As a matter of fact, the first time Raine had a fresh vegetable was at his house, her first taste of an orange.

It wasn't just mental or material. There was physical abuse, as well.

Raine had told Prescott about one of the worst punishments she'd been given. Her house didn't have air conditioning except for her parents' bedroom. In the south, with the high temperatures and humidity, this was unheard of except under poverty conditions. Raine's parents locked their bedroom door so only they could have the air-conditioned relief from the summer's heat.

The kids didn't even have fans. They weren't allowed to open their windows.

One night when Raine couldn't sleep because the heat was so

oppressive, she'd taken her pillow into the hallway and lain by the crack of her parents' bedroom door, where the chill seeped out of their polar-temperature room. She'd been thrilled to have figured out how to get some relief, but her mother had opened the door to go to the bathroom, tripped over Raine, and fell. Raine was whipped with the belt for leaving her bed until she was bruised and bleeding.

Thinking of someone hurting Raine, even in a decades-old memory, sent Prescott's system into a wild spin.

"I am hugging you from Switzerland." Todor's voice pulled Prescott back from his thoughts. "I want you to come here soon so I can put my arms around you in person. If I sent you a plane ticket, would you come?"

"We can talk about it, Todor." Even without vocal range, Raine sounded deflated. "I need to go to work now."

"I care for you, my sweet Cammy. Thank you for your beautiful honesty."

"I care for you, too, Todor. I'll talk to you later." She tapped end.

Raine swallowed audibly.

Todor was right about her swallowing. Prescott had never put it together before. He'd pay attention from here on out.

"That was a hard story to tell," he said softly. He couldn't just pop open the door and go whistling up the stairs. He needed to make sure she was okay.

"You know what my life was like."

"I know some. I never heard that story."

"I guess I've such a marvelous grab bag of similar stories. They all come from the same storage unit of shit memory boxes."

She powered her chair back upright and covered her eyes with her palms, sucked in a deep breath, and let it out. She gave herself a shake before she reached for her bag.

"That wasn't easy," he tried again. He was glad that they were surrounded by trees outside the car. Even in winter, it was a beautiful view. Trees had always had a soothing quality for Raine.

Her mouth pulled into that tight smile that meant she was done with the conversation. "It is what it is."

"Rainey Day, don't brush this off." He reached his hand out, and she laced her fingers into his, just like old times. He couldn't tell if it was because she accepted his support or if she was practicing for her new role as his pretend wife.

"Water under the bridge. Okay?" She lifted her brows.

"It didn't sound that way. There were real emotions running through your words."

"Of course, there were, or I would have picked a different story. You know there are different ways to be intimate. You seem to be worried about whom I might sleep with to get my job done. To be honest, it's having to expose my soft underbelly that I find hard."

"Why do you do it?" He kept his voice soft and nonconfrontational.

"Because *that's* what's required of me to come off as authentic. I can't make up a story. I tell too many stories to too many people to keep track of lies. The trick is to keep the lies to an absolute minimum. Sometimes, that requires me to slit my own wrist and watch it bleed. I just try very hard to watch the depth of the slice."

"It's a hell of a sacrifice."

"We're soldiers. You and I agreed a long time ago, our lives would be dedicated to the greater good." She squeezed his hand and let go. "Look, the story is the story. My life is my life. I can't change the past. All I can do is focus on my present. After my dad pulled his last crap act and walked out for good, I realized that I was all I had. And I'm better for it."

She brought that up purposefully.

Her dad's last crap act was the reason that Raine had broken up with Prescott. She'd sworn from the time their relationship turned serious that if Prescott *ever* acted in a jealous rage, she'd walk away and never look back.

Prescott had believed her at the time she'd said it. And wasn't surprised when she'd followed through by throwing their engagement ring in his face when he broke Eric's jaw after he found Raine in Eric's arms.

The question was, did Damian want to try to change Raine's mind? Or was everyone better off if they just handled the mission and went on their merry way?

24

Establish a distinctive and dynamic profile and pattern.
~ Moscow Rule

Monday morning

As they approached Strike Force war room, Raine took a step back to allow Damian an opportunity to open the door for her.

He'd reached for her hand, and she'd followed a half a step back, her shoulder tucked behind his, using Damian as a shield as they walked into the space, and he said good morning.

Raine offered up a timid smile, lifting her free hand in a wave that was held tight to her body as if she were trying to make herself as small a target as possible.

Javeed Hasan, her supervisor, sat at the computer. Lisa Griffin and Lynx had their heads together over a file.

Damian aimed for an open seat and pulled it out for her. "How's this?"

Raine offered up a little smile that signified without words that it was fine.

Once she was seated, Damian leaned over. "May I get you some coffee? Maybe something from the buffet?"

He smelled of shaving cream and cinnamon toothpaste. Her system warmed to his attention. Habit, she told herself. Her body was responding to the closeness and familiarity. Her mind flashed to the memory of his hands, caressing her thighs. His skillful touch. The hard-earned callouses and the gentle strokes. She hid her little gasp with a "Yes, thank you."

Damian rested a hand on her shoulder while he scanned the room, gave her one last assessing glance, and moved away.

"Good. That's the way to play it." Hasan was watching them over his laptop screen. His readers were balanced on the end of his nose. An empty coffee mug sat next to a plate with a few crumbs, and the last bite of what looked like it had been a cinnamon roll, stale around the edges. He must have eaten it hours ago.

"Deep reported a call came in from Todor." Hasan rubbed his thumb between his eyebrows. "How'd that go?"

"He wanted a story of personal shame, which I gave him, and he dangled a plane ticket and his affections," Raine said.

"Nice. Well, that's day one. Two more calls, and then you get the reprieve of three days of cold shoulder. That worked out okay with the phone line rerouting?"

"Seamless," she said.

"Before we hand you over to Lynx for the day, we need you two to lay some groundwork."

"Where are we in the preparations?" Raine was reading over the whiteboard.

Lists covered the surface in Lynx's neat writing. She seemed to have a very organized mind.

"The DIA has interfaced with the Pentagon, check," Raine read aloud. "Damian Prescott assigned to Delta Force Echo Team, Fort

Bragg, check. Housing is checked." Raine looked over to Lynx. "Is my housing near the other wives?"

"I was able to get you a temporary housing assignment for three months, a few doors down on the same street as Lucy McDonald's home. We're hoping the mission window ends up being significantly shorter than that." Lynx picked up a remote control and pressed the button. "This is your house." An image of a little brick house with a wide front porch came up on the screen.

"Cute."

"Yeah, not bad at all." Lynx tipped her head with a grin. "I have the interior floor plans so we can design your household needs. We'll go over that later this morning." Lynx moved to a photo of the neighborhood. "Your house." She circled the area with a red laser pointer. "There are about fifteen Delta Force families living within an easy walk. In your direct neighborhood, seven families, including you, are on Echo, Damian's team. This is the McDonald's house. Dice and Lucy McDonald are two doors down from you. This is Pelt and his wife Theresa's house. Across the street from you is Kendra Sullivan. Both families are Lima. Kendra Sullivan is a target. Her husband's re-up date comes up Saturday. He is presently downrange."

"Any updates on Lucy's situation?" Raine's brow was pulled tight as she focused.

"Sergeant McDonald is stateside. He's been apprised of the situation with Lucy and the baby. He's packing up. My Strike Force teammate Jack's with him and will drive him up to Virginia to reunite the family. I checked with the house mother at the safe location this morning, and Lucy is physically fine. The house mother thinks once Lucy's husband is reunited with her, she'll be better able to relax."

"Thank you," Raine told Lynx.

"This afternoon, after McDonald gets into place, their

commander will tell Echo that McDonald had been lent out for an assignment, and Prescott's stepping back in," Lynx said.

"Can we all go by his first name?" Raine asked. "I know Damian as Damian and Deimos. I'd like to stay in character and not think of him as FBI Special Agent in Charge Prescott. And while we're at it," she turned to Lisa, "I know you as Lisa, not as Griffin."

"That's cool," Lisa said.

"Appreciated. Okay, moving forward," Raine said. "Sergeant McDonald's moving out, the tangos will know that they're being impactful even without killing or harming Lucy. They've got one man down. Granted, another target is moving back into place. If you can get word to their commander, Hasan, it might be good for him to come right out and say, 'We have Deimos back, but it might only be for a couple of weeks. His contract is up in two weeks, and he hasn't decided on his next move.' Something like that. But specific and repeated."

Hasan looked at his watch. "He's in a meeting. We're scheduled to talk over a secure line in the next hour. The Pentagon isn't fully informed for obvious reasons. We can't be a hundred percent that we don't have a mole. They're cooperating in the dark on a classified DIA request." He focused on Damian. "You've received a promotion during your time on the black op."

Damian tipped his head.

"You're going back in as an E-8 Master Sergeant," Hasan qualified. "We had to do that to bump you to the top of the housing list. But it makes sense that in the last seven years, you'd have advanced, especially given the secrecy of your last mission. Your call sign is Echo Seven."

"Echo Seven, copy."

Damian set a black coffee and some fruit in front of Raine, exactly what she would have chosen had she gone through the line. *He remembered.*

"Is this okay?" he asked.

Raine gave him a little smile and did what she could to make her eyes look grateful and needy. "Thank you."

"I'll be right back." He paused to look at her, scanned the room, and sauntered back to the buffet that Iniquus catering kept hot and healthy during ongoing missions where leaving to find food would inconvenience the operators' efforts.

Hasan chuckled. "It's like he's trying to coax a chipmunk over to take a seed from his hand while watching that no foxes will pounce. Quite entertaining." He scratched behind his ear. "It'll probably be hard to keep the charade up. Luckily, you'll mostly have to do that when you're in public. You were already cautioned, with the new technologies, monitoring can take place from a distance. Very accurately. Even in your house and alone, you can't drop the roles. Damian, you'll want to continue to be deferential. Though, granted, Raine should feel safe when it's just one on one. It could well be that gatherings are the thing that sets her off—too many people. Let's make that a thing. Groups of, say, six or more, Raine becomes the mouse. Other than that, it's a lesser problem. One on one, you can almost see what Raine was like before her capture."

"I can do that," they said in unison.

Damian set his coffee on the table next to Raine's and cast his gaze down, assessing her as he pulled his chair out and sat.

Raine got the feeling it was only part practice for their assignment.

She'd bet dollars to doughnuts that he was glad to have a reason to watch over her after her conversation with Todor.

It had been a long couple of days. Springing Damian back into her life and soon into her bed. Telling her private stories in front of two men that she wasn't intimate with. And on top of that, not being allowed to don her personal armor, but rather having to expose her vulnerability as part of her assigned storyline.

It was a lot.

Lynx lifted the remote and aimed it toward a screen. A new aerial image came up. "This is your house with the gold star. Blues stars on fellow Echo Force wives. Red dots on those where we've documented threats."

"And the numbers?" Damian asked.

"They correspond to the dates where the operators must sign their re-up to continue their service. You'll see Kendra Sullivan with a number one. Since Sullivan's contract needs to be signed by Saturday, you'll want to stick close to her from the get-go. The next on the list isn't for another twenty-one days, but then there's a cluster of about ten women who become possible targets that week, including Laurel Jordan, Jeopardy Jordan's wife. He's in Echo. If we haven't figured this out by then, we'll have to take some more significant steps to secure the wives."

"Sullivan is downrange, you said?" Damian asked.

"Yes. And, we think he'll sign at the base," Hasan said. "The Sullivan's don't have any plans to leave."

"Do they have children I need to guard?" Raine asked.

"Fifteen-year-old boy. He's in London for a Young Ambassador's scholarship. He won't be back until May."

"How old is Kendra Sullivan?" Raine asked.

"Both of the Sullivans are thirty-three," Lynx said.

"Shouldn't we move Kendra out of the area?" Lisa asked.

"She won't go," Hasan said. "Kendra believes it's a phony threat, just like the Twitter threats that affected so many last June. She's not buying in, and she's not giving it any more thought."

"I might have agreed with her," Lisa said. "Except for Lucy. You told us Lucy kept her move to her friend's house secret. That means she was being monitored, and then she was attacked when she failed to comply. Raine can't cover that by herself."

"Iniquus can monitor Kendra if Raine can place the bugs. Can the DIA get warrants?" Lynx asked, her gaze resting on Hasan.

He gave a thumbs up.

Raine turned to Lynx. "In the meantime, do you have a file on Kendra? Let's figure out something she and I could have in common. I can make that connection quicker. I'll aim for meeting her Tuesday when we get in, Wednesday at the latest."

"She'll probably come to you on Tuesday," Hasan said.

"Oh?"

"Part of what we wanted to talk to you about this morning." Lisa stood.

"Okay." Raine pushed back in her seat and realized Damian's arm was stretched across the back. His thumb came up, brushing back and forth over her shoulder. An old move from their past. He probably did it reflexively. "It looks like when I went home to sleep, you all were hard at work." She gestured toward the board. "Those checkmarks didn't come out of thin air. Thank you."

"It's a push to get the logistics in place, but once that's coordinated, this is mostly on you and Prescott—erm Damian." Lisa shifted her feet to a wider stance. "This morning, in the guise of being Raine, Lynx will send an email to the Fort Bragg FRG—Family Readiness Group. That way, they'll know you're scheduled to arrive tomorrow evening. You can anticipate someone will greet you. It's important to get you into the pipeline. To that end, we have new .mil email accounts for you that you're to use for this assignment. We can track all activity associated with them from the burner phones and laptops we'll be giving you."

"There's something you're looking for through the FRG connection?" Damian asked.

"It's a way that the Delta operators' information might have been exposed to the Russians, especially if the Prokhorovs were using a TIA-like scraping system. Delta might not have the same exposure as others from the hack I'm about to explain, but it was postulated that if the soldiers were visible and then suddenly disappeared from rosters, moving to the Fort Bragg area might have been the red flags the Russians via the Prokhorovs were looking for."

Damian leaned forward with interest.

"Lynx," Lisa said, "why don't we play that FBI interview of SUBJECT 932871." Lisa turned back to the others. "This snip is from the female's FBI intake interview. It's about ten minutes in. If you want to hear more, I can download the whole interview for you. But this is the part you need."

Lynx used the remote to scroll. When her cursor found an audio file, she pressed the button.

The room stilled.

FEMALE: "*I never thought in my wildest dreams that I'd be targeted by Russia and have my email hacked. I'm glad to help in any way I can. I'm afraid that the Russians have a great deal of very personal data about our military families.*"

Male: "*You had quite a bit of data on your computer because of your volunteer work with the Army Family Readiness Group, FRG?*"

Female: "*I had dozens and dozens of spreadsheets on my computer. They delineate personal information. Names, addresses, family members, and their birthdates, deployment dates, general troop movement, unit functions. Parties and social gatherings and what they mark. If someone was accepted to Rangers, for example, or got a promotion.*"

Male: "*You contacted the FBI because you were approached by an AP reporter. What did this reporter tell you?*"

Female: "*That they were investigating Dancing Bear, a Russian-based cyber hacker. The reporter said the hacker got into FRG volunteer emails all over the world. He showed me evidence they'd got into my email accounts. He said it was called phishing. The hackers send letters from known correspondents, and they had a link in the letter. If people clicked the link, then they'd be able to get into your account. Put in malware or spyware or some such thing.*"

Male: *"And did you?"*

Female: *"What?"*

Male: *"Click it?"*

Female: *"I'm sure I did. If it was from a friend, and they'd sent me to a recipe or something... I'm sure I did. I don't know what the phishing email looked like, so I can't tell you. But the reporter said that the Russians had access to my computer."*

Male: *"How is it that you were targeted, do you think?*

Female: *"The reporter said that the Dancing Bear folks got the original names for the hack from when we were quoted in a national article, me along with a bunch of other military wives. The reporter said that it was the list that got them started on hacking us, then they could use the information that they found on our spreadsheets to hack others.*

Male: *"What steps did the government take? Did they inform anyone else of the hack?"*

Female: *"They told a few people that they were hacked. The reporter said it had been hundreds of us FRG volunteers. I was not contacted by the government. But... I needed to make sure I did everything possible to protect the military families from Russian attacks, so I came here. I figured you'd know what to do. All that data is out there. The Russians have it. Probably can't get it back."*

Male: *"What you're telling me is that this is still in progress. The hackers don't just have old data. They still have access, and so can update their files?"*

Female: *"Yes. I don't know anything about computers. I don't know how to stop this or what to do. That's why I'm here. All the data about all the soldiers who put their name on the roster is in the hands of the Russians. And everyone puts their names on the rosters, so they get the update emails. But this puts the families in danger, don't you think? I mean, if the troops are captured, the enemy can just ring up their buddies, the Russians, and say, 'We know all about little Timmy at this address and his birthday on the nineteenth. A soldier would do anything to protect their family. I mean, there they are fighting the war, leaving their family in harm's way. Who would stand for that?"*

Male: *"Did you bring your computer with you?*

Female: *"Yes, I have it here."*

Male: *"Do you mind if I run that up to forensics and let them take a look at it? We may need it for a few days."*

Female: *"Will they tell me how to make things secure?"*

LISA LIFTED HER HAND. "It goes on from there. While Dancing Bear is Russian based, we know that they share data with the Prokhorovs. We can assume that the family has all those personal data points the military family support group maintained. If they did and also applied a TIA-like system, it would make the Delta Force targeting very easy."

"Did they close the loop? Do they have a new protocol for maintaining the security of the military data?" Damian asked.

"As far as we can tell, no. The rosters she was speaking about are still shared over unsecured email sites."

Lynx turned to Raine. "You knew about this, didn't you?"

Raine looked at Hasan.

"Go ahead," he said.

"Yes," she said. "I've been tracking this attack along with the June Twitter attack. The DIA has evidence tying both to the Prokhorovs at the behest of the Kremlin. That's one of the reasons why I'm developing Todor, and that was why I was sent to facilitate the operation in Brussels. This has been my baby for about eight months now."

Lisa blinked at Raine then turned to Hasan. "Way to share. It would have been nice if you'd just told me this, oh, around three this morning when I first mentioned it to you."

Hasan didn't reply.

"Hasan, they're still not encrypted or password-protected?" Raine asked.

"Negative," Hasan said. "And your names will be going on those rosters today. We hope a mention of a party to welcome Damian back to the fold will show up on the spreadsheets. That should put a nice big target on your backs as soon as you get there."

25

Maintain a natural pace.
~Moscow Rules

Monday

"Usually, it takes longer than that," Lynx said, leaning forward with a smile.

Iniquus frequently put their operators in the field. In order to support their various missions, Iniquus had an entire warehouse set up with everything needed—furniture in different income ranges, ages, and styles; kitchenware, partially imbibed bottles of booze, house cleaning supplies, yard tools, picture frames ready to be filled…everything and anything needed to make it look like the next step for an undercover operation was simply the continuance of a life that had been in play. Seamless.

Lynx had entered the Prescott's Fort Bragg house plan room dimensions into the computer program. She'd tapped the boxes to indicate the number and ages of people on the mission, gender, if they would be sleeping together—yes—undercover job and income, undercover character style and palette. Then, she'd pushed the laptop over to Raine and Damian.

The computer program moved them systematically through available choices within the given parameters.

Raine and Damian had scrolled through and clicked "reserve" on the household goods that would be culled and loaded onto a moving van.

They had chosen urban comfortable in neutral colors. They picked bright splashes of color in their accent rugs, throw pillows, wall decorations, and a couple of tchotchkes.

They scrolled through the inventory, picking their kitchen plates, and cookware, and the accompanying palette of kitchen linens. Bath linens in peacock blues and toothbrush holders in white, thc system was easy to navigate as it took them room by room and category by category.

"In your linen packages, for bed, bath, and kitchen, you'll find they're not all the same. You'll have enough good ones for a nice presentation, then you'll have some older ones, torn or threadbare mixed in, so it looks like you've been through some iterations."

This was impressive. Lynx was right. Someone walking through their house wouldn't get their radar up looking for the reason why something felt "off."

With a click on Earth-friendly cleaning products, the system put up a HOUSEHOLD COMPLETE screen.

"Your cleaning supplies come with a ragbag and scrub brushes, rubber gloves, brooms, what have you," Lynx said, pulling up her tablet. "Great. With that underway, next…Damian, we can equip you to be mission-ready, uniforms and kit." She looked up to catch his eye. "You'll just need to pack your everyday clothes for, say, six weeks." Lynx made a note on her list.

"Excellent. Thank you," he said.

"You'll want to pack some books to put on your shelf." She looked back and forth between Damian and Raine. "We can't provide those because you need to have read them—Raine, nothing that speaks to your military interest. I suggest cookbooks. Gardening. Romances. Mysteries. Anything craft or hobby related as long as it fits into the stereotypical female gender roles. Damian, you should add some of your books to that mix." She picked up her phone and started pecking out a text.

"All right." Damian leaned forward, looking earnest. "Do mine have to be gender-specific, or can I bring some of my chick-lit?"

"Stop." Raine rolled her eyes. "You're not funny."

He sent her a hangdog look. "I thought that was kind of funny."

"I love it. That's perfect," Lynx said. "You sound like you've been married for a long time." Lynx put her phone in her lap. "Next steps, I've texted one of our graphic designers to come up to the war room. Thank you for bringing me the memory sticks with photos."

When Raine had handed Lynx the thumb drive, Damian was surprised. He would have thought she'd have deleted their photos. What did it mean that she still had them?

"The artist will be photoshopping together your wedding pictures to hang on your wall. You'll need to decide where you went on your honeymoon. Probably best if you picked somewhere simple. Camping even."

They'd planned on Norway to sleep in an ice hotel and see the Northern Lights. The exact opposite of Afghanistan. Hard to pretend that they'd done that.

Lynx once again seemed to read his mind. "It has to be somewhere you've both been, and it's best if you were there together, and even better if there was no way to track that. Like, I had a buddy who lent me their lake cabin or beach house, whatever. Simple is best. We can photoshop a honeymoon picture or so. You'll need those for your walls and wallets. Okay, next on my list... We touched on this before, Raine. Let's talk clothes. You're wearing a turtleneck today. I imagine you have a lot of them in your wardrobe."

"Yes. Even in my summer clothes. It keeps my scars off cameras. They're too identifying."

"You'll need a different feel to what you wear every day. Let's talk hair while I reach out…" She picked up her phone and tapped out a text while she spoke. "Can you tell me about the persona you've been living as Raine when you're not undercover? You had brown hair in the military."

"Yes."

"Let's start there. Can you go back to your natural color, and can we consider a haircut? Something with layers to frame your face to change the angles of your facial structure? We have an in-house stylist who's very good. I can red flag you to get you an immediate appointment."

"That would be okay as long as those layers are long enough to put securely into a bun or ponytail. There are circumstances when I need to make sure my visual field isn't impinged upon. And wisps aren't tickling at my cheeks, distracting me, especially if they touch my scars."

"Understood." She sent a text. "Clothes. It's January, but it's been a mild year in North Carolina. NOAA projects temperatures in the seventies for the next two weeks at Fort Bragg. We've talked about classically feminine clothes. A lot of dresses and ballet slipper shoes. We talked about you exposing your neck as much as possible."

"I hope I can find something in the stores. The winter styles this year don't lend themselves to the look you're describing. Used clothing stores are best anyway."

"We have a stylist. Let me send him a quick email and flag this as time-sensitive. Your measurements are in your file from the Cammy Burke op. He can get started on that problem. Getting you prepped for tomorrow morning means all hands on deck." Lynx sent her a smile, then picked up her phone to access yet another ready member of the Iniquus machine. This was why the government hired them to assist. They ran smooth, thorough, competent missions.

"Can I see your neck?" Damian asked quietly. Raine had said she'd give him time to explore her scars later. He wasn't sure why he'd picked that moment to ask.

Without hesitation, Raine wrapped her fingers into the top of her sweater and pulled the collar below her clavicle, tipping her head back to expose the white lines.

The scarring was wider than he'd anticipated. It circled across her neck, high up where her vocal cords were severed. And below that, near her clavicle, there was a deep indentation from the place where one of his Echo brothers had saved her with a trach tube down her throat.

Damian heard his exhale loud in his ears.

After catching her eye to check in, Damian strummed the pad of his thumb over the slash from the knife. The slices were just inside the margins of her jugular veins and carotid arteries. He felt his stomach drop like he was fast-roping off the side of a skyscraper. Ferocity blazed through his system.

"That's handled," Lynx said, and Raine put her sweater back in place.

From the look in her eyes, Lynx noted the change of atmosphere.

"This is going to be a challenging assignment." Her brows drew together with what Damian read as concern. And support. "I know they put you two together because, on paper, it's a convenient solution. Paper doesn't really account for personal emotions. We're humans."

These little talks were part of Lynx's skillsets that made her so effective at her job. But this piece of the puzzle was highly personal. And Damian didn't want any colleague involved in his private life.

"This assignment is of critical importance to United States security," Raine said, pulling her body tighter and compacting herself.

"Granted." Lynx opened her mouth to continue but was preempted.

"Prescott and I are well trained, battle-hardened. We've known personal adversity, and we come back for more."

Raine wasn't looking at him. She'd called him Prescott to add mental distance. She couldn't do that in the field.

"Our personal feelings don't have a place in our work. They're dangerous," Raine concluded.

"True." Lynx sent her a warm smile. "That's very true. But when you work deep undercover, saying that on the front end is very different than living it. We know that our brains don't differentiate what it perceives as real or simulated. You both went through training." She looked from one to the other. "You were both trained to practice operations in your minds. In return, your minds coordinated your bodies to follow the scenario you'd imagined. This isn't much different."

Raine's shoulders rounded.

"If you are looking lovingly into each other's eyes and holding hands, playing the role you are asked to play," Lynx continued. "You both need to understand that your brains will perceive this as reality. Not to expose anyone's personal information, but Damian has a teammate who was deep undercover. He was simulating a man falling in love with an asset so that he could move in with her and guard her without her knowing. He, in real-world experience, fell in love with her. And that jeopardized both of their lives."

Lynx was talking about his colleague, Steve Finley, and his case from about a year ago. Damian had been thinking along this very line when it was suggested they go undercover. He'd seen what happened to Finley. Every aspect of his life turned into a shitstorm from that case.

Knowing that his life could be upended wasn't going to deter

Damian. He just knew there was a lot riding on him getting this right with Raine.

"The scope of your relationship as it will be presented—you two are simulating a couple who has been together since high school. You worked and lived away from each other until Damian left Delta Force, ostensibly for the FBI and CIRG, but that was really an undercover program. You, Raine, at the same time, were wounded and sent home to recover. You married Damian but had to keep it quietly between you two for Damian's work. Yes, it was hard, but it was okay. At least you got to be together. And Raine needed your support as she's worked toward her recovery. Yes?"

"Yes," he and Raine said together.

"In the real-world positive column—the time that you've known each other will help in that you don't have to be staring at each other all lovey-dovey. In fact, it would be odd. Remember that. It's okay to be comfortable just being companionably beside each other. It will probably be safer for your emotional wellbeing, as well." She picked up and scrolled. "Now, about your teammates. There are four who will be at Fort Bragg who deployed with you when you were still on Echo. They are T-Rex and Ty, Nitro and Havoc." She looked at Damian. "What will they know about Raine? What have you told them since the end of your engagement?"

"They know that Raine and I were engaged just before I entered operators training course after selection and assessment for the Unit," he said. "They know what was happening for my mother and the promises I had made to my mom after my father died. Raine and I were still engaged when I needed a job closer to home when Mom got ill unexpectedly. That's when I didn't re-up and joined the FBI for CIRG. Raine was incommunicado at the time, so she was unaware of the changes, and they knew that. The next time they saw her was on the rescue mission. As far as I know, that's their last point of contact."

"With me, yes," Raine said. Her voice almost inaudible.

It occurred to Damian that as uncomfortable as their going in and playing a married couple might be, being back with the sights and sounds, the smells and the faces, might just trigger some demons for Raine.

"Okay." Lynx gave a nod. "Real-world, you didn't marry. So there was a break-up. Your Echo brothers know that. Where was this in the timeline?"

His mind flashed back to the scene in Eric's kitchen. His fist connecting with Eric's jaw. His ex-friend lying on the ground, Raine's handwritten letter asking Eric to pass along the information about what had happened to her on his kitchen table, the sting where Raine's engagement ring tagged his cheek. The CIRG call out on his phone screen. "I can't remember who all I told. But I tend not to be talkative about my personal life. I could spin it if anyone were to ask as a temporary thing, and now our relationship is right as Raine." He sent her a teasing wink. An old joke that she deflected by ignoring it.

"What were you doing at the time, Raine?" Lynx asked.

This was starting to feel more like couple's therapy than plotting their undercover story.

"I didn't know where Damian was at the time I was captured. Like he said, I'd been off-grid for months. Echo performed the rescue mission. I was taken to Germany where they stitched me back together, but I couldn't talk."

"The military didn't reach out to Damian?"

"There was a delay because of mission sensitivity. I told them that I wanted to go home and tell Damian myself."

"And Echo didn't contact Damian?" Lynx asked.

"The mission was classified," Raine said.

"The day Raine and I broke up, I had just come back from my own classified CIRG mission. I got the note she'd written out to explain her circumstances to me, and I was called out to go work the Nigerian mission."

Lynx nodded, then turned back to Raine.

"Once I was back in the US, I started vocal rehab. They were able to train me to speak again. Not beautifully, but at least I can be heard."

That was a sucker punch.

Raine had had a gorgeous voice. He had discovered that in high school. She was sitting under a tree with her friend, what was her name? The one with the flame-red hair… The sound of Raine's voice riding the warm spring air pulled his attention to her. That was probably the moment he'd fallen in love with her. They weren't even dating yet. They both hung with the athletic clique, but they got to know each other when their psychology teacher assigned them to be parents to a flour sack they named Iris.

That day, Damian had held back, just out of her view, so he could listen. Just as it had then, that song swam through his veins. He'd laughed when he told Raine about the scene months later, when they were an official couple and how he'd thought of it like a mythical siren song.

She'd cracked a smile and swatted at him. "That's so corny."

But he could see in her eyes she understood he wasn't teasing her, that he was exposing a truth. Raine also knew it wasn't like him, so she eased him out of that gulf of emotion. He'd appreciated it then. Still appreciated it.

Raine had had a way of knowing what he needed and when he needed it. And he should have reciprocated. He *should* have been there for her in her hour of desperation.

He wasn't there for the rescue.

After the fact, he'd read her letter and figured out she'd needed him. It was too late; he was flying over the Atlantic.

And then she was just gone.

26

…they must pay the price, and so must you.
~ Moscow Rules

Tuesday

The expected knock on her actual Raine Meyers apartment door came sooner than Raine wanted it to. After the requisite check through the safety aperture, Raine pulled the door wide.

"Good morning." Lynx had her hands full with a tray of coffees and a box of something that smelled delicious.

"Mmph," Raine grumped, taking the coffee tray from Lynx's hands and nodding toward the kitchen.

Raine had had a whopping two hours of sleep by the time she'd gotten through all the prep lists that Lynx had handed her. After all the kaboom and sizzle from the weekend, Raine's thirty-six-year-old body needed more recovery. *Last mission*, she promised herself, again. She needed to cook up an exit strategy from the Todor Bilov case. There was never a time when she'd have a clean plate. She'd have to leave something dangling at some point. She wasn't egotistical enough to think of herself as irreplaceable.

Damian knocked on her open door, then stepped in. His eyes scanned Raine from head to foot and then averted to Lynx.

Raine had just rolled out of bed when she heard Lynx's knock. Damian had found her standing there in her rather immodest sleep shirt with nothing underneath. She hadn't even brushed her teeth yet. "You can close the door," she said, slogging toward the bathroom. "Make yourselves comfortable. I need twenty minutes."

When she came back out, she was wearing a rose sundress with a matching cardigan. Her now chestnut-colored hair was up in a French twist. Her makeup fit the role of feminine but understated. On her feet, she wore rose gold kitten-heeled sandals that showed off her newly pedicured toes. She had been polished from head to foot by the Iniquus salon yesterday, and her clothes, now packed in three suitcases by the door, were perfect for this role. So bravo to the Iniquus team.

Raine stretched her hand for the cup of coffee Damian was holding out to her.

"Black and industrial strength," he said. He sent her a warm smile. "You look lovely, Mrs. Prescott."

"Thank you," she said about the coffee, moving off to the window when she heard a truck rumble up to the building.

"The movers are here to pick up your suitcases and boxes," Lynx explained. "The crew's just waiting for my signal that it's okay to come up and gather them."

While Deep and Lynx would continue providing team support from Washington's Iniquus Headquarters, Jack, Blaze, Striker, and Gator would be shadowing the Prescott's trek to Fort Bragg.

The four field operators had housing on Fort Bragg property a few blocks from the Prescott's house.

"Ignore them if you see them," was the standing order.

Raine pulled back the drapes to watch the parade of a moving van and two cars.

Iniquus cars.

Her loaner might look like a regular crossover, but she'd been told it sported a souped-up engine, run-flat tires, and bullet-resistant windows and doors. 24/7 360 video cameras monitored the vehicle to make sure no one did anything to the car that would be a surprise —slit tires, sugar in the gas tank, GPS on the bumper, whatever. There was supposed to be a red button on the dash that Raine could press to open up the integrated comms and speak right to Strike Force support.

Damian's Iniquus car was similarly packaged. The field operators would shuttle it down, then a moving van guy would pick it up from the satellite support house and drive it to the Prescott's house, so she and Damian could remain no public contact with Strike Force.

Damian and Raine were supposed to drive together in her mission car.

Five hours, ten minutes. Plus stops for gas and food—side by side.

It had been seven years, almost eight if Raine wasn't counting the farewell theater when Damian punched Eric in a fit of uncensored rage.

There was more to Raine's abrupt exit that fateful night.

She'd admitted that to herself all along.

Damian and Raine had had a plan for what would happen once they were both stateside, but at that moment in her life, Raine simply wasn't able to cope with the follow-through.

Raine didn't want to try to play nice or play house.

She wanted to be selfish in her recovery from the nearly fatal attack in Afghanistan.

If she'd told Damian that, he would have supported her. That was who he was.

But Raine didn't give him the chance.

The whole break Eric's jaw scene…it looked on the surface like Damian was in a jealous rage. Jealousy was Raine's line in the sand. It was convenient that she interpreted that kitchen punch as an act of jealousy, though Raine had never experienced Damian as a jealous person.

There was some piece to that night that Raine didn't understand.

At the time, she was so messed up in her head that none of it mattered. It was her excuse to exit, and Raine had latched on.

It was complicated.

Life was *complicated.*

In Raine's mind, being home had meant getting married. And getting married…well, for her, it wasn't the bright and shiny hopeful thing it was for most people.

Raine had her parents' crazy relationship imprinted on her psyche.

She'd panicked. Raine could admit that in therapy. She wasn't sure she was ready to admit that to Damian. Or if he'd even care.

And now, fate picked her up and dropped her right back into that marriage scenario.

Only, it was all pretend.

27

...anticipate your destination.
~ Moscow Rules

Tuesday

As soon as their car moved onto the highway, Raine fell asleep—despite the industrial-strength coffee Lynx had brought with breakfast that morning.

She roused when Damian rubbed her leg. "Raine drop. Can you wake up enough to listen?"

Raine nodded against the pillow she'd wedged between her seat and the door.

"We need gas. There's food here. Do you want to come in and use the bathroom and get something to eat? If not, I'll get you something to go, and you can keep sleeping."

He could tell by the way she shoved her head deeper into the pillow that Raine wanted to keep sleeping.

If she did, it would mess with her ability to sleep tonight.

She should wake up anyway. They had things they needed to talk about before they got to Fort Bragg when all their communications would be monitored.

Personal things that might come up in social conversations. They needed to be stepping forward on the same foot, so neither of them got tripped up.

He'd pushed this moment off, but the gas needle was close to empty.

Raine blinked her eyes open and pulled the pillow into her lap as she straightened up.

"I hated to wake you." He rolled up next to the pump and shifted into park.

"Thank you, it's good." She had that groggy out of body look she got after taking a too-long nap. Some jumping jacks would probably get her blood flowing. "Where are we?" She dropped her safety belt and reached for the door handle.

"We've made good time. We're over the Virginia-North Carolina border."

"I'm going in. Should I go ahead and order food for you?"

"Yeah, you know what to get. My tastes haven't changed." Something about the way he said it made Raine turn to catch his gaze. He climbed out before he needed to psychoanalyze it.

His mind flashed back to their talk with Lynx and the subtle warnings she'd offered.

Luckily, Hasan let them know that Echo would practice Wednesday and Thursday, and in the wee hours of Friday, they'd get a call out. They'd go and sit on their hands until Raine got a threat, then they'd stand down. All orchestrated to move the mission along. Three nights. How much damage could they do to each other in just three nights?

Fed, hydrated, and back in the car, they drove in silence.

"What are you thinking?" Lame, but Damian had to get the ball rolling somehow.

She turned back and gave him a one-sided smile. "I was thinking about a poetry class I took back in the day. My study partner told me that Emily Dickinson wrote almost all her poetry in common meter, which means they can all be sung to the tune of Gilligan's Island theme song. So in my head, I was singing, "To all the truth but tell it slant—Success in Circuit lies/Too bright for our infirm delight/The Truth's superb surprise." Her words were spoken tonelessly, but he could still hear the song in the pattern.

He ran those words through his head again.

"Not what you expected me to say?" she asked.

"You know Lynx back at Iniquus."

"Mmm…"

"She has a theory that has borne out in the times that I've watched her tackle mission questions. It has to do with the complex workings of the mind and how we all have our years of memories, studies, and experiences. It's all in there." He tapped his head. "Stuck on sometimes dusty shelves, sometimes misfiled in the wrong box, but still in there somewhere."

"Okay."

"She says that when things come to us, memories, images, songs…they're our brains trying to say that they've synthesized through the situation. Here's a roadmap. Blurry, perhaps. But information. When we have an odd memory pop up, it's the mind helping us."

"So what do you get from the Emily Dickinson poem?"

"'To all the truth but tell it slant,' right? 'Success in circuit lies.' Following Lynx's theory, I'd say that part of our story is truthful, but we have to be duplicitous, even to those that we know, like T-Rex and Ty and my other brothers. We're going to find out what we need down at Bragg, and it's right in front of our faces, but we're not seeing it yet."

"Conversely, this is about Gilligan, and if that's the case, there's no help to be had uncharted territory, and worst of all, we're here for a long time."

"Our scope for this mission isn't that broad," he countered. "We need to find the people who are posing physical dangers. Expose the plot. There's nothing more we can do right now. The cyber threat isn't going to go away. This asymmetrical cyberwar works the way war always worked—find a bad guy and take 'em down, hope you can take down more of them than they take down from your side. It's whack-a-mole warfare."

"Okay, as your wife," she made the effort to make finger quotes like he'd forget that this was a work assignment, and they didn't have a real-life relationship, "I should know why you left Delta for FBI. When my gear was sent to me, and I had my computer back, I saw that you'd emailed me with your new contact information and the message that we needed to talk as soon as I could swing it. Of course, you'd sent that when you left the Army and went on to the FBI. In the hospital in Germany, the Army told me that you had not been contacted because of mission sensitivity, they apologized. I told them—well, I wrote on a whiteboard—that it was fine. I had wanted to tell you—write to you—in person. I still had a trach, and my vocal cords weren't repaired. Obviously, since I couldn't speak, I couldn't call you. I went to your house, and you weren't there that night. The night of Eric…"

"I was just home from a mission."

"And you went right to Eric's?"

"No, I—"

"It doesn't matter. I wrote a note to you, and at the top of it, I asked Eric for his help. I wanted him to get the information to you. I needed to head on to recovery. Then…" She looked out the side window.

Damian gave her a moment, hoping she'd finish that thought.

Instead, she went to, "So your leaving Delta Force…what brought that on?"

"After dad died—you know this—Mom was terrified of dying alone while I was at war. I promised her I'd do my absolute best to be with her if and when she needed me."

"Yes, we'd agreed on that. She's been ill?"

"She had a series of mini-strokes. It was time for me to sign my contract, and I came home to D.C. instead to fulfill my promise to my mother. I leaned on some contacts I'd made when Echo partnered with CIRG to get a gig with the FBI. It was good timing. When I got home and got her moved to D.C. near me, she had another stroke that left her paralyzed on her left side. She has some cognitive issues."

"Is she still in her home?"

"After the last stroke, I had to move her to a full care facility. She won't go to physical therapy. I get the impression Mom's done. She's just biding time until she dies."

"I'm sorry. Your mom is a wonderful person." Raine reached out and put her hand on his arm. "It hurts me to think that she's suffered. I've missed her over the years."

"Yeah, she's missed you, too. She asks every once in a while to see if I've heard anything."

Their eyes held, then slipped off as they turned forward to look out the front window.

Silence, like a third passenger, wedged between them.

His mother's illness had Damian moving back to Washington D.C. while Raine was off in the mountains for three months with restricted comms as they hunted Osama Bin Laden's leadership in the Hindu Kush mountain range. Raine was acting as an interpreter and helped gather intel.

Raine's detachment came under attack. Four soldiers, unconscious from a bomb concussion, were captured, including Raine.

They were hauled off to a camp where they were used for propaganda films. One night, Raine was dragged in front of a camera and told to read a poster before they beheaded her.

Right after Raine threw the ring, Damian saw T-Rex at a fellow soldier's funeral. Damian asked T-Rex what he could share about Raine's rescue. T-Rex said that Echo had been called in to save a Ranger team. They'd been given the names of the soldiers. Echo recognized Raine right away and knew they were going after one of the Echo family, Raine.

Later, when it was no longer classified, Damian found out that Ty Newcome was first in the tent. He saw Raine there, her hands tied behind her back. She was kneeling on the ground in the bright camera lights. A dagger point held to her throat.

Ty exploded the knife-wielder's head with one shot, then took out the others in the room. When Ty turned Raine over, her throat was slit all the way back to her spine, missing her arteries by centimeters. Her windpipe was crushed by the blow, not allowing oxygen down her throat. In a last-ditch Hail Mary, Ty did a field trach with make-do tubing.

T-Rex told Damian Raine was awake and seemed aware through all of it. Ty hadn't had time to spare for pain meds as he did the field surgery while under fire. After the scene was secured, they were afraid to give her anything in case they dropped her blood pressure any more.

They never left her side.

Ty only let go of her hand once the PJs—Airforce Pararescue—pushed her gurney onto the waiting helo.

By miracle, she lived.

Frost must have known that story. That was why she had enlarged the photograph of Cammy Burke earlier to look for the scars on her neck. Raine must have covered them with specialized makeup. In the close-up, there was a ripple of her skin, but nothing as telltale as a scar to say that a terrorist had tried to behead her.

28

Take the natural break of traffic
~ Moscow Rules

TUESDAY

ELEPHANT IN THE CHINA SHOP.

Come on Prescott, step up.

"Eventually, we need to talk about the night you gave me back my ring." He looked her way just long enough to see her quirk a brow at him, then he settled his gaze back on the horizon.

"Tossed it in your face," she said quietly.

"I wasn't going to put a fine point on it. There is something significant you need to know. I didn't go after you that night to talk it through."

"Yeah. I know."

"For a reason." He glanced over; she was staring out the side window.

"I found your note on the table. I didn't get a chance to read it right away. I got a CIRG call out. I didn't read the letter until we were airborne." He stalled. "I got called out on a rescue mission. It turned out to be for Kaylie Street."

"What?" Her hand reached out and grabbed his arm. "Kaylie from school, Kaylie? Can you share? What happened? Is she all right? Did you get there in time?"

"Sh sh sh shhh. I'll tell you. Okay?"

"All of it." Her grip tightened.

He glanced at her.

"All of it."

"You had just banged out the door when my cell phone went off with a CIRG callout. We were sent over to Nigeria to track down a group of research scientists who had disappeared from their encampment. It was reported by their cook when they didn't come out of their tents to eat breakfast. It was a kick in the gut when they handed out the photos of the missing scientists, and there on the top was Dr. Kaylie Street. She looked like she always did—same old Kaylie. We were searching, we had K-9, both trailing and HRD—human remains detection. Kaylie's parents got there on the second day of our search."

"They recognized you?"

"Yeah."

"I bet they clung to you as their hope. This was personal."

There was something to that. He thought that about Ty. Ty was one of their hardest pipe hitters. If there was any way to walk out of a mission successful, he'd find it. In his heart, Damian knew Ty would have swum through fire to save Raine and not just because she was family. T-Rex said Ty's field operation wasn't pretty, but it was enough to keep her alive for the PJs.

"They depended on me, yes," Damian said. "Through sightings, we tracked some trucks. Listened to local stories. Iniquus was there on contract with Kaylie's university. They had their K9 unit on hand. Their HRD dogs had a hit, and they started finding body parts."

"Shit."

"Hang tight, the story goes on. So in Nigeria, there were lots of body parts eaten and scattered by wild animals. Our team found and processed all of it we could. I kept thinking I would be crawling through the dirt, and I'd find some piece of Kaylie—an ear, a finger."

"Man."

"Three weeks, we worked that case. I kept thinking about Kaylie as a little girl and how much she taught me with her attitude—that grab at life she'd had." Damian stopped himself from saying that Raine had that, too. It was one of the many things he'd loved about Raine from the beginning.

"They did DNA?" Raine asked.

"Kaylie's DNA wasn't collected in Nigeria. It had to be assumed she died with the rest, and we missed her. We didn't find whole bodies. After seven years, her parents had Kaylie declared dead and had a memorial for her. And the next day, the NSA computers picked up a likely picture of her."

Raine gasped. "They found her? She was alive?"

"Enslaved. I didn't find her. Lynx did. It was a hell of a mission getting her home. Lynx is the one who figured out Kaylie."

"Man," Raine said again and pressed her head back into the headrest.

"But that's fast-forwarding the story. When our team did all we could in Nigeria, we came home. I looked for you. But you had taken me off your papers. No one would tell me anything. All I had was your letter to Eric. And what T-Rex could tell me a little later, which was limited."

"I didn't want you—or anyone to find me. I was in my dark place. I was looking for you that night I broke it off because I wanted to give you your ring back. The scene at Eric's gave me an easy out." She pressed a heavy breath from her lungs, pressed her lips into a flat line as she nodded. "It was good that I took that time to heal and recover on my own. I needed it."

Damian had heard that same sentiment from teammates who'd been tagged. They needed space to recover. A wounded animal seeks a quiet corner to go lay low and heal. It made sense to him. Even if he didn't like it.

"Your voice. In the letter to Eric, you said your vocal cords were severed."

"Yeah. Severed and crushed. It was disappointing to lose my vocal range. Others have lost so much more. It's not just about singing, which I dearly miss. It's about communication. And a little bit about safety."

They were starting to see signs that put them near Fort Bragg. Time had flown by. Damian wished it was farther. Wished they had the space to get some closure. This felt like his one opportunity.

"As it turns out, it's not *what* people say that communicates the information the clearest. It's *how* you say it. With my loss of range, I've lost a lot of the verbal cues that people use to help them understand meaning. The things that I lost are often more important to human dynamics. It causes problems in the field. It's caused me relationship issues everywhere."

While she didn't specify romantic relationships, Damian's mind heard that as men.

As dynamic and amazing as Raine was, she could be with anyone at any time. Just look at Kennedy and what he'd said about the Brussels mission. Okay, maybe that was jealousy. Maybe nostalgia.

Damian remembered very clearly what Raine's kisses had tasted like. How she'd felt wrapped around his body. He still woke up surprised when he reached for her as he came awake, only to find she wasn't there. Each time, that sensation struck him as odd since they had rarely been "there" in the same bed. Even as their relationship had turned to something much more deep and abiding, their lives had pushed them in physically opposite directions.

It made sense that they grew apart.

But still, he woke up reaching for her. And that had been unfair to the women he'd dated over the years. They didn't measure up to the connection he'd felt for Raine. So he never pursued anything deeper when he dated than companionship and sex.

"What are you thinking?" Raine asked.

He held up a finger, and they moved through the guard station at the Fort Bragg gate.

When he rolled up his window again, he said, "I was thinking through what you said about voice and relationships. How do you navigate that?"

"There are verbal elements of speech. Those are the word choices. And there's the non-verbal element of speech, including things like pauses and speed. Varying those makes me sound less robotic. And yes, people have actually accused me over the phone of being a call-bot and hung up on me."

"I'm sorry."

"Yeah. Well… I try to help give people cues. I'll talk fast or conversationally louder, for example, if I'm excited. I'll slow way down and pause in the middle of sentences when I want people to know that I'm being deliberate about what I'm saying. But sincerity and lying can sound an awful lot alike when just picking up verbal cues from those elements."

"We've trained in this, in what to listen for in people's voices. The science is still inconclusive with detecting lies from intonation. But over the phone, like you were saying, a flat inflection would cause people to become suspicious." He glanced at the GPS that was directing them to their new home.

"Then there are things called jitter and pitch. Jitter can be used by some to tell if you're lying. So, I don't have that. That makes lying easier. But pitch helps to show emotion. When someone's excited or frightened, the pitch goes higher. Angry or disgusted, the pitch lowers. Amplitude—that's a problem, too. How loud I can be. I can't be much louder than the volume I'm using now. I can't call out for help. I can't call a warning. I have to make up for it in a different way—body language, facial expressions, my eyes."

Damian looked over to see what was in her eyes now. He read her as stoic.

Up ahead of them, his Iniquus car was in the driveway of their mission home.

The Iniquus moving van curbside, doors wide, ramp in place. A man had one of Raine's suitcases in each hand, striding toward the sidewalk.

Next door to their digs was an Echo Force house, Nitro and Laurel. A WELCOME BACK banner was hung. Beers in the cooler. Burgers on the grill. About a dozen people were milling under the trees.

Damian didn't know if this was real fear and overwhelm or Raine had flipped on the acting switch, but when she turned to him, she held her eyes wide. Her hands clenched in her lap. "Speaking of jitter. Wow."

He pulled alongside the curb and put the car in park.

Hands held beers high.

The air filled with a cheer.

Raine looked through the window with her shoulders drawn up toward her ears.

Damian reached out to cover Raine's hands with his. They were ice cold, and she was trembling. He followed her gaze and saw Ty standing against a tree, one knee bent, foot resting on the trunk. He and Raine held eye contact.

"I think I actually need a moment. The last time I saw Ty..." She pulled her gaze around to see Damian. "He saved my life. I had taken my last breath. Seconds from death."

Raine sent Damian a panicked look.

Damian hadn't asked, and he *should* have—there were bound to be triggers. Bound to be memories.

"I knew this was a possibility if not an eventuality. Ty…"

Damian cast his gaze out the side window, watching Ty set his beer against the roots. "You remember him at the rescue?"

"Flashes. Yes. Him. Yes."

"What do you want to do?"

"I want to pull myself together and go give him a hug and my thanks. Probably some of the others were there. I don't know who all. Did they tell you?"

"Echo. That's about all I know. T-Rex, and Ty for sure. They didn't say much. It was a classified mission."

She looked like she was trying to force air into her lungs.

"Wait. I'll get your door for you. It'll give you a second to adjust."

"Thank you," she said softly.

Okay, this was the real deal. She hadn't been ready for the welcome wagon—a public spectacle of a deeply private moment.

As Damian opened his door, he spotted T-Rex head and shoulder among the rest.

Raine was alive because of his brothers.

Damian thought he'd never forgive himself for not being there on that mission.

He'd failed her.

While Raine had told a story of shame to Todor, Raine's shame was that her parents didn't keep her safe and cared for as a child.

Damian's shame was that he'd done the same damned thing to her as an adult.

Someone else, somewhere else, he was always in the thick of it, trying to do right. But he hadn't done right by Raine. No matter how much Raine put their breaking up on herself as they talked just now…truth was, over the years, he'd had to confront his own failings in their relationship. Mission had *always* been number one.

As he shut his door, Damian raised his hand in salute. The party pressed forward with whoops and welcome homes! Damian bent his elbow and squeezed his hand into a fist, signaling freeze. His Echo brothers stopped on a dime. Hands went to the women's elbows or shoulders, keeping them in place. The noise dropped off.

The crowd milled as he popped Raine's door open, and Damian held out a hand to her.

She'd worn the dress they had chosen purposefully, with the V-neck, and she had her hair up in what she called a French twist, with little pearl earrings and no necklace to distract from the scars.

She wore what looked like hearing aids in each ear. They were really a comms unit; Strike Force could monitor ambient sounds and talk in her ear without anyone knowing any better. Deep thought they'd add to the fragile feel that Raine would be trying to engender.

She swung her legs from the car, ankles together, lifting gracefully from the seat. When she'd first joined, she had said that she was going to retain her femininity. Being a woman in the armed services didn't mean she had to become masculine. She could be strong and female at the same time. That changed the first time she deployed, but she could trot it out like she would a fancy gown when the occasion called for it.

"Thank you," she said with a sad smile.

Everyone hung back, waiting for a signal.

29

…immediately change direction and leave the area
~ Moscow Rules

TUESDAY

RAINE'S GAZE settled on Ty Newcome. *Big old Bear*. She brought her hands up to her throat, then down to her heart as she sniffed back her tears.

Ty sauntered forward, and she flowed into his outstretched arms. "Welcome home, Storm."

She tipped her head off his chest. "Oh now, no more calling me Storm. That was a different lifetime ago. Now, I'm just Raine. You look good. The last time I saw you, you were handing me off to the PJs."

"Can't believe you stayed conscious through all that."

"I wasn't able to say thank you."

"Not in words. But I got the gist of it from your eyes."

She swallowed audibly.

"Do you need a minute? I bet it's a surprise to see me standing here. Come on." Ty sent Damian a look, and Raine knew that like most soldiers who'd been to war together, they had a whole conversation with their eyes. Raine knew a plan was agreed on when Ty offered Raine his arm. "Let me introduce you to my dog. I live just over there." He pointed to the house next door, so two doors down from hers.

Walking away from that crowd was a relief.

Ty and Raine settled on the stairs, and the gorgeous Malinois crawled over to put his head in her lap.

Raine scrubbed behind his ears then bent to give a kiss. "Work dog?"

"Yep, his name is Rory."

"Rory," she crooned as she petted him. "Such a good boy. How'd that name come about?"

"Well, I tried to call him Glory, but he pronounces it like a dog, so I go with that."

She sent Ty a smile that didn't make its way to her eyes.

For a long moment, she focused on scrunching her fingers into the warm, soft fur on Rory's scruff. She let her feelings bubble up and drift off in the evening breeze. It took a while. She bent and planted another kiss on the dog's head. "Thank you, Rory."

Ty was pushed back against the newel post. His hand rested on his bent knee. He looked unphased by her emotions. He seemed content to sit and feel the air, strangely warm when the tree limbs were bare.

"Are you married now, Ty? Do I get to meet Mrs. Newcomb today?"

"No, ma'am, I haven't met a woman willing to put up with me yet."

"Hard to imagine, seeing how you handle your dog. A dog is a true judge of character, and Rory obviously adores you. Or I wouldn't have been allowed to come over here and be soothed."

"Old Rory here has a soft spot for ladies in pink dresses."

Raine sent him a sad smile. "Okay, Damian's looking over, feeling protective."

"He did bring you into the wolves' den."

"I think I can survive it." She moved to stand. "Though I will readily admit, I appreciated a moment to get my feet underneath me. Thank you. Seeing you standing there took me back for a moment." She wrapped her hand protectively around her throat.

"Do you need Rory?" Ty asked, standing. "I can put him on a lead for you."

"I'll let you know." She slid her hand into the crook of the elbow Ty offered her. "Thank you. Thank you. Thank you. You know I'll never be able to say it enough."

He patted her hand, then looked over his shoulder at Rory. "Stay home." Ty turned back to her. "Lots of new faces. Let's get you something to eat, then I'll make sure you get introduced around."

THEY SAT on white plastic chairs with their paper plates balanced on their knees, eating the cookout fare.

The woman sitting next to her leaned in. "Hi, Raine. Welcome. I'm Laurel. This is my house, so howdy, neighbor." She lifted her hand with her lemonade and stuck out a finger toward a guy sitting on the front steps. "The guy in the blue t-shirt, that guy's my husband, Nitro. The guy next to him in the red tee is Havoc. Tonight's welcome is from our neighborhood. Tomorrow night, though, the Echo wives have a dinner planned. You'll be busy getting unpacked. Dinner is at least one thing you needn't worry yourself about. I hear they have Deimos heading into training first thing in the morning, so you'll both be tired and hungry come nightfall."

"Thank you."

"Echo's dinner will be at Pam and Jeopardy's house." Laurel pointed toward the table, where a couple was getting their plates filled. "Over there. Pam's the redhead."

Pam looked up and waved in their direction with a smile. "They're in that house kitty-corner to Ty. The one with the snowman on the front door." She pointed. "You probably know Nitro because he was here when Deimos was. Nitro and I were married four years ago."

"Congratulations." Raine should have known that…

"The guys call you Storm," Laurel said. "What do you prefer to be called?"

"Storm was a long time ago. I go by my middle name, Raine. Thank you for all this. You've made this a lovely welcome."

"Looks like your moving crew is efficient. Not that we plan to move any time soon, but if we do, I'll get their name from you."

Raine shot a look toward the moving van. It was unloaded.

Inside, Raine knew that Iniquus would be taking this time to sweep the house for surveillance and to put their own in place. Strike Force would be watching to see if anyone was trying to gather information on Damian and Raine. Just that piece of the puzzle would be important, but following someone and getting an ID might just crack this case.

"You haven't even been in your house yet. A friend of mine used to live there, so I know the layout and most of its quirks pretty well. Don't you want to take a look?"

No, in fact, she wanted to give Iniquus the time and space they needed. But that would look strange. Raine sent Damian a *pay attention* zap. Anyone who'd been downrange could pick up on that kind of eye connection. He spun around and focused on her. Raine waved him in.

Raine, Pam, Damian, and Laurel all made their way to the house.

The Iniquus men had already set up her dining room. The boxes were set on a blanket on the table.

Laurel stopped and pulled out one of the photoshopped wedding pictures. This one was of them feeding each other bites of a tiny wedding cake.

"Not many people at your wedding?" she asked.

"There were six in all. It had to be a secretive thing." Raine tipped her head back and forth. "You know how that kind of thing goes. Damian was sad he couldn't have his Echo brothers there with him."

Raine handed Damian the framed photograph.

He held it in his hand, overlong. Long enough that Pam came over to see. "It's a sweet picture. Why are you looking so sour?"

Raine sent him a wrinkled nose. "He's still mad at me."

"Did she shove the piece in your face?" Laurel asked.

"So much worse," Raine said quickly. She had a good story that would work here. "I have a friend who saved the top of her cake. Cut it into fifty little pieces, so they could have a bite each year until their silver anniversary."

"What?" Laurel laughed.

"She got the idea off Pinterest, but she didn't tell me how she preserved it other than a sprinkle of rum before she put it in her freezer. She, by the way, sprinkled it with rum then coated the whole thing in honey. We got married within a few months of each other, and I thought, what a fun idea. So I did it. But I only used the rum."

"No!" Laurel's brows flew up.

"Yup, I did. The first year was fine." She looked at Damian and laughed. "The second year was fine. The third year, he put it in his mouth, and the taste was terrible, but he wasn't about to spit out our wedding cake, so he swallowed it down like the special forces he-man that he is." She tipped her head and gave him a look that said, *I'm sorry. I love you. And this is still kinda funny, don't you think?* "I spit mine out."

"She put me in the hospital with food poisoning."

"No!"

Raine lifted her lips for a kiss to show there were no bad feelings. Without missing a beat, Damian dropped an *I forgive you* kiss on her mouth. Soft and warm, it sent electricity through her system. She felt her face heat up. She tried to cover with a laugh. "By the way, my friend who did it with the honey said that the fourth year was gag awful. So I don't suggest this to anyone. Just eat the cake and call it done."

Laurel was pulling their photos from the box. Wedding pictures were at the top, then her diploma.

"Your university degree," Laurel said. "You were a foreign language major?"

"Yes, with a film acting minor."

"You wanted to act in foreign films and ended up in the Army?" Laurel laid the frame carefully on the table, starting another pile.

"When 9-11 happened, it was my freshman year. I had no idea what I'd study. When the towers collapsed, though, I felt compelled to protect America, so I joined the reserves. I thought that the best way I could help was to study language. I did Russian and Arabic studies, language, culture, religion, what have you. And I trained in film acting for me. I think it served me well." Raine had planned this story.

She had a reputation as Storm Meyers, and she needed to make sure the wives thought that all her big and brave, bouncing with the special operations forces was an act. That she was really a delicate flower. It was all about manipulating those around her into believing what she needed them to believe so she could get her job done. Right now, Raine's job was to keep the Delta Force wives safe.

"As a soldier?" Pam asked.

"Exactly." Raine pulled out a chair and sat down. "You see, acting—and this is something I learned from my freshman roommate who already had her drama major declared—is all about dealing with vulnerability. It's also about finding the seed of an emotion and growing it, even in an austere climate. For example, if I am having a wonderful day, and I feel ebullient, I might need to be devastated and tearful in a scene, angry in another, terrified in a third. Despite how I feel, I have to set that aside and feel what that character is feeling in that scene. In order to be successful, we were taught to find the seed of that emotion somewhere in our past experiences and focus all our attention there on the tiny potential until it surfaces. So in combat, when I was truly scared, my heart racing, my fingers shaking, I would reach inside and find a seed of courage, pull it up, and let that emotion grow big enough to shadow my true feelings. And it worked. It worked then, anyway."

Damian rested a hand on her shoulder. She reached up to interlace their fingers. Raine wondered what he thought. Regardless, it was truthful. As the DIA taught her, always speak the truth when possible. Lies are energy sucks and take up too much room in your brain for what you said when and to whom. Better to obfuscate than to lie. Better to be genuine, so you were trusted. It was all part of the game.

"That day," Raine continued, "back when I was signing on with the Army, Damian called. He had just left the recruiter's office. I was going to wait until we had spoken before I signed the papers. I was gathering information. But once I knew our hearts were in the same place, I proudly signed up, showed up, and did my part." She tipped her head to rest it against Damian and to show off her scars.

Laurel's gaze came to rest on Raine's neck.

The emotions in the room got squirrely.

A woman came through their open front door. "Heyyyy," she called, walking toward them. "I'm Theresa. I'm married to Pelt in

Lima. We live just over there." She waved her hand toward the wall. "Welcome."

"Thank you," Damian said.

"Hey Theresa, we're digging into Deimos and Raine's personal stuff, listening to stories because we're nosey." Pam reached into the box and pulled out a picture from when Raine and Damian had been on a camel safari in Egypt the year before their breakup.

"That camel's name was improbably McKenzie," Raine said.

"He had green slime coming out his mouth and back end, and he liked to spit," Damian threw in.

"Where were you going on the camel?" Pam asked.

Damian squeezed Raine's hand then let go to pull out a chair. "We were going to see a burial site where they had found tens of thousands of mummified cats. When we got there, the archaeologists were taking a lunch break, and they let us ask questions." He swung around to sit.

"I asked the head guy why the Egyptians mummified the cats and why did they bury them all together." Raine reached again for Damian's hand. "The Egyptologist said that he spent about three months there studying the area. When he went back to Cairo, he went to the guy in charge of the Cairo Museum and asked the very same thing. The guy wrote down a name and number and handed him a piece of paper. 'We don't know what that's all about,' the head curator said. 'But this guy has been studying them. I suggest you contact him.' The man walked out of the museum, pleased to have a resource, opened the folded paper only to find his name and address written there."

"What?" Pam asked.

"Crazy. Right?" Damian said. "And that's how he became the foremost expert in Egyptian cat mummification even though he knew next to nothing about Egyptian cat mummification."

"You two make the cutest couple," Theresa said. "You have a very romantic story, high school sweethearts, putting your lives on hold for the greater good, finally coming together and marrying. Raine holding down the home front while you…well, we don't know what you've been doing for the last seven years, Master Sergeant. I'm thoroughly fascinated by that black hole in your military history." She held up both hands. "Not that I'm asking."

Damian smiled, but his lips stayed shut.

"Where are you in your contract? Did you re-up during that time?" Laurel leaned forward.

"No, I'm just about due. Four weeks?" Damian turned to Raine.

"Two," Raine said, letting fear and sadness slide across her face. She homed in on Theresa, then Pam, and finally rested on Laurel, watching their reactions closely. Laurel's name was on the list of women the DIA had flagged as having received a threat.

Laurel had ducked her head into the box.

"But you will re-up, right?" Theresa asked. "I mean, you didn't move all your stuff back here for two weeks."

Damian and Raine's eyes locked. "It's a matter of discussion at this point," he said after a long pause.

"We're trying to figure out what the future holds." Neither had moved. "Right now, we don't know what's in store for us."

30

Never fall in love with your agent.
~Moscow Rules

Tuesday night.

Raine and Damian had taken turns in the bathroom, getting ready for bed.

She was putting her comms hearing aids into their holder on the chest of drawers. Raine had turned them off for the night.

Now, they were alone.

With the bed.

It was going to be interesting how they'd navigate this. God, he hoped he didn't snore. Or…anything else in his sleep.

Damian set the alarm on his watch. He had to get up in six hours and get over to Ty's. As he pressed the crown back into the watch face, Damian's phone buzzed with the Iniquus tone. Damian opened his encryption app to read the message.

There's an unsub outside your bedroom window. Deep used the shortened version of unknown subject. **I have them on the night vision camera—right distance for binoculars.**

Damian stood by their king-sized bed in a pair of gym shorts and a T-shirt. Normally, he slept naked, but that wasn't going to work.

He signaled Raine over and held out the message for her to read.

She took the phone from his hand. **Leave it or go out and chat?** She tapped out.

Deep: **You might have raised suspicions at the party. If you want to put them on their back foot, confront. Though that might drive them underground. If you want to protect your cover, take other action. Support will jog by in the next five minutes.**

Raine flipped the phone to Damian, threw her head back, and laughed, peddling backward until she was right in front of the window.

Damian read it and moved toward her, grinning. "Make it good, Mrs. Prescott."

"Yes, sir, Master Sergeant." When he stepped close, she opened her arms to reach around his neck.

"What should we do here?" he whispered as he slid his hands down her arms, following the curves of her waist to her hips. "We could pretend to slow dance."

She pressed her body against him. Her nightgown, while it covered her to her feet, was mighty thin. She wasn't wearing anything underneath, he discovered as he pressed his hands into her lower back and began to sway. His body caught up to that thought immediately. "Sorry about…" he said. "You've always had this effect on me. Hard to teach an old dog new tricks."

She laughed. "There's a joke about a bone in there somewhere."

"Probably."

She pushed to move them around. "Look out the window. Do you see anyone?"

He tucked his head; his cheek rested against her hair as he peered out. Sure enough, there was a silhouette just there at the back corner of their lot. "Yup, out behind Laurel's house."

"What are they doing?"

"Human shape. Black against black. Hard to say if they're even looking this way. We'll have to assume."

Raine twisted and tipped her head up. "Then we should give them a show, don't you think?"

Before he could *actually* think, his lips found hers. He stilled their dancing sway to kiss her. She opened her mouth to him.

Their tongues tangled.

He was thirsty for her. Every cell in his body begged him to take her to bed. To explore her body. He missed her. Missed this.

This is work, he reminded himself.

When he'd taken her home Monday night, Raine had let him explore her body – her scars anyway. She'd sat there under a bright light in her bikini bathing suit, pointing out all her scars and telling him their vague stories. Shrapnel. Burns from an explosion. Fell from a ten-foot wall. Chapters in the story of her long career. He'd skipped over her throat scars. At that moment, his imagination was filled with all the times and all the ways that Raine had been in real life or death survival scenarios.

Raine was doing her job then. She was doing her job now. Damian would follow Raine where she wanted to go on this part of their operation.

After the mission concluded, maybe…

She reached her hands up to his head and stood on her toes as she deepened the kiss. Still, it wasn't nearly enough. Damian wanted more. Had wanted more since he dropped that innocent kiss on her lips in the dining room for the Delta Force wives to see when

Raine was holding the cake picture and looking up at him like she had so many years ago.

The phone buzzed between their stomachs, where he'd shoved his cell into the elastic of his shorts.

Clear. Whatever you did, did the job.

"Whatever we did. They don't have cameras in here?" Raine had only moved her head enough to glance down at the phone.

Damian tossed the phone toward the mattress and turned back to their kiss. "Master bedroom and bathrooms are audience free."

Her kisses were as aggressive as his.

They weren't kissing for their job anymore. They'd entered new territory.

Raine lifted back just enough to say, "I don't think this is a good idea to do more than absolutely necessary." Then her mouth found his again.

He kissed his way toward her ear and whispered, "Oh, I'm *sure* this isn't a good idea."

She giggled and squirmed against him when he lowered his lips to her tickle spot just behind her earlobe. "We should stop," she gasped.

"Absolutely." His mouth found hers again.

Her lips opened, and their kisses deepened. It did nothing to bring him satisfaction.

He wanted more.

She turned her head and panted into his ear. "We should stop. Right now."

"This conversation would probably feel more convincing if your hand wasn't wrapped around my hard-on."

"And your thumbs weren't painting over my breasts."

Their words were stopped with more kisses.

Damian backed Raine toward the bed. He stopped himself, running the tip of his nose up the bridge of hers until he reached her brow and planted a kiss there. "Where are we going here?" He needed Raine to give him a clear green light. Or red. Something. He couldn't keep coasting on yellow.

"Down memory lane, maybe?" Her heels hit the ground, and she dropped her forehead to his chest.

"That's not what I'm feeling," he said, pulling her hips closer.

"Fuck."

"With no inflection, I'm not sure what that was." His lips pressed into her hair. "That could be an invitation. Could be you cussing me out."

"With all the words spinning around in my head, that's the one that tumbled out. It hasn't attached to any particular thought," she panted. "It sort of slipped out in the wash."

She's not sure. Got it. "I think maybe hit pause." He rested his hands on her shoulders. He waited for her to look him in the eye. "You and I like to tuck our emotions into the back closets. It makes the work we do doable." He slid his hands down her arms, taking her hands in his—away from his dick, so he could move some blood away from his head and back up to his brain. He let their hands hang, clasped together. "These last four days, people have been poking and prying into our feelings. Maybe we churned some things loose."

"Ghosts."

"I don't like to look in my rearview mirror. I just press my foot on the gas and try to move forward. Running up against it now is… well, it wasn't on my playlist Friday afternoon. I thought I was going to spend the weekend on the basketball court and grilling out. Instead—"

"It's a lot all at once. I hear you. I've been wrestling with my demons since Saturday for sure."

He ran a finger over her cheekbone, down the side of her face, across her jaw, then tipped her chin up until their gazes met. "I have to apologize to you, Raine. For so many things." His voice was gruff with emotion.

"Stop."

"Not for this kiss. I… yeah, I'm not apologizing for this," he said. "But... I've failed you."

"Stop. I wish I could inflect, and you could hear my feelings in my voice. I need you to stop."

They stood there, perfectly still.

"We've made choices together about what life looked like," she said. "When life threw us our curve balls—you with your mother, me with my injuries—we did what we had to do. I know I did the only thing I could at the time and survive. I think we can probably each make a good case of framing things as how we failed each other. And we can both regret our failings deeply. You're right. This mission has lit up some of my dark times. I'm dredging up my childhood, my physical realities, the results of my choices all along my lifeline. And the one thing that could do that? Not Echo, not Ty, not being back here at Fort Bragg with the Army. *You.*"

"Same."

She dropped her head back to his chest. "Damian, I have to be careful. Your arms feel like home."

He felt her heavy exhale through his shirt. "I'm with you on that," he whispered.

"Fuck."

"Still could go either way with that word." He tried to tease away the mood. He lifted her hand to his lips and kissed her palm. "How about we go to bed and sleep. See what's going on with us tomorrow."

31

Pick the time and the place for action
~ Moscow Rules

WEDNESDAY

DAMIAN HAD BEEN UP and dressed at zero five hundred hours. He'd grabbed breakfast and a ride with Ty. Echo would train today and tomorrow, then they'd spool the team up tomorrow night, getting Echo out of the country to go sit on their hands somewhere, so someone could threaten Raine.

Damian was gone long before Raine dragged herself from their bed.

It had been hard to sleep with him just on the other side of the pillow barricade she'd put in place. It seemed childish to do, but she couldn't guarantee herself that she wouldn't roll into his arms during the night.

Damian was gone, but she wasn't alone. Strike Force was monitoring her house and the cars 24/7. Raine wandered over to the chest of drawers, turned on her hearing aids, and slid them into place.

"Wednesday morning," she said.

"Blaze here. Good copy and good morning, Sunshine. We were starting to get worried. We thought maybe someone should stop by and do a welfare check on you."

She glanced over at the clock. It was zero eight hundred hours. He was teasing her.

"Say coffee if you're following the plan for today."

If someone was listening in, they wouldn't be able to hear Blaze or her through their comms because they had end to end voice encryption. But they could pick up Raine's words as they left her mouth using a parabolic listening device.

"Man, I need some coffee," she said.

"Kendra Sullivan went for a jog at seven." Kendra was the Delta wife who was most imperiled. Her husband, Budge Sullivan, was due to sign his contract by Saturday. She lived right across the street from Raine's house. "Kendra's not home yet," Blaze said. "We've got eyes on her, and we have Jack jogging just out of sight. I'll let you know when she goes back to her house. Maybe you can introduce yourself and borrow a cup of sugar."

"Coffee."

"Other than that. We expect you to have curious wives stopping in to see if they can lend you a hand. When I hear their names, I'll feed you any data I have on them."

"Coffee." She moved down the stairs to the kitchen. The red light on the coffee maker was on, which meant the coffee was ready. *Damian, I love you,* she thought, and then told herself that was said in the general tenor of thanksgiving, not in the hearts and flowers sense of the word.

She moved over and lifted the carafe. Full, hot, and—she put her nose over the opening to sniff—high test. "Thank you, god."

"I'm assuming you just got to the coffee pot?"

"Mmmm."

"Good luck today. Build those bridges. Make the contacts. We have the computer looking for anything that might need a heads up in ambient conversation in your house. It'll be harder to track outside of there since we'll only have your hearing aids. But either way, we can cue you if we think anything needs a follow-up. Say 'shower' if this is the way you want things to play. If not, I need you to take a quick drive, so we can make a new plan. Say 'milk' if you need the drive."

"Shower."

"One more thing, Raine. We'd appreciate it if you wore a camera today, either glasses or contact lenses."

"Shower," she said on a sigh. Raine really didn't like wearing those things.

Raine ran through her to-do list as she poured her coffee. Kendra, of course, was number one on her list. Laurel had received a threat, too. But Raine had twenty days now to take care of that. She'd keep her focus on the two burning issues, keep Kendra safe, and find the terrorists who were functioning on American soil to neutralize the threat on the Delta Force wives.

Her mind flashed to a woman she'd run across while working in Eastern Europe. Zelda Fitzgerald. Not her real name, as it turned out. A pretty stupid undercover name. It was even worse than Raine's Paisley Moorhead cover. But the Zoric family had christened Zelda that way. Raine had focused in on Zelda because she was an American hanging out in Slovakia with a known crime family. Raine and the DIA ran surveillance and then were warned to back off by the US military. The US military was hitting the same Zoric target just from a different angle. This operator, Zelda, was the point of that military spear.

If the Zorics had been the boots on the ground for Todor's tunnel stupidity, could the Prokhorovs be using them for boots on the ground for their cyber-attack follow through?

Raine thought back to the precision of action in the tunnel. It was a ridiculous scenario, but the execution was razor-sharp.

"I need milk for my coffee," she mumbled, putting her mug down and walking the few steps from kitchen to living room, where she grabbed the key fob from the bowl on the table by the door.

"Copy."

She snagged a raincoat from the hall closet. She was still in her nightgown, and in the sunlight, it would probably be see-through. She padded, barefoot, to the car, climbed in, and drove three blocks before she said, "Blaze."

"Go for Blaze."

"I had an idea. I'm not sure…maybe Hasan?" She drove, trying to figure out how to reach out to Zelda. It was dangerous to make contact if Zelda were in Slovakia. Raine didn't want to do anything to blow the operator's cover.

"When you have that thought together, I'm here," Blaze said.

"There's a woman—her name is Zelda Fitzgerald—she might have some information about the Zorics' involvement with the Prokhorov family."

"You're suggesting that the Zoric family is the muscle against the Delta Force wives?"

"Maybe?... Something to look into."

"Steve Finley has been investigating that family for a while now in terms of domestic terror for the FBI. With your permission, before I reach out to Hasan, I'll contact Finley and see if he's heard of Zelda Fitzgerald and has a communication channel. We'll see if there's any information there."

"Appreciated. Now, I'm going to go and get into an actual shower. I'll have my hearing aids out. I'll signal when I'm back online."

"Raine, I know you hate them. But glasses or contact cameras, please."

"Wilco."

Raine was putting the dreaded contact lenses in her eyes. They were supposed to be okay for thirty days. Sleeping in them was fine —so was showering if she kept her eyes mostly shut. It was the whole blinking them into action thing that she found distracting. But the glasses on her nose all day seemed worse.

She looked at her reflection and saw Storm Meyers in her facial expression—ready for action. Raine absolutely needed to lose that look. Reaching inside, looking for a seed of vulnerability to pull up, she remembered the sensation when Ty let go of her hand as he crouched by the rescue helicopter. In that moment, she gave herself even odds she would live through the helo ride to the hospital.

Vulnerability and pain. She pulled those sensations through her body and watched herself transform into a delicate petal, easily bruised. Hmm, too much. She dimmed it down a bit with domestic thoughts about finding the groceries and getting some ice cream for the freezer.

The Delta Force wives needed to believe she was one of them and didn't cleave to her soldier past. They needed to trust her and share. There had to be something that happened here at Fort Bragg, maybe even in *this* neighborhood, that clued the terrorists in to Lucy McDonald's secret escape up to D.C. at her friend Martha's house.

Lucy arrived, and that very night, the hit was in place.

Raine couldn't bring up Lucy McDonald by name, Raine reminded herself. But she could ask who lived in the house across the street between Pam and Theresa.

The DIA said Lucy's phone was clean. Her computer was compromised, but Lucy hadn't contacted anyone over her computer. Lucy said she had talked to her friend Martha about housesitting while she was outside because Lucy was afraid that her house was bugged.

Where Lucy had been when she was outside, she couldn't

remember. Maybe walking. Maybe at the park. Maybe in her own yard. She was so stressed that all she could remember was that she was outside in January in bare feet.

Raine went down the stairs, dressed in a pair of stretch jeans and a low V-neck. She had swept her hair up in a ponytail to show off her hearing aids and her scars.

She pulled the front door open. The day was a little chillier than yesterday, but the air was dry and smelled fresh. Raine bent to place a book against the door to hold it wide.

Kendra's house was dark. Maybe Raine's open door would be enough of an invitation for Kendra to slip by and introduce herself when she got home.

Until they tracked down the bad guys, Raine had to assume Kendra was in mortal danger. Saturday was the day. That thought was the hammer banging in the back of Raine's mind. The last day Budge Sullivan had to sign and come home, or not sign and stay in the Unit.

"I wonder who lives in the house across from me," she muttered as she walked back to the kitchen. "It doesn't look like anyone's home."

"Blaze here. Kendra's leaving the store. It looks like she's with a friend. Heading toward a car."

"Coffee." She fixed a fresh mug of coffee and eyed the boxes that stood ready for unpacking.

A few minutes later, softly in her ear, she heard, "Blaze here. I have an update from Finley."

"Mmmm."

"Finley knows Zelda Fitzgerald personally. Zelda's stateside. As we speak, they're in conference about the question of the Zorics' involvement with this case. Do not. I repeat, *do not* mention this name in any circles or to *anyone*. How copy?"

"I have a *good copy* of my manuscript around here someplace…" she murmured.

Looking around, Iniquus support didn't leave her much unpacking to do. Some of the cookware in the kitchen, some books to go on the bookshelf. Just enough to give people something to do if they came over to help. Raine decided to start with her art table. Maybe she'd even sit down and start a painting.

"Knock knock," someone called from the front room.

Raine rounded out of the kitchen to find Theresa and Laurel standing at the bottom of her stairs, looking up. "Hey, there," Raine said.

The women turned to her.

"I'm getting a second cup of coffee. Can I offer you ladies some?"

"Yes, thanks," Theresa said.

"I'm good," Laurel answered. "We thought we'd stop by and see if you'd like some help getting your boxes unpacked. Pam's getting ready for tonight, so she won't be coming by."

"Oh, I hope she doesn't go out of her way. I mean, we could maybe order some pizzas or something…" Raine said.

"She loves this kind of thing." Laurel waved her hand through the air. "Let her do it so she can be happy. There are eight guys on the team, adding in Deimos. Three aren't married. Ty, T-Rex, and Havoc."

"I don't know Havoc."

"He's a sweetheart. Tonight, you'll get to meet him and all the other men on Echo except Dice McDonald. He's on leave. His wife, Lucy, is eight months pregnant and had some complications."

"I'm sorry to hear that. Is she nearby? Can I help?"

"Their house is across from Ty's place. But no, she went to stay with family."

"You're Lima?" Raine asked Theresa.

"Yeah, my husband, Pelt, is Lima, and your across the street neighbor, Kendra Sullivan, is, too," Theresa said. "Her husband's

Budge. He's been on the teams about as long as Deimos went black."

"Our contract is up in the next couple weeks." Raine looked in the direction of the Sullivan's house. "I guess they'll be making the same decisions we are."

"Budge signed yesterday," Laurel said. Her face was strained as she said it. Her eyes shifted toward the door with a frown.

Raine turned to see Theresa's reaction, but she had her hand in the box of books and was pulling up a novel.

"Good for them," Raine said. "That's lovely."

"Blaze. Copy. Sullivan signed his contract. Will verify." Raine heard softly in her ear.

Her phone rang with an Iniquus tone. Raine scowled as she answered it.

"Deep—Call coming in. You are at work."

"K." The phone disconnected then rang again. "Hello?" Raine said.

"Kitten!"

"Hi. How are you?" Raine held up a finger to the ladies, picked up the keys from the bowl, and went out to her car, transforming into her role as Cammy Burke on the way.

32

There is no limit to a human being's ability to rationalize the truth.
~ Moscow Rules

Wednesday

Raine needed to balance getting Todor off the phone and keeping Todor feeling comfortable in their relationship, so he wouldn't call for the next three days. She had Laurel and Theresa in her house.

And since Todor didn't have a phone with encryption, she had to keep everything benign for anyone listening in.

A car pulled up and parked in Kendra's drive across the street.

"Hey there. Poo! I'd love to talk to you, but I have a meeting with my supervisor. You caught me at a bad time. I don't know how long I'll be tied up, something very concerning has come up about the contracts, and I need to see if we can't figure out the problem."

"I'd be happy to listen to you if you need to—what you say —vent."

"Believe me, I'd *love* to vent." She adjusted the rearview mirror and watched a woman exit the passenger side of the car and start toward Kendra's house with a wave of her hand. She'd turned too quickly for Raine to see if it looked like the picture she'd been shown of Kendra Sullivan. "This is the most stressful thing that's happened since I've been here. I would lose my job if I told you."

"I don't want you in that position. I won't ask."

"Listen, I'm so sorry. There's nothing I'd like better… Can we talk tomorrow?"

The car in Kendra's driveway pulled out and drove away.

"Tomorrow?" Todor repeated. "No. I'll be gone tomorrow."

"I could get up early, or you could call me late? I know the time difference is sometimes complicated."

"I'm sorry tomorrow, I can't." He did a good job of sounding regretful, though. This was an acting job for Todor, just like it was for Raine.

"Okay, later in the week then."

"Blaze. That's Kendra Sullivan," he whispered as a woman in a jogging outfit and hugging a houseplant made her way across Raine's lawn. She must not have seen Raine sitting in the car. Kendra walked up Raine's porch steps and through the open door.

"Have a good meeting, Kitten. I hope things turn out well."

And he hung up.

Raine grinned. She'd be Todor free until at least Sunday.

With a deep breath, Raine focused on the vanity mirror to see how she looked now. Her face was painted with the pragmatic, efficient expression that Cammy Burke tended to wear. Raine closed her eyes, remembering Ty releasing her hand. The push of the backboard sliding into the PJs' helicopter. The I.V. that went into her arm.

"What is that the hose from a camel water pack?" the PJ asked his buddy as the helicopter wop-wop-wopped, lifting into the air.

"That's exactly what it is. Hand me a trach kit and a bag. Looks like she wasn't getting air through the stab wound. Good that he did the field surgery. I think we can stabilize her."

Then the medication, or the exhaustion, or the relief of being away from the terrorists…something peaceful slid through her, and she fell into nothingness.

Raine lifted her chin and put her finger into the dimple left over from Ty's desperate field surgery and the trach tube she used until reconstructive surgery could be performed.

Ty…if it wasn't for him, she'd be dead. Now, it was her turn. Payback. Starting with Kendra.

Raine checked her face one last time, decided that what she saw fit her character, and got out of the car.

"Sorry about that," she said as she walked back through the door. She smiled at the two new ladies. "My therapist is trying to get me lined up with someone new down here."

The three women nodded sympathetically.

Raine stepped toward Kendra. "I'm Raine."

"Kendra," she held out the rubber plant, "a house warming."

Raine accepted the plant into her hands and looked at it sentimentally. "So lovely." Raine gestured. "Please sit. Can I offer you something to drink, Kendra? I have water, coffee, and tea. Does anyone need anything?" She let her gaze take in all three of her neighbors.

They demurred.

Raine went to the kitchen and came back with a decorative plate, which she put on the coffee table and set the plant on top. The best way to break the ice was to share a personal story that had all the feels. It made people think they were closer than was reality, well, as long as it wasn't too personal. Luckily, Raine had a wonderful story to tell about a rubber plant.

Raine took a seat in the chair nearest Kendra. "Before I was born, my Uncle Ralph bought a rubber plant, which he brought home and christened Herman. Uncle Ralph *adored* Herman. He babied that plant, trimming its leaves, carefully watering—never too much, never too dry. Herman was a great rubber plant. A fabulous listener. Every single day Uncle Ralph would have a long conversation with Herman. When I went to visit, I would talk to Herman, too. Herman heard about all my childhood woes, my unrequited middle school crushes, my teenage angst. Uncle Ralph was right. Herman listened and absorbed it all. Plant therapy." She smiled.

The ladies chuckled.

"Herman grew and grew and grew. By the time I started dating Damian—I was not quite seventeen—Herman was tall enough to touch the ceiling. When Damian and I got engaged, I went to tell my Uncle Ralph our news, and, of course, to tell Herman all about Damian's and my future plans. By that time, Herman had grown so big he stretched across the ceiling. When I got home for good," Raine petted her finger slowly across her scars, "I went to see Uncle Ralph. I wasn't able to talk yet. I couldn't have a chat with Herman. On that trip, I found out that my uncle had been diagnosed with throat cancer and was becoming frail."

"Oh, I'm so sorry," Laurel said.

"Thank you." Raine sent her a grateful smile. "Every day, through his cancer treatments, Uncle Ralph babied Herman. But despite all that Uncle Ralph did, Herman began to wither." Raine reached out and touched a leaf, delicately rubbing it between her fingers and telling her story directly to the plant. "My uncle passed away about two years later. At that point, Herman was only three feet high. He had almost no leaves left." She glanced around at the women with a nostalgic smile. "My aunt tried to care for Herman, tried to rouse him, and make him healthy again." Raine let a sad exhale past her lips. "It wasn't even two months after Uncle Ralph died that Herman died too. Every single one of us *truly* believes that Herman died of grief."

Tears glistened the women's eyes. Kendra reached out and

squeezed her hand. "Your uncle sounds like he had an amazing capacity to love."

"Uncle Ralph, yes, he was a one of a kind. Thank you for this gift. Rubber plants equal goodness to me." When Raine once again took in the woman, she didn't need to conjure up a right emotion. She felt the right feelings. Here was support and camaraderie. "It looks like you've been out for a run, Kendra. I run every day, rain, or shine. I was hoping to meet a fellow runner who might be able to show me some good paths."

"What's your distance?" Kendra asked.

In her ear, Raine heard, "She ran ten miles today at six miles per hour."

"I like to vary, but six to ten miles feels good to me. So an hour to an hour and a half, depending on slopes. The prettier it is, the longer I want to be out."

"Nice. Well, we're about the same then. Tomorrow, I was planning to run in the park if you want to join me."

"I'd love that, thank you. It's been a few days now since I've run, and I can feel it in my body."

"Theresa, can you come?" Kendra asked.

"Maybe. Let me check and see if I can't arrange a playdate for the kids. I'll call and let you know."

A handful of women showed up at Raine's door. It looked like they were each bearing food. Casserole dishes went into her fridge and freezer. Cookies and other baked goods dotted her counter. "Wow, thank you. This is so helpful."

Raine moved the dining room chairs to the living room. Then added the kitchen chairs as the room filled. She put out the cookie trays and made a pot of tea and one of coffee.

When she finally got the niceties out of the way, Raine walked in and picked up on a conversation. A dark-haired woman swiveled toward Raine. "There aren't many American women at the bases in the Middle East," she said.

"No." Raine scrambled for a way to shut that conversation down. She was a wife, not a soldier.

"If I were a woman at the base, and I had my pick of men, I'd pick from the special operators." Theresa leaned forward to pick up a paper napkin and two chocolate cookies. "Why not have the best of the best?"

"I read an article once about women's choices in men," Kendra said. "It turns out that women have a biological propensity to pick men who are taller and stronger when they live in a dangerous neighborhood. Women who come from elite neighborhoods chose more on earning potential as the alpha, and they could have any shape or size. It would seem to me that the women at the bases would feel the physical danger and want the very most protection. A Delta, for example, might look good to them from their physical capacity, their military prestige. If that were true, though, first, I wouldn't have married Budge. Second, Ty and Havoc wouldn't be single."

"Or T-Rex?" Raine asked.

"He's widowed," Laurel said. "His wife was a police officer. She was shot trying to intervene in a domestic dispute. Four years ago, now."

"Oh, my goodness." Damian hadn't mentioned that. There were a lot of details to catch up on. Four years ago, she and Damian were supposed to have been married. "I…I…I'm so sorry."

"Still with the male to female ratios over there. A woman could find plenty of fine men to choose from if one was that kind of woman," the dark-haired woman said.

"Single?" Raine asked.

"Not necessarily," the woman said. She was kind of prickly.

Raine would have to watch her tongue. In general, Raine wasn't great around prickly people.

"If a married man has an affair, it ruins his career," Kendra said.

"No one would need to know, though, would they?" Prickle girl seemed to be stuck in a groove.

"Everyone would know," Laurel said. "In the camps? With the communal tents and no privacy? Absolutely everyone would know."

"Not always," Prickle puss insisted.

Raine picked up the plate of cookies and held it out to her. Maybe she had low blood sugar, and that would explain this line of thought. Raine needed to move them to something more informative, like Lucy McDonald.

"Look at you, for example." Prickle Puss accepted a cookie and a napkin. "Your job was to go out with the special operators to interact with the women along the way and to be a translator, right?"

Wife, not soldier. "That was so long ago." Raine poured herself more tea.

"It was you and them—not a whole camp. No one was watching you, and you know nothing gets leaked out of the brotherhood. You would be safe."

Raine blinked at the woman.

Theresa's hand hit her hip, and she twitched her head like she was ready to rumble. "Are you accusing Raine Prescott of having *sex* with her team?"

Raine heard, "Blaze here. Focus on the agitator and snap a picture." Raine turned to Prickle Puss and blinked—one Mississippi. Opened her eyes, one Mississippi. Then blinked twice to turn the video camera back on.

"Photograph received," Blaze said. "Video functioning."

Raine hoped he'd feed her some information into her ear.

"No! No. Of course, I'm not accusing Raine of anything. I'm using her experience to illustrate a point." Prickle Puss laughed.

"That's not an experience I had," Raine said quietly.

"I mean, she *could*. Not that she *did*. I'm commenting on the possibility. But no, I'm not accusing her of that. I'm interested in the culture of the camps is all. The men never discuss it and won't mention any women they meet on deployment."

Ah, the bitterness of jealousy, Raine thought. Fear that while home alone and worried, some other woman was offering comfort to her husband. "I'd take that concern off my radar. Almost all the women that I knew being there with the men significantly challenges them. Most women I know rethink ever wanting to have a relationship with a man again."

Laurel put a hand on Raine's shoulder. "You and Damian are fine, though. I mean, you look very committed to each other."

Raine let a shy smile light her face. Good, back to tender wife territory. "I have loved Damian since we co-parented a flour sack back in high school." She winked at the women. "You know, in high school, Damian Prescott was a big man on campus. Water polo, wrestling, track and field. The cheerleaders were all abuzz." She held up jazz hands. "I did athletics too. Volleyball, soccer, swim team. We had some AP classes together. Otherwise, we didn't cross paths except in the hallways. Then we were in a class required by our school called "Whole Lives." It taught us survival basics—insurance, taxes, resumes, and job interviews, budgeting, and relationships. And, of course, parenting. That's when our teacher Mr. Camden—"

"A man taught that class?" Theresa asked.

"I actually think it was best. He did a great job. Assistant head coach, ex-marine, he wasn't messing around about diapering our flour sack—Damian's and my little sack was named Iris—and doing our best to keep Iris safe and well-loved. Where we grew up, there was still a lot of gender role-playing. Guys didn't cook. It's the wife's job to raise the child until it gets to the age when they can be fun and taken out to the woods for hunting and fishing. When the Marine said pat the flour sack on the diaper and sing, the guys patted and sang." Raine grinned. "Damian was an excellent flour sack father."

"But not in real life?" Prickle Puss asked.

"Wow," Blaze whispered in her ear.

Raine knew this was going to come up. "I had a lot to overcome once I got back. Parenthood is something we're looking forward to." Raine stood up, lifted the empty cookie plate, and walked to the kitchen.

"Take your bitch pills this morning, Mary?" someone hissed behind her back.

"What?" Pickle Puss Mary asked.

Raine was glad to move out of the room. She hoped her absence would mean that the ambient conversation might yield up something interesting to the AI on Blaze's computer. She took a moment to clean off the plate then opened a container with brownies to arrange on the dessert plate.

Babies. What a faraway thought that had always been. Raine remembered lying with Damian, wrapped tightly together as they imagined their future. Raine had stipulated she wanted to get to her fifteenth year with the military, and then she wanted to have two babies, one after the other. If they had married when they said they would, seven years ago, and if things had gone to plan, right now Raine would have a desk job and two little ones at home. Raine was thirty-six. She'd just turned thirty-six. It wasn't too late. She was strong and healthy. She was leaving her field job...

But in her little future picture of what life could be, Damian had been there, handsome in his uniform, strong and steady. Yeah, she hadn't taken those old goals off the shelf and dusted them in seven years.

Not since Damian decked his best friend when his friend was overcome with emotion after reading her letter and was hugging her.

It was almost an exact replay of what had happened between her mom and dad.

The last Raine had seen of her father, the neighbor, a rosy-faced man who fed stray cats and hugged everyone, came and gave Raine's mom some church literature and a hug. Raine's dad walked through the door, saw the hug, slugged the guy, and left forever. He'd accused Raine's mom of having an affair when it was Raine's dad who had been screwing around with one of his post-docs and had been for years.

Before Damian could accuse her of having an affair—like Mary just did—before Damian could storm out the door to go live with some other woman, Raine had ripped the ring off her finger and tossed it at him. She had been the one who left.

Unlike her dad, Damian had a good reason to be gone after that —it was his job.

Unlike her dad, Damian said he'd come looking for her as soon as he was back on American soil, but Raine knew that she had made finding her impossible.

Maybe she should ask Damian why he punched Eric.

"Blaze here. The name of the woman that you pictured is Mary Greasley. Her husband didn't make it through Delta training. Sounds like there's a chip on her shoulder. That puts her in the running for someone who could be manipulated for information. We'll take a deeper dive."

"Coffee."

33

Betrayal may come from within.
~ Moscow Rules

Wednesday Night

"I like this," Damian said, as Raine turned her back toward him so he could zip her up. He could see the top of her satiny panties that matched her coral dress. As he dragged the zipper up her back, the dress hugged her curves to her waist, then flared out with a full skirt. In the past, it was the kind of dress that allowed them to have sex in some pretty risky places without ever being caught.

"Good day today?" Raine pulled Damian's mind back to the bedroom, away from the memory of a closet escapade with a similar dress.

"Great day. I was right back in sync like I'd never been gone. It felt good," he said as Raine stepped away, smoothing down her skirt and sliding into her heels. "They have a new night-vision helmet that we're going to be working with tomorrow night. So don't expect me home until dawn. How about you? How was your day?"

"A little overwhelming. Lots of new faces dropped by. To be honest, I'll be glad when that settles down." Damian knew she was speaking in character for whoever might have ears on them. "I met a nice lady. Her name is Kendra Sullivan. She's our across the street neighbor. We're going running tomorrow morning. The rubber plant on the coffee table downstairs is a house warming gift from her and her husband, Budge." Raine stood, so they were face to face.

"Did you tell her about your uncle and Herman?"

"I did! Yeah, I had forgotten all about that. And somehow, I had also forgotten that T-Rex was widowed."

Since they were standing in front of the window, Damian drew her into his arms and kissed her hair. He bent his head and whispered, "Sorry. I'm sure you covered for that just fine," into her ear. "Did you get your work call?" he asked in a conversational voice.

"It was brief."

"Good?"

"Good enough."

"How was everyone who stopped by?"

"Well, Kendra's husband re-upped, according to Laurel. He'll be staying with the Lima team," she paused. "Have you decided?"

"I'm sorry. I know you'd like a handle on what comes next. I'd like to spend these next two weeks seeing how it feels to be back with the guys. Can you handle that? Is it okay?"

"It's a big decision."

He nodded. "Big for both of us."

She held up a finger. Her eyes went to the wall. She must be hearing something in the comms. "Roger that," she said to Iniquus support, but it sounded like she was answering Damian. It was his reminder; this was a mission. She was here for the job. He was here to support her in that job and make it feasible for someone to threaten and possibly attack her while he was downrange. That was everything he didn't want to happen.

Raine focused back on him. "Can we go for a quick ride? It always calms me down when I'm starting to get anxious."

IN THE CAR, down the street, Raine said, "Clear for communications."

"Blaze here," came the voice over the in-car communications system.

"Long day, Blaze," Raine said.

"Sitting at a desk doesn't take a lot of energy. Hold for TOC." Blaze used the acronym for tactical operations center. For this mission, it was the Strike Force war room.

"Good evening. Lynx here. I have some information for you from the earlier name."

"Earlier name?" Damian asked.

"Classified," Raine said.

"Copy." Damian didn't like that at all.

Raine leaned forward, staring toward the dash, focused. It must be something significant. Now, he *really* didn't like being in the dark.

"Did that name take you anywhere?" she asked.

"We had an interesting conversation," Lynx said. "On background, the Zoric family had a sex trafficking scheme for hiring girls out of the post-USSR countries, especially Slovakia. They signed them on to modeling contracts and as maids then brought them to America on visitor's visas. Steve Finley, along with Damian and his joint task force at the FBI, shut down a major stream of Zoric sex traffickers last year about this time. During their interviews, the FBI found out that it was a two-way stream of girls."

Raine turned her head, her gaze caught on Damian in the sudden burst of oncoming headlights. They slid apart as Damian refocused on the road ahead of them, driving nowhere in particular.

Okay, Damian had worked that case with Finley. If this player was one of Finley's contacts, Damian probably knew who it was.

"They sex-trafficked American girls to Slovakia?" Raine asked. "How does that make sense?"

"This is one of the intersections between the Zoric family and the Prokhorov family," Lynx said. "The Zorics would entice girls to Austria on a scholarship. Carefully vetted girls."

"You know about this?" Raine turned to Damian. He could feel her shooting daggers at him. "You didn't say."

"First, we joined this case Saturday." Damian adjusted his hands on the wheel. "We haven't had a chance to share much of anything. Second, I wouldn't have thought to put Zoric sex trafficking, which we shut down last year, into this mix. And third, that case was assigned to another working group once we saved the kids and made the arrests. So I don't know anything about it other than what we prepared for the court case about sex trafficking to the United States. This information about American women in Slovakia is a piece that my task force wasn't working on."

"Lynx, can you tell me more about sex trafficking being a two-way street?" Raine asked. "And why would that be of interest to what's happening with the Delta wives?"

"The American girls got the scholarships to Vienna, Austria. They were then encouraged to stay in Europe, in Bratislava, Slovakia to be exact, to work at one of the Prokhorov disinformation offices."

"Bot farms? Because they knew the American culture and could interact with the right voice and grammar on Facebook and Twitter?" Raine asked.

"Some of them worked at the bot farms, yes. Others, according to the resource you sighted, were used to gain access to military information by interacting with our troops."

"How?" Damian asked. As far as he knew, this wasn't an avenue the FBI had been tracking.

"The girls developed relationships by being pen-pals, to use the term loosely," Lynx explained. "Handwritten letters but also through social platforms. The women would reward the men's detailed information about their lives and work by sending them photographs with increasing sexualization, even acting out fantasies, with say, certain clothing or another girl. They might write the kinds of things that led the men to believe that they were in an emotionally based relationship with a future. Whatever worked to keep the soldier hooked and sharing information."

"Specific information about their units?" Damian asked.

"Exactly. Little things can accumulate, especially when they're interacting with maybe a hundred soldiers each."

"That's a lot to juggle— a hundred each." Raine drummed her fingers on the armrest. "But I guess they have the Prokhorovs' computer system to help them. How does that inform this case?"

"Since this case is seemingly run by the Prokhorov family, in conjunction with or without the support of the Zoric family, looking into their known activities is interesting. The idea of American girls getting jobs in Slovakia is a new one to Frost and Hasan. Our source indicated that American girls' interactions with soldiers was of concern to the military, and so her employer was following it. She emphatically warned Finley off any kind of deep dive. She insisted that anything the FBI or DIA did with her information had to be invisible. The resource's employer is using that avenue for counterterrorism by having American military operators take over that correspondence from the targeted soldiers. The military is using those contacts for a disinformation campaign, feeding the girls incorrect intelligence. That's one concern. The other is that if the pen pal scheme was exposed, the women's lives might be endangered."

Yup, this has to be Finley's girlfriend Anna, aka Zelda Fitzger-

ald, who works with the Asymmetrical Warfare Group. This is exactly the kind of thing they did.

"If the Zoric or Prokhorov families thought the women would carry tales back to the U.S. intelligence communities, I could see the families removing that threat by disappearing them," Damian said.

Damian flicked on his left turn signal to start the car circling back toward their house. They couldn't be late for a dinner in their honor.

"If and when they decided to shut that piece down, I was told," Lynx said, "they'd exfiltrate all the women. At this point, we don't know if these American women are there by their own volition or if they're held against their will."

"Copy," Raine said. "Does this resource believe someone associated with Delta Force, someone in their support, for example, could be a Slovakian pen pal?"

"No one in the ranks is actively corresponding now," Lynx told her. "Like I said, the resource's employer is interceding when they find a point of contact. What that means is a matter of conjecture. It sounded like the intelligence group had a high confidence threshold for finding the soldiers who were being targeted, and they took over, posing as that guy, continuing the correspondence. There must be some tell. A similar date of mail delivery, a similar zip code…"

"There's a leap there," Damian said. "For this to have any bearing on this case, one of the women who worked for the Zorics would have had to make her way out of the pen pal world and get physically involved. The information the terrorists have is too precise. Too quick. And the pictures of the wives too candid and current. If it's one of those pen pals, she took it up a notch and married the soldier and is here at Fort Bragg."

"Damian, from your understanding of the Zoric's functioning here in America, is that possible?" Raine asked.

"They play the long game. I wouldn't put it out of the realm of possibilities," he answered.

"That's the conclusion we've come to," Lynx said. "That is *if* we found the right lens to look through. In that case, the pen pal started many years ago, the relationship became real, or the woman pretended it was real. They married. She's at Fort Bragg spying on the families. Again, not definitive, but there was a meeting today where Frost and Hasan were briefed. The DIA and the other entity are supposed to provide Lisa Griffin with access to pertinent data. Lisa's using her software programs to comb the data for anything that falls into the scope of this mission. Lisa said if she can get hold of the data soon, she could have this running tonight. She's programming the computer to look at circles, starting with primaries then move out to secondary and tertiary connections. The FBI had already been hitting that hard, anyway. Another avenue is the possibility of someone in a Delta Force neighborhood, the people who might be able to see the comings and goings and pick up gossip. That's where Hasan thinks we'll find success. Low military pay, high risk to life, and limb—it could leave someone wanting a better slice of the pie."

"You flagged Mary with the chip on her shoulder?" Raine asked.

"Affirmative, Blaze brought her to our attention," Lynx said.

Damian turned onto their street.

"Thank you, Lynx," Raine said.

"Have a good night."

"Blaze here. I'll be with you for another hour, then Jack will cover your comms. Enjoy your evening."

"Thank you," Raine and Damian said together.

Today, while Damian was running through shoot houses with his brothers, Raine had moved their case picture forward. Zelda Fitzgerald was working on a case with satellite communications interference for the Asymmetric Warfare Group. How Raine picked Zelda out as the person who could inform this case would have to remain a mystery. He'd check in with Frost or Finley tomorrow and see if his guess was right, that Zelda was the mystery operator. Damian bet Raine didn't know that Zelda was dating Finley and had a connection to their joint task force. Raine would be trying to protect the woman's cover and was probably under orders not to share the identity. He got that, no hard feelings.

As Damian drove slowly back to their house, he reminded himself that this was Raine's baby. He was there to make her work possible. Tomorrow, Echo would train with night vision at the base. Damian expected their callout to happen immediately after. He'd be off sitting in a tent somewhere, twiddling his thumbs while Raine took the brunt of the danger. *Yeah, this pretty much sucked.*

34

Never fall in love with your agent
~ Moscow Rules

Wednesday night

So far, Damian had had a great night. Back in camaraderie with his brothers, hanging out, getting to know the new team members. Their wives were fun. He had the luxury of being himself. Raine, on the other hand, was on stage being vulnerable-Raine instead of one of the best intelligence officers that the United States had. Skillful. Cunning. Deadly. He sent her a searching look, and she caught his eye. In return, she sent him a small, "I'm okay, thanks for checking in" smile.

"I have a surprise!" Pam called as she emerged from the kitchen with a two-layer cake done up beautifully with flowers in the shade of Raine's bouquet in the photoshopped wedding picture that was now hanging on the Prescott's new living room wall. Two little turtle doves sat on the top of the white icing.

"Oh," Raine said, her hand coming to her heart and reaching the other one for Damian.

Jeopardy was right behind Pam, carrying champagne flutes and a sparkling white wine bottle on a tray.

"We didn't get to celebrate with you for the real wedding. And you know how we love to celebrate life's happier moments. So I put this together for all of us." She set the cake on a table then ran back into the kitchen to bring out another tray with dessert plates, cutlery, and a knife decorated with ribbons.

She set it next to the cake and moved out of the way, gesturing Damian and Raine to a place behind the cake while Jeopardy served out the wine for a toast.

"This is so beautiful. You are so kind," Raine said softly, leaning into Damian.

Damian ran his hands up and down Raine's arms while Jeopardy finished handing out the flutes.

Laurel took two of the glasses and walked them over to Raine and Damian. "Damian, you should toast your bride, don't you think?"

"Toast. Toast. Toast," the chants went up.

Pam pulled out her camera and snapped a couple of pictures. "Toast your bride, Damian, and make it a good one," she called with her phone extended, probably taking a video.

Raine turned and looked up at him.

Damian pressed his forehead against hers, trying to come up with something he could say. He thought about what Raine had told him about the importance of telling the truth in order to build trust, and he reached back into his memory to remember who they had been when they were together.

He turned to face the party-goers. "When I was a junior in high school, I planned out a first date. Raine was special, and I knew if I was to stand any kind of chance she would date me, I'd have to do something other than movies and ice cream." He smiled down at Raine, remembering just how nervous he'd been inviting her out. He looked back at the faces welcoming his story. "I took Raine to the golf course and walked her out to lie on a blanket under the stars. I'd made a thermos of hot cocoa and had a box with some of Mom's spice-flavored cookies. That night, under a sky dancing with stars, we kissed for the first time. In that very moment, I knew my heart was gone. I just put my soul in her hands and trusted it would be safe forevermore."

The women sighed.

Damian put their drinks onto the table, then took Raine's hands in his. "Raine drop, I've been blessed that we've had this life together. I'm in awe of how strong you are. How caring and gentle. How fierce and protective. You are singularly the most astonishing person I have ever met. I count myself among the few in this world who doesn't question their place. I have always belonged in your arms."

He looked down to see a storm brewing in her eyes. He'd gotten carried away and said too much out loud of what had been simmering under the surface of his thoughts.

He'd need to apologize for this later.

"Kiss," the others chanted.

Raine swallowed hard.

He whispered in her ear, "One good one, okay?"

She nodded. Lifting onto her toes, Raine tipped her head back. When his mouth found hers, he was back on the golf course under the stars, back in love. The kiss was sweet and soft. Before the sensation could turn to need, he put his hands on her cheeks and pulled back.

Her long lashes batted open.

Damian left two more little kisses on her lips, not fully able to pull himself away and stop.

The whistles and clapping helped to break the spell.

Damian swung around behind her and reached on either side of her for the cake knife. This was how he'd imagined it would be, slicing the cake and feeding each other pieces.

But it was just an act.

DAMIAN GOT INTO THE SHOWER. He figured he needed to relieve some sexual tension before he climbed in bed with Raine, or tonight was going to be miserable. He couldn't be running through practices with live ammunition when he was sleep-deprived. It put his brothers at risk.

Jeopardy had tossed back a few too many and had tripped with his moonshine punch in his hand. Damian's slacks had soaked it up just fine, and none had gotten onto Pam's rug.

Sticky from the fruit punch, it was a good excuse to be in here.

Damian let the hot water sluice over his shoulders. The tension from carrying a heavy pack all day eased from his back. He tipped some shampoo into his hand and sudsed up.

There was a knock at the door, and it opened.

"Before things get too steamy in here, I need to take my contacts out."

Those contacts were thirty-day camera lenses. They were either bothering her, or she didn't want Strike Force to see what she could see. And without an inflection in her voice, he couldn't tell if that was pragmatism in the steamy comment or if there was a sexual innuendo in those words.

Damian decided to pretend she wasn't there. If she didn't turn toward him, she wouldn't see how hard his dick was. If she turned that way? Well, the see-through shower curtain wouldn't protect her from anything. But hey, Raine had walked in on him. She was a big girl, and this wasn't anything she hadn't seen before.

He continued to wash his hair and chest and would leave rubbing one off until she walked out. Gentlemanly of you, Damian chided himself.

"I can see you in the mirror." Raine closed the contacts case and moved it to the top drawer. "It looks like you're having an argument in your own head."

"Which head is that?" he asked with a smile.

"The one on top of your shoulders. Your other head looks like it's trying to get your attention."

"Oh, believe me, it's got my attention and has ever since I zipped you into that dress tonight."

"Go ahead." Raine moved over to the toilet, put down the cover, and sat.

"Go ahead, and what?"

"Didn't you come in here to get some relief?"

"Raine…"

"Do you want me to leave so you can have your privacy?"

"I'd rather you get naked and join me."

"Slow steps."

"You think coming in and watching me jerk off is a slow step?"

"We've been through all the steps since we were seventeen. You didn't tell them tonight with your toast how that first date ended. You stopped at the kiss."

"I'm a gentleman. I figured you wouldn't mind my telling them about one little kiss."

"One hot as hell, take me now, kiss."

"Now you're teasing." He stepped back and rinsed the suds from his hair, and swiped a hand over his face to clear the water.

"Little steps. We've kissed on this mission. I thought that went pretty well."

He laughed.

"And now, I want to see you touch yourself. I've always loved that."

He smiled. Yeah, he remembered. "I get a little step, too."

"Okay." She slid her hands down her thighs and back up.

"As I get going, I want you to strip. Slowly. If you're going to be there ogling me, I get to do some ogling back. And if I'm going to masturbate, so are you."

"Okay to the striptease, but with no music?" She laughed.

"I could hum something if it would help." He was enjoying the back and forth. This was the familiar sexual banter that usually landed them in bed. He flashed to the image of her on all fours, his hands wrapped around her hips as he took her from behind. *"Harder. Do me harder, Damian,"* she'd call out, and he'd pound into her until she collapsed her chest to the mattress, panting from her release and letting him finish up at his own pace. Perfection. He blinked his eyes open.

Raine sat there with the thinking tilt to her head.

Damian poured some conditioner on his palm and reached under his cock to fondle his balls. "No show until you strip, Raine drop." He sent her a quirk of his eyebrows.

She held his gaze for a moment, deciding. That was good. She needed to be sure. And if all she wanted to do was sit there and watch him, well, he'd do his best to make it a good show.

Raine reached for her phone and tapped at the screen. The first strains of Delibes' *Lakmé - Duo des Fleurs* rose out of the speaker.

Damian wasn't an opera fan by a long stretch, but *this* one—he pushed his breath out and pressed a hand on the shower wall for stability. This one, Raine had sung in college. Her voice had been so beautiful it hurt. He could feel his heart squeezing down, remembering how he'd sat in the audience, panting as her notes swelled through his system.

Ever since then, when they wanted the kind of sex where they hit that painful spot—the point where making love felt like it was pulling him apart and slamming him back together again—they'd played that song. Never had he experienced that kind of bittersweet, painful glory with anyone else. That *thing* that he couldn't describe but made his cells hum with recognition.

He balled his fist against the wall as he thought, Raine will never sing that again.

He'd failed her. He wasn't there to protect her from the terrorists. In his fantasy mind, he had been with Echo when they went on her rescue. His bullet was five seconds sooner than Ty's. That dagger didn't pierce through her skin and throat. She could still sing. They were still together. Everything was fine.

But he wasn't there that day.

And they weren't fine.

They were colleagues, pretending for the world of bad guys that they were something they were not.

She caught his eye, and he shook his head. "Playing that song is like diving off the cliff, Rainey day. You'd better make damned sure this is what you want."

"I'm sure," she said and reached behind her to unzip the dress. She peeled one sleeve down, then the other. Slowly, she let the fabric's weight pull the dress toward the ground. It slid over her breasts, then her tight belly, revealing her coral satin panties with creamy lace, finally pooling on the tile.

Damian wrapped his hand around his cock, sliding it to the tip, circling, and gliding back up his shaft.

Raine licked her lips as she stepped out of the puddle of cloth.

Bad idea. Damian rinsed off quickly and turned to shut off the water.

"Please don't," Raine said.

Bad idea, he told himself, as he cut the water back on.

The music swelled and bounced off the walls. The room was filling with hot steam. He had just enough alcohol in his system, mixing with his testosterone, to make this a heady trip. He reached for the bottle. Popped the top. This time, the warm spices of Raine's conditioner rose up to his nostrils.

"Yes, I like that one. Use that one. Nice and slow," she said, kicking off her shoes. She sat and peeled her stocking gracefully down her leg.

Damian let his dick lie in his open palm, feeling the weight of it, how thick and long he got for her. He was aching for relief.

She slipped off her other stocking. Her legs parting, curls of her pubic hair tantalizing him from the edge of her panties.

He fisted his cock and found a rhythm in the music's bass notes.

Raine circled her fingers over her nipples. They were erect, showing tight and hard through the lace. Damian wanted them in his mouth. He was straining not to reach for her.

Slow was agony.

She unclasped the bra and tossed it to the floor. She lifted first one breast, licking her nipple, then the other. "I loved it when you put your mouth on me."

Damian's abdomen clenched, sending a convulsion through his body. A ripple of lust running all the way down to his toes.

"Do you remember how you used to tease me?" She wiggled her panties down to her thighs. "How you'd scoop your thumbs into the sides of my panties. How slow you went as you dragged them off me. How you'd inhale deeply as you knelt at my feet."

He pictured them together, the pillows pushed to the side, licking her, her thighs crushed together around his head as her orgasm raced through her body. How she'd moan as she stretched her arms for him. He'd crawl up and bury himself deep inside her, feeling her after-orgasm pulses, sending him toward the edge. He'd try to slow it down, rocking in and out, making those moments last.

Raine slid her panties down and off, letting her legs fall apart so he could see all of her.

His beautiful Raine.

He felt thick emotions pressing behind his eyes. He was glad for the veil of steam. Glad that his masturbating gave him a reason to hold his face taut.

She posted a bare foot on the edge of the tub, letting him look at her, pink and open, her clitoris swelling with her own desire.

She leaned back, reached between her legs, and started massaging herself, her fingers pressing against her flesh in the same rhythm, like a hummingbird's wing, that he'd watched so long ago.

"Do you like this?" she asked.

"No." Damian turned to cut off the water. He yanked the shower curtain from between them. "I can't. Will you turn off that song, please?"

Raine reached for her phone and tapped the music off while Damian grabbed for a towel.

"I can't go slow when it comes to you, Raine. I can't do it this way. I love you too hard. I've loved you too long. I apologize. I can't be what you need me to be here." His voice broke. "It's killing me not to touch you."

Raine sat there, unabashed. Her hands rested lightly on her open thighs. She looked up at him, her long dark hair caressing over her back. The image of her riding him, her hands planted on his heaving chest, her head bent low, sweeping her hair over his stomach, then throwing her head back as she gulped at the air as she came.

"Yeah." He took a step back. "For your safety and my sanity, I can't play at this."

She stood up, took the single long step that separated them, and pressed herself against his body. "What does that mean?" she asked. And her eyes meant that question. This wasn't a tease.

"It means that I can't play at loving you. I love you. I can't play at having sex with you. Your body already fills my dreams. I reach for you in my sleep, Raine, to this day. I can take a date home and find some relief. But you aren't relief. You're a torment."

"What do you want to happen?"

"I want us back." He put his hands on either side of her face. "I want an *us*." He released his hands to his sides.

Her forehead rested on his chest.

Hot tears dripped from her eyes and ran down his stomach.

He stroked her hair and tried to breathe. He remembered the grief he felt when their relationship was over. This was opening old wounds.

After a long moment, she tipped her head to lay a kiss over his heart. "I want that, too."

His breath stopped. The world stopped. There was no sound for a nanosecond, and then all he heard was his heart racing.

"Say it again." His voice was thick and gruff.

She looked up at him. "I still love you, too. I miss you, too. I want an *us*, Damian."

35

Never fall in love with your agent
~Moscow Rules

Thursday

Raine grinned up at him. Her hair fanning across the sheet. "Whew."

Laughing, he scooped under her to pull her tight as he collapsed to the side.

"I'd say let's do it again because we have years to make up for," Raine said as she pushed her leg between his and rolled her hips. "But I'm going to say three times the charm. I'm sated."

"Not an easy task to accomplish, riding out the Storm. It takes a special forces operator to have that kind of stamina." Damian wouldn't mind one more round. He'd find an opportunity before the team deployed tomorrow. With that thought, he grew hard again.

Raine reached down and draped her warm hand over his hard-on.

When he and Raine were together, it was for short bursts of time. The opportunities when their missions lined them up, they'd spend most of that time in bed, leaving the communicating and storytelling to their correspondence.

She stretched against him luxuriantly. "After the Storm comes the calm."

He combed her hair away from her eyes, looking down at the peace that relaxed her face.

Damian always thought of their sexual feasts like he was a grizzly gorging, trying to get filled up for hibernation when he couldn't get that contact he craved.

"One more?" he whispered.

That smile, *god!* His body snapped to full attention.

She licked her lips. "Okay, one more. But I'm not going to be able to walk, let alone run, today if you don't make it a quickie."

His phone, propped on the bedside table, buzzed with the Delta Force ring tone. He reached out and snagged it up. Zero-two-thirty hours. His mind and body shifted into focus.

He tapped the screen.

The number flashed **0000000**. They were spooling up.

He rolled from the bed and landed on his feet. His cell rang. "Go for Deimos."

"Ty, I'll drive."

"Roger."

"Spooling up?" Raine was on her knees. The sheet swirled across her hips, covering her legs.

"Roger." He grabbed his shorts and T-shirt, yanking them on. He had everything he needed up at Headquarters. They'd gear up based on what they were jumping into.

"This isn't what we expected," Raine said. "This must be a real-world scenario."

"Agreed." He pulled his tennis shoes from under the bed and shoved his feet into them.

"Are you up to this?" She posted her hands on the bed and leaned forward. "Forgive me for asking. You could endanger the others…Sorry. Sorry. I'm…talk about emotions moving from one extreme to another."

"I hear you about the emotions." He leaned back to give her a kiss, then bent over to lace up his shoes. "As to your worries. Absolutely, yes, I'm up to this. They put us through our paces all day today to make sure of it. They watched my execution and my performance with these guys. It was right as Raine." He twisted to reach out and tug a lock of her hair. "You don't need to worry about me. And you have people at your back. Make sure they know what's going on. Even so, I need your head on a swivel, eyes wide."

She nodded. Her jaw was tight as she ground her teeth together. She swallowed as she tipped her head back. "I love you."

He kissed her hard. "Always," he said, then raced down the stairs, threw open the door, and vaulted into the bed of Ty's truck where T-Rex and Jeopardy were already sitting. Nitro was up front riding shotgun.

Up at the TOC, the men piled out and jogged in to get their briefing.

Madison, CIA, stood at the front of the room. Their commander had his game face on. Maps were already up on the screens.

Echo pulled out the metal chairs and sat around the long tables.

"Gentlemen," Madison said once the whole team had assembled. "At approximately twenty-two hundred hours local time earlier tonight, a CIA officer, staging as a civil engineer, was kidnapped along the roadway near Soto Cano Air Base." He flicked his laser toward the map and circled an area. "This airbase in

Honduras is roughly seven kilometers to the south of Comayagua. This base does humanitarian outreach but is also a launching point in our efforts to stop drug flow into the United States. At this point, it's not clear if the captors know they snagged a CIA office or if they simply think they can ransom an American and get a good price. Either way, we need to get him out. This CIA officer has too much information about our movements and resources in this region to allow that information to get to the bad guys. If the captors know that's a CIA officer, our guy is probably already in a world of hurt. If the kidnappers think he's an engineer and all they want is a payday, that may buy us a little time. Either way, we need Echo in the air while we continue to gather intelligence on the matter. Plan for time in the jungle, boys. Don't forget the bug spray. Transport is on the tarmac ready. It's a five-plus-hour ride straight in. We expect you on-site at zero eight hundred hours. Let's get this underway."

Damian went through the door to his cage, his hands shooting out, gathering what uniforms and kit he would need for a jungle op. This was it. He was back in his world. It felt good and right to be here with the boys.

If anything went wrong at Fort Bragg, he wouldn't be there. Damian trusted Raine's skills. He trusted Strike Force. But man, if anything happened to her… He couldn't let his emotions distract him. It put too many people at risk. She'd run dangerous operations without him her whole career. This was no different, he tried to convince himself.

Ty's hand slapped Damian across the chest. "You good? Squared away?"

"Let's do this."

36

Any operation can be aborted; if it feels wrong, then it is wrong.
~ Moscow Rules

THURSDAY

RAINE HADN'T BEEN able to go back to sleep after Damian's callout.

She took a long bath, working to get out of her head, put her personal life to the side, and get back focused on the mission.

Distractions were deadly. This was exactly why the Delta Force wives hadn't told their men about the threats on the home front. It was brave of them. Patriotic. Caring. But Raine wasn't convinced that secrecy—which the terrorists had demanded—was the smartest action.

Now that Raine was on post, saw the women involved, and thought this through…

None of them was any more prepared than Lucy McDonald had been to handle an assault.

Lucy was actually the single threatened wife who took the actions that Raine approved of. This ostrich act, burying their heads and pretending they weren't really endangered—or equally bad, believing the threat and working on their husbands to end their tenures with the forces—played right into the terrorists' hands.

If the husbands quit, they won.

If the women were hurt or killed, they won.

The only way the terrorists didn't win was if the women pulled themselves out of the situation long enough that the task force could figure this out and shut it down.

What if the military made a public announcement? What if they talked about keeping the wives safe on the home front? They could tell the wives what they could and couldn't do until this was resolved. To Raine, that took some of the power away from the crime families.

Last night, when Raine had slipped into Pam and Jeopardy's guest bathroom to hear the report from Strike Force, Jack confirmed that Kendra's husband had re-upped.

This next time frame should prove interesting.

Would anything happen to Kendra? Budge Sullivan's contract date wasn't until Saturday. If the terrorists were going by a paper trail, there might not be any action brought until Sunday and beyond. Lima was still downrange, possibly leaving Kendra more vulnerable. If the terrorists had someone with direct access to the contract information, the DIA would be able to follow that easily. All the affected women, who had been interviewed, had agreed to spyware on their computers and phones until this was resolved.

Even so, last night, Hasan contacted Kendra and told her to report daily—anything and everything. He gave Kendra a support number that routed her to the comms for Strike Force. Monitored 24/7, the Strike Force team could commit operators to her in minutes.

Not that Kendra knew that.

Hasan asked Kendra not to leave the post before Monday, thinking that would give Raine a few more days to make progress.

But, of course, Kendra chose their running trail off post for later this morning.

Raine thought through what weapons she could take on their run. Her hairpins were probably going to be it. She'd had them made for specific needs. She always wore her get out of jail card—the one with the handcuff keys and lock picks. She had another one that clasped across her head with decorative rings on either side. Like the bracelet she wore the night of the tunnel attack when Raine grabbed at the rings and yanked, she'd have two-inch double-edged blades extending from her fists. She'd had to use her bracelet knife like that for the first time in Brussels last fall. When she'd punched the guy in the crotch, he screamed the loudest, longest, highest-pitched scream she'd ever heard in her life. He was out of the fight without her taking a single hit. And now she had the reputation as a woman who was fine stabbing a guy in the dick.

Which was A-okay with her.

Yup, the barrettes would have to do. Strike Force would have her six.

She climbed from the tub and patted herself dry. She was pretty sore from last night's gymnastics with Damian. She hadn't dated much in the last year, so her body hadn't been stretched that way in a while. Like it or not, that inner ache was going to be a reminder that her personal life and her professional life had…intersected.

Damian must have foreseen that possibility of their intersection because he had a ready supply of condoms in his Dopp kit. Of course, they might not have been placed there for her. He might just carry those around for whoever tumbled into his bed.

Huh, a little bite of jealousy. Interesting... Raine slipped her athletic bra on, dragged on her running tights, then pulled a tank over that before she put in her camera contacts and blinked them online.

As she moved through the bedroom on her way down to the kitchen, she plucked her hearing aids from their box.

"Thursday morning," she said.

"Jack here. I saw a pickup come and get Damian. That isn't to plan. They spooled up?"

"Coffee," she said. This morning, Damian hadn't had time to set up the pot for her. And for some reason, that made the kitchen feel cold and lonely.

It had taken Raine so long to get Damian out of her bloodstream, to learn to live without him. Grief over what she had lost when he threw that punch at Eric had mixed in with the recovery from her abduction and physical healing. It had been rough going.

"It's early. Are you still planning on your run?" Jack asked.

"Coffee." She thought that anyone listening would think she was crazy mumbling coffee over and over every morning. Well, as long as she did it consistently, no one would mark it as important.

"We have plotted the route that you agreed to with Kendra. It's off the base. We're on high alert for her when she's off base. We'll have a car staged in the area equipped for a medical emergency. I'll be on comms. Striker will be on foot, following on the path. Gator will clear the path from the end toward you. Once he's passed you, he'll circle back behind Striker. Striker will sprint forward ahead of you on a second sweep. Blaze will be in the car."

"Coffee."

"The DIA reached out to Kendra. She doesn't want protection. She doesn't want a safe house. She thinks it's just cyberbullying. It's her call, up to a point."

"Mmmm." Yeah, well. It was one of those catch 22s. If there was going to be a physical attack, it wouldn't happen on base. Someone had to leave base for the attackers to show themselves. The team couldn't run down the bad guys, capture them, and get answers until someone was in harm's way. In order to keep the wives safe, Raine needed to be threatened, then Damian needed to re-up, so she could put a bull's eye on her own back. Since Budge Sullivan had signed early, it was probably a good thing that Damian's callout happened already. It might unravel the plot sooner.

KENDRA BACKED out of her driveway, and Raine scampered down the front steps. She climbed into the passenger seat of the Honda. "Good morning. It's a glorious day for a run."

"Yeah, it is." Kendra slid a water bottle into a cup holder as she started down the road. "It's cooled off just enough to stay comfortable. I swear the heat and humidity suck my energy like a vacuum." She pulled off her sunglasses and perched them on top of her head as they drove away from the sun.

The two women fell into a comfortable silence as Kendra drove through the guard gate and out.

Kendra turned right out of the fort. That wasn't the correct direction. "Are we taking the scenic route?" Raine asked.

"What?" Kendra tapped her turn signal and slid into the left-hand lane. "Oh, Theresa and I were talking this morning, and we thought we had a better idea. She wants to meet us just up here at Kiest Lake."

"Kiest Lake, that's a fishing spot, isn't it?"

"Jack here. Kiest Lake, copy."

"No one's fishing in January. That means the lake is populated with migrating birds, and the wildlife is out. Sand in the shoes, so weird little cuts on your feet, but peaceful and wonderful. Are you still game?" Kendra asked with a quick check-in glance toward Raine.

"Sure." Raine smiled at her, then turned her head to look out the window.

"Jack here. I have satellite images. There won't be any other joggers in this area. There won't be any through cars. There isn't much cover. You can see right across to the other side of the lake and into the trees. This is not an optimal site."

"Why didn't Theresa drive with us?" Raine asked.

"She's taking the kids to a friend's house for a play date. And she wants to run some errands when we're done."

"Oh, okay."

As soon as they pulled off the pavement onto the dirt road, Kendra's phone rang. "Hey! We beat you here, looks like," Kendra said brightly. Her face drooped, a frown tugging at the corners of her mouth. "Well, that's a pain." She paused to listen, then replied, "As far as I know, they don't sell sanity over the counter yet. But I'll stop by later with a bottle of wine, best I can do." Kendra chuckled, then said good-bye.

"What's up?" Raine asked.

"Theresa's tire's flat. Looks like she ran over something yesterday when she was out. She has AAA on their way over."

"Bummer," Raine said.

"Pretty much." Kendra tapped the car off and put her keys on the floor. "Ready?"

"I don't mind carrying your keys if you'd like."

"Nope. No one's going to be out here this time of year. It'll be fine. Just don't lock the door, or the alarm will yell at you."

"How long is the run around the lake?"

"Not nearly long enough. I thought we'd follow the dirt road until it ends at the top of the lake and double back, then we can cross over the main street. Up the way a short distance is another road. We can run out toward the Little River. There's a dead end there to turn us around. That should be enough tree therapy and running to get your mind and body humming."

Raine shut the door and slowly scanned the scene, so Strike Force had the video.

"Jack here. We're rerouting your support team. We're putting together a plan on the fly. Updates as we have them. Cough to indicate good copy."

Raine coughed as she jogged in place and did some warm-up stretches.

"Ready?" Kendra asked.

"Sure," Raine said, but the truth was, she wasn't thrilled to be out here without support on hand.

37

Murphy is right.
~ Moscow Rules

THURSDAY

THEY ARRIVED in Honduras ahead of schedule. Echo was greeted on the tarmac by a soldier who conducted them into a hangar where a command center had been set up.

Long tables with computers and a whiteboard with no writing, it didn't look like they had a plan cooking.

An American commander and his Honduran counterpart stood shoulder to shoulder, each with their arms crossed over their chests, focused on a satellite map.

Honduran troops sat on wooden benches, waiting for their orders.

Echo moved into the space as a huddle. The men held back as

their number one, T-Rex, and number two, Ty, walked over to get the sitrep.

Their team leaders shook hands with the Honduran leader.

Damian heard "EBT" as the Honduran commander indicated his men.

EBT was the Honduran special forces, trained by U.S. Navy SEALs. Tough as nails. It would be good to have them along for the ride. They'd know the terrain, the locals, and the dialects. They'd also know what worked to coerce information—carrot or stick.

Damian chucked off his kit. They lined the bags up by their number, so it was easy to grab and go, knowing everyone had their own equipment on their back.

On this mission, Damian's call sign was Seven.

End of the line.

As Damian straddled the bench, a phone call pulled the EBT commander off to the corner, where he listened intently and replied in rapid-fire Spanish. With the phone still pressed to his ear, he stalked back to the maps. His finger traced over an area, then he tapped it, verified, and put a dot on the paper.

Damian watched as the leaders bent their heads around the table, focusing on the map and discussing information.

The sooner they got a plan in play, the sooner they'd get the CIA officer safe, the sooner they'd get back to Fort Bragg, and he'd be with Raine, working his main mission.

This seemed like Shakespeare's Hamlet with the play within a play, Damian mused, while they waited for orders.

T-Rex signaled them over. "It's like this," he'd said. "We'll be working with EBT. As long as we're working with the *Escuadrón de Buzos Tácticos,* EBT, the Honduran government has green-lighted us for a kinetic op. We're going to take electric-motored crafts to keep our sound to a minimum. That'll save us from humping our way in. We travel the river to this fork, then here, up here, here, here." He moved his finger over a thin blue line that traced through a dense mass of trees on the satellite map. "Here there's a cliffside, I'm being told that thick vines run along this face, and we can climb them like repel ropes. There's a natural concave area that'll keep the craft out of line of sight where we can tie off the boats."

"Trust the vines?" Nitro asked. "How about we send one guy up, and he can send us some lines down."

"I'll be first man up," Damian said.

"Affirmative, Seven." T-Rex nodded in his direction. "If we get the ropes rigged, we'll have our exfil prepped in case it's balls to the wall. And we'll use the rope ladder to make it a little easier on Ty and Rory."

"What's at the top?" Havoc asked.

"Forest. Thick vegetation. And a hard hike for three klicks to a hut situated here." T-Rex's finger came down on the satellite image.

If Damian squinted, he could just make out a dark spot amongst the leaves.

"There's a group of locals who have a permanent camp over here." T-Rex's finger came down on the topo map laying beside the satellite image. On this map, the men could see the lay of the land and the elevations. "The camp knows the EBT is coming to check out the area, so they're removing over the ridge. Still, if things go hot, I'd rather position so we can keep the Honduran civilians out of the line of fire."

The men took a moment to orient themselves from boat, to cliff's edge, to location of the hut. Damian visualized the time of day and the position of the sun. They liked the sun to their backs. It helped blind the people searching them out with their scopes. In this case, it would aim those bullets right toward the camp.

"No drone or current satellite visuals?" Nitro asked.

"The canopy's too dense." T-Rex took a knee, so the men formed a huddle.

"Why do we think our PC is in there?" Jeopardy used the

acronym PC for precious cargo, the name they used for the hostage they were going in to rescue.

"The encampment heard screaming." T-Rex planted his forearm on his knee.

"Screaming?" Havoc repeated. "That could be an animal…" He shrugged.

"Or someone caught in a hunter's trap," Ty said. "Which is why a couple of the men from the encampment went up there to render help. They spotted four armed men around the exterior perimeter. They said there's a white-skinned man with blond hair sitting inside. Which meets two of our missing CIA officer's descriptors. The encampment has been working to keep criminals away from that area. Not fully trusting local authorities, the first thing their leader did was to call the American base." T-Rex pointed over his shoulder at the head of the EBT. "That call got patched through to our host over there. That's what all the excitement was about."

Nitro rubbed his chin as he focused on T-Rex. "We could be going in to find someone cooking meth."

"That's all the information we have," T-Rex said. "The locals said the hut had been abandoned because it's haunted. No one goes near it. That there are suddenly four armed guards and screaming is highly unusual. We might as well do a little recon while the CIA works their ground game." He clapped his hands and rubbed his palms together. "Okay, so we're going to put eyes on and see what there is to see. When we talk to our counterparts, since we use numbers, they'll use letters. That's their Alpha and their Bravo. The rest you can meet en route. Any questions?"

The men shook their heads.

A man had come in with a Ziploc bag that he handed Ty. It had held a blue button-down shirt, presumably a scent for Rory to track if they got on the right trail.

"Load 'em up, gentlemen. We'll finesse the course of action on our way to the X."

That wasn't the way they liked to run missions. For them, it was all about preparation, preparation, preparation. But the clock was ticking, not only for the CIA officer but the intelligence that he was protecting. That meant they'd have to go for it.

THEY HAD BEEN on the water about an hour.

By now, Raine was going about her day. She'd be jogging with the Lima wives, Kendra and Theresa, getting close to them, trying to figure out how Delta Force re-up timelines had been obtained by the terrorists.

With him gone, Raine should be getting her own threat.

That anyone would threaten Raine sent a fire through Damian's system that must have glowed in his eyes because T-Rex kicked his boot.

"You square? Head in the game."

"Roger that."

They were slowing. Up ahead was the cliff with the indentation for the boats. Just as was described, vines draped over the top of the rocky face and hung all the way to the water.

Their electric motors had been silent on the way in. Their drivers slid the crafts behind the vines that were as thick as a man's arm.

Echo performed a comms check.

The EBT soldiers jumped from the boat seats, grabbed at the vines, and went up hand over hand.

Damian clipped a rope to his belt, jumped, and grabbed at the vine. Once he was topside, he could drag the rest of the lines up and get them securely anchored, ready in case they needed to fast-rope out of there. If the CIA officer was physically capable, they'd have the rope ladder for him to clamber down. If not, someone would wear him as they descended.

At the top, Damian threw a leg over the edge. One of the EBT clamped his hand on it, which made it easier for Damian to scramble up with the weight of his full battle rattle and heavy pack.

Damian set the ladder first.

Ty would climb up with Rory hanging from a K9 sling under his pack.

The EBT maintained a perimeter while Echo got everything in place. Damian's hands moved with the comfort of someone who had done this same task a thousand times before.

The EBT was brought up to speed on the exfil. They fanned out into position, and the teams headed into the tree line.

Moving was good. It kept the mosquitos and gnats out of their eyes. Bandanas covered the lower half of their faces. Their heavy combat gloves dragged the thorny vines out of the way as they crept forward.

The wind rose. Ty looked down at Rory, whose body was rigid with excitement. Ears twitching as they homed in on something.

There.

Damian could hear it too, screams riding the wind.

Shots rang out.

They were still a little over a klick out.

The teams shifted slightly to line up with the new information and proceeded forward, slow and steady, heads on a swivel.

The forest was eerie silent following the blast of gunfire.

As the men progressed, Rory was crouched low to put his weight and muscle into dragging Ty. Ty had to drop his rifle on its sling so he could hold on to the lead with both hands. Rory was excited to get to his work, find the missing person, and maybe get a chance to bite the bad guy.

T-Rex's fist came up in the air.

Everyone froze.

Damian lifted his arm to move the foliage, and there ahead of them was a cabin with two open windows in the back and no door.

Alpha signaled, and the EBT team went to check the perimeter for the guards that were mentioned over the phone.

Ty pulled out the shirt they'd brought for a scent sample. He opened the bag. "Rory, target. Target." The command Ty used to tell Rory that this was the scent he was to trail.

Rory circled his nose in the air.

Ty released the dog's lead. The K9 jetted forward, leaped in the air, and through the window. They could hear the clacking of his nails across the wooden floor. If anyone had been in there, Rory would have signaled.

Damian, Ty, and Havoc bent low and jogged forward, taking up places on either side of the windows, then rounding on the openings, their rifle barrels pressed into the cabin, tactical lights glowing.

"Clear," Ty said into his comms.

They moved around to the front door, where Ty grabbed hold of the handle on Rory's tactical vest.

Rory's nose went to the ground, and Ty followed behind, a tight grip on the lead.

Damian and Havoc went in to look for clues that the CIA officer could have been there.

The hut was small. A filthy mattress with no linens topped a rusted foldaway bed set in the corner. A chair sat in the center of the room. On the floor around the chair, Damian's light picked up a pool of semi-coagulated blood being feasted on by a swarm of flies.

"Blood trail," Damian said, following drops of blood out the front door, down the steps, and into the forest. The same direction that Rory had led Ty.

Ty came out of the woods. "I've found him, gentlemen. We have a fallen eagle."

They didn't make it in time.

"He's down in a deep drain. I think we can take the path," Ty said.

"How can you tell he's KIA?" Jeopardy asked.

"He took two taps to the forehead." Ty turned his attention to Rory. He offered the dog the scent again. "Find it."

Rory's nose went up in the air, his head twitched as he looked around for a way to get to his target. Quickly, Rory took off past the tree line.

Jeopardy dropped his backpack to pull out the handled bag that nobody ever wanted to use.

They'd take the CIA officer home.

Damian flashed back to the pain in Kaylie Street's family's eyes, the torment of not having Kaylie's body when her team was killed in Africa all those years ago. The CIRG hadn't found any sign of her, and Kaylie's family suffered the not knowing.

At least Echo could save this man's family *that* pain.

Rory strained at his lead ahead of Echo as the team followed behind Ty to collect the CIA officer's body.

Suddenly, Rory lay down.

Ty's fist came up to signal his brothers.

Everyone froze.

Squatting, Ty pulled his green light from his thigh pocket. "HOLD! Tripwire."

T-Rex called, "Four, get on it."

Echo Four was Nitro, their demolition ordinance guy. He moved up to check the situation.

As Damian turned to pass that information to the EBT, his body lifted into the air.

Damian was in a space of nothingness, no sound, no sight.

The heat all around him made Damian squeeze his eyes shut and hold his breath.

He clawed at the air, not knowing up or down.

Flying backward, the last thing Damian thought was *Raine!*

38

Break your trail, and blend into the local scene.
~ Moscow Rules

Thursday

"I hope you don't mind." Kendra stuck an earbud in place. "When I run, I go into my own headspace. I'm not conversational."

"That works," Raine said. "Lead the way."

Kendra sent her a smile, put the other earbud in her ear, and adjusted the music up.

They took off at a slow lope, building up speed as they left the car and headed toward the lake. It looked deep and cold. But Theresa and Kendra were right. It was beautiful out here.

The pounding of their feet sounded rhythmically amongst the occasional bird calls.

"Jack here."

Cough.

"We've moved our vehicles into your area. You have three support operators minutes away. Your location is difficult to secure. We can only put our cars in the general area. This is the problem—Kendra refused any security support. We've run different scenarios, and it all comes out that if Kendra sees us, she'll know she's being surveilled even though she said not to. And it would mean you're somehow involved in that. It would burn your cover. Kendra might mention something to the other women. Since we don't know the channel of communication, the operation could be blown."

Cough.

"Head on a swivel. Let us know first sign of anything that catches your attention. Chances are good that any attack wouldn't come until after Saturday."

The women ran the entire arc of the road curving along the lake, turned, and ran back toward the car. As they approached, Raine thought of various reasons that she could get Kendra back in the car and headed home. Twisted ankle would take days of faking. She could say she got her period early. Gross. Way too much information for a new acquaintance. Especially if she had to sit on the woman's beige cloth seats.

With her earplugs in her ears, Kendra was in the zone.

Raine would probably have to swat at her to get her attention.

"We just passed the car. We're up on the road," Raine ventured after letting Kendra get several strides ahead of her.

They ran down the road and hung a left onto another dirt and gravel road.

"Off the main road, heading back toward the river," Raine said.

"Jack copy. Gator and Striker checked out that road. They used thermal vision to the distance of line of sight. They didn't pick up anything bigger than a raccoon. There are no cars. It's a one-way road, and we're watching the opening. It looks like you're good to go. We can drive down the road if you need us."

"Copy," she said.

Raine hoped that with Damian downrange, she'd get the threat. Once that came in, she'd immediately announce everywhere that Damian had re-upped and pull the target on to her. Damian and Raine had planned to spend a lot of time off base once Damian "signed the contract." Of course, when they did, it would be highly orchestrated with plenty of support. And bullet-resistant vests.

Yeah, even though they cleared the area, Raine's bones just didn't feel right.

They made it all the way down to the end of the road. Kendra circled and high-fived Raine as they passed each other. Raine was rounding the end to come up behind Kendra.

"Your shoelace has come undone," Raine called out. Her voice didn't have much in the way of volume control. Her words were barely above conversational.

Kendra didn't hear her.

Raine sped up to get closer. A pop song blared from Kendra's earphones.

Raine pushed to collapse the space so she could tap Kendra's shoulder. Just as Raine reached out her arm, a bullet whizzed through the space between their heads and cracked into the tree to the side.

Bark exploded outward.

"Suppressed shots fired. Shots fired. Shots fired." Raine leaped forward and tackled Kendra to the ground.

"Roger. You're taking suppressed fire. Our team is moving."

"What in the name of Heaven are you doing?" Kendra asked, squirming and kicking at Raine.

Raine yanked the earbuds from Kendra's ears. "My voice, I can't yell to warn you. Shots fired. We have to get into the tree line."

"Oh, you poor thing," Kendra said. "This is your PTSD, isn't it? You're hallucinating? Can you let me up? Let me take you home and get you some help," she said kindly.

"Yeah, it's PTSD only if I can explode bark off the tree with the power of my mind," Raine said as she shifted down and tied Kendra's shoe, pulling a quick triple bow so they wouldn't get tripped up in the woods.

They were going to have to run for it.

There was an explosion of dirt next to Kendra's head.

Kendra's eyes stretched wide. Her facial muscles froze in place.

Raine didn't have time to coddle her. She scooped up a handful of Kendra's waistband and grabbed up a chunk of shirt. Raine shoved into her feet, bodily lifting Kendra along with her. Keeping her hand on the woman's pants, Raine grabbed hold of Kendra's ponytail, so she had control of Kendra's head. Bending them both over, Raine hightailed it into the tree line, dragging Kendra with her.

There, the women bobbed and weaved from tree to tree. Raine was hoping to gain distance.

Though Raine well knew, you can't outrun a bullet.

Raine rethought the suppressed fire call.

"Be aware, I haven't seen anyone. That could be a sniper like the one in D.C. instead of a pistol with a suppressor."

"What?" Kendra panted out. "D.C. sniper?"

"Heading for the water," Raine said.

"Jack. Copy."

A bullet whizzed past her ear.

Their feet tangling into each other was slowing them.

"Kendra, for the love of god, you have to run as fast as you have ever run in your life. We're aiming for the Little River and over the bank. Do you hear me?"

"Yes!"

Raine let go of her. "Run. Go. Go. Go."

A bullet tagged Kendra in the arm.

Raine saw a sudden bright red streak but couldn't tell how bad it was as Kendra pumped her arms and sprinted forward.

"Kendra's been hit. Left arm wound," Raine panted out.

Kendra didn't seem to notice. Adrenaline had its benefits. The two women flew through the woods and slipped down the bank. They were up to their chests in fast-moving water coming down from the mountains after a recent storm.

"In the water. Hurry. It's freezing cold."

"Hurry, and do what?" Kendra was pressed up against the bank, holding herself steady on a root and gasping for oxygen.

She still hadn't noticed she was bleeding from her wound. It was hard to tell with bullet wounds how bad they were.

While her wound was low priority, Raine took a moment to focus on it.

"Jack here. I have a visual on the wound. I am apprising the team and first responders. It looks like she's not aware. For now, I wouldn't call any attention to it. We don't know how she'll respond. If she screams, you've got bigger problems."

Raine coughed.

Yeah, sometimes ignorance was bliss, Raine thought. She quieted her mind, focusing on options.

If the shooter came up on them here, it would be as easy as shooting fish in a barrel.

Raine pointed up toward the bend. There was a log where debris had gathered. They could hide behind that—if the shooter didn't have thermal vision.

As Raine slogged through the slippery clay, crouching to keep her head below the bank, she set the timer on her watch for fifteen minutes and a vibrating alarm. That was the most time the two of them could stay in the water before they were in real danger of succumbing to hypothermia.

She looked at her watch.

"Good copy. We need to get you out of the water in less than fifteen mikes." Jack used the military word mikes to mean minutes.

At the nest of sticks and leaves, Raine looked for an entry point.

She waded up to the log and went under, finding her way to a little hollowed area that gave her a visual upstream.

Raine had been careful to keep her eyes shut while she was underwater. Those video contacts were doing a great job keeping her in communication with her team.

Jack would be able to analyze where she was and what she was seeing back at the Strike Force command post.

Raine slid herself back out to direct Kendra.

Her movements loosened the mud, making the water opaque. Raine hoped that the swift current would clear it, so the bad guys didn't have a trail to her hideout.

Raine glanced up at the far bank and contemplated that exit, then rejected it. They'd still be in line for another bullet.

Grabbing Kendra, Raine pulled her back into the space she'd found under the debris.

Surely, the shooter saw the women jump into the water.

Now their fates depended on what arrived first, her backup, the shooter, or hypothermia.

The two women were up to their necks in water behind their debris screen.

"We can't stay here. We'll die of exposure." Raine looked at the timer for Jack's sake.

"Jack here. The team is searching for the sniper. No sense pulling you out of there if everyone's in his scope. First responders were alerted and are coming lights and sirens."

"Roger that." She turned to Kendra. "We have to hug each other tight and try to protect our core heat. Pull your legs up. Tuck everything in, but try not to agitate the water, that mud has to clear, or they'll find us."

"Ok-k-k-k-k-kay," she chattered.

"Kendra, be brave. We're not alone. Help is coming."

"No, it's not. No one knows we're here. No one would find us here. Probably ever. It's a hunter. We just need to make noise, so he knows we're not a deer."

"You're wearing neon pink pants, Kendra. You're not a deer."

She was silent and scowling.

"He shot the tree head height. I've never seen a deer that tall, have you?"

"He might not be able to see height from where he was."

Time to shine a little light on the situation for her. "Kendra, is there a reason why someone might be shooting at you?"

Kendra stilled. Her trembling stopped. Her face shifted to a look of horror. "I didn't believe them."

"Who? What?" Raine asked.

"Jack here. An unidentified subject has been spotted, running in the direction of Little River. Our computer listening systems picked up his voice. I've augmented the sound. I don't recognize the language. I'll put it through the AI language system for translation."

"Let me try," Raine said.

"Try what?" Kendra asked.

Raine wasn't ready to give up her undercover status yet. "I'm trying to get into a better position with my foot."

"Jack here. This is the recording."

Raine listened, picking out several words in Slovak.

"One more time," Raine said.

"Do you need me to move somewhere?" Kendra asked.

Jack played it again. Then Again. And a third time. It was hard to hear through the man's panting. "In the river. We thought this might happen. Check the video feed and give me her location," Raine said.

"In the river. We thought that might happen. Check the video feed and give me her location. Copy. Which language was spoken? Cough once for Slovak, twice for Bulgarian, three times for Russian."

Raine coughed once.

Suppressed shots popped, and pistol fire answered.

"Jack here. We don't have eyes on. Gator fired into a tree. Hopefully, we can trick the bad guys into thinking they've been located."

The water flowed past them.

Kendra moaned.

"Sit rep," Jack said, asking for her situation report.

"C-c-c-c-cold." Raine checked the time. It always stunned her how the brain played tricks. She could swear they were in the water for two or three minutes, but the timer said twelve.

Kendra's lips were blue. Her skin pale.

"We'll need a rescue squad for hypothermia," she said.

Kendra nodded her head, emphatically.

"At the fifteen-minute mark, we're getting out of the water. We can die down here as easily as with a bullet."

"Roger. Ambulance and police one mike out," Jack said.

They could handle a minute for the sirens to blow the bad guy out of the area.

"Okay," Kendra chattered. "We'll get out then and run toward the car. That'll keep us warm. Running."

Raine tapped her ear then pointed at the air so Kendra would listen.

The sirens blare came closer, and closer, and closer.

"Gator's going over the side of the bank. The splash you hear is Gator in the water. How copy?"

"Good. Help is here."

"Ma'am?" Gator hollered. "Ma'am? Where are you?"

"Here!" Raine tried to call out with what vocal capacity she had.

Kendra slapped a hand over Raine's mouth, glared into her eyes, and shook her head no.

39

Hide small operative motions in larger non-threatening motions.
~Moscow Rules

THURSDAY

AT THE HOSPITAL, Raine was processed through the emergency department, declared stable, and moved to a room for warming therapy.

Kendra headed into surgery. The bullet was lodged just under the skin in the fleshy part of her arm. The FBI wanted that bullet. And they wanted to have a talk with Kendra about the choice of moving to a safe house versus protective custody.

They needed Kendra out of the picture, so the only target was a trained operator, Raine.

Striker came into her room. "You have more color. How long are they keeping you here?"

"I don't know, whatever's convenient for them, I'd suppose.

They have warm liquids in my I.V. They're not pleased that my chest was underwater for so long."

"I wasn't pleased either." Striker had moss-green eyes that held intelligence and compassion.

"Blaze is outside your door and will take you home after your release. Gator drove Kendra's car back to her house. We're getting you a new phone. Yours isn't salvageable."

"Thank you. My hearing aids did a great job. Deep told me water resistant, I wasn't sure if they'd survive my plunge."

"We'll change those out too, just to be sure." Striker stood beside her bed.

She wondered why he didn't pull the chair over. "I was lying here thinking about Theresa being a no-show for today's jog. One, I was glad I didn't have both women under my protection. Two, that flat tire was convenient."

"Agreed. Though we went back and checked video. Her driveway is at the edge of the lens's view. She drove in last night and parked. This morning she saw the tire. A truck came and changed it out for her."

"Looks innocent."

"Raine. I need to apprise you of a situation," Striker said.

Raine didn't like that his face had gone stoic. She held the heating blanket to her chest as she raised her bed up to sitting.

"This information was passed to me through Frost at the FBI. They've asked me to share this information with you. But it's considered classified."

Cold splashed through her system. Raine started trembling again.

"Echo was on their mission and sustained casualties."

She gripped at the sheets. "How bad?"

"This is what I know, the military contacted the FBI since Damian's their agent. They have no further updates other than operators for the host country and from Echo sustained casualties.

Frost was told that she would be updated as information became available. Frost wants you to know that she will immediately reach out to Strike Force, and we will *immediately* tell you of anything new."

"Thank you," she chattered out. "Our missions went sideways for both of us. Are they not saying if there were any KIA?"

"I'd imagine they would be very guarded with that information and absolutely sure before they presented it as fact."

Raine nodded.

"Can I get you anything?"

"Thank you. I'm fine." Masking her emotions in a professional setting was one of the only reasons Raine might be grateful that her voice didn't inflect.

She waited for Striker to excuse himself before her face crumpled and the sob escaped.

Damian!

RAINE SIGNED the hospital papers and walked out of the door, where she found Blaze standing. He wore jeans and a T-shirt and fit right in with his military-short haircut, though his russet curls seemed to have a mind of their own.

She was wearing fleece-lined pants, a T-shirt, and a thick sweater, though it was in the lower seventies outside.

Gator had brought fresh clothes and dry shoes by earlier with a new phone and the new hearing aids.

Concierge service. She could get used to this.

Without a word, she and Blaze moved out of the hospital. The sky was black and moonless.

Blaze rested his fingers on her low back as he steered her toward his car. Raine knew it was a security tactic. Blaze did that so if shit hit the fan, he could either grab her pants and yank her to the ground or slide his hand up to her neck and push her head down as they ran, similar to what she'd done to Kendra earlier.

Raine hoped to get a sit-rep on how Kendra was doing.

And Damian.

Blaze opened the passenger door for her, his head on a swivel, doing his close protection specialist thing.

It was good that someone was clear-minded.

Raine wasn't firing on all cylinders. Her mind was on Damian. And her earlier hypothermia was doing a job on her brain functioning.

"Anything?" she asked without giving any context as Blaze shut his door and started the engine.

Blaze had been a SEAL. He'd know that the only thing she cared about in this moment was that the teams were safe and getting the medical help they needed.

"We don't have anything new about Echo. We don't know what the military has disclosed to the wives. Until they bring it up, you are not authorized to share."

"Copy."

"We're going to take a drive, so you can get an update on your mission."

Raine sat quietly, watching out the window.

A cold hand wrapped her heart. She tried to shake it off.

After a distance, Blaze pulled into the empty parking lot of a church. He tapped the red button.

"Blaze and Raine available for communications."

"Deep here. Copy. I'm bringing the others online. Hold, please."

Raine started trembling again.

Blaze reached out and turned up the heat.

She sent him a tight-lipped smile as a thank you. Raine was exhausted. She'd love to blame her shaking on the hypothermia, but she knew that wasn't the problem.

"Hello?" It was Hasan's voice.

"Raine and Blaze on comms," Raine said. "We're in a Strike Force car off property."

"Hasan here. I'm in the Strike Force war room. Present are Deep—Strike Force, Frost—FBI, and a representative of the organization that supports the work of Zelda Fitzgerald."

That unidentified third party meant that Raine couldn't ask for an update on Echo. *On Damian.*

"Congratulations, Mrs. Prescott," Hasan said. "You got your threatening email. We timed opening it so if anyone was cross-checking, you opened it on your phone, and it had the hospital GPS coordinates."

"Amazing that we have the technology to do all that." She tipped her head. "Can I ask, did it come in before or after the attack?"

"You had already arrived at Emergency. It's interesting timing, isn't it?" Hasan asked rhetorically. "I've asked our guest to stay while we caught you up. Once we've had our background discussion, our guest has another meeting to attend, and we can further advance our mission."

"Yes, sir," Raine said.

"With our permission," Hasan continued. "Zelda looped her organization into this case, and they were able to provide insight as to what's happening. We have a target."

"A target?" That was a surprise. "Good. Start at the top."

"As we discussed, Dancing Bear hacked into the military spouses' email accounts on a phishing expedition. Their spyware was able to attach to the spreadsheets of personal information of military families. As these spreadsheets were shared through unsecured email sites, the spyware reached more and more military families. This data was collected, and the Prokhorovs' AI system scraped the data. This has been happening for years. The last Twitter hack by Dancing Bear merely exposed the crime."

"Okay." Raine leaned forward, put her elbows on her knees, and hung her head, focusing past the chitter of worry about Echo team that wouldn't be quieted.

"Another point that we've touched upon. American girls—who were selected for being attractive, rebellious, and from difficult homes—were recruited by the Zoric families to work at the Prokhorov bot farms."

"Where they worked as pen pals for the American troops," Raine said.

"They focused on soldiers who could give them information about troop movements." The unidentified man had a low gravelly voice. "They tried to pick out and focus on the guys who were heading toward special forces. They continued their relationships even as the men married others. The girls weren't jealous. They would keep writing. Very supportive. Very loving. They were bringing joy."

"And by joy, you mean very personal photos for the guys?" Raine asked.

"Exactly. Those photos were rewards for detailed information," the gravel voice added. "Lisa Griffin, FBI, tasked the computer to search our data systems to see if any of the American women recruited to the bot farms either joined the U.S. military or married into the military."

"And you found someone?" That was shocking.

"We found thirty-two instances of this occurring," Gravel said.

"My understanding," Raine said. "Is that you've known about the women and intervened for a while now. Out of curiosity, how did you track down the targeted soldiers so you could pursue a disinformation campaign?"

"We followed the women's correspondence in different ways. At one point, for example, over a hundred female pen pals listed a single apartment in Virginia as their place of residence. The soldier's mail was received at this location. It was then put in a box and two-day mailed to the bot farm in Slovakia where the girls worked. The women listing the Virginia address all had the same paid job in the United States, data information specialist. They all paid US taxes. On the surface, it looked like they were young women living an everyday American life in the United States. This is simplifying the structure, but the end result is that in a background check, they would come up clean. All electric correspondence was routed through that location. Therefore, to anyone who knows about finding locations, it would also seem legitimate."

"Thank you," Raine said. "And you're going to leave the women in place?"

"Yes. As far as we can tell, they are working in Slovakia of their own volition. If we find out otherwise, we will help them. But if they *want* to be there, trying to gather intelligence on the U.S. military, we will use them for counterterrorism measures."

"Thirty-two pen pal women were discovered in our ranks," Raine said, feeling overwhelmed by the duplicity.

"That cannot continue," Hasan said. "We are determining what to do with this information."

"Thank you, sir," Raine said. That hadn't been what she wanted to know. What she wanted to know was. "Hasan, you said a single target. Has the target been narrowed down from the thirty-two women to one woman at Fort Bragg?"

"Affirmative," Hasan said. "Your neighbor Theresa."

"Theresa, Pelt's wife from Lima?"

"Yes, that's right," Hasan said.

Raine's brow furrowed. "Lucy said she was outside."

"I'm sorry?" Hasan asked.

"Lucy McDonald said she was outside when she arranged to go to Martha's house in D.C. We didn't know how the Washington attackers could get themselves organized that quickly. If Lucy had been outside her house, Theresa lives next door. It's been hot out. People have their windows open. Theresa could have heard the whole conversation. Zoric had a specialty team in the area to attack

Todor. If Theresa let her handler know about Lucy's escape, Theresa's handler could pass the information to the Zoric team, and the Zoric team was free Friday night. Saturday night, they'd be doing the tunnel kidnapping."

"That timeline works," Hasan said.

"Theresa…" Raine went back in her mind thinking about their interactions. "She encouraged Kendra to change her jogging path to the remote area that wasn't securable. She could have driven anywhere, pushed a nail or two into her tire, and driven home to have it deflate overnight. Acted it out, just to complete the cover."

"Yes," Hasan said.

"Out of curiosity, how did Pelt meet her?"

"We called Lucy McDonald to see if she knew the story. It turns out, Theresa was Pelt's buddy's pen pal. The buddy mentioned Pelt was off to Ranger school. When he was there, Theresa started sending him encouraging mail. They hit it off, and they met up in various places when Pelt was on leave."

"The Prokhorovs flew her home for that?"

"Her passport seems to line up that way," Hasan said.

"You've had a busy day. Kudos."

"Hold, please," Hasan said. Then over the ambient noise, Raine heard everyone thanking the unidentified man, a door opened, a door shut. "I'm back. We are now Hasan, Frost, and Deep."

"Okay, next steps?" Raine asked. "Have you heard anything back about Echo?"

"Echo sustained casualties to their team."

"The whole team?" Raine thought she might vomit. She looked around and put her hand on the car's door handle.

"That's my understanding," Hasan said. "Both their team and their support team from the host nation. We don't know anything more other than a rescue effort was underway. I know this is difficult, but I need you to focus."

Raine decided it was best not to reply. She sat there and glowered out the window.

"What's going on with Kendra?" she asked after a moment of silence. "Theresa is going to ask when she sees that I've shown up without her."

"Truth as much as possible. Let's reframe. How about this," Frost asked. "You were out for a jog. You were on a road near a farm. You guessed the owner was target practicing and didn't realize anyone was out there in the remote location. You both ran to the Little River, jumped in, tell them you have an app that calls 9-1-1 if there are unusual body movements."

"With their computer capabilities, they could see that's not true. I have to tell the truth, or they'll know I know."

"Lynx called 9-1-1 and pretended to be you. We routed the call through your phone. Luckily, it was still functional at that point."

"That was well organized. Thank you, Strike Force."

"Continuing your story, Kendra got tagged by a bullet." Hasan laid out the cover story. "Kendra's fine. It was just a graze. The police got the farmer to stop shooting. They pulled you out of the river. She had stitches, and one of her friends picked her up. You don't know where she went from there. But the friend was going to take care of her for a few days."

"I don't know the friend's name?" Raine asked.

"Call her Peggy," Hasan said.

"Peggy is the friend. Peggy. Peggy. Got it."

"You will tell everyone that Damian signed his new contract on the way out the door on this mission."

"Depending on what went down on their mission…" Raine couldn't finish the thought.

"At this juncture, with so much at risk," Hasan said. "No matter what, we'll need to press forward. If…*if* there is a reason for Damian not to be back working as your partner, we will declare him to be on another black op, he's re-upped, and you will continue functioning in your role. I'm sorry, I know this is hard."

"Keep going," Raine said.

"We'll say that he's black ops and keep you in play. Each of the attacks has happened within twenty-four hours of their telling people the contracts were signed. You should tell Theresa tonight if she comes to check on you, which we think she will find out what happened to Kendra. Certainly by tomorrow. This should mean that depending on when you tell her and when you leave the fort—Friday or Saturday—you should get attacked. We're developing a scenario that will be as safe as we can make it for you, protecting citizens as well as drawing out the attackers. We need them in custody. Theresa, by the way, is now under FBI surveillance. We have an arrest warrant for her. We'll take her in for questioning as soon as we know she can't tip off the sniper. We want them so we can flip them."

"In reality, Kendra's not with friend Peggy. She's in a safe house." Raine rubbed her hands over her knees. Her feet had gone numb. "Right? I don't need to worry about her?"

"Affirmative," Hasan said. "So, Raine, that's where we are. Strike Force will continue to support you in any way they can."

"They've been stellar," Raine said.

"Good. Get some sleep. It'll be a big day tomorrow."

"Wilco. Good night everyone."

Blaze ended the comms and turned her way. "Home?"

"I'd prefer a bar and a bottle of rum. But yes, thank you, Blaze, home, I guess it is."

Hopefully, she'd get the all-clear call letting her know if Damian survived.

40

Keep your options open.
~ Moscow Rules

Thursday Night

Blaze stopped at the curb in front of her house to let Raine out.

She turned once she reached her front door and raised her hand to Blaze as a good-bye and thank you, then pushed her key into the door.

As she was pulling the door closed behind her, Raine looked across to Theresa's house. The curtain in Theresa's living room fell straight. Raine couldn't deal with Theresa tonight. She locked the door and turned off her outdoor lights. Raine figured if Theresa banged on her door, she'd say she'd taken out her hearing aids. Sorry.

She climbed the stairs and headed straight for the bathroom, where she filled the tub with hot water.

Raine had been on missions when her friends and colleagues had been injured or killed. There was a brief moment when they were honored, then everything continued as usual. A war was a war. A mission a mission. There was no time out for personal grief and processing. There was pushing forward.

The thought of losing Damian again felt too big to put inside her body.

Until she took out the contacts and hearing aids, she didn't have the luxury of privacy to let her emotions explode out of her. She didn't want to let go of her comms in case they had any word on Damian. But damming it all up wasn't working. Her emotions leaked from her nose—that wouldn't stop running—and her eyes. It escaped with sighs and little groans.

With the bathroom lights off, Raine climbed into the tub and steeped until the water became a dark tea of distress, then she let the water swirl down the drain.

Raine didn't know what else to do, so she went to bed.

She lay on her back, wrapped in a bath towel. The light on. Raine held up her left hand, examining her fake wedding and engagement rings. And she tried to hold her thoughts in check.

She was mobilized on a mission.

Lives were on the line.

No matter how much pain she was experiencing, she was mission first.

This one last time, she promised herself.

For Echo.

"Gator here." She heard softly over her comms as if Gator was trying to ease into her headspace, not wanting to startle her.

Raine bolted to her feet anyway.

"You turned your front lights off. We have an unknown subject walking up the lawn toward your front door in our night vision."

"Theresa?"

"A figure."

Raine pulled open a drawer and grabbed at a T-shirt and a pair of yoga pants. She pulled them on and raced down the stairs.

"Stop," Gator said in her ear. "You'd have no way of telling that someone is approaching your house."

He was right—*Head in the game, Raine.*

She bounced on the balls of her feet, desperate to pull the door wide. And just when she couldn't stand it another second, the door popped open.

There stood Damian.

Her hands came to her mouth, and she sucked in the scream that Raine wanted to expel from her lungs. She swayed as her legs tried to buckle.

Damian stalked two steps forward and caught her by the arms.

She closed her eyes so Gator wouldn't see him kissing her. "Before I open my eyes. Tell me what happened. How badly are you hurt? Frost said Echo team all took a hit."

"It's okay to look. Nothing gross is hanging out. I have all my limbs."

She blinked her eyes open.

"Slight concussion from an explosion. Cuts. Bruises. First degree burns."

"You smell like burned hair. And the others?"

He turned and looked down in the bowl by the door, snagging up the car keys.

Raine nodded and followed him out, barefooted, checking that the door locked behind them, even if Strike Force had their eyes on the place.

"Can you drive?" Damian asked.

She accepted the keys and slid behind the wheel.

Three blocks from the house, he said, "That mission was FUBAR. No one on Echo was seriously injured. Some of our partner forces are worse off than we are. They were closest to the explosion. We mostly got the blast concussion. A wild boar stumbled across a tripwire. The pig was vaporized."

"Man, you didn't even get BBQ out of the deal."

"Disappointing. That partnering team will be getting the care they need. Echo got patched and released back into the wild. We flew home."

"Was your mission successful?"

"We found what we were looking for. But we were late to the scene."

"I'm sorry. That always feels so wrong."

"Okay, your turn. You have a hospital bracelet on your wrist. I was told hypothermia, which is quite the feat when it's in the mid-seventies."

"I have specialized talents."

"Some I know personally." He chuckled. "Frost caught me up on what happened while I was up at the TOC. So let me give you the newest brief. Kendra and Lucy are in a safe house. No one else is scheduled to re-up for three weeks. You've received your threat. You're supposed to communicate to Theresa that I signed before I took off on this mission. Then we go out and try to lure the killers into the open."

"I've been thinking about that. I'm not sure it'll work if you're there with me."

"If they're trying to damage the Unit, they'll attack when your husband is there and unable to keep you safe. You want to talk about breaking a man? That would do it. They'll want to watch me watch."

"Huh." She processed that idea. "Sadly, I think you're probably right."

Raine pulled into a darkened parking lot. "Turning off comms," she said.

"Gator here. I'll ping you through the car's system if there's an emergency."

Raine pulled out the hearing aids and put them in the cupholder.

She sighed over and over as if her breath could move this burden out of her system. "Damian." She swallowed hard as she looked at him.

They held hands in the quiet for a long time.

"Tell me," he said.

"I can't do this anymore. I can't."

The silence became thick between them.

"Do you mean us?" Damian finally asked, his voice barely above a whisper. "We moved pretty fast. I'm sorry if that was overwhelming."

She tapped his thigh with her free hand. "No. I'm so sorry you thought that. Not us. This. My job."

He tipped his head.

"When is it enough? When have we done our share? The bullets and the explosions. The fear. The pain. I've done my bit, I think. *You* have." Then a thought snagged her. She shifted her body to better face him.

"When I left the Army, I went to work for DIA as a field operator. When you left Delta, you went right back to the same work in the CIRG. But now that I'm thinking about it, you left that behind. You're Special Agent in Charge Damian Prescott. You run a joint task force. You don't do fieldwork. You're a strategist. A decision-maker."

She looked down at how their fingers entwined while she thought.

"When you went out last Friday and followed Todor's car into the tunnel, you had already seen my face. You planned to be on hand that night but sent Finley and Griffin in to the event. You were in the field knowing I was going to be there."

"Yes."

"And you came down here to Fort Bragg because you knew that if it wasn't you, it would be someone. They'd go grab someone with a Delta background, unmarried, out of the CIRG and put them on this case. I would have had to make up some story about falling in love with someone else, and I would have slept in their bed. But you came instead to protect me from that. And here I was dodging bullets, and you were…blown up." She shook her head. "Why would you do that, Damian? You were out of this crap. Why come back?"

"That's easy," Damian said. "It's because I wasn't there the last time, Raine drop. Because I wouldn't be able to live with myself if I wasn't here this time."

"You know what I do for a living. You *can't* protect me."

"No, but I could be here this time and try."

"God, Damian, I feel horrible. You were *blown up* because of me."

"I was thrown by a blast concussion. Admittedly, not something I want to do again."

"Me either." She exhaled forcibly. "I can't."

"That's where this conversation started. What can't you do?"

"My job. This is going to be my last mission. I'm resigning."

"And Todor Bilov?"

"I'm not convinced he's my ticket into where I needed to go. I'll have Cammy Burke die in a car crash, or easier, maybe I'll just tell him I've thought about it, and I'm not interested in him. Block his phone number." She gave a little chuckle.

"This is serious? You mean this?"

"This work is never done. Our friends have died, their blood has spilled into the soil, and the war goes on anyway. At some point, I have to say I've done my share. I need more to my life. I want *you* in my life. And I don't want you in my life worried about me all the time."

"Before my mom got sick before you were hurt, we had a good plan. Children, a family, warmth, we talked about our house and our garden. I miss those dreams."

"It wasn't my injury that stopped us. It was the punch."

"In Eric's kitchen. I know what you thought was happening. You're wrong. Mostly."

"I would very much like that to be the case." Raine held her breath.

"I was never jealous. I promised a friend that I'd never tell her story, so I won't. Eric did something that I never thought in a million years Eric would do."

"But you're sure he did?"

"While I was in Nigeria looking for Kaylie, my friend brought Eric up on charges, and he went to prison with a ten-year sentence."

"Oh, wow. Eric… That's unfathomable."

"I showed up that night to put the fear of God into him, to keep him from going anywhere near her. When I saw you in his arms, something in me snapped. That punch came from a place of rage. I am sorry that you were there and saw it. I'm *not* your dad, Raine. I trust you. And I trust that you'd tell me if you were done with our relationship, and you wanted to move on. It's your life to do with as you wish. But Raine, I wish I had been there for you while you were recovering."

"I couldn't have you there. I would have tried to be all right for you, and I wasn't. I needed that time, to be honest, and fall apart, so I could put myself back together again."

"I can understand that." He played with the fake wedding rings around her ring finger. "Where are we now?"

"I have always loved you." Her words in her ears seemed insincere without an inflection. It was too dark for him to see her expression.

"Yes."

"I *still* love you," she said.

"I love you, too. I want to love you better. I want to hold your hand. I want to make love to you without hesitation. I want to be angry and sad and quiet with you. I want you to be you. I want you to give us a chance."

"No." She shook her head.

"Not even a chance, Raine drop?"

"No. I don't think so. It never really works out when you give something a chance. I mean, then there are even odds that you'll fail. I think it would be better if we—"

She scratched at her forehead.

"I want to have this conversation, Damian. But it's too important. I need to be clear-minded. Kendra's attack and then you… They told me there were casualties. I didn't know if you'd survived. Making declarations tonight is a mistake. Damian, I need us to get through this mission. You will understand this when I say I have a debt to pay. Ty, T-Rex, Echo, and the whole Delta Force family."

"Focus on the mission. Then we can make decisions. Okay." He smoothed his thumb back and forth over her hand. "Raine, what do you need right now?"

"I want to go back to the house and get into bed with you. I want you to let me look at your body, so I know how you've been hurt. Then, I want you to hold me tight all night long."

"Good, I need that, too."

41

Once is an accident, twice is a coincidence, but three times is enemy action.

~ Moscow Rules

Friday

Raine was getting ready to head over to Theresa's house. She needed to make sure that Theresa knew Damian had re-upped. Then she'd hand Theresa the story about Kendra. Raine would make sure that Theresa knew where and when the Slovakian team could tag Damian and her.

"Jack here. Hold."

Raine's hand had just landed on the front doorknob.

"Theresa's on her way over. It looks like she's bearing food. I wouldn't eat it unless she does." Jack chuckled.

"Yeah, no kidding. That's something to watch for, Novichok nerve agents on my doorknobs and polonium tea."

"That would suck for sure," Jack said as the doorbell rang.

Raine answered it with a smile for Theresa. "Hey, there. Come on in."

Theresa pushed the plate toward her. "I was making banana bread and thought you might like some."

"That's awfully nice of you." Raine took the plate and gestured toward her kitchen. "Want to come in and have a slice with a cup of tea?"

"Actually, that sounds nice." Theresa followed Raine into the kitchen. "Hey, Damian. I heard Echo had a rough time of it. I'm glad everyone is home and mending. How's your head?"

"I need to lay low for a couple of days. The military is starting to take brain injuries more seriously. They want to make sure they keep their operators in top condition."

"Will this impact your decision making about staying in? I hear Budge just signed on again." Theresa pulled out a chair and sat.

"Raine and I decided it feels good to be back at the fort. I signed my contract as I was heading out the door to our last mission. Looks like we'll be neighbors for years to come."

"Congratulations to you both." Theresa turned calculating eyes toward Raine.

"Tea or coffee?" Raine asked.

"If you already have coffee made, I'll have that. I drink it black." She ran her fingers down a strand of hair in a self-soothing gesture. "How was your jog yesterday with Kendra? I was disappointed I didn't get to go. I love the lake when no one's there. It's so peaceful."

Raine wandered over with three plates, a knife, and some forks. She stood behind Theresa's back and mouthed to Damian, "Don't eat the bread."

His eyes flashed to Theresa and back to her.

Theresa turned toward Raine. And Raine immediately put her

hands in a little heart shape over her chest and sent a wink Damian's way to cover.

While she set a coffee mug in front of Theresa, Raine fed her the decided upon Kendra storyline about the farmer doing target practice, the bullet wound, the quick swim.

"How did the police cars know to come?" Theresa asked.

Raine sliced the bread while she heard Jack in her ear. "Remember, you have a danger app on your phone."

"When the first shot hit the tree, I grabbed Kendra, and we fell to the ground," Raine explained. "I have a safety app on my phone that alerts the police if I move in a certain way like I fall, or it thinks I'm in a fight. Well, first it buzzes me, and if I don't answer, it opens up and records and sends the information to the police. Lucky us! The phone heard me tell Kendra that there were shots coming in our direction, and they sent police and a rescue squad right away. You should get it on your phone, too. It works great, apparently."

Theresa shook her head. "Selfish as this sounds, thank goodness for my flat tire. I would have been terrible in that scenario. Wow. I'm so glad you two are okay."

Raine shrugged. "Farms and target practice, one should kind of expect it out in the country. Can I cut you a slice of banana bread?"

"Maybe in a little bit." She turned to Damian. "What are your plans while you're lying low?"

"Today, I'm binge-watching some TV." He lifted his chin toward Raine. "Raine wants to get going on her art for the new book."

"Oh! I ordered three of your books for my kids. I'm excited to get them in."

"I didn't write them. I'm the illustrator," Raine said.

"Still, I want you to autograph them." She turned back to Damian. "You'll be home today. Looks like rain on Saturday. Are you going to cocoon?"

"We're going out to Shadow Ridge and park the car," Raine

said. They'd been given the specifics of the takedown last night. And she needed to feed just the right story to Theresa.

"When we were deployed to separate areas back when I was in the military, Damian and I would listen to the same books on tape and talk about them. With so little that could be discussed from our jobs and our lives, it was one of the ways that we had something in common to talk about. Anyway, once we got home, we've kept up the tradition. One of the things we like to do is go to a pretty site and hold hands while we listen to a book together." She stopped and sent a loving look toward Damian, no seed needed to be searched for or pulled up. "It's especially nice if it's raining."

"That's romantic. Shadow Ridge is a well-known make-out spot. But not on a rainy Saturday. You'll probably have it all to yourselves."

"We hope so," Damian said.

Theresa stood. "I should be getting back. I left the kids in front of the TV. I can let myself out." And she left.

Jack was in her ear. "She didn't eat the bread."

Raine walked over to the trash. "Yup, I'm going to save you lab tests. I'm dumping it in the bin."

Saturday

They were on chapter fourteen of their book on tape.

They'd eaten a picnic lunch.

Draped in rain ponchos, they'd risked getting out of the car to go behind the bushes to pee.

Raine was rubbing circulation back into her legs. "I hope I don't have to run anywhere. My feet fell asleep," she grumped.

Her phone rang with the Iniquus tone. "Deep here. Todor's calling in. You're at your apartment."

"Let it go to voice mail," she said. "Thanks, Deep."

"Yes, ma'am."

Damian tapped the radio to pause their audiobook. "Todor's a day early."

"Interesting, huh?"

"Maybe. You can't read too much into that."

The phone rang again. This time it was Hasan's ringtone. Raine answered on speakerphone. "Hello?"

"Todor just called you a day early. You didn't want to feel him out? You're just sitting in a car." His voice was terse. "You could juggle both aspects of this mission."

"No, I don't want to do that."

"I'm sure you have a reason." Hasan's inflection moved toward pissed off.

"Yes, I'm giving you my notice. I'm finishing up the Delta Force mission, and then I'm resigning from the DIA."

"Are you serious right now?" His tone immediately changed to something more placating. "You're one of our best. We need you out in the field."

"I'm serious, yes. This will be my last mission."

"It was a lot to put you in the field with Damian. I'm sorry we had to do that, but you shouldn't quit."

"I'm not a quitter, Hasan. I'm resigning to move on to other things. I had made up my mind prior to seeing Damian. He was not part of my decision-making process at the time. But I will admit, this mission solidified my conclusion."

"All right. Well, let's get through this. We can talk when you get back."

Raine rolled her eyes for Damian's benefit.

"It's getting dark. It doesn't look like the sniper is taking the bait," Hasan said. "We're calling it. Go back to your house. Stay on base until we make a second plan. Oh, and Raine."

"Yes?"

"Don't eat anything that Theresa cooks."

Raine tapped end. "Home again, home again, jiggery jig."

Damian reached back and touched Raine's barrettes. "And you didn't even get to deploy your super-secret weapons."

"I know. That kinda sucks. Well, maybe another day."

He laughed as he pressed the button, and the engine started up, blowing warm air into the cab. Damian put the car in gear, and they rolled down the hill toward the bridge. Along the way, they picked up a Strike Force escort car in the front and back.

Raine reached forward and was trying to find some atmospheric music, something slow with a jazz feel. Movement out the side of the car pulled her attention around. A rental moving van barreled toward them from between two sheds.

"Damian!" she yelled with all the sound she could get out of her throat.

Bang!

The cab hit her door. The airbag exploded toward her.

The truck pushed their car sideways between the parallel sheds on the left.

Damian slapped the red button on the dash to open comms.

There was nothing to be done as their tires scraped sideways.

Their bumpers grazed the metal shed siding. High pitched screeches—fingernails on a chalkboard, a hundredfold.

Raine set her teeth.

"Hold tight. We're with you," Jack's voice was soothingly deep against the high-pitched cacophony.

The truck increased its speed as their car was pressed through the gap in the buildings and now out the other side.

Damian pressed down on the gas to move them forward, but the speed of their sideways momentum wouldn't allow it.

There was a sudden *thunk* as their carriage hit the ground, their tires dropping over the side of the bank.

Another big push and their car slipped into the river.

"We're in the water," Damian said.

Heavy from its body armor, the engine immediately tipped straight down.

The water here was swollen and angry from the rush of rain up in the mountains.

Nose down, Raine and Damian dangled from their safety belts, looking through the front window at the murky brew.

"The backseat collapses to give access to the trunk," Jack said. "Pull the seatback with a quick jerk to release the catch."

"Have you got flotation devices back there?" Damian asked while they tried to unlatch their safety belts.

"See if you can pop the trunk and stay there until we can get to you. Strike Force is trying to acquire the tangos and secure the area."

The operators' weight pressing against their seatbelts locked the safety mechanism.

Raine reached back and pulled the knives from her barrette. "So I do get to use them." She pressed one toward Damian.

The water was rising fast. Raine's legs were wet to her shins.

They sawed furiously at the webbing of their belts.

Raine sliced through hers first.

"I'll get out of your way. I have more maneuverability." Raine twisted in her seat, grabbed the back, and pulled herself up, trying to give Damian space to get out from under the steering wheel. Her bottom was getting wet as she scrambled into the space in the back seat, reaching out and yanking at the cushion to drop down the hatch. When she looked up into the black trunk, a glow-in-the-dark T dangled, showing her the emergency exit latch.

"Come on, Damian. *Hurry.*"

Damian was wet to his neck as he pressed into the backseat space. He planted his feet and pulled and pressed his legs straight.

The car rocked with his movements and Raine fought panic.

If they didn't get the trunk open by the time the tide tipped the car, the pressure of the water would seal them in.

The water was filling to her shoulder. She pushed her head into the trunk area.

Damian pulled the latch and was shoving at the trunk lid, trying to prop it wide.

"Sit rep," Jack said into her hearing aid comms.

"I'm sucking in the last of the oxygen in the back seat. Damian is working on the trunk lid, but we're straight in and sinking fast."

"Strike Force is taking fire. They're pinned down. Anything you do right now is high danger. We have emergency responders headed to your area."

With a grunt and a desperate push, Damian got the trunk lid up.

Waves made from the rushing water hitting the solid surface of the car rained down on them.

Damian reached for her. Stabilizing with his left hand, Raine climbed his right arm like it was a rope. She grabbed on to the lip, pulled, and got one leg on the outside of the car. She braced, then reached to help Damian get there too.

Now they had decisions to make. An attempt to swim to shore was foolhardy.

"We should stay here as long as possible," Raine stated the obvious.

They didn't have long. Her shin out the back of the car was in the onslaught. In the car, it was up to her ankle.

"Wait sounds good," Damian said.

That's when the first bullet pinged against the opened trunk lid.

Raine's body flinched when she heard it, making her slip to the side. Her body was in the cold, rushing water. One leg over the lip, she had a death grip on the edge.

Damian reached down and pulled her Glock from her ankle holster. He left one hand on her ankle, helping to anchor her to the car as he aimed.

Raine fought against the thundering current to hold on. If Damian didn't get his shot, they'd be sitting ducks or drowning. She needed to give him every opportunity to get them out of this mess.

Long. Every second. Every breath. It felt like an eternity.

She clenched her muscles hard against the water that threatened to rip her away.

Bang! Damian's gun shooting at close quarters with the water augmenting the sound exploded in her ears. Two. Three. Four. Five shots. A pause.

Her head went under. She came up sputtering. With gritted teeth, she renewed her grip on the slippery interior carpeting.

Damian had her leg in a steely grip.

Bang!

Another set of three shots. She knew her gun was out of bullets. Raine wasn't sure if Damian could get to his own gun or not.

The car slipped to the side.

Damian lunged and trapped her in a hug. They were together when they spilled into the river.

The car disappeared beneath them.

They flipped onto their backs and focused their feet downstream.

"We're in the water," Raine called, hoping her comms worked. Hoping she could be heard over the river groans.

"Roger. We have eyes on you. They're rigging a throw line."

"I see them," she gasped as she bobbed up over the crest.

She and Damian gripped each other's wrists as they fought to stay afloat.

The men were still twenty yards up ahead.

Just as the two were about to pass, a rope with a floatation was tossed across their path.

Raine and Damian grabbed on, and they were pulled to shore.

"Shooters?" Damian gasped out. He was on all fours, panting for breath.

"Tangos down."

DAMIAN AND RAINE sat on the back of an EMT truck, getting checked out.

"That team must have had us staked out all day waiting for us to leave. Must have been bored out of their mind sitting there waiting for us to move."

"Sucks for them, bet they didn't even have an audiobook."

"Jack here. I have an update."

"Hold," Raine said. She took a hearing aid out and gave it to Damian so he could listen too. "Go for Damian and Raine."

"The FBI is going in Theresa's house now. They've pulled Pelt out and have him up against their car. I'm watching the new cameras we installed Thursday night. I can see into their house. Theresa's on the ground in the hall handcuffed. Looks like they have a team gathering evidence. They're walking out with electronics."

"The evidence is solid?" Raine asked. "We know for sure that this isn't circumstantial?" She focused over on the first responders who were packaging the wounded tangoes for transport.

"Theresa called in your update on Kendra, Damian's signature on the contract, and your plans for today, including your location to her handler. It's all on tape."

"Roger that," Damian said. He twisted around, so he and Raine were face to face and grinned. "Another successful mission, Rainey day."

She sent him a smile and reached for his hand, looking down at her fake wedding and engagement rings, then up to his eyes. "I think we should probably extend this successful streak." She tipped her head. "Don't you think?"

"I do indeed." Damian slipped down to take a knee in front of her. He kissed the hand that he held, then sought out her gaze. "Raine Meyers, I'm done pretending to be your fake husband. I'm ready to take on a real-life role. Won't you marry me?"

She knew everyone had just heard that over their comms because Striker, Blaze, and Gator all turned their way to see her respond.

Raine didn't care. The whole world could know.

She moved to her knees alongside Damian so she could lay her ear on his chest and listen to the strength of his heartbeat. "Without a single hesitation, yes." Then she tipped her head back so Damian could press the kiss on her lips that sealed their fates and their love together, forever.

The end

Thank you for reading Raine and Damian's story.

The Iniquus World of books continues to grow with more great stories from the ex-special forces security team members who live, work, and love in the tightly knit Iniquus family.

Would you like to learn more about K9 Rory, who did such a wonderful job of soothing Raine when she arrived at the fort?

Take a look at book one of the Cerberus Tactical K9 Series, Survival Instinct.

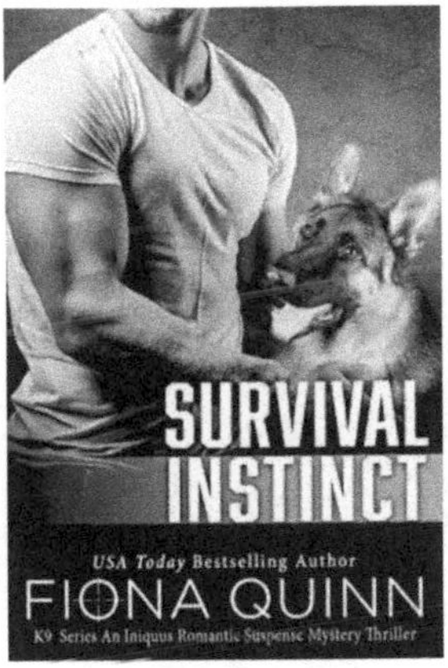

Readers, I hope you enjoyed getting to know Raine and Damian. If you had fun reading Even Odds, I'd appreciate it if you'd help others enjoy it too.

Recommend it: Just a few words to your friends, your book groups, and your social networks would be wonderful.

Review it: Please tell your fellow readers what you liked about my book by reviewing Even Odds. If you do write a review, please send me a note at FionaQuinnBooks@outlook.com so I can thank you with a personal e-mail. Or stop by my website www.FionaQuinnBooks.com to keep up with my news and chat through my contact form.

THE WORLD of INIQUUS

Chronological Order

Ubicumque, Quoties. Quidquid

Weakest Lynx (Lynx Series)

Missing Lynx (Lynx Series)

Chain Lynx (Lynx Series)

Cuff Lynx (Lynx Series)

WASP (Uncommon Enemies)

In Too DEEP (Strike Force)

Relic (Uncommon Enemies)

Mine (Kate Hamilton Mystery)

Jack Be Quick (Strike Force

Deadlock (Uncommon Enemies)

Instigator (Strike Force)

Yours (Kate Hamilton Mystery)

Gulf Lynx (Lynx Series)

Open Secret (FBI Joint Task Force)

Thorn (Uncommon Enemies)
Ours (Kate Hamilton Mysteries
Cold Red (FBI Joint Task Force)
Even Odds (FBI Joint Task Force)
Survival Instinct (Cerberus Tactical K9)
Protective Instinct (Cerberus Tactical K9)
Defender's Instinct (Cerberus Tactical K9)
Danger Signs (Delta Force Echo)
Hyper Lynx (Lynx Series)
Danger Zone (Delta Force Echo)
Danger Close (Delta Force Echo)
Cerberus Tactical K9 (Team Bravo)
Marriage Lynx (Lynx Series)

For more information visit
www.FionaQuinnBooks.com

My great appreciation ~

To my editor, **Kathleen Payne**

To my cover artist, **Melody Simmons**

To my publicist, **Margaret Daly**

To Jeanne Boisineau for sharing the beautiful tale of her Uncle Ralph and Herman. It made me cry bittersweet tears. I've included their story in this work with Jeanne's permission. I am charmed by the magic of Herman and Ralph's friendship and bond.

To Dr. Carlon for helping me find this story and for her help throughout.

To my Beta Force, who are always honest and kind at the same time.

To my Street Force, who support me and my writing with such enthusiasm. If you're interested in joining this group, please send me an email. **FionaQuinnBooks@outlook.com**

To **H. Russell** for creating the Iniquus Bible – so I can keep it all straight in my head.

Thank you to the real-world military and FBI who serve to protect us.

To all of the wonderful professionals whom I called on to get the details right. Please note: this is a work of fiction, and while I always try my best to get all of the details correct, there are times when it serves the story to go slightly to the left or right of perfection. Please understand that any mistakes or discrepancies are my authorial decision making alone and sit squarely on my shoulders.

Thank you to my family.

I send my love to my husband and my great appreciation. T, you are my rock and my resting place. You are my encouragement and my adventure. Thank you.

And of course, thank YOU for reading my stories. I'm smiling joyfully as I type this. I so appreciate you!

ABOUT THE AUTHOR

Fiona Quinn is a six-time USA Today bestselling author, a Kindle Scout winner, and an Amazon All-Star.

Quinn writes action-adventure in her Iniquus World of books, including Lynx, Strike Force, Uncommon Enemies, Kate Hamilton Mysteries, FBI Joint Task Force, Cerberus Tactical K9, and Delta Force Echo series.

She writes urban fantasy as Fiona Angelica Quinn for her Elemental Witches Series.

And, just for fun, she writes the Badge Bunny Booze Mystery Collection with her dear friend, Tina Glasneck.

Quinn is rooted in the Old Dominion, where she lives with her husband. There, she pops chocolates, devours books, and taps continuously on her laptop.

Visit www.FionaQuinnBooks.com

COPYRIGHT

Even Odds is a work of fiction. Names, characters, places, and incidents either are the product of the author's imagination or are used fictitiously, and any resemblance to actual persons, living or dead, business establishments, events, or locales is entirely coincidental.

ISBN: 978-1-946661-23-4
Chesterfield, VA
Library of Congress Control Number: 2021910734

Cover Design by Melody Simmons from eBookindlecovers
Fonts used with permission from Microsoft

Publisher's Note: Neither the publisher nor the author has any control over and does not assume any responsibility for third-party websites and their content.

CPSIA information can be obtained
at www.ICGtesting.com
Printed in the USA
BVHW032025101021
618635BV00005B/21

9 781946 661234